House of Many Gods is a work of fiction. Names, characters, places, and incidents are the products of the author's imagination or are used fictitiously. Any resemblance to actual events, locales, or persons, living or dead, is entirely coincidental.

Published in the United States by Ballantine Books, an imprint of The Random House Publishing Group, a division of Random House, Inc., New York.

BALLANTINE and colophon are registered trademarks of Random House, Inc.

Portions of this book originally appeared in "Bones of the Inner Ear": *Story Magazine, The O. Henry Awards Prize Stories* (Anchor Books, New York, 2000) and *The Best American Short Stories* (Houghton Mifflin, Boston, 2000).

Grateful acknowledgment is made to Darhansoff, Verrill, Feldman Literary Agents for permission to reprint two poems from *Poems of Akhmatova* by Anna Akhmatova, translated by Stanley Kunitz and Max Hayward, copyright © 1967, 1968, 1972, 1973. Reprinted by permission of Darhansoff, Verrill, Feldman Literary Agents.

Library of Congress Cataloging-in-Publication Data
Davenport, Kiana.
House of many gods : a novel / Kiana Davenport.—1st ed.
p.   cm.
ISBN 0-345-48150-X
1. Hawaii—Fiction. I. Title.
PS3554.A88H68 2006
813'.54—dc22   2005048174

Printed in the United States of America on acid-free paper

www.ballantinebooks.com

2 4 6 8 9 7 5 3 1

First Edition

HOUSE OF MANY GODS

A NOVEL

Kiana Davenport

BALLANTINE BOOKS

NEW YORK

HOUSE OF
MANY GODS

To my beloved cousin,
Rosemond Kehau Aho

To Anita and Robert Yantorno

And to the memory of Rostov Anadyr,
who disappeared

PULE HOʻOLAʻA HALE

E ʻoki i ka piko o ka hale . . .
He hale noho hoʻi no ke kanaka . . .
Oia ke ola au e ke akua—amama ua noa.
E Kū, E Kāne, E Lono
Kuʻua mai i ke ola . . .

(HOUSE DEDICATION PRAYER)

Cut the umbilical cord of this house . . .
A house for man to dwell in . . .
Let this be the life granted to us by the gods.
O Kū, O Kāne, O Lono
Let down the gift of life . . .
—from THE POLYNESIAN FAMILY
SYSTEM IN KAʻU, HAWAIʻI.
By MARY KAWENA PUKUI and CRAIGHILL HANDY

I drink to our ruined house . . .
to lying lips that have betrayed us . . .
and to the hard realities:
that the world is brutal and coarse,
that God in fact has not saved us.
—ANNA AKHMATOVA, "The Last Toast,"
Poems of Akhmatova
Translated by Stanley Kunitz

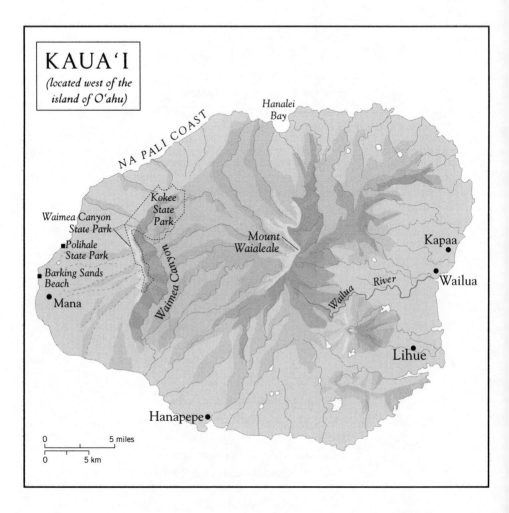

KAUA'I
(located west of the
island of O'ahu)

Hanalei
Bay

NA PALI COAST

Kokee
State
Park

Waimea Canyon
State Park

Polihale
State Park

Barking Sands
Beach

Mana

Waimea Canyon

Mount
Waialeale

Kapaa

Wailua River

Wailua

Wailua

Lihue

Hanapepe

0   5 miles

0   5 km

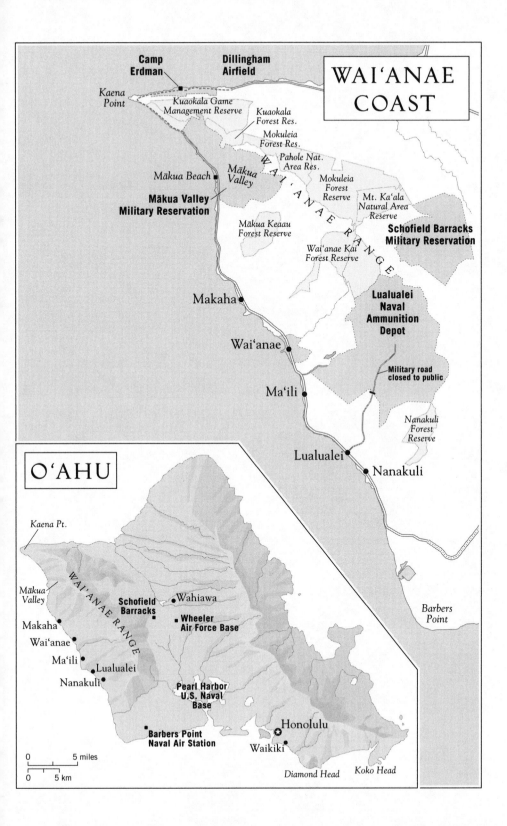

WAI'ANAE COAST

Camp Erdman
Dillingham Airfield
Kaena Point
Kuaokala Game Management Reserve
Kuaokala Forest Res.
Mokuleia Forest Res.
Pahole Nat. Area Res.
Wai'anae Range
Mākua Beach
Mākua Valley
Mākua Valley Military Reservation
Mokuleia Forest Reserve
Mt. Ka'ala Natural Area Reserve
Mākua Keaau Forest Reserve
Schofield Barracks Military Reservation
Wai'anae Kai Forest Reserve
Makaha
Lualualei Naval Ammunition Depot
Wai'anae
Military road closed to public
Ma'ili
Nanakuli Forest Reserve
Lualualei
Nanakuli

O'AHU

Kaena Pt.
Wai'anae Range
Mākua Valley
Schofield Barracks
Wahiawa
Makaha
Wheeler Air Force Base
Wai'anae
Ma'ili
Lualualei
Nanakuli
Barbers Point
Pearl Harbor U.S. Naval Base
Honolulu
Barbers Point Naval Air Station
Waikiki
Diamond Head
Koko Head

0   5 miles
0   5 km

PART ONE

KE ALA KE OLA

—

The Road of Life

PUNAHELE

Favored Child

MORNING, THE AIR ASTONISHINGLY CLEAR. THE SKY SO UNBLEM-
ished and wide, there is divinity in the light. Sun and heat already strong, the
shapes of all things are revealed. Old roosters crowing, shopkeepers yawning,
rolling back iron window grilles. The absolute poise of women with blood-
leaping grace walking dusty roads to market.

In shanty houses, in rumpled beds, the piping cries of humans waking. A
dozing father's muscular, copper-colored arm falls from a bed to the floor. An
infant crawls across the floor, picks up the father's hand, and drools. The hand
scoops up the child, cupping it like a well-loved toy. It lifts the child up to the
day. Here is the still life. The sudden, static poem of being.

Down no-name roads, children stare from windows of abandoned, oxidizing buses, like little clusters of roe. Fresh from sleep, their faces are lovely to
behold. Some windows have curtains, there is even a tilting mailbox near the
road. A boy appears in a doorway, shaking out a sleeping mat. He rubs his
eyes and stares as if in deep remembrance. An old man waters his taro patch,
whispering to heart-shaped leaves that it is morning.

Life is not weary of these folks. They have held on to ancient rhythms in
this world that was bequeathed to them . . .

THIS WAS THE WILD PLACE, THE UNTUTORED PLACE, WHERE THE
Grand* Tūtū of the coast, the rugged Wai'anae Mountains, watched

---

*Tūtū—meaning grandmother or grandfather—is pronounced "too-too." A Hawaiian-English,
Russian-English glossary is provided in the back of the book.

over the generations. Here, thirty miles west of Honolulu, were the
rough tribes of Wai'anae, native clans that spawned outcasts and felons.
Yet their towns had names like lullabies—Ma'ili, Nanakuli, Lualualei—
until up past Makaha and Mākua the coastal road ran out, coming to a
blunt point like a shark's snout.

And there was history here, many-layered legends. A reverence for
the old ways, the good ways. Each town was set apart by a valley, by
plains of weedy, rust-red dirt dotted with patches of taro fields and herds
of sharp-ribbed cattle. The soil was coarse and punishing; it was unforgiving and bit back. Still, old *tūtū* men and women planted their taro at
Mahealani Hoku, the full moon. And when they harvested the taro, un-
derneath was good. And slogging in the *lo'i*, the taro mud, was good.
Good for arteries and circulation. Good for hoof-thick fingernails.

And they ocean-fished by the dark moon when plankton came,
bringing the big fish. And they gave back to the sea what was not
needed. And they rested and worshipped according to moon phases. Living by the old Hawaiian moon calendar, honoring their gods, they prayed
that theirs would be a good death. That their bones would not lie
bleaching in the sun.

Here too, among steep ridges in valley recesses were ancient ruins,
sacred *heiau*, prayer-towers, and sacrificial altars. Here in caves hidden by
volcanic rocks, in bags of rotting nets, eyeless skulls watched the land to
see what *kapu* would be broken. And what the gods would do. In ancient
days the coast had been a place of refuge for warriors weakened in battles. Here they had hid, tending their wounds, regathering their strength.
Here, at night, across the valleys folks still heard those warriors marching back across the land to battle. Some mornings there were giant footsteps.

Seaward, the Wai'anae Coast was untouched and magnificent, its
beaches great strands of soft, white powder. Yet only the boldest strangers
ventured there. Last holdout of pure-blood Hawaiians, it was the skill of
Wai'anae to keep outsiders out. Dark, husky local boys stalked foolhardy
tourists at beach parks, vandalizing their rented cars. They ambushed
soldiers venturing out from military bases. Sultry girls tossed back their
hair, breathing self-esteem, hips swaying insolently as they strode by on
crumbling rubber slippers.

Homestead youngsters raised on Welfare, their lives were circumscribed by landlessness, poor education, drugs. Outsiders saw in them
the criminal intent, the wish to self-destruct, not looking deeper where

hunger for beauty lay. Not hearing the suck and lisp of dreams, despair, then resignation. Yet here was tribal confidence, a sense of deeply rooted blood, of elders standing behind them for now, for good, for always. And the youngsters grew insolent and fearless. Even hardened surfers from Honolulu, out to catch the waves at Yokohama Bay, showed respect. They did not enter the sacred Kaneana Caves. They left the coast before moonrise.

In the town of Nanakuli, off the coastal highway, a house stood halfway up Keola Road, a sprawling Homestead house that vaguely resembled a shipwreck listing to the left. Generations earlier, it had been a house of pride, of people vivid with ambition. Then life, and neglect, had made the house seem very old. But scandals made it new again, embellishing its history.

The town itself was like that, constantly renewed, rewritten by its tragedies. There were shootings. Whirl-kick karate death gangs. Marijuana farmers were hauled off to Halawa Prison, while girls gave birth in high-school johns. But there was Nanakuli magic, too. Wild-pig hunting with uncles, their boar-hounds singing up jade mountains. And torch-fishing nights—elders chanting, bronzed muscles flashing, strained by dripping haunches of full nets. In tin-roofed Quonset huts, and ancient wooden shacks, women sang at rusty stoves, their shadows epic on the walls.

HE LEANED FROM HIS WINDOW, LOOKING OUT AT A BLOODRED VALley, the color so beloved and worshipped by the ancients. A silent man, an empty room, only the white rectangle of a bed. He was Noah, and he had come home from combat in Korea without the will to speak. He did not, in fact, remember that war. When folks mentioned it, he shrugged, sure that they were making it up. This was his life now, leaning from his window, the windowsill grown shiny from the years of his forearms.

Having dismissed the past, he was acutely aware of the present, watching the comings and goings of his family, the neighbors, the progression of their small town, Nanakuli, slung like a hammock between mountain and sea. Knowing he watched them, folks behaved a little better. Sometimes while he dozed, children tiptoed close and left things on his windowsill. A mango, a green apple. He woke and leaned down, watching how the apple focused the glow of afternoon.

Since his niece had departed, he did not really sleep. He listened for the cries of little Ana, her abandoned child. He had watched the mother go, driving off with her arm waving out the window of Nanakuli's only taxi. A graceful arm, a careless arm, looking severed from the elbow. She never looked back. Her face was already looking toward the sea, already going *makai and makai and makai*, out into the world where life, real life, awaited her.

She was leaving behind intractable red dust, valleys that seized up and swallowed livestock, forests of mean kiawe trees whose barbed-wire thorns could skin a human clean. She was leaving, she said, a place of hopelessness, a coast of broken, thrown-away lives.

Noah heard a voice call softly in the dusk, like someone calling in a dream. "Mama . . . Mama . . ."

The child she left behind. Sometimes in the shock of early morning, he heard her chattering to herself. He rose, looked out the window where she was leashed by a harness to a wire clothesline. For hours she played alone in the gritty yard, building a little house with scraps of lino-leum, then tidying each cranny.

In the heat of her chores, the child ran up and down the clothesline so it seemed to hum and sing as if she were a note running up and down a scale. After several hours, her hands grimy, her face bearded with dirt, she would grow lonely and would scream, which started the boar-hounds barking. She would scream until someone ran from the house and picked her up.

One day she screamed and no one came. Her screams grew so pierc-ing, a young goat tethered to a tree fainted out of terror. Finally, Noah left his room, walked outside, removed the harness from the child, and pumped it with his shotgun, watching it leap and dance around the yard. Then he took Ana in his arms, humming while she slept. After that folks paid more attention, holding her more often. She grew up feeling loved, but quiet, a pensive child who sat alone like an old woman tired of talk-ing.

THERE WERE SO MANY ELDERS IN THE HOUSE, FOR YEARS SHE COULD not keep them straight. Fight-full uncles and great-uncles smelling of to-bacco and gun bluing. Big-breasted aunties and great-aunties whose hands reeked of Fels Naphtha. At dusk they gathered on the *lānai* in com-petitive fugues of storytelling, and often they talked about her mother. Ana sat in the shadows and listened and, sensing her nearby, they fell silent, or sent her off to her cousins.

For years, she thought that sleeping alone was what people did when they were contagious, for she and her cousins grew up sharing beds; sleeping head to toe—husky boys with bronzed shoulders, and girls with names like Rosie, Ginger, Jade, one girl named Seaweed. Girls whose mothers were all headstrong beauties, famous up and down the Wai'anae coast—Emma, Nani, Ava, Māpuana, and for a while there had been Ana's mother, Anahola.

Along with its tempestuous women, the big house was famous for its damaged men. Ana's great-grandfather had come home from World War I with his nose shot off. Doctors had built him a metal nose which he removed each night before he slept. Folks said that's why his wife had gone insane, lying under his empty face. Great-uncle Ben, his son, came home from World War II without an arm. Ben's younger brother, Noah, returned from Korea silent as a grub.

Their cousin, Tito, a champion swimmer, had been a diver for the U. S. Navy. Deep saturation dives, day after day, year after year, until nitrogen bubbles trapped in his bone marrow turned his bones to rotting crochet. Now wheelchair-bound, he had become a poker master. There were other families, other vets. And sometimes they all came together, remembering war with fierce lyrics and metaphoric dazzle, as if peacetime were the nightmare.

Once a year on Veterans Day, folks came from up and down the coast, bringing baskets of food. They sat watching the veteran sons, and sons of sons, like people at a zoo. The damaged men would drink too much, strip off their clothes, and rave and dance with savage grace, while light hung in the space of a missing limb. Their mutilations glowed. Then they would wrestle their boar-hounds to the ground, play pitch and catch with great-grandpa's bronzed nose till everyone went home.

OF ALL HER COUSINS IN THAT HOUSE, ROSIE, FIVE YEARS OLDER, grew to be Ana's favorite. Smart and feisty with sightly darker skin, the girl gave Ana a feeling of security, a deep sense of okayness. Rosie's mother was Ava, and she was the one Ana kept her eye on. The woman had grown up wanting to be an Olympic swimmer, but then she turned beautiful and the dance halls found her. Folks said she looked like Lena Horne. Slow-hipped, honey-colored, each night Ava and her sisters dressed for the Filipino dance halls, rice-powdering their cheeks and arms to make them pale, puckering and rouging their perfect lips.

Sometimes an aunty mentioned Ana's mother, Anahola, how she

had loved dressing up and going to the dance halls. How she had stood alone, measuring the men who never measured up. She hardly remembered the woman's face, but often in sleep Ana climbed behind her mother's eyes. She slipped into her skin. She glided with handsome mix-bloods at the dance halls, legs wrapped around thighs that ruddered her round the floor.

One night Ava turned to her, grinning in a twisted way. "Poor little bastard. Your mama didn't want you."

One-armed Ben took her aside. "You got one *loko 'ino* mouth. Every time you open it, you swallow yo' damn brain. *Nevah* use dat word again."

Remembering what Ava had said, on her seventh birthday Ana walked into the kitchen full of elders. "Am I still a bastard?"

They cried out and scooped her in their arms. Great-aunty Pua took her on her lap while she mixed poi in a tub of pounded taro.

"Listen, child, anybody call you that again, you tell them *pa'a ke waha*! Keep the mouth shut. You our precious *punahele*. You going to be somebody, going make this family proud."

"If I'm so much, how come my mama left?"

Pua looked up at her sisters. "Your mama's on a voyage. One day when she's *pau*, then she come home."

Ana watched Pua add water to the tub, watched her squeeze the pounded taro, watched the poi ooze through her aunty's thick brown fingers. She listened as Pua instructed, telling her the secret to two-finger poi—not too thin, not too thick—knowing how much water, how much to squeeze.

"You squeeze too much, poi comes watery and runs away."

While she talked, the poi made sucking sounds, swallowing her hands and wrists. "Your mama's a little bit like poi, not always easy to hold on to. Have to let her go her way."

THERE WERE NIGHTS WHEN ALL THE AUNTIES BROUGHT THEIR MEN home, and the house bulged and rocked with human drama. In the mornings while they slept, Ana and her cousins slicked mulberry juice on their lips, turning them a ghoulish blue. They scraped green mold from the walls and smeared it on their eyelids, then pinned plumeria in their hair and slow-danced in couples like the grown-ups.

Rosie's father came, a handsome Filipino. He closed the door to Ava's room. Their singing bedsprings, call and response of human moans. Then, the sound of him slapping her, a series of screams, Ben aiming his pig-hunting rifle, the drummer running down the road. Ava stood in the doorway flicking ashes, throwing off perfumes.

One day for no reason, she hit Rosie so hard, the girl flipped sideways, landing on her head. Her eyes rolled back, showing white, a trick that took Ana's breath. That night it was quiet, Ana was careful where she looked. Then Noah silently appeared, walked up to the chair Ava sat in, lifted her and the chair over his head, and threw them both across the room. Ava just lay there, her cheekbone's shadow on the floor.

Ben stood over her. "You going end up Kāne'ohe State Hospital, like Grandma."

Gradually, her face began to change. It grew bloated, blister-tight. She threw Rosie headfirst through a window. She slammed the girl's head with an iron skillet. One day she held Rosie's hand over open flames until Ben pinned her to a wall. Ana found Rosie hiding out behind the goat pen, and they slept wrapped together in a blanket. Through the years they grew so close, they could just look at each other and feel safe.

WHEN ROSIE WAS THIRTEEN, AVA HAD ANOTHER CHILD. THE FAther, a graceful Chinese famous for his tango, was only five years older than Rosie. Ben threw Ava out of the house; she never made it to the clinic. Her baby slid out on the backseat of Nanakuli's only taxi while the driver knelt in the bushes vomiting.

Much later she told the girls how she bit the umbilical cord, swung the baby upside down, and slapped it till it screamed. Then she wrapped it in her skirt, climbed up to the driver's seat, stuffed the man's jacket between her legs, and stole his taxi. For years, Ana pictured her speeding off in a rusty Ford, her newborn yelling itself purple while she shifted gears and struggled with her afterbirth.

Ava and the tango man hid out in Honolulu's Chinatown, living off the sale of the stripped-down cab. When they were finally arrested, Ben posted bail, Ava was put on probation and he brought her home. The baby, Taxi, was beautiful. But when Rosie bent to lift her little brother, Ava lunged at her.

"Touch him, I break your arm."

The girl stood straight so she and her mother were eye to eye.

"Guarantee. I never again come near your little bastard."

That word again. It was the first time Ana saw her cousin's edge. She saw something else that day. Rosie's walk was becoming obvious. For several years, she had listed slightly, as if her right foot were deprived of a natural heel. Each year the lopsided walk was more pronounced. Ben took her to a foot doctor who found nothing, but an ear specialist said her equilibrium was off. Tiny bones of her inner ear were permanently damaged.

Ana thought of Rosie flying headfirst through a window. She thought of Ava striking Rosie's head with an iron skillet swung like a baseball bat. Rosie's flame-scarred hand that took away her lifeline. Ana crawled into bed and held her.

Though folks in Honolulu called the Wai'anae Coast a "junk kine" life, somewhere in her early years, Ana began to see the forbidding beauty of her land. Slowly, the distant jade mountains and red valleys gained entry to her upcast eyes. The road past her house was paved, but dust lay so thick, it had always seemed a dirt road. Some days she stood on that road, hands on hips, as if barring entry to her valley, her attitude defiant even when neighbors drove by.

She would be a big girl, strong legs, wide, *lū'au* feet. She would never be a beauty. From her father, she had inherited wide cheekbones and slightly slanted eyes that went from green to brown, like *hapu'u* ferns. Her hair was black and curly and if not pulled back in a braid, made her look wild, electrified. She had the brown/gold skin and full, pouting lips of a local girl, so in that sense she did not stand out. But there was something in her eyes, always probing, asking why? that made her, even young, seem formidable. What folks remarked upon most were Ana's shoulders. Wide like a boy's, they gave the impression of double pride.

Some days when harsh, sobbing winds dried the membranes of throats, and left eyes gritty and raw, something would break loose inside her. Like a hunter of rain, she would run shouting up Keola Road, hair flying behind her like barbed moss. Boar-hounds—brawny warriors of the back roads—leapt alongside her like dark muscles exploding from the earth. And then the pounding of hooves, the gleaming, sweaty flanks of horses who shook their manes and galloped through meager grass beside her.

She would pass Inez Makiki's house where the Hawaiian flag stood waving in the wind, which meant a newborn baby. The Makikis were full-bloods and flew the original Hawaiian flag, showing a *kāhili* in front of two crossed, pointed paddles, nine red, yellow, and green stripes for the major islands, and one to represent the entire Hawaiian archipelago. Twins ran in that family and folks were waiting for the day Inez would fly two flags.

Ana always slowed down as she passed Uncle Pili's house, an old bachelor who rented beds to field-workers and construction crews. "Dollah a day and suppah." There were eight rooms, two beds to a room, his kitchen so small, the table, chairs, and Frigidaire were chained outside to trees. No phone, no TV, no indoor toilet. For twenty years Pili's rates had stayed the same. Instead, each year he had lowered the wattage in the lightbulbs, leaving the house so dim, folks called his place The Lights-Out Inn.

"Beds fo' sleeping," Pili said. "Folks like read, go library."

Now guests brought their own lightbulbs, and neighbors watched them flickering on as folks screwed them in, and flickering off as folks moved out. With all the in-out traffic, sometimes at dusk the house resembled a mother ship signaling her pods for the final voyage home. As she passed, Ana would wave to Uncle Pili sitting on his porch in a broken-down obstetrics chair retrieved from Angel's Junkyard, his feet propped in the stirrups, his head thrown back, watching the day advance between his legs.

She would huff along, passing dozens of Quonset huts on either side of the road, left over from World War II, when the military occupied the land. Families lived in them now, and some were neat and hung with curtains, even miniature gardens. But some yards looked like dump sites—pyramids of rusted cars, skulls of hog heads, naked, running children, their bodies sequined with flies.

She would pass the chicken farm of the Chinese-Portuguese brothers, Panama and Florentine Chang, and then at the end of Keola Road, where it began to trickle out, Ana would slow down. Here were the turnoffs, degraded dirt roads that people stayed away from. Down these roads were rusted-out Quonsets long ago condemned, hideouts for the death gangs. Men who dealt serious drugs and kept arsenals of guns. They were seldom seen in daylight, but at night they rumbled, their trucks skidding up and down the road. Gunshots were heard. A body found floating facedown in a feeding trough, nudged back and forth by the snouts of pigs. When police raided the huts, they always found them empty. The gangs had melted farther back into the valley.

Sometimes after a long run, Ana would hose herself down, then come in and sit under a big, translucent light globe, watching a gecko warm its belly against the genial glow. She would whisper to the small, transparent thing, observing its internal workings as it digested mosquitoes. She adopted a toad and three stray cats.

Ben shook his head. "This thing with animals, too much. She take that toad to bed with her, make conversation."

"She's lonely," Pua said.

"Why, lonely? She got a house of folks who love her."

"She doesn't have a *mother*. Not the same."

Each time Ana heard that word, a ship eased out of the corner of her eye and into the horizon. She would lie in the raw yellow light of a naked bulb, holding a textbook behind which she studied old snapshots of her mother.

"Maybe she never left the islands."

"What you mean?" Rosie asked.

"Maybe she's in Honolulu. Could be right now she's with some handsome beachboy, sipping Mai Tais."

Rosie gathered her in her arms. "Ana, when she's ready, she'll come home. She only got one home."

"When she comes back, I'll make her beg."

Newscasters on their black-and-white TV described the long hot summer on the U. S. mainland, whole cities burning during "race riots." Then riots escalated into assassinations. It happened to men named Martin and Bobby, names that did not mean much to her for they were far away.

But in that same year, 1968, Duke Kahanamoku died. Handsome, regal, pure-blood Hawaiian, he had been their living royalty, a fearless swimmer and record-breaking Olympic champ. When the sixty-five-year-old Queen Mother came from England touring the Pacific, Duke Kahanamoku was the man who charmed her so, she had got up and danced the hula. Now a wailing went up across the islands, people mourned for days.

Life suddenly seemed to escalate. Ana's cousin, Lopaka, enlisted in the Army, and was on his way to Vietnam. Ten years Ana's senior, he was a wild "park boy" who rumbled all night and came home at dawn when the frogs went to sleep. Sometimes he smelled of liquor and the musk of women. Yet he was fearless, hunting wild boar—wrestling them to the ground bare-handed—slaying them without a knife or gun. He swam spearless through caves of sleeping tiger sharks, and one day he walked into a burning house and walked out with his hair singed off, carrying two children.

And Lopaka loved her. She was the one to whom he brought jars of fresh bamboo hearts. He taught her how to swing a machete. How to dive in the wildest surf, and how to eat a fish head. And when some girl broke his heart, Ana was the one he turned to, his damp, smoky sweat like eucalyptus fires, exciting the air around her. He took her net-fishing, and taught her how to pick *'opihi* off the rocks. How to use *limu* as a poultice when she cut her foot. And days when she seemed irretrievably sad, he blew cigarette smoke into her ear, leaving her shivering with laughter.

Before he left for 'Nam, Lopaka drove her round the island to the wet side and took her up into the rain forests, the two of them trolling streams for *'ōpae*, succulent, freshwater shrimp.

"Don't go. We could run away, get married." She was eight years old.

Lopaka laughed. "*Ei nei*, you're just a kid. Besides, we're blood. Anyway, I got to go. I'm bored to death."

"I love you," she said.

He scooped up *'ōpae*, threw them in a can, and sat down next to her.

"I love you too. We're both orphans in a way. Look, Ana, if I don't come back . . ."

She began to cry.

". . . promise me you'll be brave. That you'll remember everything I taught you. Never go surfing alone. Do that thing with banana peels I showed you, so your hands don't get so chapped. Stop eating so much *kimchee*, that's why you don't have friends. And when you make bamboo kites, what you do before splitting the wood?"

"I soak it first. But maybe I will kill myself. No one left for me, but Rosie."

He laughed. "Silly girl! You got to learn to hit life back. Be *ikaika*. Strong. You want to love something for me while I'm gone?"

He spread his arms out, encompassing the forest, then he pointed out to sea. "Love this. All this. The *'āina*, and the *kai*, and the *wai*. These things will always honor you."

"I will," she said. "I promise."

He made her a thick lei of *'ōpae* and settled it on her shoulders, the fat things wriggling and writhing in her hair. She wore it round her neck until the *'ōpae* died, the smell so bad Ben had to cut it off her while she slept. Ana stood brave when Lopaka left in uniform. But for weeks she walked bent like an old woman.

EVEN WITH HIM GONE, THE HOUSE SEEMED LIKE A BREEDING SHED, bulging with children, and sometimes she got lost in the shuffle. On full-moon nights while people slept, she got up and counted bodies, adding up the younger kids, taking stock of the adults.

She took Rosie aside. "Now we're getting older, they might soon need our beds. They'll have to throw us out." She heard thunder in the distance. "See? Even the gods are warning us."

Rosie laughed. "You crazy? Families don't do that. And that's not god-thunder, *lōlō*. It's the Army testing bombs up in Mākua."

Aunties still laundered her clothes, braided her hair, and sent her off to school. They taught her manners, even instructed her on how to nibble cookies, always delicately in a straight line.

"Young ladies don't leave teeth marks."

They taught her how to Vaseline her fingers to get rid of stubborn dirt. "Young ladies don't have red cuticles."

Uncles still took her hunting and fishing, and "talked story" for hours. They taught her how to make "Wai'anae wallets" by wrapping dollar bills round straws and sticking them in empty soda bottles so she would not be robbed. She walked down the highway past tough "park boys" pretending she was sipping a Nehi.

And when letters arrived from Lopaka, they called Ana to read them aloud because she was his *punahele*, his favorite. Sometimes her aunties wept, afraid he would be killed, and Ana took them in her arms, as if she were the elder. And no one threw her out.

ANAHOLA

Time in a Glass

. . . LIGHT HAS ITS OWN EMOTION. ITS BLIND STITCH OF YIN AND
yang. *Sometimes a woman in a distant city dreams of light, the way it struck a
swinging gangway as it was slowly hoisted up. The sense of massive shifting as
a ship, the* Lurline, *pulled away, in its wake, coin divers surfacing with quar-
ters in their teeth, light striking the coins and shattering their faces. She dreams
of dockside crowds calling out and waving.*

*She remembers that she did not wave. There was no one to wave to. She
had simply stood on deck watching as the harbor faded, then the land. Then she
had closed her eyes and breathed in deeply, a woman running. She had run
away. She had left suddenly, taking nothing, not even her child.*

*Now, in the ethers of morning she wakes, feeling the city outside waiting
to offer itself to her as raw material from which she continually constructs her
new identity. She hears a man in the bathroom rinsing his razor, calmly encas-
ing it, then gently slapping his cheeks with cologne. She starts to rise, to greet
the day, and the past comes rushing in. As if it has been lying in wait, as if it
were not behind but in front of her.*

*A gauntlet of sunlight on her arm inflames an old surfing scar. Even now
she feels the surfboard crack, waves taking her down, the mean, contentless
undertow. Someone humming in the kitchen below, slapping around in am-
phibian slippers, summons up old sweet-faced aunties with a buttery caste to
the whites of their eyes. Memories persist with relish, with ingenuity.*

*Sometimes near the wharves of San Francisco, old fishermen with crooked
gaits conjure old tūtū men back home dragging their rotting nets out of a sun-
set. Urchin street dogs bring memories of Digger and Squid, brave hunting*

hounds with long, rough tongues. Winds blow and it is still the sea she inhales, tossing her dreams of an arid coast, a child's plaintive calling.

Some nights she feels that the man asleep beside her—the whole city—sees right through her. In a flash of insight people see she is a woman who has run, who has shed everything, and so she has no background and no worth. Sometimes she hates the city, hates the people born there, who are part of its history. And she hates how the city made her pay before it allowed her entry.

She lies back in her bed recalling those early days, though she never quite remembered the first sight of the bridge, or the Lurline *entering the harbor, or the skyline of San Francisco. What she remembered was how, at that moment, she had felt grateful for not having had a happy childhood. Whatever happened next, she was not a lamb being led to slaughter . . .*

WHEN THE *LURLINE* HAD DOCKED, SHE FOUND HER WAY TO CHINA-town, the only place she could afford until she got her bearings. Down narrow streets of sterile, asphalt frightfulness, she saw people cupped in the shadows like effigies. Then gold shops, pagoda'ed temples. An old woman in slippers dragged a promethean handbag while beside her a barefoot child thriftily carried new pink rubber boots. Ana stepped from a bus into a slippery tide of discarded shrimp heads, the sound of wind chimes, odor of burning incense. Then she had relaxed somewhat: Things looked so familiar she could have been in Honolulu.

In broken English, a vendor had offered her a mushroom big and vir-ile as a steak. Or, dried camel eye from some doomed caravan traversing ancient spice routes. Dong Quai for "happy womb." She moved on, struck by the smell of singed ducks hanging in doorways, the offal of rab-bits being disemboweled on-site. An amber hand waving the blue meat of monkey.

Streets were almost suffocating, but with a redemptive squalor, a sense of hustle, of focus, immigrants struggling toward better lives. Here and there the old and the new world meshed, the 1960s moving in. Young Asians in blue jeans slapped fresh paint on storefronts. A couple flew by on a Harley. But then across the street, old men squatted, throw-ing dice, and in an alley a child emptied its bladder into an abandoned shoe.

She bought a slithery square of barbecued mock meat and a bag of moist, pink *li hing mui*, and gazed at cheap curios and smiled. Even litter on the ground seemed beautiful. Even tiny women in doorways, hurling bright balls of spittle into open drains. Passing a barrel of fresh pig's feet,

Ana had suddenly slowed down, remembering midwives bringing bouquets of pig's feet with which they had made soup to shrink her womb. She remembered how, after childbirth, they had tenderly kneaded her belly. She put those thoughts away.

Light rains began to fall, undyeing Chinatown as colors ran from posters and clothes on racks. Down Fifteen Cent Alley she had found Tung Lok, the Happy Together Hotel. The lobby smelled rancid, and she heard people coughing in their rooms. Her walls were flocked with dead roaches, but there were no bloodstains on her mattress, and her sheets were clean.

At dusk she had walked the streets again, asking for work in several shops. People passed her arm in arm. Even the gods had company: icons of Buddha, Jesus, and Confucius lined up abreast for sale. She felt the fog curl up her sleeves, a chilly sense of loneliness, the sense of one who has crossed frontiers and sees that what was left behind is already fading into flashbacks. There was only now, the aftermath.

For weeks she labored in a sweatshop, stitching pockets into cheap dungarees. Around her in palpitant, moist heat were Mexicans, Asians, and Latins—robust, velvet-eyed women nursing their infants as they bent at ancient Singers. Ana stood the heat until one day, exhausted, she fainted between blue pyramids of dungarees. The owner woke her by pinching her, punching her with his fist between her shoulder blades.

After that, she served dim sum in a restaurant where four-generation families ate, holding each other in their laps. Each day, in the abrupt turbulence of beaded drapes, she exploded from the kitchen, pushing carts loaded with metal and bamboo steamers, lifting and replacing the scalding lids hour after hour until whole constellations of blisters lined her palms. Skin peeled from her fingertips, which bled.

When Chinese customers were rude, she had the manifest advantage of being an "immigrant" not understanding their language, pretending not to understand English. They cursed her, waving her away, and she reflected on how, at home in her islands, she had never thought of Chinese as rude or cruel. She had only thought of whites that way.

At night she swept up hair in a beauty shop, then sat with the owner sewing hair-pillows which women bought to cushion their elbows in the sweatshops. They sewed till dawn, when the sun lit little rainbows in a toothbrush glass. Years later, she would remember those nights as luminous—two women gloved in human hair, lost in hanging strips of brilliant silks, a small rotating fan lazily wafting the silk this way, and then that way. Long hours drew them close, coaxing out confessions, their life stories knotted up in bits of thread they bit off with their teeth. And in the mornings, a roomful of brilliant pillows that often they fell asleep upon, waking at noon like concubines.

Still, in the permanent twilight of exhaustion, Ana could not seem to make progress, to save enough money for proper clothes, a better job. She began to see how lack of money engendered shame, how without it people allowed themselves to disappear. She lost the dim sum job. The hair-pillow woman moved back to Hong Kong. She tutored English in the back room of a laundry. She waitressed, washed dishes. Graveyard. Swing shift. One job rinsing into another.

One night a sailor offered her a fifty-dollar bill. Balanced on the girders of indecision, Ana reached out and thoughtfully touched the bill before she walked away. She was beginning to know hunger, what it was to lie awake and hear her insides working on almost nothing. She began to learn how far she could go on water and air, how far she could divest herself of herself without collapsing. She avoided open markets and food stalls. She began to despise food a little.

In a mirror her face was becoming narrow; she imagined it all frontal like a cat's. Increasingly she felt weak, intimations of how easily her system could fail, her organs ignore the chain of command, how hunger could drive verbal and motor skills back in evolution so that movements suggested a human being learning to walk upright. It was not quite starvation, which had manners. Starvation just walked up to folks and knocked them down.

Hunger, near hunger, was sly. It allowed her to get up and move around, gave her a sense of mission: pay rent, find food. Hunger became her escort, walking her through the antique pungency of Chinatown, through viruses germinating in puddles under streetlights. Through a succession of jobs in little holes-in-the-wall, until she began to lose track of what it was she wanted, of what might be worth having.

And she began to recognize certain women like her who had run away. Women of every color and hue who had tried to reinvent themselves, shedding their names, their languages, their backgrounds, everything but their skins. Women worn down, their edges blurred, on the verge of sinking out of sight. Ana began to find these women essential, their tragic incoherence proof that there were others worse off than she. She began to see how life could be brought to a standstill.

She pored over discarded newspapers looking for odd jobs, even blood banks. And one day she saw the picture of a man she recognized. She stared at his face, etched with lines like an outdoorsman, a rugged, rather handsome face. An older man, a strong, straight nose giving him an unperturbed and rather noble profile. He had sailed on the *Lurline* out of Honolulu, bound for San Francisco.

She sat back remembering how she had hastened to the ship, remembered it as huge and regal, yet something feminine and graceful in its lines. She remembered how, as she drew near, the ship seemed to look at her, to focus on her. Seeing the full size of it up close, she had felt everything around her drop away.

Her first night on board, in the ship's boutique she had bought one good dress and a pair of leather shoes. Later she stood on deck with her tattered suitcase full of island clothes, then stepped back and heaved it overboard. She had forty-eight dollars to her name.

In the morning she had strolled the decks, studying passengers in third class and second class. Then she had ventured to the top deck, observing those in first class, how they dressed, how they talked. The way they seemed to move in slow motion. That was when she first saw him, a solitary stroller, a tall man lost in thought. He moved with the natural grace of someone privileged, and as he passed she felt the clean male scent of lime cologne settle over her. For a moment their eyes had met, he slowed his pace, but then she looked away. He appeared to be somewhere in his midforties. She was twenty-three.

Day after day she had watched him stroll the decks, perhaps because she had sensed he was watching her. Yet, as if by tacit agreement, they never introduced themselves.

What would we have said? What would we have had in common?

At night as couples floated past her dying upward into fog, she had stared at the sea, wondering where she would go when they reached San Francisco. What she would do. The morning they docked, she had glimpsed him at Immigrations, then lost him.

That night at Tung Lok Hotel she scanned the newspaper article under his picture. "... Recent relaxation of immigrant restrictions in Chinatown ... 50,000 people congesting the area ... alarming rise of syphilis, tuberculosis ..." She studied his photograph, his features, hoping he would be kind. In the morning she bathed, and washed her hair, then oiled it into a smooth French twist and slipped on her one good dress, now frayed and rusty at the seams. Then she made her way to a local clinic.

The line was long, the sun intense. The old man ahead of her removed his shirt, his back so thin he seemed to be wearing a larger man's skin. She wiped her face, then stood counting the long jade vertebrae of his backbone. Inside there was such a mob, the nurses looked in need of nursing.

One of them regarded Ana disdainfully. "We don't buy blood. Unless you're here for TB examination."

Ana shook her head, then pointed to the newspaper she was carrying. "I'm here to see him, Dr. McCormick."

The woman frowned. "For what? He's very busy. Look how long these lines. You understand? We have bad problem now in Chinatown."

She was about to retreat when she saw him in the corridor. He was wearing a white lab coat, holding the hand of a mortally thin Chinese woman, talking softly, as if she were a child about whose future he knew a sad story.

"I know him," Ana told the nurse.

"So? You go now, or wait for other doctor to see you."

She remembered the way he had looked at her aboard the ship—as if she were beautiful—and knew that somehow he would help her. He *must* help her. A man shouldn't look at a woman that way if not prepared to perform a kind of exorcism over her loneliness and desperation.

People coughed. She smelled their fragile, humid bodies, the condensation of sweat on amber arms. She felt her owns arms, so thin. In that moment she was no one. She had nothing to lose.

"Look, it's highly personal. Please tell Dr. McCormick I need to see him. Tell him . . . it's the girl from the ship, the *Lurline*."

The nurse studied her as if she were both novel and absurd.

But minutes later he peered out from an examination room, smiled faintly, and came forward.

Timidly, she took his hand. "I'm Ana. I hope you remember me. I used to watch you stroll the decks . . ."

"Of course I remember. I should have introduced myself then. How can I help you? Are you ill?"

She shook her head. "I'm here because I saw your picture in the paper. I came to ask if possibly you knew of an opening here, receptionist or anything. I'm afraid I haven't been able to get my bearings since I arrived."

In a glance he took in her dress, her worn-down shoes. He sat her down in a corner. "Ana, I don't officially work here. I'm with a lab outside the city. My field is immunology, and they've called several of us in for consultation. It's pretty serious."

She had never felt so desperate. "Well . . . do you know someone who could hire me? I had two years of university at home, a science major. It's just . . . I left the islands quickly, with no forethought."

"And it's your first time in San Francisco."

"My first time anywhere."

Months later he would tell her how he had seen her coming up the gangway of the *Lurline* in her island clothes. He had watched her stand alone on deck, waving to no one as the ship's bow slowly turned and headed out to sea. She had looked so brave and lonely, something touched him. During the crossing he had thought to introduce himself, but she was young and he felt he had already thrown his life away.

MAX FOUND HER A SECRETARIAL JOB AT A COMMUNITY COLLEGE where eventually she would complete her degree. At first he puzzled her, a man who dressed impeccably as if to compensate for something lost in his expression, something sad, used-up. He asked few questions. He did not seem to ask much of life either.

But as weeks passed, they began to talk in such a natural way the hours seemed calibrated into periods of stillness and motion, coolness and warmth, a flawless, almost timeless ease. Yet Ana was careful, leaving blanks rather than lie so that she would not have to cover her tracks, lie to protect earlier lies. Rather, she told him half-truths.

She had dropped out of university. She had left home because her family stifled her. With seeming modest dignity, she spoke of her Hawaiian father, a well-known lawyer. And her uncle, a celebrated trumpeter who had played for heads of state in Europe. Testing Max's credulity, she began to see how near truths and half-truths could ease her way into the world.

And so she told of her great-grandfather who had owned a phaeton and matching steeds with which he had raced through the cobblestone streets of Honolulu to play checkers with the queen. And as she continued, Ana saw how in telling her tales, she assumed a kind of power over Max, how in linking sequences of made-up events she captured and held his attention, making him her accomplice.

She told of a thieving ancestor who had stolen all the land from her father's side of the family.

"We never speak of him in public. Hawaiians believe the tongue is the steering paddle of the mouth. Better to hold the paddle still than speak offending thoughts."

She told of farmers of the valleys whose torches zigzagged through the nights, folks so poor they still went forth to borrow fire.

"Some nights our fire god *Lono-makua*, sends them fire from the hearts of bursting rocks, which we call *pōhaku*. With these, folks light their torches, until each rock says it has had enough."

Max had leaned forward smiling, only half believing her tales. But by patiently listening, he saw how very slowly, like an image in a developing tray, her truer self began to emerge. And later, recalling the stories she had told, Ana realized that some of them were true.

She remembered Nanakuli nights rippling with running flames as folks without electricity ran through the fields with borrowed fire. There *was* an uncle famous for his trumpet-playing, though he had never played for heads of state. And in fact, her father *was* a well-known lawyer, though he had started out a beachboy. What she did not tell was that for the first sixteen years of her life, she did not know he was her father. And the woman she believed was her older sister turned out to be her mother.

. . . *She birthed me in a tub, in wartime during blackout. My mother, Malia. Stifling her screams by biting down hard on a bar of soap. Then wiping her birth blood on her mother's thighs, and calling me that woman's child. In that way, I was born to lying. I was born a lie . . .*

When they had finally confronted her—telling her who she was, and who they were—she understood there was such a thing as truth with taste, and truth without taste. She had been unplanned, a mistake. And even after they told her, her parents virtually ignored her, so impassioned they looked right through her trying to get at each other. And so she had made her own mistake, and finally got their attention.

All in all, she had not entirely lied to Max. Her background, if not happy, was interesting. She was interesting. Only, she never told him of the child. Perhaps when the girl was older, perhaps when they were in touch again. She fell asleep thinking of the metaphysical quality of the word *perhaps*.

IN TIME SHE AND MAX HAD BECOME LOVERS, NOT BECAUSE SHE loved him but she felt he had earned her, more than earned her. And because she was weary of being alone, weary of self-loving, and self-loathing. She wanted someone to do it for her. They lived in his house in Pacific Heights, a rather formal house—all was foreground and exact. But one room held only a grand piano and a terrace overlooking a garden of blooming orange trees. Ana thought she could live in that one room. She could grow old and die there watching the gardener rake the gravel driveway slowly and thoughtfully, like a croupier.

A stately Siamese prowled the house and some nights it padded across her stomach. Something breathed softly in her face. Paws like little clutching hands. She dreamed of old midwives, their voices shouting "*Pahū. Ho'opāhūhū!*" Push. Push hard. She remembered how in those moments she wanted to reach up and strike them. Let them lie down and push. She thought how her mother must have pushed, wanting her out, unborn.

And some nights she dreamed of the father of her child, handsome, reckless, eyes of shave-ice green. Handcuffs jangling at his hips. Then she and his child had been banished to a dehydrated coast. *Four years I tried. A bastard raising her little bastard.* In the end she had loved the child. She had thought of marrying the father. But then a gunshot, a sound so innocent. Like someone opening a flip-top can. And there was nothing but to run, find a better life. Men did it all the time.

As she and Max grew closer she began to perceive how the act of conversation was a gift, how that exchange between two humans made one feel less alone, feel just a bit more capable of bearing things. And so she came to love the give-and-take, the miracle of cells jostling and combining, the slow adagio of minds proceeding in the same direction.

When he saw how bright she was, how hungry for knowledge, he sent her back to college to finish her degree. Then he steered her to certain medical texts which introduced the interlocking brilliance of the human immune system, the difference between T-cells, antibodies, and antigens. The makeup of phagocytes and lymphocytes. The genius of the thymus, a tiny gland that produced tens of millions of killer-vigilantes of the human immune system—lymphocytes or T-cells—and then proceeded to kill off those cells, keeping only the most "intelligent," with the sharpest powers of recognition.

As her fascination with Max's work grew, Anahola earned an advanced degree in biochemistry, became his lab intern, and eventually his assistant. It was extremely solitary work, perfect for a woman who had always proceeded at a tangent from the crowd. There was something urgent about sitting poised on a stool over a microscope, completely focused and alert; she lost all sense of artifice and vanity. The world outside melted away. Time itself seemed to dissolve, as a second world—the truer, minute world—made itself known to her.

Such moments gave Ana a deep sense of fulfillment, as if she had finally found the answers to life, its riddles. When, in the future, she occasionally grew bored, suspecting she had not sufficiently challenged life, had not tested the limits of her daring and her drive, she would remember that first grueling year in Chinatown.

. . . . IT HAS BEEN FOUR YEARS SINCE ANAHOLA LEFT THE ISLANDS *and one day Max asks her to accompany him to a conference on immunology. It will be held on the outer island of Kaua'i, a forty-minute flight from Honolulu. At first she is terrified, fearing the island will take her hostage again. But he is a kind man, and has asked for very little. Her company would give him pleasure.*

When they arrive, she is extremely uncomfortable at the Coco Palms Hotel, hating the nightly blowing of the conch shell, the theatrical torch-lighting ceremony on the lagoon, entertainment geared for tourists. As she enters the dining room, men lift their heads like game dogs tracking spoor. Pale-shouldered women stare with anthropological interest. She sees herself through their eyes: rich, honey-colored skin, full lips, a languid sultry body. Except for the waiters, she is the only nonwhite in the room. She pulls herself in, her movements exaggeratedly chaste, and makes her way to the table.

In one glance the staff of the hotel recognizes her as local, and that she is this older man's kept woman. As Max becomes engaged in seminars, she is left more and more alone. Painfully self-conscious, she wears suits and high heels even to breakfast. She ignores the maids. But after a few days she begins to lose her bearings. The perfumed island air becomes a drug, making her eyelids heavy. Flowers drop in her lap, big and pale like the ears of priests waiting to hear her confession.

An old bronzed man with aged-dove hair sits mending a fishing net, "talking story" like tūtū men from her childhood. She hears the blending of Pidgin and Hawaiian Mother Tongue that in the mouths of soft-voiced elders becomes intrinsically poetic. One night, hearing the wounded music of the sea, she runs barefoot to the beach and dives into moon-shot waves. She feels the harmony of things, the bliss of letting go. She thinks of the child and her 'ohana.

The next day she takes a forty-minute flight to Honolulu, then a cab out to the west coast. She stares at the stark Wai'anae Mountains, at cattle thirsty for so-plenty rain. Alongside the highway are trash bags spilling chicken heads, used-up cans of Roach Motel. Skinny poi dogs run in packs. Kids in an abandoned truck seem to be sniffing glue rags.

At a traffic light, a woman pulls up beside them in a car that looks welded

together from many cars. Her face is bruised, one eye shut. She sees the cabbie staring and leans out of the window.

"Ey! Wha' choo looking at, manong?" Then she floors the gas and takes
off.

The Filipino driver glances at his passenger in the rearview, a pretty woman
in a suit. "Rough neighborhood out here. Sure you know where you going?"

Anahola smiles at him. "This town holds all of my mistakes."

They turn up Keola Road and drive past a pond where piggeries discharge
their waste, past an old school bus oxidized to rust, then small neat houses with
pretty yards full of flapping laundry. They turn into the potholed driveway of
the house.

In high heels and a pongee suit, she stands in the living room amongst
them, self-consciously handing out cartons of cigarettes and See's Candy from
San Francisco. She has forgotten to take her shoes off at the door; the family
stares as her heels sink into termite-ridden floorboards. She totters slightly, stylish, well cared for, out of place.

Yet here she is to show that she has not forgotten them. She sits and drinks
a beer that someone offers, and dips her hand into a bag of soggy, boiled
peanuts. Food seems to float across the room, great bowls cupped in big, dark
hands. Laulau dripping good, good grease. Poi, and lomi salmon. Steaming
mounds of rice and fish.

While she eats, she glances round the room. Same old rusty flit gun on the
windowsill. In the kitchen, same Bull Durham bag wrapped round the faucet
for the drip. She shifts her weight, looking farther into the kitchen and sees the
kerosene string still tied round each leg of the Frigidaire to ward off ants. Food
relaxes her elders and makes them somewhat confident. They ask about California, the weather, about jobs. Do folks eat poi there? And kimchee? They do
not ask who she is living with. She will tell them that in time. Or not.

"How is Uncle Noah?" she asks.

They laugh, pointing to his room, where he sits at his window, a sentry at
his post. Later, she knocks and steps into his room.

"Noah. Pehea oe?" How are you.

He turns from the window, her father's younger brother who saw too
much combat in Korea.

She moves forward and holds him. "Don't hate me. I had to go. I had to."

What she wants is for him to say that it's all right. That life will be right.
Instead, he pulls her to the window and they gaze out for a while. His hands
are broad like her father's had been and now he takes one of her hands in his,
following her lifeline with his finger. He turns it over, smoothing her knuckles,

then balls her hand into a fist and squeezes it over and over, as if to say, Be strong. Be strong.

For a while she sits in the bedroom with little Ana, surrounded by rickety bamboo furniture, and old flower leis gathering bugs and mildew on the walls. She smokes a cigarette, watching the child dig under the sheets, hiding from her, too frightened to talk to her. Each time she reaches out her hand, the girl scuttles deeper and deeper away from her, so that only her feet show, sienna-tinted from red dirt.

"Who can blame you?" she whispers.

Wanting to give her privacy, folks had moved out to the lānai. Now she stands in the living room alone, and in the silence hears the drip. drip. of stewed guava sieving through a cheesecloth. She knows it will drip all night for 'ono guava jelly. She writes a check and leaves it discreetly under the sugar bowl. Finally, she steps outside and hugs each one good-bye, then slides into the cab, still smelling stewed guava, and the iron-rich soil of Nanakuli.

KULA ʻIWI

———

Here My Bones Began

THE SUMMER OF HER TENTH YEAR WAS SO DRY, BARKING DEER stumbled down from distant mountains, licking windows of air-conditioned stores. The piss of boar-hounds sizzled on tar. Ana watched mongooses crawl under their house, coughing and sucking at the pipes, while everywhere the earth cracked open like a gourd. In ancient times the word for wealth was *waiwai*, double water, for it was the fundamental element in their lives. Now elders stood in fields, praying to *Kāne*, keeper of water. But no rains came.

Instead, a letter from her mother. A word that always silenced her. Through the envelope Ana smelled the woman's perfume. She heard her smoky voice. Rosie read the letter to her through a closed door, so it would not mark her. Afterwards, she burned it. Watching the pages curl to embered rags, she recalled her mother's visit two years earlier. On that day folks had rushed out to the *lānai*. A woman stood there in a silk suit that flowed down her hips and legs like water. She was wearing toe-pinch high heels, a matching handbag.

Rosie had put her arms round Ana protectively. "Your mama."

Her vision blurred, she felt her heart pulsing in her shoulders. "What's her name?"

"Anahola. Same as you. Don't worry. I'm not going to let her take you."

As the family moved indoors, the woman gliding in the midst of them, the girls had run to their bedroom and shut the door. Yet she could smell her mother's perfume breaking down the walls.

"What does she want?"

"Nothing. She just came back to look and see."

For hours they listened to rags of conversation, imagining blue smoke coiled in the air as uncles sucked on cigarettes, exhaling audibly like runners at the tape. She heard her mother's voice, a strange and foreign-sounding voice from which all Pidgin-richness had been rinsed. She heard the sharp staccato of her mother's high heels. She had not removed them at the door.

Hours had passed, a half-moon rose. Rosie dragged her off to bed. When Ana woke, the woman was sitting beside her, studying her face. She had whispered something soft. Hello. Ana pulled back, terrified.

"They say you're smart . . . a good girl . . . one day you will understand. When you're grown, you'll see things differently . . . the world is always waiting to ambush a woman."

She looked beautiful, unreal. She sat in the dimness smoking, turning the room into a dream.

"You're better off here, with family . . ."

She had crushed the cigarette, then bent to kiss Ana's cheek, but the girl recoiled, scrambling under the sheet. Her mother had sighed and patted her foot like a little paw. She left her cigarette case behind. When Ana found it on the bed, she stroked its buttery-soft leather, reading tiny gold words in a corner. *Genuine calfskin.* Ben mailed the case back to San Francisco, and for years Ana thought of her mother as a woman who carried her cigarettes in a former calf. And she thought of San Francisco as a place women went to who did not want to be mothers.

Now, watching the letter turn to ash, she heard a subtle whispering, felt a dampness on her back. At last, at last, the rain. A gentle rain, like mist, that brought earth back to life gradually, almost thoughtfully. In the months of the Dry, taro leaves a full foot in diameter had knotted up like papery fists. Now they slowly unfurled, stretching out like great green hands. Ana reached out to them, letting her body go.

The rains continued for three days while folks ran through the fields with their faces up, mouths open like flowers, their ankles socked in wet red clay. Only Rosie moved alone, her big body steaming in the wet, arms lifting dreamily like something adrift on the ocean floor. Then she seemed to pivot and go rigid, aiming her body and her profile at some distant point.

At fifteen she had discovered dancing, that when she danced, she did not limp. She began to smell of aftershave. Someone was teaching her to tango.

One night she knelt beside Ana's bed. "I'm in love. With Gum, father of little Taxi."

Ana sat up scared. "You crazy? What about your mama?"

"She never loved him. Or anyone."

Gum, the tango dancer, tried to explain it to Rosie's mother, Ava. Hearing her screams, both girls ran up the road, on into the valley, toward deep, ridged mountains that swallowed them. For hours they climbed up lava boulders, clinging to roots and knotted vines. Up to their refuge behind a hidden waterfall, formed through centuries in the flutings of the rocks. Years back when they first braved the falls, they had discovered behind them an eerie grotto draped in moss, full of scattered bones.

Now, crawling behind those thundering drapes, they fell exhausted into the cave, into man-shaped hollows centuries old. In the dimness, bones glowed blue and green. They lay down side by side feeling warmth from the sun the earth had swallowed. They were children again, cradled in stone.

"Sometimes I see things," Rosie whispered. "I hope they don't see me. I hope they don't come after me."

Ana suspected Rosie was afraid she would inherit her mother's and grandmother's craziness. It seemed to run in that line of females.

"Do you think your mama's mama did the same things to her?"

"Maybe. Maybe if Mama shaved her head, we'd see the scars."

They stayed behind the falls all night and in those hours Rosie tried to change her life. Take it off like a coat, leave it behind.

"I'm a woman now. Next time Mama hit me, I strike back."

The next day they shot out of those falls like bullets, plunging feet-first into a swirling stream. Ben, out searching for them with his boar-hounds, found them exhausted on the rocks. They marched home like women warriors, full of resolution.

Ava must have sensed it. She never mentioned Gum, but at night she stood in Rosie's room, staring at the empty bed. One day Ana heard little Taxi scream, then muffled silence. Blue moons appeared on his arms and legs, small bruises the size of a pinch. Ben saw them, too, and started throwing furniture, telling Ava to get out for good, he would raise her kids. She fell to her knees, pleading. Ben relented and she stayed, but he sent the child, Taxi, to his father.

For days Ava sat in her room, whispering and rocking. Then without warning, she stood in Ana's doorway, crept close and, with dreamy precision, tapped Ana's hand.

"Your papa was real mischief. He once put a lizard in my handbag."

Ana sat stunned. She felt like something with its mouth stitched shut. "You knew my father?"

"The cop. Ho! What a dancer."

She leaned so close, Ana saw her fillings, blue-black as lava. Strands of saliva clung to the roof of her mouth.

"I had him first you know. But he was nothing. He just lived. I gave him to your mama."

Ana looked her in the eye. "What was his name? What happened to him?"

"Johnny. Shot to death. That's what men do. They shoot each other."

She stood up, full of hate. "I don't believe you. You're crazy, you beat your kids. Look at Rosie . . . all those scars."

"Scars make her *interesting*." Ava's skin grew tight, her cheekbones whittled down to knuckles. "Where's my boy, Taxi?"

"I won't tell you."

She grabbed Ana's wrist. Shook it like a club. "You get him back. Else I burn this house down."

One night Ana woke, gasping for air. She had been dreaming of the sea, and now her dream of water was put out by flames, the sounds of men shouting. Uncle Tito flew past her in his wheelchair. Someone lifted her and ran. Then the bright yellow jackets of firemen, their hoses snaking through the yard. Only Ava's room had gone up, charred bits of which now fluttered in the smoky air, then descended with infinite listlessness.

They found her semiconscious with her neck slashed, having attempted to cut her jugular. The box of matches beside her. She followed her mother to Kāne'ohe State Hospital, and for weeks folks drove past their burned house taking pictures. Ana ran out with Ben's old camera and shot back.

It took two years to repair the house and shortly thereafter her mother showed up in her life again. Still exuding that steady, quiet perfume. Folks dispersed, leaving them alone. From the kitchen, the empty sea sound of a ticking clock telling the wrong time. Ana was wearing ragged shorts and roller skates, elbow and knee pads.

Her mother puffed a cigarette, creating a nice boundary of fog between them. "Hello, Ana. You look like a roller-derby queen."

For a while she just stared. When she spoke her voice was rough and careless. "Why you keep coming back? What you want from me?"

"Well . . . what do you think I deserve?"

"Nothing." Perspiration made her aware of the shape of her face, so similar to her mother's.

"Ana. You have no idea . . ."

"Don't tell me what I have and don't have. You don't know nothing about me."

Her mother stood and walked into the kitchen. She reached out and set the hands of the clock right, then drank a glass of water at the sink. She wrote a check, left it on the counter, and moved to the front door. There she paused, gazing through the rusty screen, addressing her daughter behind her.

"I'm thirty-two years old. If I had stayed here, I would be locked up now. Like Ava. I'm not trying to apologize. I love you. And I think of you. But I made a decision, and stuck to it." She turned and looked at Ana. "May you have such convictions."

The girl cursed her and left the room. Her mother pushed open the door, hugged the family, and carefully walked down the steps to the waiting cab.

Why Ava was released from Kāne'ohe State several years later was never clear. Crowded wards. Her age, her edges soft and blurred. Ben signed the papers and they brought her home. In her absence her boy had been brought home, too, and each day Noah sat in a chair rocking him to and fro. That's how Ana knew how much he loved little Taxi.

Now Ava wore an ink-colored wig, and most days her forehead was pressed to her bedroom wall, telling her confession. Her eyes empty craters, her neck a pearly grid of scars. When Ana passed her room, Ava turned and ran at her headfirst, then jerked back like something leaping the length of its chain. She didn't remember the girl. But she remembered Taxi, the child they had stolen from her.

And she started on Rosie again, whispering outside her door, lurid, obscene things no daughter should have heard. Ben packed Rosie's bags, planning to send her to cousins in Pearl City, but she retreated, up to her elbows in pastries. Gum, the tango man, had moved to Seattle, and after that, Rosie stopped dancing, she stopped everything. All she did was eat.

Ava kept stalking her, and then she stalked little Taxi, baring her teeth at him as if she might consume him.

Ben watched her closely and kept the child beside him. But, then, emerging from a midnight swoon, he saw the child was gone. They found Taxi unconscious in Ava's bed, her hands clasped tight, trying to crush his windpipe.

"You not taking him from me again. I warned! I warned!" In the ensuing struggle she bit Ben's arm down to the bone.

Little Taxi survived, the bruises faded from his neck, and he was sent to his father in Seattle.

Lightning season came, the air so electric the fillings in their teeth hummed. Everything they touched just sparked. There were flash floods, the seas gave off a yellow glow. For days, lightning zigzagged up the valley. It hit a wild pig that rolled into their yard completely roasted. One night, herringbones of ions, lightning striking everywhere. No one saw Ava leave the house. But they heard her awful scream, and found Ben standing over her, his hair electrified a gaseous blue.

She lay facedown, spread out like a pelt. Paramedics said lightning, but her body seemed untouched. Then they said she must have tripped and fallen. The medical examiner found a big crack in the back of her skull from a powerful blow. He thought lightning had hit a branch which struck her. Folks said Ben had struck the blow. Or Rosie. The skies calmed down. The family buried Ava, then sat back tipping long-necked beers, letting the wounded world become green glass.

Only Ana saw how Noah smiled at an empty chair still rocking to and fro, remembering the boy who had sat there. Months later he called her to his room and pointed to his closet. Inside was something big and round, wrapped in moldy cloth.

"Bury it," he said.

That night she unwrapped it in her room. Rusty now, the way iron gets. The weight of the skillet profound. The back still matted with blood, gray strands of hair, bits of skull like ice chips. She wiped it clean and buried it.

IN A HOUSE EVER BURGEONING WITH INFANTS AND YOUNGSTERS, love for the older ones became general, rather than specific. Less and less the center of attention, Ana became a watcher. Elders were only vaguely aware of her standing in the shadows, or half-buried in a book, but always attentive, listening to their conversations.

She began to see how books could be a shield, a bulwark behind which she hid—only her eyes and the top of her head visible—observing. On dark days, when she felt totally forgotten, invisible even to herself, she learned to turn her attention to the book before her, lost in a landscape of words that lifted her out of herself.

She sat with Noah while he kept watch over the valley, reading to him about the discovery of penicillin, or the thermoscopic eyes of squid which perceived heat-generating objects through photochemical reactions. The boar-hounds gathered outside his window, laying their dark, wet muzzles on their paws. Ana's voice seemed to calm them down. And children gathered too, making her the center of attention. And in that way, she became a lover of books, pirating them out of the library, dragging them up Keola Road.

One day a young man followed her. When she stopped for a rainbow shave-ice, he stopped, too. He was wearing blue jeans, a T-shirt with a pack of cigarettes rolled up in one sleeve like a Merchant Marine. He looked sort of local, and yet not, a sloe-eyed *hapa-haole* with long surfer hair.

"I know who you are," she said. "Your father's called Steve-a-dor."

"Who calls him that?"

"My uncles."

"They making fun of him because he's Jewish?"

She didn't know what "Jewish" was. "They call him that because he works the docks. They got nicknames for anybody with a job."

He moved closer. "No need to lie. I know folks hate us because my dad was Army, and married a local girl. And because he's Jewish."

She watched her shave-ice melt through the hole in the bottom of the cup. She felt its coolness hit her feet.

"So, what's your name?"

He stood up straighter. "Tommy . . . Suzuki . . . Goldberg."

It didn't sound right. It didn't sound wrong. It just didn't sound usual. He wore two chains around his neck. One held a small crucifix, the other what looked like a six-pointed star.

"What's that you're wearing?"

"Catholic cross. And Star of David. My mom and pop have different kind religions."

". . . . .is that hard for you?" she asked.

He shrugged. "Sometimes confusing."

He reached out and caught a drip from beneath her shave-ice, then licked it from his hand. She held her breath, caught by his scent. Tobacco, young man sweat. He smelled different from the boys she knew. She wondered if it was because he was "Jewish." His hair was brown, but blondish at the ends. His skin was brown too, but with a yellowish undertone like when brown skin was wet. His almond-shaped eyes were ordinary for a local, but he had the longest eyelashes she had ever seen on a human. She found him rather beautiful.

He asked her name, then rolled down his sleeve, flicked a match with his thumbnail and lit up a cigarette like a pro. She watched him exhale, watched the smoke drift like a thought. They sat on a bench facing the sea, and almost in one breath he told her how his grandparents, German Jews, had settled in someplace called New Jersey. Wanting to see the world, his dad had enlisted in the Army, got stationed in Honolulu, and married a Hawaiian-Japanese girl.

"So, what's *your* story?"

Ana shrugged. "My parents died. No big deal. So tell me . . . what does 'Jewish' mean?"

In stops and starts, he tried to explain what he understood. How they were people descended from ancient Hebrews . . . who were descendants of northern Semitic people . . . who claimed descent from the prophets Abraham, Isaac, and Jacob.

"Pop says they were also called . . . Israelites. Folks who shared one heritage based on, ah . . . Judaism."

She tried very hard to follow. "And what is that?"

"A religion based on the Bible and the Talmud."

A dozen words she had never heard before.

"Pop says there was once an ancient kingdom called Judah in this place South Palestine. Between the Mediterranean and the Dead Sea. But it disappeared."

While he talked about Moses and the parting of the Red Sea, Ana sat back overwhelmed. This boy was opening up a brand-new world, people and places she could never have imagined.

"I like the sound of that guy, Moses. I've always been suspicious of Jesus Christ."

"Yeah? Why?" Tommy fingered his crucifix.

"Well, he makes plenty mistakes. He lets folks get away with murder."

She was thinking of her mother. If Jesus was fair, he'd burn down her house in San Francisco, so she would have to come crawling home.

Walking her up the highway to Keola Road, he touched her elbow.

"I heard about your family, too. All those wounded vets. Who takes care of them?"

She suddenly wanted to impress him. "I do."

"Don't they have wives and things?"

"Yeah. Sure. But folks always coming and going. You know, real island style."

That night, all the youngsters asleep, she watched her Aunty Pua sit in a chair with her Bible. As she got into the swing of the text, the woman swayed backwards and forwards rhythmically, ducking her head in great nods of moral affirmation. Each night when she opened that Bible, she seemed to have the time of her life.

Ana glanced round the room at her elders, then took a deep breath. "How come we're Christian, instead of Jewish? Jesus never parted the sea like Moses."

In the silence, Pua stood and swerved across the room, and smacked Ana's head with her Bible. She sat on the floor in shock, watching her uncle and aunty go at it. Ben finally pushed the woman into a corner, using his arm as a club.

"You evah touch dis girl again . . . I going broke yo' face."

Pua held up her Bible. "She said a sacrilegious thing!"

"Oh, you!" Ben shouted. "One day you spouting Christian, next day you calling on our ancient gods. Why you think dis girl's mixed up?"

"Not mixed up," Pua said. "Too clever. Going be just like her mama."

Tito slapped down his playing cards. "I think you jealous of her mama. She got momentum. What you got?"

They squandered half the night, arguing, while Ana studied the heavens, wondering which star was David.

MEETING TOMMY SUZUKI GOLDBERG WAS THE BEGINNING OF awareness, of how small her island world was. And of how she could love someone, knowing they would not love her back. He would become the thing she rested her eyes upon. His mere existence in the world—the knowledge that tomorrow he would walk down a hall toward her—would help Ana survive the random atrocities of high school, the knifings, and pregnancies, the murky smell of the public lav where gang girls nodded out in the sweet declensions of drugs. Even the sentencing of two drug-running cousins to five years at Halawa High-Security Prison, which locals called the "Halawa Hilton."

Mostly, she would be grateful to Tommy for awakening in her a deeper awareness of her damaged uncles, that fraternity of broken men. Sometimes she stood in the center of the house and looked around. She had never known if it was patriotism or love of combat that drove the men in her family to volunteer for every war. And now each week Ana wrote letters to her cousin, Lopaka, recovering somewhere from bomb fragments that had shattered his leg in Vietnam.

This is what we live on, she thought. *Their military pensions, their veteran's disability checks.*

Folks said her uncles had it made. No more grinding ninety-hour workweek, no more union dues. No need for food stamps, or Welfare. But some nights she watched Tito in his wheelchair, staring at his lap like a child wondering what had happened. And one night she saw Ben standing in the field, waving his arm and shouting at the sky. Later, she found him weeping in his room.

"No mo' pride! So many years now, useless."

Before his war he had been a heavy-equipment operator, one of the best on the Wai'anae Coast. When he came home without an arm, the VA tried to train him for clerical work.

He had gone into severe depression. "Sitting at one desk . . . like a girl!"

Now Ana put her arm around him, softly scolding him.

"Uncle Ben, pick up your eyes. Look how you keep us safe in this crazy family. Without you, we'd be killing each other. You feed us kids, make us do homework, buy our clothes. You give us plenty pride, reminding us what's right, what's wrong. You're our papa, our *ali'i*. Folks up and down Keola Road respect you. How can you say you're useless!"

He sat up and wiped his eyes, and scratched his belly with his big, bronze hand. "Ana. You my best medicine. My best t'ing."

Perhaps that was the beginning of caring on her part. A conscious need to look after the men of her family, men who had chosen to look after her.

SHE ENTERED HER MIDTEENS FULL OF TREMOR, A LUSTFUL RANCOR at the world. A young woman training for adversity. Some days she stood in the yard slugging a ratty old punching bag, then wiped red dirt from her feet, ran into the house, and studied her face in a mirror. Pale probing eyes, defiant cheekbones. A stubborn jaw. She twisted in front of the mirror, studying the reflection of her skinny behind. She wanted muscles, the buttocks of a horse! She wanted to be desired but powerful, a woman beyond possession.

She spent long hours in the sun until she was dark as *kukui* nut. Dark showed she was local, and tough, not a girl to kid around with. But she avoided Tommy's gang, the "park boys," who hung out at beaches, drinking and breaking into cars. In less than two years, all goodness seemed to have been rinsed out of him. By now he was seasoned, with a tough, *hapa* look, yet sometimes she felt his eyes on her. An uncanny sensation: to be held in the eyes of a handsome young man. A surfer and a stoner, he kept a rolled joint over his ear, always in a crowd, yet watching her. Maybe admiration, maybe curiosity.

"No need for friends. Ey, Ana?"

She wondered if that was good or bad. She tried to sound world-weary. "No time for fun. I have responsibilities."

"You mean your uncles, all those men you take care of?"

"Yeah. Cooking, cleaning, laundry."

Tommy smiled. "Liar. I know your pretty cousin, Rosie, does all that."

Hippies had started flooding the coast in psychedelic-painted vans, lying on Nanakuli's beaches stoned, exulting in the syntax of grass. In clashes with locals, there were knifings, even shootings. One day Tommy broke into a van. He brought her a tie-dyed scarf and showed her four ten-dollar bills.

Ana looked at him, disgusted. "You think this makes you interesting?"

He began to reek of bad deeds. Next time it was a silver bracelet he had lifted from a shop. He put it on her wrist and tried to kiss her. Ana flung the bracelet to the dirt.

"Well, what you want, then?" he asked.

"Not you. You think you can have what you want from me with stolen goods?"

She walked toward the beach, shouting back at him. "It's all downhill for you, Tommy Two-Gods! You trying so hard to fit in, you going wind up at 'Halawa Hilton.' Know what they do to boys in there? Pretty . . . young . . . *Jewish* boys?"

He stared after her in shock, as she dived into a wave, feeling the undertow, wanting to drown out of shame. Why did she say that thing to him? Where had it come from? She stroked into another slamming wave, then picked herself off the ocean floor, remembering what a girl had told her about Jewish men. They were different. They had gone through something called "circumcision." Whatever it was, it was painful. It made them more gentle in bed, yet made them better lovers. Ana realized her rudeness to Tommy, her pushing him away was because she wanted him to touch her. She simply wanted him.

One morning she heard the skies crack, reverberating thunder. She sat up in bed listening to her uncles curse.

"Sounds like next war starting *here*."

"Army testing bombs again up in Mākua, blowing that whole valley to hell."

Mākua, up near the tip of the Wai'anae Coast, had once been a beautiful mountain ridge overlooking the sea, a sacred place of temples and grave sites. For over twenty years the mountains and valley there had been so heavily gouged and gutted by bombs in Army war maneuvers, it had turned into a no-man's-land.

Across the island, high-school and university students who had protested the war in Vietnam now demonstrated against the military's continuing use of their homelands for war games. Every other weekend Ana watched students march down the highway carrying banners. GET OFF OUR ISLANDS. BOMB YOUR OWN BACKYARDS.

On such a day Tommy walked up to her. "Ana. I'm dropping out. Going to enlist."

She saw his face, even his posture, had changed. "Don't you want to graduate high school?"

He shook his head. "What I want is action. See some combat."

"But Vietnam is over."

"My pop was a sergeant for twenty years. He says there's always going to be a war. The military *needs* wars." He almost shook with anticipation. "So, what you think? I'm going be one *hapa* Green Beret."

She reached up and touched his face. "I guess it's better than prison, Tommy."

He took her hand and held it. "What you said, it made me think. There's more to life than this dead coast. A whole world to see. I hope you see it, too."

He sounded like Lopaka, like all the wounded men she knew.

"I will," she said. "I will."

"Look. I'm sorry I stole. Sorry I disappointed you. I know your mama didn't die, she left you. I'm sorry about that, too. You know, you're not the prettiest girl at school. Not even the smartest. But . . . you're different, Ana. Something proud about you. Even just the way you walk. I think I'm going to miss you."

They stood under a plumeria tree and trade winds blew the petals past their shoulders. Deep shadows of Nanakuli now determined they must enter them. They walked for a while, hand in hand, then lay down in vines and weeds and struggled awkwardly, becoming lovers. At first she felt terror. She had spied on couples and knew the posture of love, knew he would climb on top of her. He could possibly crush her in a moment's passion.

Just before he entered her, she asked, "Tommy. How much do you weigh?"

He lost his erection. But then he was hard again, trying not to collapse on her. It seemed to be over in a minute. Later, they tried again and it was better. Better, for the incredible smell of his hair in her face, his bittersweet tobacco breath. Better because he lasted longer before he shuddered and sighed. She felt pain. She bled, and cried a little. They both cried. Not out of guilt, but out of astonishment. Was that all there was to it?

Tommy lay down beside her. "There's got to be more. There must be something we don't know about, something we left out."

She looked at his handsome face, his features so perfectly aligned. *This is enough*, she thought. *I will remember this.* She would relive these hours for years, remembering every word he uttered, knowing he could never utter them again, because there would only be this one first time. They made love each night for weeks, and it got better. They had left nothing out.

Then one day as he approached, she saw a different face. There was nothing there she recognized. Very tenderly, like a priest, he put his hands on her shoulders.

"Yesterday I enlisted in the Army."

She stared at sunlight varnishing his forearm. She smiled, and stroked that arm like someone gently stropping a razor. She was already moving ahead, building her life without him. Already wise to the truth: that no one stayed. That no one stood beside you, defending you, for now, for good, for always.

Tommy left. She sat with Noah in the dark.

"I know we have to take what comes. To forget, and then move on. But sometimes I wonder . . . where does all this forgetting lead? I mean, when we're older, what's left when we look back at this thing that was our life?"

Noah hung his head. She was too young to ask such questions. Too young to sound so old.

"I wonder if I would understand things better if I had had a mother."

He tried to respond. But just now he had no words for her. His hands shook as he lit a cigarette, trying to introduce order to his mind.

. . . here's a match, here's a ashtray on da sill. Careful, careful. Yesterday, knocked it out da window, butts all over chili pepper plant . . . auwē! Little chili pepper shriveled. Hosed it down . . . picked up butts . . . threw dem to da goat. Same goat used to faint when Ana screamed, tied up to da clothesline . . . Cannot be! How old dat damn goat now? . . . Here's her hand, soft and warm in mine . . . here's her sweet face crying in da Kleenex . . .

He wanted to whisper "Ana! Live!" He wanted to tell her it did not matter if folks went away. That she was richer because other humans had loved her, even hurt her. And that those humans were enriched by her. He had come back from a horrible place, but that place had let him live. He wanted to tell her how life was a miracle. Each moment of living, each living thing, a miracle. He had so much to tell her. He did not know how.

NIKOLAO

Nikolai

TWELVE YEARS BEFORE ANA HAD COME INTO THE WORLD, A BOY was born in a place so bleak and cold, his first breath was visible. Years later Nikolai Volenko would swear he could remember the moment of birth—bursting from between his mother's thighs, his screams creating little clouds of vapor. He would remember a smoke-blackened ice hut, smoldering carcasses, women who smelled like great, wild beasts.

The ice hut sat in a virgin forest surrounded by the subarctic tundra of north Russia. It was a region called Archangel'sk that faced the White Sea, only ice-capped waves between them and the North Pole. A forsaken place at the edge of the world, as forbidding as Siberia.

In his first few months of life, the infant, Nikolai, slept inside great greasy pelts of bear and elk sewn together with needles made from bone. He lived pressed against his mother's breasts, held fast in her arms like ice holding fast to an inlet. Thus, he would always carry the cold of Archangel'sk in his marrow. It paralyzed everything, even thought, so that the women lived mostly in silence, communicating with grunts and gestures.

Here daylight was weak and fleeting; they huddled close and slept with their nightmares unbroken. And when there was no food, the snows too deep to hunt, they slept for days, unaware of the passage of time. Perhaps out in the world empires were rising and falling, perhaps another world war had started. Here, it only snowed. And then the wind howled. Sometimes his mother roused herself and passed the child around, and women held him like a tender roast.

"*Goloobka. Our little goloobka.*" Our dove. For he was life. He gave them hope.

It would be these women he remembered most indelibly—how they gathered round him, sitting hunched and neckless, their shoulders on a level with their eyes. Great crones in birch-bark boots and leggings tied with animal gut, and ragged Army greatcoats so thickly padded their bodies were spherical. They appeared wrinkled and ancient, with breath rank as wolves, yet some of them were still in their thirties. Life in Archangel'sk had reduced them to creatures of animal cunning with a touch of remembered tenderness.

As he grew out of infancy, their stench became a comfort to the boy. He learned to clutch the toylike skulls of lynx or fox, and to inhale the lonely madness when a woman screamed. They did not scream often. Rather, when one of them learned that the husband they had followed to this place had perished, they simply stepped out of the hut into shriek-ing winds and temperatures far below zero, and died frozen into standing blocks of ice.

Those who survived watched him take his first steps in the hut, and they smiled and patted his footprints, so tiny and lovable. Sitting him close to the fire, they blew warm breath on his naked toes, rubbing them briskly, and sang little hunting chants of the strategy of foxes, the scru-ples of wolves.

When temperatures rose a few degrees and daylight endured for an hour or two, they rubbed bear grease on his cheeks and strapped him to their chests inside their padded coats and plunged with snowshoes through the virgin forests of Archangel'sk, through birch and pine and giant fir, while they stalked wildlife, checked the rusty, cold jaws of their traps, and set fish lines in ice holes of a frozen pond. Some days they har-vested gray human skulls protruding from the snow.

Occasionally they took Nikolai when they trudged fifty miles on homemade skis to a wood-pulp mill across the frozen Dvina River. There they traded fish and pelts and even sex for a rifle, bullets, fuel, tobacco, muddy green vodka made from rye, and matches whose wood was tipped with phosphorus and wax. Days later they struggled through snows for-ever crisscrossed by men in chains back to their ice hut near the perime-ters of the *lag*, the labor camp, of Archangel'sk.

And as they traveled, the great forests gifted the boy with miracles. Rising from seemingly fathomless snow, the shimmering, golden dome of a gutted church with its shattered, tongueless bell. Redberry bushes like bonfires suddenly bursting through the ice. One night his mother cried out and popped his head from inside her coat, and he saw in the endless expanse of Eurasian skies, fantastic dancing lights.

"The Northern Aurora!"

As he grew old enough to venture out in snowshoes, the little boy's senses grew sharper. He learned how the mute frozen world came alive when he stood still, so that he heard the sigh of a dying crow crucified on iced branches. The bubbling up of blood as deer lay down to a flash of wolves. Following behind the women as they stalked prey, he heard their hunter heartbeats, thundering like drums. He heard glass shattering: ice cracking through the forest, a sound old as time.

He learned how to listen for the panting of the lynx, and to eat snow so the hunted fox could not see his breath. He learned to blink rapidly to keep his eyes from icing shut, but to move slowly and breathe evenly. To move fast would create a sweat under so many layers of fur and cloth. Sweat would freeze, and slow the heart. A sleepiness would come. Then coma.

Other things he would remember: how frost crystallized on the gray fur of wolves so they seemed to be running in coats of diamonds, silvery green against blue arctic snow. And he would remember how, as light deepened into purple dusk, a freezing mist hovered, then rose from the ground and gave the impression the women were floating like saints as they glided home.

WHEN HE WAS FOUR YEARS OLD THE FOREST TURNED ON HIM, leaving a hole in his life where his youth should have been. One day, following behind the hunting women, Nikolai heard the sound of barking voices, and then dragging chains. The women grew still and moved behind a grove of firs. From there he saw long lines of men in ragged clothes, so vaporously thin he thought he was imagining them. They semed to hum as they stumbled past, skull-like heads hung with cold, exhaustion. Armed guards in trucks followed alongside them aiming machine guns, and now and then a guard dog leapt. Teeth scraping bone.

He began to be aware of them in the distance through the trees. The clanging of leg chains as they sawed logs, nearby a campfire where guards played with their dogs, making them beg and roll over. Some guards, half-drunk, shot at prisoners for sport. Each day the sound of shifting gears—trucks fighting for traction on the ice as they hauled a dead man back to camp.

One night when temperatures rose above zero, Nikolai's mother walked him down a path of frozen footprints humpbacked with ice and mud. Slowly, laboriously, she hoisted herself up into a tree, high into snow-laden branches, and pulled him up beside her.

"That's where your father is."

He gazed into the distance at razor-wired fences, above them barriers of rolled barbed wire. Along the fences were guard towers and emplacements holding machine guns. Every few seconds a spotlight from a tower swept the camp. From inside one of the towers a man with a rifle seemed to tilt drunkenly, tossing a bottle to the ground. There appeared to be nothing else to see, but endless boxcars on rusty tracks, and long gray buildings, dismal and decrepit, that seemed to go on for miles.

His mother whispered, "They pack them on those cattle cars . . . and run them north . . . until the tracks run out."

Nikolai grew impatient. He was cold and he wanted to take his father home. "Where is Papa?"

Just then a truck with watery headlights moved across the campgrounds, its lights falling on the form of a man facedown. Guards stepped cursing from the truck, picked up the body by the ankle, and flung it aside. Even with leg chains, it seemed so light, so weightless, it hung in the air like cloth, then appeared to thoughtfully float down. Guard dogs made sport of it, growling and dragging it to and fro, tearing at it till they grew bored. Nikolai started to cry out, then he saw that his mother had sucked her fist into her mouth with such force she seemed to have partially swallowed it.

After that night he listened more closely when the women talked, hoarding phrases until he began to vaguely understand them.

"Niki's father . . . a hero in the war. But after war, two careless words sentence him to death . . ."

Like thousands of wives whose husbands were condemned to labor camps across Russia after World War II, Niki's mother had followed her husband from Leningrad to Archangel'sk, a grueling journey that took over a year. They had trudged through war-ravaged towns and mined fields, held each other up in winter snows and summer swamps filled with deadly mosquitoes. Begging their way till half of them were broken, diseased, near-dead.

It was summer when the women had finally reached Archangel'sk, a brief month or two when temperatures rose above freezing. They dug deep holes in the earth to sleep in and that was how they lived, deep in earth, eating birds and berries. When men came in chains to chop down trees, the women had popped their heads up from the earth, asking for their husbands. And so they made contact.

In time, camp guards had heard of women hiding in the forests. They aimed rifles down the earth holes and ordered them out, then used them like goats for sex and pushed them back into the earth. Some guards took pity, tracking down a prisoner, and in that way, after many months, Nikolai's mother, Vera, had found her husband.

She made a sturdy slingshot from small birch branches, then traded homemade cigarettes with guards for pencils, rubber bands. She wrote to her husband on bits of rags, balled them up and shot them over the prison fence. How many were received she never knew.

But one night a slender missile flew back at her. The next night another. Messages signed with his name. Sergeivitch Volenko. He aimed them over the fence with a kind of homemade blowgun, notes rolled up tight as darts, written on paper scraps in lumpy, rusty red. She learned that he had scratched dust from barrack walls to thicken his blood, with which he wrote his messages.

As winter returned and snows came, the women had built ice huts deep in the forests near the *lag*, and there they lived like Eskimos. Each day they ran into the woods where prisoners felled trees, men bent and skeletal from disease and near starvation. They hid behind the trees looking for their husbands. And when they found them each man and wife stood dumb, pressing their heads to each other's shoulders.

Months passed, then one day Vera saw him. Sergeivitch, just eyes and bone, his filthy skull now bald. At first they stood and stared as prisoners started fistfights to distract the guards. Then Vera ran forward. Her husband hobbling toward her like a child. No words, just cries, and holding on.

It happened for weeks, their running together, holding each other while trees crashed around them. And in that way, Nikolai was conceived midst the white firs of Archangel'sk. One day they stood braced against a fir tree, making love, Sergei's leg chains singing against the bark. In that moment they had both looked up, their cheeks stroked by the blind tenderness of snow, frost patterns overlapping their eyes as they created him.

Months passed before she saw her husband again. She held him while he shuddered, so weak and starved he had no words. She pushed bits of deer liver into his mouth and watched him swallow them whole.

"I am carrying your child," she whispered.

In that moment his eyes had lit up, he found the strength to smile even though his teeth were gone. Vera never saw him again. Week after week she ran through the forest, stood outside the camp fence at night and slingshot messages to him. And finally, the child was born. Still week after week, month after month, she stood outside the fence and waited.

One day a woman caught her hand in the jaw of a trap and hacked her hand off at the wrist so she would not freeze to death. Her wrist turned black and stank, and then the arm turned black. She kissed Nikolai on the cheek and walked out into the snow. That was how it was for some. When death came for them they did not seem surprised, they did not mind. Their men had already perished here.

In time, some of the women became like trees. Their ragged coats grew filthy with grease and resin, attracting leaves and dirt which stuck to them. Under layers of *babushki* and rank pelts, their hair and skin became like bark. Mold grew in their ears, in their armpits, and inside their birch-bark boots. They carried this dank smell of rot, and they became the rot. When they died, they fell like trees and they became like logs. Sometimes during a brief thaw, a corpse was found before wolves came. One with berries sprouting in her hair. One whose groin had become a thriving nest of beetles.

Yet, month after month, year after year, each woman waited. Vera still stood outside the prison fence and slingshot messages. Sometimes she even called his name.

"Sergeivitch Volenko!"

One night his blowgun was thrown over the fence. This was how she knew. She lost her mind a little, then she found it.

Nikolai was six years old the year Archangel'sk finally released them. It took Vera two more years to work her way back to Leningrad, dragging her child through the same ravaged villages and blown-up fields of a country that would never quite recover from its wars. They survived by stealing, sleeping in barnyards amongst half-starved sheep for warmth. Or, they slept in wet manure which, as it hardened, became a warm sarcophagus. At dawn they drank from cow's teats, then sliced tiny cuts in their flanks and drank their blood, so nourishing. Ever after, the boy would have great affection for cows.

IN LENINGRAD, EVEN BEGGARS STARED, FOR THE MOTHER AND child looked and smelled like death. But Vera rejoiced, they had survived. As they scavenged for food, they began hearing of new purges across Russia. Stalin was making clean sweeps through major cities. Leningrad, Moscow, Kiev. Wanting to beautify them again, make them architectural gems. He wanted to show the world that Russia had recovered from World War II, how healthy and handsome the people were, how well they lived. And so he had begun deporting all of the wounded, deformed, and disabled.

He rounded them up in every city, poured them into trucks, freight trains, cattle cars, and sent them south to regions the outside world had never seen, had hardly heard of. Even disabled soldiers were thrown away, to Uzbekistan, Tajikstan, Kyrgzstan. Most deportees froze to death in vasty, empty mountain ranges. The world would not know this for many years. Even Russians would not know, and many of them would not believe. Heroes, whole families, faithful Communists—millions tossed aside.

Vera was still young but the years, and Archangel'sk, had turned her to a crone. Her spine bent to a spider's hunch, she limped with the pain of arthritis. Her features had always been mismatched, distinctly asymmetrical, a face that frightened strangers. To Nikolai she was beautiful. At night her arms enfolded him, her body smelling of monthly blood, as she forced food between his lips, depriving herself and growing thinner.

For a year they hid, living in drainage pipes outside the city. Dirt kept their skin dark and filthy so flashlights could not find them. He learned to stand so still he melted into walls. Once they pressed their faces against a wall for fourteen hours. In that way he learned that if one looks at a thing long enough, they become that thing. But then, the sound of boots running in formation. Another roundup. He saw the shadow of his mother as it limped beneath a streetlight. The shadow of a soldier's hand reach out and grab her.

His mother turned and cried, "Run, Niki! Run!"

He could not. They threw her on a truck and he climbed up beside her, as soldiers flashed lights on his face, and up and down his body. A skinny, filthy kid, but not deformed. He could be useful as child labor in the city. They pushed him off the truck. He watched his dear mother's face grow smaller as they pulled away, her hand still reaching out.

That day consumed his boyhood. Consumed him into manhood. After that he pretended he had lost his tongue, that he was mute. They would deport him south, and he would find his mother. But gnawing hunger betrayed him. During a roundup, soldiers hoisted him onto a truck with dozens of broken children. A soldier studied him, then offered him a candy.

"Hungry?" he asked, holding out the sweet.

Near-starving, foolishly Nikolai answered, "*Da! Pazhalsta.*" Yes. Please.

They threw him off the truck.

Now he lived in typhus-ridden streets, hobbling in shoes of rags and ropes. He slept with gangs of street boys, huddling end to end in straw like corpses. He stole and cheated and lived how he could, depending on his wits. And maybe that was the end of truth for him. That was how Nikolai Volenko learned that, deprived of blood—a mother to protect him—lies were his only salvation.

NOI NO KA ʻIEWE

Request for the Placenta

ANA HAD BEGUN TO LEARN THAT WHAT OTHER HUMANS HAD, they kept. It made her sharpen her boundaries, dig deep trenches in order to protect herself. The one person she allowed into her heart fully and with total trust was Rosie, and together they watched as life in the larger world accelerated. The Vietnam War had ended. American and Soviet spacecraft had linked up in outer space, and somewhere in those years, direct long-distance dialing came to the islands.

She discovered she could, simply by dialing a number, hear her mother's voice. One night she crept into the kitchen and looked at a slip of paper, the number in San Francisco. She picked up the receiver, put it down, picked it up again and dialed. Her heart beating so hard, her hair shook.

"Hello . . . ?"

She hung up and sank to her haunches on the floor. The voice sounded soft, educated. A woman out there fooling the world. Then she remembered that her mother *was* educated, that she had earned a degree and had a job.

She crawled into bed beside Rosie. "She answered the phone."

"And you hung up." Rosie yawned and rubbed her stomach. "You know what that tells her? That she's still important in your life. You want her to come home so you can forgive her."

"She doesn't want forgiveness."

"*Everybody* wants forgiveness. A chance to wipe the slate, start clean again."

They lay in half-light, staring at Rosie's bulging stomach. In the past year she had diligently stopped gorging on food and begun to slim down. Then, a chance encounter, a semi-romance and she grew big again. Just twenty-one now, she announced that she was *hāpai*, and that the child's father had left the coast. When Aunty Pua heard the news she careened through the house waving her Bible, flicking holy water at the walls.

"A slut. Just like her mama! We got to pray the devil out of this house of illegitimates."

The family ignored her, for "illegitimate" was a Western, not a Hawaiian, concept. The next day Pua moved from room to room, slapping the walls with ti leaves, muttering old Hawaiian chants.

From his wheelchair, Tito laughed. "Ey, sistah, make up your mind. You one missionary Bible thumper? Or one *kahuna pule?*"

Week by week, Ana watched Rosie's body change. Her nipples enlarged and turned brown. A dark line grew upward from the bottom of her abdomen. Another line started down from the top. This was *alawela*, the scorched path, and when these lines met and went into the navel, the baby would be born. Rosie spent restless nights as ancestors entered her dreams, discussing the coming child's *inoa pō*, its name given in darkness.

Cousins took turns rubbing kukui oil into her breasts and stomach, for strength and lubrication. They walked her down to the sea, where she stood in calm waters, moving her stomach back and forth to loosen the baby so it would not "stick" during birth. Ana stood faithfully beside her, holding her round the waist during the sea bath.

"Do you think our mamas did *'au 'au kai* like this for us?"

Rosie nodded. "My mama told me that was when she loved me most, when the ocean took my weight."

Ana pictured her own mother in the sea, asking it to take her weight. Take it forever. She pictured her mother pounding her stomach with her fists.

A powerful old *kahuna pale keiki*, a midwife, came and laid her hands on Rosie to see if the baby was placed right.

"No more wearing of *lei*," she said, "or baby could be born with *piko* choking neck." The *piko* was the umbilical cord.

"No stringing of fish, baby could have rotten breath. No eating mountain apple. Baby might be born with red birthmark."

Strangely, Rosie had no cravings for salt, or sours. What she craved were fresh hearts of bamboo. Day after day, she woke begging for bamboo. Uncles drove to the wet side of the island, chopping down bamboo trees for the hearts. They watched her eat them by the bowlsful.

"Not good," Ben said. "Sharpened bamboo our first weapon before we knew metal. Still symbolic of cutting. Means child will be cruel, unkind."

The *pale keiki* tranced Rosie, taking away her craving for bamboo. Untranced, she looked around bewildered, and said she wanted squid. Hunks of juicy fried squid, and squid creamed in coconut milk. She craved squid every day and folks sighed out, relieved. It meant the child would be loving and clinging. Ana looked askance at the doings of the midwife.

"Rosie, you believe all this foolishness?"

"*Pēlā paha. 'A'ole paha.*" Maybe. Maybe not. "But it is better to believe."

Then, in the last two months of her pregnancy, Rosie began eating *'ilima* blossoms and drinking *hau* tree bark tea, lubricants that would help her in the birthing. Some days she lay back planning her child's future while Ana *lomi*'ed her stomach with kukui oil.

"She's going to be educated. A prideful woman. Like you."

"Like me?"

"Yes. I been thinking about you plenty, Ana. Fate cannot shape itself to you. You don't sit still. You're going to *choose* your fate, be something in the world. You're going to finish high school."

Rosie glanced at their uncles in the next room. "Never used their GI Bills. Can you believe? Could have got high-school diplomas, gone to trade school, university. Even I once dreamed of college, now too late for me. You got to do that, Ana. We got to break the pattern in this family."

Long before her pregnancy, Rosie had begun to carry herself with extra care, giving her Polynesian beauty and massive size a certain dignity. Since Ava's death, she had even begun to speak differently, seeming wiser and sure. Folks said her mother's death had birthed her. She was slowly becoming the link between the generations, the one the family turned to for advice.

Now she patted her stomach. "Put your hand here, on my child's beating heart."

Ana gently laid her hand there.

"Now. Swear you're going get a higher education. You're going make this family proud."

She swore, and then she whispered, "I already know what I want to be. But I don't want to say it."

"Then swear on my child you going to accomplish it."

Ana snatched her hand back. "Cannot . . . not yet."

She was curious and smart, but seldom volunteered in class, afraid she would stand out, "make ass" of herself as an achiever. And so for a while she ditched classes, got into fistfights and ran on the fringes of a girl gang. It was a matter of pride, of upholding Nanakuli's toughness, its "country" reputation. Teachers evaluated Ana as bright, but "noncompliant," one step from becoming delinquent. She looked at her report card. C's, all C's. She looked at Rosie's stomach, remembering her promise.

"I swear, by the time that baby's born, I'm going to make upper third of my class."

Perhaps because someone believed in her she began to push herself. With unswerving focus, she rose to the upper third of her class and then pushed on, aiming for Honor Roll. And she began to see how language could give her access to higher learning. One night she made an announcement.

"Today my teacher said we got to learn 'proper' English, so we can study things like math and science. Ho, man! Kids got plenty angry. Everybody yelling. 'How we going talk to parents widdout Pidgin? Pidgin same as English.' "

She played with her fork, slightly embarrassed. "I raised my hand and said Pidgin is *not* the same as English. It's not an inferior kind of English. It's a *different* language than English. Like French, or Spanish. Like Hawaiian Mother Tongue. My teacher said that was a good point. So now I have to write a paper on it."

The family sat quiet, not understanding.

"So now . . . she punishing you?" Ben asked.

"No, Uncle. It's sort of an honor, and I get extra credit for the paper. She wants me to write about how it's important that we speak all three languages. Hawaiian, Pidgin, English, so we can keep up with the rest of the world. We going to be what she calls . . . trilingual."

A cousin argued. "But, we already know da kine . . . English."

Ana shook her head. "We only know it as slang. When we're happy, or sad, or have to say something important, we always say it in Pidgin."

"Dat's right," Ben said. ". . . 'cause Pidgin real! It what we feel *pu'uwai*, from da heart."

Ana sighed. "Yes, but could anyone understand physics if Einstein had talked Pidgin? 'Da kine = mc squared.' My teacher said that to study chemistry, math, even world literature, we have to learn 'proper' English. We have to express ourselves that way."

Two cousins pushed back from the table. "English fo' *haole*. *Haole* buggahs stole our lands."

"Fuck English. Fuck yo' teachah. And fuck education."

Ben smacked them on the shoulders and forced them to sit down while Rosie pointed at each boy.

"That's right. You kids keep messing with your lives, your *pakalōlō*, your six-packs. One day be heroin, and crime. Couple years from now, no English, no education—dropouts or pushouts—you'll both be on Welfare. Or pulling time at the Halawa Hilton."

One of the boys spoke earnestly. "Aunty, I going finish high school, 'kay? But I like fixing cars, I like engines. Smell of oil, stuff like dat. Maybe one day I like have my own garage. You telling me I got to learn *haole* English fo' dis kine work?"

Rosie studied him. Her fingers tapped the table. "No, Jason, you don't. But I will tell you this. In Taiwan, folks speak Taiwanese. In Spain, they speak Spanish. Probably in Africa, they speak African. But when folks leave their homes and go out in the world, the universal language that is spoken most . . . is English. Proper English. Now, unless you plan to stay in Nanakuli all your life, you better think about it."

Later they sat on the *lānai*, watching dusk decanting off the fender of a truck. Ana felt alternately sad and pleased. Sad, because the world was invading their language, their traditions. Pleased, because Rosie was trying to prepare them, to arm them in a way. The two of them swung back and forth, chains of the old porch swing barking and whining.

Rosie splayed her hands across her stomach. "You know, this house is full of interesting, intelligent folks. Our men went halfway round the word. Ben saw Paris, Naples. Great-uncle Willy saw the pyramids in Egypt. Look at the lives our great-aunties lived. They remember when we had a queen! But they never tell. And no one asks. We don't talk-story anymore. This family was once *pulupulu ahi,* real fire-starters! Now we're just decaying into silence."

She grunted and slowly shifted her weight. "Time we wake up. I don't want my baby born into a tongueless clan."

For six nights Rosie dreamed of constellations. On the seventh she woke and saw the Pleiades above her, the seven major stars gleaming so brilliantly they seemed to be aiming at the house.

"So. That is the name our ancestors have chosen for the child. Her *inoa pō* will be Makali'i, for the Pleiades, and for our seven major islands of Hawai'i Nei."

When the lines of the *alawela*, the scorched path, had met and gone into Rosie's navel her labor pains began. The old *pale keiki* was called. Boiling water, towels, and clean sheets were readied. Ana prepared herself as *ko'o kua*, Rosie's back support. With the elders gathered on both sides of Rosie's bed, the old midwife coached them on how to give physical support if Rosie needed an arm to grip, and emotional support when she needed women to bear down with her. And she acknowledged the psychic forces of her great-aunties who had birthed many babies through the years and now stood praying and chanting to *Haumea*, goddess of birth.

With each preliminary pain Rosie was tossed backwards on her bed, but she never cried out, a thing *kapu* during childbirth. The old midwife looked round at the elders.

"Who will accept *ho'okau ka 'eha*? Who will carry this girl's pain?"

Fearful, most of the men looked down. Only silent Noah stepped forward. The midwife nodded, pointing her finger at him.

"Go then. Lie down. And be a woman!"

Noah fell back, as three younger cousins helped him to his room.

The old midwife threw her hands in the air. "*Ē hāmau! Ho'olohe!*" Be silent. Listen. "Have not the dark lines of the *alawela* met at the *piko*? Has not the cry of *'Ewe'ewe-iki*, ghost mother, been heard singing on the roof? And look. The *'ina'ina* has appeared." First bloodstains. "It is the time of *Hānau*." Childbirth.

Folks gathered, watching and waiting as Rosie's pains became intense. They lifted her and carried her to *lauhala* mats piled high on the floor. They took turns with the midwife, gently bearing down on her stomach. Even children were involved, for this was life's most natural process. Girls ran back and forth with towels, scissors, and water. Boys stood at the window calling out the shape of a cloud, the flight of a bird, omens that would tell elders many things about the coming child.

They prayed and continued bearing down gently on Rosie's stomach. They did this for hours in watchful acceptance until the *pohā ka nalu*, the amniotic sac, broke, and they knew birth was near. Now Rosie was lifted to her feet and placed squatting on the mats. Her knees well apart, her arms round Ben's neck in front of her, giving her support when actual birth began. Later, when he tired, it would be another uncle's neck she clung to.

As pain became more intense, Ana moved behind her as *koʻo kua*, sat with her legs spread, and wrapped her arms around her tightly. Following the midwife's instruction, Ana pressed down and stopped, pressed down and stopped.

Now the midwife spoke softly to Rosie. "*Ume i ka hanu.* Draw the breath. *Koke. Koke.* Soon."

Contractions began to come so strong sweat cataracted down Rosie's body, drenching Ana. They heard the rumble from Noah's room as cousins came running.

"Ho! Uncle Noah moan and groan, all twisted up in pain. Three cousins try hold him down. How long it going take?"

Ben shouted back. "However long da gods decide. Tell him he scream, I break his leg. Screaming in childbirth is disgrace!"

"*Pahū! Ho ʻopāhūhū!* Push now. Push hard!" the midwife called, and suddenly the head emerged.

Ana moaned, pressing down with Rosie as if she herself were giving birth. The whole family seemed to moan, weeping and praying, even breathing for Rosie. Gently, the midwife held the baby's bloody head, guiding the little body through its narrow passage. Ben's eyes bulged from the strain of Rosie's arms pulling on his neck. Her knees began to give out.

It was then the midwife cried, " '*Ike ʻia na maka I ke ao!*" The eyes are seen in the world. The child was born.

Closest to a grandfather for the child, Ben now stepped forward, his cheeks wet with tears.

"*Ola ke kumu, I ka lālā hou!*" The branches of the tree were green again. The family line continued.

Very gently, he stuck his finger into the baby's mouth and gagged her just enough to disgorge her birth fluid. He rinsed his own mouth and sucked the baby's fluid from her nose, then wiped her eyes, as she let out a healthy scream.

The infant's *piko*, umbilical cord, was handled with great care as her link between the backward time to ancestors, and the forward time to her descendants. It was cut and blessed by the midwife, and dusted with arrowroot to stanch the bleeding. All the while, Rosie continued squatting, grunting, trying to expel the *ʻiēwe*, the placenta. Suddenly, she gasped, expelled the thing, and then collapsed. Shaking with exhaustion, Ana fell forward to her knees. Someone bent and wiped her face and neck with cool, wet cloths, then lifted her and held her in their arms.

The child's *piko* was wrapped in tapa cloth. Within days it would be taken by canoe out beyond the reef, a gift to *'aumākua* dwelling there, assuring that the child would be safe in her travels. Then the midwife requested the *'iēwe*, which she thoroughly washed and prayed over. It would be buried beneath a young tree to ensure that the child would always find her way home and not become a hopeless, wandering spirit.

Observing the rituals, the washing and the wrapping, in spite of extreme exhaustion, Ana wondered, *When I was born, did someone take my piko out beyond the reef? And where is my 'iēwe buried? Under what tree?*

While Rosie was bathed and lay with her child, the old midwife sat with the family. "I am tired, nearing my time. This child, Makali'i, is my last birthing. This is my last request for the placenta."

A year hence, there would be a celebration to commemorate the child's first year. *But* because this was the firstborn, on this day the family gathered for a quiet, solemn meal. This was the *'aha 'āina māwaewae*, "clearing away feast" which, through ritual and prayer, and shared food, would keep the child's pathway into the future safe and unobstructed. It dedicated Makali'i to the family *'aumākua*, and started her on the road of honor and responsibility.

During the preparation of the meal, Ana observed how elders assumed importance in their duties. Tito leaned forward in his wheelchair, carefully pouring cups of *'awa* to be passed around. Noah held down a slippery *ulua* while Ben delicately sliced into it, tracing the flashing knife along the soft white belly. Aunties cut pork butt into luscious hunks for *laulau*. A cousin washed taro leaves. Another spread Hawaiian salt, rich with the memory of seaweed. Rosie was also given food which, by word meanings or sound, conveyed the idea of "clearing and freeing"—*mahiki*, shrimp, for "peeling off," Limu *kala*, seaweed for "release," *'a'ama*, crab, for "setting loose." All symbols of freeing the child from forces of misfortune, illness, harm.

And as they prayed for the mother and child, Ana saw how her family honored the holiness of things—the food, and the tools that served the food. Before he filled the cups, Tito poured a bit of *'awa* onto the ground, thanking *Lono* for this year's batch. Ben stroked the belly of the *ulua* and bowed his head, thanking *Kanaloa* for what the sea had yielded, and honoring the fish's soul still spiraling in waves. Her aunties gave thanks over bowls of *poi* and *poke*, and even asked blessings for the cooking pots and the fires that heated those pots.

Reflecting on the long, exhausting hours of that day—the birthing, and praying, the taking and sharing of pain, and love—in that moment

Ana saw how rich they were, how thick their blood coursing the generations. It was a family that did not keep up with time, but rather allowed time to pause, stand still, and catch its breath. A family conjoined and condemned to each other for now, for good, forever. In those moments she understood that these people, and this house, would always be her solace. Her language. And her place. Though she would try to overcome it.

'ŌULI

Portent

NIGHT UNDRESSES HER, REMOVING THE WEIGHTS AND EPHEMERA OF *memory, so that, unencumbered, she is no longer sure if what is remembered is what actually occurred. In her youth had there really been a young man who had loved her? Had they really been wild and reckless? And, had he lived, would she have married him, giving his child a proper name? Or, would she still have abandoned everything, and run?*

Now, each morning, Anahola irons her hair straight and wedges herself into high heels and somber-colored suits that do not quite fit the shape of her body. She is almost fastidious in how she looks; even her handwriting has changed. Yet she suspects that the city will always read something in her as foreign, a woman to be taught the socially acceptable way.

She still feels the terror of revealing her class, her lack of culture. The dissonance between appearance and voice, opinions and vowel sounds. Proper English has become like a delicacy to her. She takes each word into her mouth carefully, her tongue attaching itself to every syllable. English redeems her, gives her worth. With each mouthful her past is further silenced.

Yet in conversation sometimes she hesitates, glancing at Max the way children look at parents for guidance in their reactions. Her gestures are fraught with flourishes she has adopted, her speech with fragments of phrases she does not quite understand. Sometimes she mimics Max, his opinions hers, even his expressions, so that altogether she is looked upon with mild curiosity.

There is her dark beauty, and her youth, and the subtext of vitality—an undercurrent of electricity with which she charges even trivial exchanges. There is also her devotion to Max, which suggests a certain gravity and maturity. But then there are the blanks—her past, her origins, which she avoids speaking of to his friends or colleagues.

She is a woman who seems to change form and definition, which gives her an air of inauthenticity. And so, in spite of him, she feels peripheral, a minor character at their events. She will feel this way for years . . .

SHE HAD COME TO UNDERSTAND THAT MAX HER LOVER, AND MAX the scientist were different people. He was something of a brooder, so that large chunks of his life were closed to her. He could even seem aloof, the way a distracted child can seem aloof. He didn't know how often he was watched by her, how his silences gave him a glow, a puzzling and solitary loveliness. Anahola thought that if she could grasp the secret there, if she could know one or two things more, she might more fully understand him.

Some days she felt he was simply not there, that she was looking at empty space through which Max was the foreground. Then, unaccountably, what seemed certain shifted. He left her in the lab for entire afternoons, but when they met over dinner he was anxious. To hear her opinions, to confess his apprehension that she might be growing bored with their life together. Some nights when she stood behind him, he asked her to move closer and put her hand on his shoulder.

When they made love, he exausted her, as if he were trying to press through her, to get beyond her, beyond the present and the past, his eyes seeming to look into another dimension. At such times Anahola felt unreal, felt their world was unreal, that Max could snap his fingers and it would disappear.

Yet he was fiercely protective of her. When they entered a room together, she felt the tension in his arm, the muscles shift, alert to her slightest discomfort or lack of ease. He was quick to assume a courtly, almost soldierly aspect, as if ready to defend her position against aggressors, overwhelming odds. But some utterances were so sly, he missed them.

During dinner at the home of a wealthy industrialist who funded scientific research, Anahola fell silent as a Chinese servant unfolded her napkin and placed it on her lap, a drift of stiff linen that startled like a cat's tongue. While he poured her champagne, she sat transfixed by the fragile beauty of the tulip-shaped glass.

The hostess was a tiny, impeccable woman with irises so pale they seemed to defy the focus of one's eyes. In her blue-veined hands, knives and forks looked like giant weaponry wielded by an agile child. Throughout the meal she observed with darting glances, Anahola's hair, her brown skin, while weaving curiosity and disdain into a delicate cross-examination.

The house was huge, the dining room cavernous. Anahola watched Chinese servants drift in and out of endless rooms, then vanish down winding marble halls. The champagne made her feel momentarily elated and forthcoming, and leaning forward she half jokingly asked.

"Your help . . . don't they ever get lost?"

The old woman stared at her, then spoke with a downward finality. "They built railroads. They'll find their way."

With a fussy exactitude, she folded her napkin and, in hushed tones, explained to her guests why Chinese made the best servants.

"That superb silence, which makes them virtually . . . invisible. They know their place."

The words like a knife chime on a tulip glass. Ana felt herself step back.

SHE TRAVELED EVERYWHERE WITH MAX WHEN HE ADDRESSED CONferences on immunology and on the direction of America's Energy Program, and how those fields were related, since much of his research dealt with people exposed to radiation. Sometimes at receptions in smoke-filled rooms, Anahola saw Max's colleagues eyeing her, winking back and forth over her shoulder.

A man said to be brilliant in particle physics seemed to bark at her in octaves. Was she Italian? Hispanic? Lebanese? But no, he said, her features were too broad. How did she meet Max, he asked, and did she enjoy all the travel? Pretending to be amused by her to conceal the fact that he was. In time she understood that to these men she would only ever be Max McCormick's "woman." And so she navigated the slights, the subtle insults, and stood in crowds smiling brilliantly, refusing to feel reduced at having so little to offer.

ONE DAY MAX SAT ON THE TERRACE SIPPING SCOTCH, WATCHING ice cubes shimmer, little arctic explosions inside his glass. It was early evening, the kind of dusk that closed all wounds. Air going blue, the smell of mown clover bringing a reverie of wistful, boyish dreams. Anahola sat beside him bent over a textbook, her hair swept up in a twist.

In that moment the back of her neck glowed, the color of a summer tint. He saw how she could withdrew from the world, her utter, trance-like concentration. He saw how finely made she was, how dowered with the dignity of grace, how hard she was trying to be equal to this life. And how her presence erased his sense of loneliness, reminding him he once loved life, and that he loved it now.

For a while he was aware of very little, only the hard chair he sat in, his dry mouth. "Ana . . . I want very much to marry you."

She looked up, shocked. "Why would you want to do that?"

Max shook his head and smiled. "You like your ambiguity, don't you? The sultry young woman at my side. Probably my mistress, no one is sure. Marriage would tell the world you're not my toy. And it would give you security."

"I don't care what the world thinks. And I don't want more from you than we already have."

"Perhaps you feel not marrying me gives you the moral advantage. Then you'll never be a failure as my wife."

She frowned, groping for words. "Max, I'm not that complicated. It's just . . . my life has already been a series of mistakes."

He fell silent for a while. "Look, you have no idea how life can strike you down. If something should happen to me, you'd hardly have enough if someone needs you, an emergency back home. A child . . . its educa-tion . . ."

". . . .I never said there was a child."

He folded his hands together and his voice turned soft. "Ana, do you think I'm blind? I see how you stare at children in the street. I've been with women through the years, and know the physical tautness of a woman who has never had a child. Their bodies are almost angular and sharp, not really sensuous. Yours has the softness at the breasts and hips of a woman who has given birth, those tiny phosphorescent marks below your belly. Stretch marks, which I find beautiful."

She felt momentarily chilled, a pricklish hollow in her stomach. She lit a cigarette.

"The child was a mistake. I was already planning to leave the is-lands. Anyway, the father died, a young policeman. She's well taken care of. She's fine. What else do you want to know?"

"Do you miss her?"

"To miss her would imply that I would like to be with her. No, I don't miss her. But do I think of her? Yes, now and then. It's natural."

"You never wanted . . ."

"No. I never wanted motherhood. Some women don't feel that urge. It's a biological function, not a holy calling."

She stared at the glowing eye of her cigarette, then took a thoughtful puff. "Now you know all my secrets, Max. It's your turn."

And so he told her of his past. His father a physicist, his uncle, a Nobel Prize laureate, something to do with nuclear fission. Together they had founded McCormick Labs north of San Francisco, a huge complex involved in research and in the production of military defense weapons. Following in their footsteps, Max became a physicist and worked in the desert at Los Alamos. But there had been an accident, the reason he never married.

"We were working on a new bomb, testing for criticality—trying to find the precise amount of plutonium needed in the bomb device. A potentially deadly experiment. They call it 'tickling the dragon's tail' because you're observing a split-second chain reaction, and have to stop at the critical point just before the thing explodes."

"One day in the lab, the head physicist, Pelevini, brought together two halves of a beryllium sphere that would convert plutonium to a critical state. The point was to bring them as flush as possible without blowing up the lab. He went too far. The two halves met, the assembly went supercritical. Pelevini stopped the chain reaction by knocking them apart, but in less than a second, deadly gamma and neutron radiation had burst from the assembly. I remember how a blue glow lit the room as the air was momentarily ionized. We were all exposed. Pelevini died within four days, totally out of his mind."

Max clasped his hands, remembering.

"At Los Alamos Hospital, they monitored our blood counts and bone counts while we lost our hair and vomited. On the ninth day another colleague died. I had been farthest from Pelevini and thought I might be spared. How terribly naïve. Fearing gold inlays in my teeth were sending damaging rays into my jawbone, doctors tried to shield my teeth with a mouthpiece made of solid gold. I wore that thing for weeks until the radiation in my inlays subsided. A hole in the mouthpiece allowed for a straw through which I was kept alive on liquids. It was hideous. I still have nightmares—the bottom of my face muzzled, locked shut like a dog's. I wake up trying to rip that mouthpiece off."

Ana looked down, shocked.

"I'd already seen what bombs could do at Hiroshima, Nagasaki. I was horrified. And I knew what we were going to do at Bikini, the mother of all bombs, the one called BRAVO. I had told my uncle I wanted out, but he appealed to my sense of morality. 'You can help us beat the Russians,' he said. 'Or you can let them vaporize half the United States.' So I had stayed."

"But after the accident, I got hold of my medical records . . . depression of lymphocytes, abnormally low number of leukocytes, patient's exposure significant. Radiation sickness. My passport out of Los Alamos. That's when I switched my field to immunology. A lot of Los Alamites were exposed, a lot of them dropped out. You just don't hear about us. We live quietly, rotting on the hoof."

His voice grew soft like the faint edge of a curl of smoke. "I'm sorry to tell you these things, Ana."

She sat quiet for a while; anything she said would sound like charity. And maybe she was quiet because she could not quite grasp his point.

In years to come, when she finally understood the import of Max's words, she would marvel at her narrowness of vision. The signs she missed, the silences that fell mid-conversation. The way Max muffled his snores when they began to sound like something else. She would gaze at snapshots of him, searching for an expression, some giveaway that he knew what was coming. The pictures would tell her nothing.

HAʻI MOʻOLELO

The Telling Wind

THE NIGHT BEFORE HER FIRST DAY OF UNIVERSITY, ANA FELL INTO a terrified half sleep. *I'll study like a maniac. I won't pick up my eyes. I'll do the hardest thing on earth for me. Suppose I fail? Suppose I don't have what it takes?*

In the dark, something ancient answered. *"Aia no I ke ko a ke au."* Time will tell.

All night aunties had banged round the house, afraid Ana would disappear in Honolulu, "Sin City," where sailors took girls in alleys. Rosie tried to reassure them, reminding them that the university was miles from all those military men.

But Aunty Mapuana argued. "What need for books? Books only good for termites. Look all the termite holes in Pua's Bible."

Pua leaned forward, the world of her eyes so floaty the irises seemed to be melting into white.

"Not from termites! From missionary gods. All they tell is holes. Lies. I prayed for our sister, Emma, they let her die. They let Anahola run away. Now we going lose Ana. Why she need to go so far? Good nurses' training school right here in Waiʻanae."

Ana had talked of wanting to heal, of maybe becoming a nurse. Now Rosie got to her feet, looking somewhat formidable.

"Ana's going to be more than a nurse. That's what university's for, find out what she wants to do. She could even become a doctor . . ."

She saw she was over their heads and slowed down. "Aunty Pua, you talk about Emma. She had the healing gift. Have you forgotten what happened when she died? She gave that girl all of her mana in the Ritual of *Hā.*"

They fell silent, remembering. In her last moments, their sister Emma had called young Ana to her bedside. With great effort she had put her hand against the back of Ana's head, pressing the girl's face to hers. Whispering hoarsely, she had forced Ana's mouth to her mouth and, inhaling deeply, had expulsed all the air inside her body into Ana's. The girl seemed to swoon on the verge of collapse. The family had rushed forward, holding her.

Through wracking pain and morphine, Emma had whispered, "Child. This is my last will and testament. Through this *Hā*, you have received my mana."

In the moment of her passing, Ana had touched her great-aunt's face and seemed to wipe it clean. All pain dispelled, she had reflected peace.

"Emma gave that girl special gifts," Rosie said. "She's got to go out in the world and use them. You stop her from getting education, Emma's going come back and *scoop out your eyes.*"

Pua hobbled out to the yard and gathered ti leaves. "Let her go then. Let her educate. No more drippings from my bitter mouth."

All night she walked through the house slapping ti leaves for protection, draping several leaves over the sleeping form of Ana.

And she prayed to her dead sister. "Emma, *Ē ʻoluʻolu!*" Please. "Don't let those gripping cuttlefish of Honolulu get our girl."

Next morning, Ana started down Keola Road. Their house sat on a rise half a mile up from the highway, in the distance, the leaping morning sea. As she descended, she passed a yellow house that looked blown sideways, socks stuck in rusty window screens. Outside the house, a heavily tattooed man in a purple sarong sat polishing his rifle, then tilted the barrels up to the light so that they glittered blue and became an extension of his tattooed arms. Seeing Ana, he jumped up, aimed his rifle at the sky and shot off a round, giving her the Shaka sign. "Ey, Ana! . . . Geev'um at dat university!"

She smiled and waved. Just past the blue's man yellow house, from atop a Quonset hut, a goat magisterially surveyed his domain, observing her passage from her old life.

At the bottom of the road, even the intersection looked condemned—abandoned cars, a malfunctioning stoplight that seemed to hang by a single thread. Tow trucks screeched to a stop as ragged kids shot into traffic on skateboards. Then life, the highway, waiting to consume her. Near the shopping strip, surfers and druggers crawled half-awake from their pick-

ups, draping themselves across the fenders. The young muscled turks of
Nanakuli.

They called out as she passed by. "Ey, Ana! Hear you going university. Going hang out wit all dem . . . homolectuals."

"What you trying prove wit all dem books? No fo'get, you one
Nanakuli girl. Only good fo' do one t'ing."

She turned and lashed out with a country mouth. "Suck rocks, you
mokes! Don't fuck wit' me. My uncles going broke yo' ugly faces."

Yet they were not ugly; most of them were beautiful, with the beauty
of mixed "chop suey" blood. Hawaiian, Chinese, Japanese, Portuguese,
Scotch, Irish, Filipino. Half a dozen other bloods. Their skin tones ran
the gamut from sun-tinted white to gold to deep dark brown, their
almond-shaped eyes sometimes blue, or green. They were muscular and
fit from surfing, but their hair hung long and greasy. Some heads were
garishly shaved with only topknots. Their arms and legs a grid of scars
and tribal tattoos. She saw their drug-shot eyes and shook her head, their
future written all over them.

Shifting her heavy book bag and lunch bag, she walked on. Five
mornings a week she would make the two-hour bus trip to the university
up in Manoa Valley, and in the evenings, the two-hour trip back to
Nanakuli. Stepping into the bus, Ana glanced at faces heading into the
city, folks looking anxious and alert. It was not her first trip off the
Wai'anae Coast, but apprehension made her feel it was.

Her dress was homemade. Her shoes were new and pinched. She was
not beautiful, nor was she brilliant or accomplished. But she carried herself as if she were. Crossing her legs, she opened a textbook and thoughtfully smoothed down a page, ignoring the sea paralleling the highway.
Now and then she looked up at the ruby-strung necklace of taillights
bound for Honolulu.

KNOWLEDGE DID NOT ENTER HER WITH UNWAVERING LIGHT. AT
first it glanced over her. She could not keep up, even in basic chemistry,
in which she had excelled. Called upon in class, she stood dumb and shy.
Sometimes she thought of killing herself. Nights at the kitchen table,
she pressed her forehead to the pages of a book, trying to literally absorb
convoluted equations. Comprehension did not come.

"The problem," Rosie said, "is that right now you're stuck in that
place where you know too much and not enough. Why not just *pretend*
you know? Memorize, keep repeating it, and see what happens next."

Slowly, miraculously, things began to coalesce. Ana memorized every lesson, every assignment, repeating and repeating it, until comprehension approached like a buzzing in her brain, and then a midnight Eureka. Once deciphered, certain equations became brilliant in their simplicity. Thereafter, each time she was mired in confusion, she remembered Rosie's words: Sometimes life was just about holding on, waiting to see what happened next.

She also learned that an honor student from Nanakuli High was not held in the same regard as a student from an elite private school in Honolulu. Each night she scrubbed red dust from her clothes and shoes, and from her book bag. Still, on campus, people knew. They knew from the giveaway pink of her cuticles and nails, and sometimes a faint pink tinge to her hair, that she was from the Wai'anae Coast. Students walking behind her rolled their eyes, even their bookmarks stuck out at her like tongues. She hid her hands between her knees in class. She dropped behind and fell into depressions. Then she snapped out of it, running to catch up. The rest of life fell by the wayside.

One day she looked up from her books in shock. Younger cousins seemed taller. Spring had come and gone and it was autumn, the wet season. Ana felt she had given life the slip, that she was moving through it like a shadow. She worked summer jobs but would not remember them. She forgot the name of her favorite boar-hound, the one with almost human eyes.

Rosie waved checks at her from San Francisco. "Silly girl. With this money you wouldn't have to work your way. You could live in the dorm, not have to commute."

Ana stared at her, pupils enlarged to an anthracite gleam.

Some mornings she left the house so early it was dark, stars still hard and bright, the moon dropping blue notes on her shoulders. Wearing her rubber thongs, she grabbed her heavy book bag and her lunch and set off down the road, carrying her good shoes in a plastic bag. At night, walking home from the bus stop, she found her rubber slippers where she left them in the weeds, removed her good shoes and put them in the plastic bag. Then she started the steep climb up Keola Road. In *malo'o* season, when red Wai'anae dust blanketed the valley, she wore a kerchief across her face like a bandit. Neighbors watering their yards stepped out to the road and hosed it down so Ana could breathe on her long walk home.

Some nights, halfway up the road, she sat down, so mentally and physically exhausted, her eyes ached, moonlight on her head like a concussion. She looked up the badly lit road, saw the outlines of houses impossibly distant, and imagined her form trudging upwards like a crone. She imagined her tired face in conversation over supper, her half-conscious body laying itself down. She saw all this in a dream.

Later she woke, still curled up in the weeds beside the road, and heard them calling her name. They bent over her, Noah and Ben, faces like dark angels leaning out of paintings. They gently scolded her, lifted and half carried her, while youngsters dragged along her books and shoes. She smelled their perspiration, their clean uncle-smell and she was all right then. She knew where she was in the world.

". . . waiting fo' you, worried half to death . . ."

Barking dogs fell silent as they passed. So did two men fistfighting in their underwear. The silhouette of a woman in a doorway. Then, their house ablaze with lights. Rosie washing Ana's face, her hands, her feet. A clean, fragrant sheet beneath her, and one billowing out over her. And then, the ecstasy of letting go.

By the end of her first year at university, she had refined her life almost to a point. Her studies, sleep, and food. A life of such unrelenting focus, it was like the workings of a clock. Ana looked down at textbook illustrations, the machinations of the human anatomy. Respiration. Digestion. Reproduction. Where was the illustration for the need to laugh, to touch and be touched? How did one illustrate longing, or loneliness? She dreamed of Tommy Two-Gods and woke up missing him, wondering where life had taken him. She slept curved inward, like a child.

PERHAPS BECAUSE SHE WAS READY, ONE DAY IN HER SOPHOMORE year a young man wandered out of the rain and into her life. He was drenched but his hair was perfectly intact, so sleekly gelled it looked bulletproof. His wet skin glowed like chrome. His name was Pak Morelli. Mother Korean, father Italian American.

"Is that hard for you?" she asked.

He laughed. "You know anyone that's pure-blood? I grew up on *kimchee* and lasagna."

They spent their first nights fused together in the backseat of his car, making love with such abandon the car shimmied and bounced on its springs. Passing street dogs paused, listening to their cries. Then, a friend loaned him an apartment where they began meeting between classes twice a week.

On late bus rides back to Nanakuli, Ana crossed one leg over the other, still smelling their yeasty coupling. She felt a different kind of exhaustion then, her body fulfilled, aglow. Most days they didn't talk much; what they physically gave each other seemed enough. Yet she was struck by his scrupulous lack of curiosity about her life, her aspirations. They saw each other several months before he broke it off.

"This girl found out about you . . . she's Chinese."

Ana shook her head confused. "And?"

"She says it's you or her."

"Why? Because I'm 'country,' from Nanakuli?" She sat up slowly. "Or because I'm *kanaka*?"

His hesitation set up a keen attentiveness in her.

". . . Both. I guess."

She rose from the bed and dressed, keeping her tongue still in her head, swallowing back profanities. Sighing, he half stood, pulling on his shirt and pants.

"No. Take *off* your clothes." Her voice was suddenly different. It wasn't kidding.

Puzzled, he stripped down to his underwear and sat on the bed.

"Lie down. Turn your face to the wall."

He thought she wanted to lie behind him, and hold him. Maybe beg him.

He lay down, facing the wall. "Ana, I'm really sorry that . . ."

"Shut up. Don't turn around until I'm gone. And don't *ever* look at me again. Not on campus. Not anywhere."

She picked up his shoes and shirt and pants, flung them from the eighth-floor window, and walked out the door.

This breakup hurt more than losing Tommy Two-Gods. It was a hurt that went deeper than her pride, striking her psyche and her very soul. The family saw her pain and tried to distract her, make her a girl again, their Nanakuli girl.

Noah sat her beside him at his window, the nights so humid termites drowned in the creases of his neck.

"Horse races," he whispered, pointing at the sky.

And she saw how the clouds did look like horses, huge, winged piebalds racing up the stars. They sat looking up for hours. He taught her how to smoke, to purse her lips and form smoke rings which, as they lazily expanded, field bats flew in and out of. Ben taught her how to torch-fish, how to play the *'uli'uli*, and how to open a bottle of Primo with her teeth.

Some nights she and her older cousin, Lopaka, sat silent in his truck. He had come home from Vietnam a bitter man, his right leg shattered by shrapnel. For several years, he was a dropout, ignoring Ana, drugging and drinking with older gangs who hung out in the Quonsets at the end of Keola Road. Then he grew bored, tired of rehashing combat every night. He took stock of his life and went into rehab, and learned to walk again with a leg brace.

Then he had shocked the family by entering university on the GI Bill. Now he was preparing for law school, but he was still a loner, angry and bitter. The war and constant pain had bent him down, leaving his big, muscled shoulders weighted with that burden. He talked mostly with other vets and now and then with Ana, but cautiously.

Until he left for Vietnam, he had been the center of her life, and while he was gone, she remembered everything he taught her. In those years she had stood in fields flying her kites, watching their shoulders rub against the sky. And she had prayed, "Bring him home. Bring him home." Until one day he was carried off a plane with wounded vets.

Now she was a full-grown woman sitting in Lopaka's truck. He had become bookish, his Pidgin less pronounced. He spoke "proper" English now, but carefully, like someone new to it.

"So this guy put you down for being Wai'anae?"

"And for being . . . *kanaka.*"

He shook his head. "These people . . . they don't see that Hawaiians are slowly rising . . . One day when they're finally ready to treat us with 'fairness' . . . they might find we are prepared for violence."

She reacted slowly, because he had spoken slowly, in the old slow tribal rhythms.

"We're not a violent people," she said.

"No one is . . . till violence is done to them."

He shaved every day now, and kept his nails and toenails clean, so parts of him looked new. But his face was the same, still so rugged and *kanaka* handsome, she found it hard to look him in the eye. Instead, while they talked, she looked at his muscular brown arms, the blue veins bulging and forking. She looked at his hair, so thick and curly she wanted to put her hand there. Wanted to tell him that he was still her hero, that she would always love him, that life would be okay.

She and Rosie sat under a sickle moon, contemplating men.

"Not worth the trouble," Rosie said. "All little boys. Handsome, rich, ugly, poor . . . still the same, all looking for their mamas."

Ana laughed. "Then how's come you can't get enough of them?"

Rosie was in love again. Her third, or fourth, or seventh lover. This one wanted marriage.

"What for?" she asked. "I belong here, with 'ohana. A husband would take me away, make me his slave. Or else live here, and put his two cents worth in."

She nodded toward their elders, dozing in the shadows. "How could I leave them? They saved me from my mother."

"I think of that, too," Ana said. "This old place is falling down. The termites own it, really. But, how could I ever leave? Maybe when I'm older, when they're gone. I'll be nursing in the city then. You can come and live with me."

Rosie studied her. "Nursing? He lalau! Nonsense! You want to count syringes the rest of your life? You're going to medical school, and you know it."

"I don't know that. I'm not sure I have . . ."

"Ey! You remember that night you promised on my belly? On my baby's head. You had a dream, to be a doctor. You promised you would try. You break that promise, you will kill me."

She talked softly now. "Rosie. You've seen me these past two years. I've never worked so hard. I don't remember anything but textbooks. Formulas. Equations. Med school means another four–five years. Twice as hard. Can you imagine? Even if I got accepted, I'd need to take out a loan. Then internship, residency. My God. I'd be twenty-seven, twenty-eight before I earn a decent income."

"And so? And so? We talked about it nights when you were climbing up the road. You, and Lopaka. You're first-generation college in this house. First-generation anything. You are our dreams. Lopaka's going to be a lawyer even though he started late. All our savings go for you and him. What else are savings for? All you got to do is try. Then you kōkua kids coming up behind you. That's 'ohana. What life is for."

She hesitated, not used to doing things that weren't her idea. "Rosie, do you know how many students drop out of med school every year? Suppose I try, and fail?"

"Ana. You never try, you never know."

"I'm tired. I'm not that smart! I thought I was, I'm not. I have to cram and pray for every grade."

Rosie stood now, hands on hips. She looked out at the night, then turned and looked at Ana.

"Let me tell you something, girlie. You can do anything you set your mind to. You don't want to hear this but . . . you're just like your mama. Nerves of steel when you make up your mind. I don't care if it takes ten, twenty years. Just say you want to be a doctor. That you'll try."

She cried then. "I want it more than anything. I want to make you proud."

"I will be proud," Rosie said. "You will be a healer."

One day after classes she found the family gathered in front of the TV. There had been an accident on the U.S. mainland.

"Place called Three Mile Island, state of Pennsylvania," Rosie said. "One of those reactor things broke down. Oh, look . . . people vomiting." She held Makaliʻi in her lap, while younger children gathered round, asking if they were all going to die.

"Shhh," Ben cried. "Saying thousands of folks breathed in dat stuff. Even in dere water now. Ho! Look dem cows, lying down. Say radioiodine already in dere milk. Look dat field, hundreds dead birds. All da flowers black."

The newscaster quoted experts as saying that half the residents of central Pennsylvania were affected by the Three Mile Island meltdown. "America's worst nuclear disaster."

Ben quickly turned off the TV. Then one of the old aunties spoke.

"Aʻole pilikia! No worries. We're thousands of miles from that state Pennsylvania."

Lopaka slowly turned to her. "You think we're safe? The U.S. military is our biggest industry."

"So? That makes our islands safer."

"No. It makes us potential victims. Right now we've got two dozen nuclear subs homeported here in Pearl Harbor. You think they don't have accidents on those ships? Millions of gallons of radioactive waste from those subs have already been dumped into the harbor."

"Lopaka, hush," Rosie said. "Wait till I get these youngsters off to bed."

She herded the children from the room, then returned and sat facing him. "Now. How do you know all this stuff?"

"My professors. Most of them are liberals. Environmentalists."

He glanced round the room, his handsome dark face flushed. "You folks have any idea what's going on? You know what's just down the road at Lualualei Naval Reservation? They got chemical and biological weapons stashed in underground arsenals. Why do you think that whole valley is restricted? It's also a nuclear-weapons depot. Armed soldiers patrolling day and night."

Ana shook her head. "I don't believe you."

"You ever try driving into the valley at Lualualei? You want to see? Come on."

She followed him out to his truck, then Rosie followed, squeezing Ana in between them. He drove up the coastal highway to the town of Lualualei, then turned right onto a road that took them deep into the valley, toward what was known as Lualualei Naval Reservation, a high-security military base no local had ever been inside of. Along the road the signs began. TURN BACK. RESTRICTED AREA.

Rosie glanced at him, alarmed. "You been out here before?"

"Plenty times. Now watch what happens."

He suddenly swerved off the road into deep grass and drove along a chain-link fence topped with barbed wire, until he saw a truck-sized hole. He drove through the hole and they entered deep woods, dense groves of trees. Through the trees they saw another high-security perimeter fence topped with barbed wire.

"They got them set in deeper and deeper, like Russian dolls."

He swerved through the trees and drove along the inner fence until it suddenly became a double chain link, topped by blinding high-intensity lights. Every few yards was an electronic surveillance detection system. Then more signs. RESTRICTED AREA. USE OF DEADLY FORCE AUTHORIZED.

"Turn around," Rosie said.

"Not yet."

In the distance, they saw what looked like armed guards in watchtowers.

"Now tell me, you think they'd have security like this if it was just a boot camp?"

Without warning, Lopaka bounced onto a paved road intersecting the groves of trees. Dead ahead to the right was a gate with posted sentries. Before they ever reached it, they were surrounded by three jeeps, half a dozen soldiers pointing rifles.

He skidded to a stop and stuck his head out the window at two approaching soldiers. "Sorry. We took a wrong turn."

One of the soldiers moved close, squinting like a marksman.

"Yeah. Through a high-security fence! You people like fucking with us, don't you? You know this area's KAPU. Now, turn your *kānaka* butts around before we blow your tires."

"You blow our tires, how you going get rid of us?"

The soldier flung the door of the truck open and grabbed Lopaka by the arm. "Okay, wise guy. Out. Out of the truck!"

Four others dismounted from their jeeps and gathered with their rifles aimed. They looked wired, ready to explode.

He was wearing baggy shorts, and now he swung out with his braced and damaged leg. "So, what you going do? Shoot me in my good leg?"

Rosie slid out of the truck, yelling her head off. "Shame! Shame on you, pointing rifles at us! You know how this boy got crippled? Vietnam. He came home with four medals for bravery and scar tissue for a leg. Fighting for America. For you! You like shoot us? Go ahead. Shoot us all!"

The soldier who had pulled Lopaka from the truck lowered his rifle. "Get back in the truck. Get outta here."

Lopaka took one step closer, and spoke softly. "These lands are our lands. You stole them from us. You're storing nuclear weapons here. You're testing bombs up the highway at Mākua. You think we're stupid? We don't know? . . . You think this is what I fought for? To watch my homelands blown to bits?"

The soldier looked down. He looked at his buddies. "Please. Get in the truck. Go home."

As they backed up and pulled away, Lopaka shouted out the window, "Hope you guys are wearing dosimeters! This whole base is leaking radiation."

On the drive back, they were silent, still in shock.

Ana finally turned to him. "You've known about this all along, haven't you?"

"Be blind not to." He tapped his fingers on the steering wheel. "Frankly, that's not what really bugs me. It's the day-to-day stuff. Radioactive water from the harbors and rivers seeping into our soil. The stuff we stand in, in our fields. Stuff that seeps into the grass our dairy cows and pigs eat. And I'm bugged by those big naval radio towers out on Pa'akea Road up the highway toward Ma'ili. Those things emit electromagnetic radiation. The Navy has even admitted their hazard zone is two and a half miles in radius. That means all those farmers and kids could be contaminated . . ."

His voice trailed off, exhausted.

"I hear things on campus, too," Ana said. "They've installed high-frequency radar-tracking stations on each of our islands. Those things leak that same electromagnetic stuff. They say it causes Alzheimer's. Blindness. Mental retardation. Our trade winds blow that filth back and forth. We breathe it, it builds up inside us. One day we'll end up like those Three Mile Islanders."

Lopaka pulled up to the house and they fell silent, seeing the fields hung in moonlight. Then clouds suddenly enveloped the moon as if a hand had brushed a light switch.

Rosie stepped out of the truck. "I'm sick at heart. Don't discuss this stuff in front of the elders, or the kids. Good night."

Ana felt the heat of his arm touching hers. She didn't even have to look at him. "Why didn't you tell me you knew all this?"

"I didn't want to scare you. So many ugly facts, it takes time to understand it. To even *believe* it. This whole damned coast, from Pearl Harbor all the way to the tip at Ka'ena Point, has become a nuclear playground. And now we're a priority target for terrorists."

He finally turned to her. "I don't even know the words for this, an injustice so immense. And I don't know what we do about it."

"Yes, you do. We fight back."

ANA JOINED A WATCHDOG GROUP ON CAMPUS, ATTENDING VIGILS and rallies. She marched, carrying banners. DESTROY BOMBS NOT PEOPLE. NO MORE WAR GAMES ON OUR SACRED LANDS. She was arrested for throwing a water bag that hit a policeman in the neck. Livid, Ben bailed her out.

"Where's your respect? Your father was a cop. And you had to hit a *white* cop."

"His skin wasn't white. It was . . . room tone."

Even Rosie scolded her. "You crazy? You're a student, not a gang girl."

"They were tearing down our banners. I lost my temper."

"Well, you better find it, girlie. You're beginning to remind me of my mama."

Ana stared at her in shock. "Your mama was insane. She tried to kill you. I, on the other hand, would die for you."

But she suspected Rosie was partly right. There was something that now and then took hold of Ana. She thought it might be rage. Residual rage. It started with a buzzing in her head, then a slow constriction in her breathing as if she were choking, like something on a leash. Something running up and down a clothesline. She wondered if it was something else she felt, not rage.

"Maybe I use my temper to hide fear. Maybe I shout to get attention. I'm afraid if I don't shout, people will forget I'm there. I'll be ignored."

Rosie looked out at the clothesline, remembering. "Okay. We had it rough. The worst is over. I think God has big plans for us."

"Tell God I'll make my own plans."

"Don't get too high-tone, Ana. You already got the profile of a bitter mouth. Next comes empty heart."

Empty heart. Hard heart. Bleeding or broken heart. She was always amazed at how folks threw that word around. When she tried to envision her own heart, it came up plum-colored and prickly. A moody muscle in its solitary cage.

But some nights, hand pressed to her heart, Ana stood up from her bed and, like a mystic on hot coals, crept cautiously to the kitchen. She stared at the phone, then picked it up and dialed in a frenzy, before she lost her nerve. She listened. Sometimes she listened for thirty rings, imagining a perfect house with perfect rooms, echoing each ring.

One night when her mother answered, Ana did not instantly hang up. They listened to each other's breathing.

Finally, her mother spoke. "I'm very proud of you."

She stared down at the holes in the plastic mouthpiece and carefully replaced it in its cradle. She had not seen the woman in seven years.

NIKOLAO

———

Nikolai

BY THE TIME HE WAS TEN, THERE WAS NO PITY IN HIM, NOT EVEN for himself. Through brief summer days—when statues of war heroes saluted the luminous twilight in this dusty corpse of a city—and through long winter nights—when numbing winds blew from the Bay of Finland, sheathing trees in ice—Nikolai learned to move through Leningrad by stealth, his movements pivotal and quick.

He learned where the best pickings were, what garbage heap, and to limp with a "deformed" leg while begging for kopecks outside hotels, his large black eyes giving his face an urgency. He learned to pilfer odds and ends and to sell them for black bread and sausages, and with his natural aptitude for stillness, he became expert at picking pockets in spite of his oversized hands.

Still parsimoniously thin, he navigated across the perilous aisles of skidding traffic on wide Nevsky Prospekt without looking left or right. When a street beggar died, he would listen for that final breath leaking out like an old Russian epitaph. Then he stepped forward, unlaced their boots, and ran. These he bartered, or when they fit he slept with them against his chest, his fingers calmly discerning the spectral shape of the former owner's foot.

At night, against the shivery sounds of balalaikas on the Neva River, he ran home through arctic *souks* and labyrinthine streets that bled out to narrow muddy lanes where he slid back into his netherworld of drainage pipes that swallowed humans whole. Here he nested with tribes of street kids, some so scarred and used up they were already old.

He would never look youthful. The years had inscribed on his face
the harsh lines of their text. But he was curious, tenacious, more clever
than the boys he ran with. At night, half-asleep, he thought of all he had
seen that day, the want, and squalor, and sometimes even beauty—old,
crumbling Tsarist-era palaces bursting out of the snow in hot Italian
palettes of greens and pinks and ochers.

Most boys spoke a street argot with tongue-tying speed but, Nikolai
lived mostly in his head, not knowing he was already observing the
world, preserving it in images. When he did speak, he never mentioned
his childhood in Archangel'sk, afraid words would erase the memory.
When asked his name, he gave different names, retreating behind lies,
wearing those lies like a lead apron that shielded him from the world.

Some folks thought he was retarded, especially in summer when he
seemed to languish, not knowing how to feel, how to behave. Missing
the sensation of near freezing, of shivering and seeing his breath made
visible, he sought out the city's parks and sat alone amongst the trees.
They were not the giant firs he remembered, but still they comforted
him. Sometimes he laid his cheek against their bark, remembering the
warm, beastly smell of women who had turned to trees, and then to logs.
Remembering the smell of his dear mother. Seasons changed, the schiz-
ophrenia of autumn, then winter when Nikolai came alive, kneeling on
blocks of ice breaking up in the frozen Neva, flinging his head back like
a young wolf and crying out in stellated brightness.

No matter where he roamed in the city, he was always drawn by the
abattoir smell of the old Haymarket's slaughterhouses. The metallic
scent of blood and freshly skinned animals tranced him in a moment,
transporting him back to a smoke-blackened ice hut. One place special-
ized in wild game as well as pigs and cattle. Sometimes Nikolai slipped
inside and stood dreamily fingering the dripping antlers of an elk, or the
white hide of a hare, recalling the bright wonder of red-eyed hares leaping against the snows of Archangel'sk.

When they caught him, slaughterhouse guards hauled him out to
the street and beat him. And each time, he cried out how he had grown
up hunting wolf and lynx while strapped against his mother's chest. How
he had been teethed on cured strips of bear meat. One day a worker
threw him a hairy slab of raw bacon, and in return Nikolai showed him
how he could skin a grouse expertly, even with his eyes closed.

He seemed so desperate and eager, the slaughterhouse foreman took
pity on him, giving him a few kopecks to sweep bloody sawdust off
the floors and keep the outside pavements clean. In time he grew famil-

iar with the workers—stun-men, and skinners and dyers—huge, virile, bare-chested men swinging sledgehammers and butchering knives. With brute locution they shouted and cursed, scooping out and devouring raw animal organs—still-quivering beef hearts, livers alive with bloodworms. Yet somehow the white rags on their heads tied up in dainty points like cat's ears made them seem half-playful and endearing to the boy.

On breaks, they stood outside in the cold, smoking cigarettes while wrapped in fresh, bloody cowhides, their steaming torsos flocked with offal.

And they would call to him. "Niki! Come, take a smoke! Be a man!"

He would stand amongst them stupefied, as if surrounded by rampaging Huns.

Some days women and children brought them baskets of lunch, and Nikolai began to understand that these men were fathers. With no sense of it, he drew closer, thinking *This is what a father is*. He studied men on the stun line, and then the skinners—who sliced off hides while the eyes of the cattle still flickered. He studied the sausage makers, skating across floors of salt as he helped squeeze out waste and shit from animal intestines, then hose them clean and fill the casings.

And once, he ventured into a room whose stench was like a judgment. Here were the hide dyers, men bent over huge bubbling vats, lifting and dipping sheets of skins, their chests and arms dyed turquoise blue, canary yellow. These were the foulest-smelling men, for each animal's death entered their pores with the dye, and lodged deep in their flesh, and in their lungs. It never washed away.

Nikolai went back to the skinning room, the work he seemed best suited for. This, he decided, would be his life. He would labor surrounded by men who were fathers so he could understand what he had lost, what it was he lacked. The workers humored him, explaining that to become a skinner he would first have to apprentice on the stun line. For this it would take years to build up muscles, and he was only ten.

And so he remained a sweeper and a waterboy, waiting for his body to grow muscular and hard. Some days he idled round the foreman's desk, listening to exchanges with tradesmen who hauled off carcasses for butcher shops. The endless transactions in rubles and vodka, the arguments over profit and loss. And in that way he learned how to add and to subtract, and in time to tally up purchases faster than with an abacus. Eventually he could do figures in his head without pencil or paper and slowly, painstakingly, he learned to divide and multiply.

Perhaps it was the alchemy of fate and luck: the foreman detected in the boy a yearning beyond curiosity. A driving need to know. He encouraged him to study the newsprint used to wrap offal, and began to teach him the rudimentaries of reading, and of writing, astonished at how fast he learned. In time, Nikolai could repeat headlines, whole paragraphs, though not quite sure of their meaning. Workers began to bring him old, cast-off books from their children, some with words accompanied by pictures. These he studied at night under streetlights.

Still, it was numbers that fascinated him. He amused stun-men and skinners by strolling through hanging carcasses of marbled beef, using them as punching bags while he multiplied columns of figures they called out, dividing and subdividing them in his head and shouting the answers within seconds.

Month after month, the foreman watched him, and then one day he made a call. An officious-looking man showed up and sat with Nikolai, asking questions. So many young people had died in the war, so many superior minds sacrificed, that the Party was now scouring the country, even testing farm children—tearing them from their parents' arms—in an attempt to fill schools with the brightest and most promising.

And so he was sent away to state school. The slaughterhouse workers cheered him when he left because he had been rescued from their life, but somehow he felt captured.

FOR A WHILE HE WAS IGNORED, ESPECIALLY BY HIS SCHOOLMATES. He did not possess the natural ease of discourse, and so they looked right through him. When asked about his earlier life he lied; each history he offered hid other histories he would not tell. He seemed to reek of indifference, so that at first even his teachers ignored him.

Then he began to flourish, to excel at math, his progress so accelerated, teachers walked in circles around him, giving him their full attention. While most youngsters struggled over written examinations, Nikolai worked out equations in his head, then impatiently stood, shouting out the answers. Officials came and probed his mind, this strange quiet boy with an affinity for numbers. They sat for days, challenging him with seemingly insoluble mathematical problems, many of which he solved. But no one engaged him in real conversation. No one asked if he was lonely, if he wished for a friend to talk to.

By the time he arrived at Moscow University, he had learned that people could be kind or cruel, tactful or blundering, and that most humans possessed both qualities, which made them unpredictable, never to be trusted. He avoided making eye contact, keeping his eyes slightly out of focus with the effort to look confident, at ease. He learned to think that way, too, sizing up situations quickly, seeing what his advantage could be, or backing off altogether.

He passed himself in crowds—loners, eccentrics—whatever the term the world had bestowed on him. He dressed in gray, head to insole, hoping to blend, but he never quite did. He had grown into a wiry young man with taut skin and muscles, a body tense, never at ease. His dark, probing eyes ever restless. Each passing year seemed to prove to him that things other humans thought crucial—hoped-for pleasures, accomplishments, even grievances—did not mark his life. Only his earliest years came at him with clarity and boldness.

He found Moscow an ugly place, lacking the faded, haunting beauty of old Leningrad. Rather, it was a city of menacing and clumsy façades housing offices, bureaucrats, the Kremlin. What was left of its people had been boiled down. Their gray faces invaded him—people alone, in crowds, staring out of subways. Faces pained, without vision, as if life were over.

And yet in those university years, there were times when Moscow spoke to him. In winter Nikolai stood near fires in empty lots with other humans congregating for warmth and conversation, even songs. Men played violins with icicled brows. He watched people hunched over, padding through the shadows of snow-sculpted buildings that seemed to be floating astride Moskva River. The river itself spread like a sheet. He liked how blizzards paralyzed everything, erasing the acoustics of the city. This was when he most felt Moscow's heart, the pulse of the ancient, invading Tartar.

At first his university colleagues found him clever and intriguing, then they found him rude, and they began to understand they could not grasp or trust him. He stood in the homes of professors, stuffing silverware into his pockets, his narratives of childhood scalded into outrageous lies.

"You've a superior mind," a professor said. "You could go far. Why do you do have to steal and lie?"

Nikolai did not know how to answer. He suspected that he would never be completely at home here—not in this city, and not in the rigid academic life where the Party dictated what was truth and what was perceived as lies. He had come from a place where people died with their lungs slashed naked to the wind, their frozen hearts slung down their backs. If that was truth, reality, then what was fantasy? What constituted a lie?

And so he responded to the question. "Perhaps lies are merely a form of longing out loud. It's how we survive."

He continued to be shunned, a social pariah, though he was favored academically. Finally, an official took him aside.

"Is tragic, that you have no manners, Niki. Nonetheless, we are grooming you to go to Novosibirsk, Siberia. Huge honor! New city built exclusively for scientists, physicists, their families. Country clubs, motorboats! Only for cream of Russia."

By then he had begun to see how their young minds were being warped, primed to make weapons of extinction. The stink of Russian invasions still hung in the air. Poland. Hungary. Czechoslovakia. He began to see his government as depraved, run by idiots and sadists. And slowly he stepped back. One day he walked away from Moscow University. He simply gave up mathematics. Numbers now seemed futile to him.

With no one to live for, nothing to hold him back, he dropped out of life completely, inventing a new name every week. *I absolve myself of all sense of morality, a word lost in my inner ear.* He went back to the streets, became all things to survive. Black marketeer. Thief. Bodyguard to gangsters. He paid for women and never asked their names. And nothing touched him.

IN AN ALLEY HE GLANCED AT A REFLECTION IN A SLAB OF GLASS. Himself, dagger-sideburned, wielding a gun, a man hulked and brutal. By then he had joined up with protection rackets, becoming a "roofer," thugs who preyed on shopkeepers and street vendors, taking a percentage of their profits for "protection." Those who held back were viciously beaten. The country was becoming so corrupt, even policemen worked as "roofers." Even Army officers.

Several times in self-defense he had to kill. After that Nikolai stepped back, he even thought of suicide, but then it seemed that all of Russia was committing suicide. In time he stumbled back to math, to the contemplation of numbers, the only thing he loved. He tried to explain it to a prostitute.

"It's like morphine. Mathematics deadens pain."

He would sit up all night, struggling with equations, old propositions he had never solved. He liked how the logic of numbers led *away* from words, remembering how numbers turned into words became deadly.

This saved him for a while, then he grew restless and went back to the streets. One night outside Moscow, he helped hijack a truck transporting computer terminals and cameras. A box fell open at his feet, revealing a video camera recorder. Examining it, he felt an odd sensation, as if nothing were real but the weight of this camera.

Nikolai went home and slept and woke still holding it, marveling at how well it fit the shape of his hand. As if he and the camera were invented for each other. He taught himself how to use it, liking how he did not have to speak when he stood in crowds. He could be an observer, enter rooms and no one would get hurt.

He started walking the streets, pointing the thing. He was armed and people left him alone. He shot quietly, unobtrusively, not sure what he was doing, not knowing that he was registering events. He photographed the young, the old, even the sick and dying—always admiring how they were so very much themselves. He did not see what he was doing as bizarre, but rather a retreat, a way to keep life out of range when it was too much for him, allowing him to step out of the frame.

He walked through cemeteries, shooting epitaphs. He edged close to funeral crowds, shooting solitary mourners. People allowed him because they thought he knew what he was doing. For a long time, he didn't. Then, he did. When he needed money, he shot corpses boxed in satin for their families. The newly dead for medical researchers. He shot honeymooners.

And he saw how subjects became trusting and vulnerable, taking directions like a child. Sometimes he felt a warmth for them. He began to see people in a different way, because usually while he shot them, out of nervousness they would talk about their lives—their jobs, their dreams, their childhoods. The whippings and the scars. Nikolai never saw them again. They had confessed: They had found a place to leave their burdens.

When he had enough rubles saved, he stopped. He shot without film; subjects seemed irrelevant. For, what was left to record of a country that was dying after centuries of war, revolution, genocide? Outside "modern" cities like Leningrad and Moscow, life was medieval, people roving the countryside in droves, eating roots and soil. Millions were starving to death, but this was an old story in Russia. The only thing new was industrial gloom, terrible pollution.

He began traveling the countryside, shooting footage of rivers of sludge, bent-over coal-miners lined up each day to breathe through oxygen masks. A town just south of Moscow was so toxic with industrial emissions, 90 percent of the children were born missing an arm. Officials hid them from the press, but a sympathetic doctor allowed Niki to film them.

As the years passed, he learned to assemble his films into rather crude documentaries, and he showed them to old university friends, some of whom smuggled them out of the country to Sweden, and Germany, where they were eventually aired. He was invited to a film congress in Stockholm, where he was asked to address issues of "future global toxicity."

In that way he learned how easy it was to enter the world by embellishing one's background. Moderators introduced him as a "noted mathematics scholar" who had dropped out to become an environmentalist-filmmaker. Small audiences welcomed him as symbolic of the "new Russia" with a conscience. He bluffed his way through everything—interviews, speeches. Then he began to realize he was not bluffing.

"I shoot conditions in my Russia many years," he told reporters. "I am expert on what I speak of."

He drifted through Europe for months and he was welcomed. People now seemed to love Russians, though Nikolai knew that deep down they pitied them. He shot everything he saw, though often his camera was just an excuse to study Europeans, to try to fathom them, why they seemed so different, so superior to Russians. Why Russians did not assimilate well into their countries.

A French girl he slept with tried to explain. "Europe is composed of small, tight countries, side by side, keeping each other in check. We co-exist by being polite, diplomatic. But Russia! It is too big, too wild."

"Da," Nikolai agreed. "Eleven different time zones, spanning one-third of the earth—vast, empty, godless. Many cultures, many different tongues. Not even Tsars could watch us all the time. Not even Stalin. We were allowed to be insane."

When his visa ran out, he always returned to Russia. With the country increasingly in chaos, it was easy for him to go back to the life of hijacking and "roofing." And when he had enough rubles, and yearned to travel again, he bought new passports and visas on the flourishing black market. And he drifted—eventually to Asia, Australia—always armed with his camera. A man recording a world that did not seem to touch him.

POLIHALE

Home of the Spirits

FOR YEARS THERE HAS BEEN ONLY MAX. NOW HE LIES BESIDE HER IN *the dark and tells her that his illness is progressing, that he might not recover. His words so soft, so evanescent, they almost pass for air. At first she feels disbelief, then fear, confusing it with anger, all the little impermeables between them switching places. And he cries out, weeping from the heart, for all the unlived days and mortal indecisions still stored up inside him.*

Anahola touches his long, hollow cheeks, and finally, after all these years, begins to grasp the depth of her love for him, that she has always loved him. A love he earned by slow industrious kindness, and the stern will of human nobility. She gathers him close and tells him they will fight this, they will overcome it. In her resolve, she feels a powerful quality of goodness, an untouched grace.

And so the sleepless nights begin as she learns to eavesdrop on his body, the meditative lisp and growl of organs. Some days there is no rattle when he breathes, and some days there is pain, a watery impulse in his inhalations. In conversations his words come unmoored, his syllables lengthened to slow tides . . .

THE DAY MAX WENT IN FOR SURGERY HE WAS VERY CALM, AS IF HE were having a tooth pulled. She sat beside him in recovery.

A little high on drugs, he smiled. "Not to worry, Ana. One can live with a single lung."

She told him a story then. "After I found out who my real father was, they told me he had lost a lung in World War II. A German sniper. Doctors removed several ribs to get to his lung, and he inscribed them and sent them home to my mother. That's how he courted her."

"Yet she never married him. Even though she loved him."

"He was dark-skinned, pure-blood Hawaiian. Even though she had had his child while he was overseas, she thought she wanted to marry 'up,' a *haole*."

"Still, they ended up together."

"Yes."

"Well, perhaps I should offer you my ribs, as I would most definitely like to marry you. Today would be a good day. You look splendid."

Through the years she had re-created herself, slimming down somewhat, wearing her wild hair slicked back in a French twist, her clothes always simple and expensive. Now she was wearing a new suit, smart high heels, a Chanel handbag with the signature shoulder chain. Later the chain slipped off her shoulder as she stood in the hallway talking to Max's surgeon.

The man was cold, noncommittal, and Ana tried to see herself through his eyes. *Brown-skinned. Ambitious. Squeezing her older, white-skinned lover for all she could get.* She felt like compounding his disdain, telling him that her best friend was a Mexican, their cook. That together they ran Max's house, even balanced his checkbooks. And that sometimes she cooked dinner for the cook.

"There's also a small tumor on his shoulder," she said. "Can you tell me why that was not removed?"

He fidgeted, clicking a ballpoint pen. "There are higher priorities presenting themselves . . ."

"In other words, the cancer is metastasizing."

He nodded, staring at the floor. "Unfortunately, that's what these cells do. Run amok. Divide and conquer."

"You know he once worked at Los Alamos, that he was exposed . . ."

"Of course. A lot of those physicists got sick. Occupational hazard. Like chimney sweeps."

She moved closer. "I'm sorry. Like what?"

The surgeon looked out the window. "In the eighteenth century there was a high incidence of scrotum cancer in chimney sweeps. From carcinogens, hydrocarbons in the soot. Of course, back then who knew?"

Her face flushed hot. He was so chatty, so contemptuously nonchalant, she felt like wrapping the chain of her handbag round his neck.

"Doctor. Is there any chance he'll beat this? Any hope?"

He seemed to address the floor again. "There is always hope . . ."

Ana grabbed his arm and shook it like a child's. "Oh, be a man! Pick up your face and look me in the eye. Is . . . he . . . dying?"

He looked up, unflinching. "Yes. I'm afraid so."

"How much time does he . . ."

"That I honestly cannot tell you. Six months. Two years. This is where God steps in. And chemotherapy."

She sat down in his room and took his hand. "The news is not good. But you know that."

"I'm way ahead of you," Max said. "Thing I can't figure out is why it isn't in my bones yet. Strontium 90 is a bone-seeker." He half laughed. "Maybe I'm already dead and don't know it."

Ana leaned forward, desperate. "Max, we're not quitters. We're going to fight this all the way."

Postsurgery treatments left him weak but he recovered. He seemed to recover. He put on weight. His face grew fuller and less lined. When they made love he was as ardent as a young man.

"I remember flowers in the desert after the bomb tests. They sprang up like giants overnight."

"Then what happened to them?" Ana asked.

"They thrived. For a while."

A year passed with no recurrence, no signs of new tumors. The lump in his shoulder grew smaller. Each night Ana went to the bathroom and locked the door and got down on her knees. She prayed while walking down the street. She prayed while they made love.

SHE SPENT HOURS PORING OVER MAPS, RECALLING CITIES THEY had visited, Munich, Madrid, even cities she had never heard of as a girl. Oslo, and Minsk. For over a decade they had traveled to conferences, wherever Max was invited to lecture on immunology and physics. In years to come, when she looked at a map of Europe, her eyes would always be drawn to the ancient city of old Prague. It was there that Max began to die.

Folks said Prague was most beautiful in spring. That was when chestnuts blossomed pink and white, and palace courtyards were fragrant with lilacs. Most beautiful in spring. But they had come in March when Gothic spires and red-tiled roofs were covered with snow so the medieval city seemed a dream.

Max bought her an old-fashioned fur muff, and for hours they walked cobblestoned streets lit by gas lamps. They stood on a fourteenth-century bridge over the Vltava River, a bridge graced with thirty giant statues of saints that seemed to be floating toward them in the snow. Then the entire bridge seemed to be floating, carrying them over the gilded city.

She would always remember this moment of timelessness beside him. She would remember the chill of his lips pressed to hers. Ice on the rim of his hat, the tips of his eyebrows. She would remember the warmth of his hand shoved down inside her pocket. The roughness of his coat against her cheek. The scent of his cologne, the softness of his skin, even as she imagined his blood, his marrow, his white cells, his T-cells. His cells that were running amok.

Afraid she would break down, she dashed away from him, scooped up snow and threw it at a gull. They walked off the bridge backwards for, according to legend, if one turned their back on them, the giant statues followed them home.

It was dusk when, full of dark beer, they stood outside a ballroom, formerly a convent for Ursuline nuns. Through tall mullioned windows, they watched couples in suits and long dresses dance mazurkas, the czardas, the waltz. Seeing their faces pressed against the panes, the small orchestra threw open the windows and played for them. Schubert, Brahms, Kricka. And as they played, flakes began to fall again, big and fat as petals.

"I want to waltz out in the snow."

She had never waltzed, but now she followed Max and they were flawless, moving like skaters leaning into the wind, circling the edges of a courtyard. Spinning in his arms, for a moment Ana felt that all sins were forgiven, all wounds healed, the world was in balance, and they would grow old together.

The next morning she sat in a lecture hall, listening to talks on Prague's enfeebled stonework, its precious, deteriorating buildings. Coal and coke, the main fuels for heating and cooking, were largely to blame, producing sulfurous exhalations that penetrated and corroded. Officials promised that within twenty years Prague would be heating with gas. But corrosive exhalations would still come from cars burning gas and diesel oil.

An official beside her explained. "You see, we sit in a valley. When there's high pressure, there's inversion. For weeks no fresh air comes, especially now in winter. Don't you feel it? The fog is like a pillow pushed against your face."

It was true. Ana had begun to feel she was breathing through a cloth.

"When rains come, it cannot wash the soot away. Streets turn to blackest goo. This is why we need a nuclear reactor."

That afternoon when talks resumed she noticed three men with their heads together who suddenly stood and rushed up the aisle. Max had just been asked how much low-level radiation from a nuclear reactor was safe. His voice grew loud as he responded.

"My opinion is . . . *no* radiation level is harmless. There is no safe level of exposure. Your question should *not* be, 'Is there a risk for low-level exposure?' Or, 'What is a safe level of exposure?' The question *should* be 'How great is this risk?' "

He paused as if breathless. "Most of you know my background. I was a nuclear physicist. Our work on bombs paved the way for these reactors. You've seen what bombs can do. So can reactors when they break down. I'm dead set against them. There is no safety in this industry because there is no such thing as a peaceful atom. We are simply not ready for atomically produced energy. Now, maybe I'm out of step, a barking watchdog with no teeth. But if . . ."

A man in the audience stood, his accent Dutch, or German. "Has anyone heard the news? There has been an accident in the United States. One of those reactors has had a close-to-total meltdown. There are reports . . . large quantities of radioactive isotopes pouring into the air and water of that region . . ."

People jumped up from their seats. A man crossed the stage and took the mike. "If you please. We have an update. The nuclear station is called Three Mile Island, located in central Pennsylvania. They are evacuating in the thousands."

A woman stood, clutching her briefcase. "Are we in danger of winds from this accident?"

The moderator shook his head. "We think winds will hit France and Germany first. As for Great Britain, they are already tracking wind patterns that will blow directly across the Atlantic. They would be affected first . . ."

People crowded the aisles, wanting to get home to their families, gather their children safe inside.

When Max reached her, she asked, "How bad is it?"

For a moment he winced, then shook his head. "Three Mile Island? I've been there. High-leak rates. They're careless, sloppy. I'd say a twenty-mile radius will be severely hit. Thirty–forty thousand people affected, especially downwinders."

New snow began to fall. As they walked along the Bridge of Saints, Max gazed down at her. "What a mess we've made of things. I wish . . ."

She laid her hand against his cheek. "What do you wish?"

"That I had met you when I was a younger man. That we had lived life more intensely."

"Oh, Max. It has been intense. It's been extraordinary. Much more than I ever dreamed my life could be."

He seemed not to be listening. "I wish we could have lived in deep, green fields with winding roads. A farmhouse, kids on swings. Dogs trotting by our side . . ."

He winced again, his face grew pale. "It might be time to go back now."

In their room he swallowed pills, then they quietly undressed and burrowed under thick old-fashioned comforters.

"I think . . . this is the beginning."

She took his face between her hands. "Don't talk like that. You promised we would fight this. It's been all right for a year."

"No. It hasn't."

"Max. Don't give up. What would I do? How could I go on?"

"You have no idea how strong you are."

She started to weep, then struggled to compose herself.

"Why does it take so long to see things clearly? I stood on that bridge today, and nothing mattered anymore. But you. I don't want to live without you."

He took her in his arms. "Thank you. For telling me these things. I have never been sure you really . . ."

"I have *always* loved you. How could you not know. It's just . . . I could never say that word. I never trusted it."

"Ana. It's just a word. A way to say a dozen things. 'I admire you. I respect you. I like your bank account. Your socks.' "

She tried to smile, thinking how only in death or near-death did people become real. "Help me. Tell me what to do."

"We're going home to San Francisco. You're going to marry me."

She began to shake her head.

"Ana. I'm dying. This is what I want. That way no one can touch you. You'll be, not rich, but financially secure. Besides the house, the bulk of what I'm leaving you is money. Use it wisely, and in some small way it will teach you what power is."

"I don't want power."

"You mean you don't want to abuse your power. You won't, you were never greedy. Money will give you the means to help others. I hope you will do that for me."

"I'll try. I'll find a way."

He coughed, bent forward slightly. "I promise you this. I won't give up till it gets rough. I won't put you through that."

Her heart felt shattered. Her whole chest ached. They fell silent for so long, it seemed they had both got up and left the room.

"I wish I could take you back to Hawai'i. There are healing people there. Sacred, healing places . . ."

"I'm not going to heal. You have to face that now. But . . . there seems very little left for me in San Francisco. And I have always loved your islands. Once when I visited Kaua'i, I heard Hawaiians chanting in your native tongue. I blacked out. Something beat me up. I woke up bruised and weeping, knowing I'd been punished. Then, I'd been forgiven."

She took his hands in both of hers. "Maybe, when the time is right, I'll take you back. I think it's where you've always been."

THEY WERE MARRIED BY A JUDGE IN SAN FRANCISCO, A CEREMONY so perfunctory it left her depressed. Then she began to know what it meant to wait, what it meant to dread the future. Some nights she paced for hours. Max filled a glass and swallowed several pills, then followed behind her, watering her footsteps.

Finally, he told her. "I'd like to go back to Kaua'i now."

"Soon." The longer she put it off, the longer he would live.

"Ana, before it's too late."

They flew to Honolulu and, waiting to change planes, she felt trade winds embrace her, felt her past drift through her hair. On the island of Kaua'i, they landed on an airstrip sliced out of cane fields, and rented a bungalow on the quiet, north shore of the island, reached by a creaking one-lane bridge. Their house sat nestled on a cliff, cantilevered out over Hanalei Bay, the rain forest crowding in behind them.

Ana settled them in, lined up Max's medications, and set up a portable oxygen tank. In a few days when he was ready, she took him out driving, showing him sections of Kaua'i.

"This is our oldest island, very spiritual. You can feel the *mana* everywhere. The coral layers tell the history of millions of years. At eighty-five feet down, you're in the time of Christ. At one hundred and eighty feet, the age of the Pyramids."

She showed him a bay filled with magical swarms of thimble jellies, and millions of lobster larvae like spun glass.

Max looked down in wonder. "Our predecessors. Which proves we're just little bags of atoms at the mercy of chance."

"Darwin. And you don't believe that."

He laughed. "Right now I do. Tomorrow I might quote Jesus, the Upanishads. My die is cast, my deck is shuffled and dealt. I'm game to believe in anything."

Beneath his humor she heard the subtext of a man who knew he was beginning to die. Some days she drove for hours, and while she talked, Max felt his senses rush out to the landscape of his new, his last, life. He began to let go of other things, even his personal history. Sometimes they drove in silences that lasted so long, when Ana spoke she hardly recognized her voice. She sounded almost formal, using the landscape to camouflage her sorrow.

"Folks say this is our most beautiful island. Here is one of the world's great annual rainfalls high up on Mt. Wai'ale'ale."

"Which means?"

"A Rippling on the Water. Because of the pond up there on the plateau of that peak. Also Wai'ale'ale was the wife of the god Kaua'i."

She pointed to a peak five thousand feet above them, where clouds hovered over the mountain. "The wettest spot on earth. Five hundred inches of rain a year."

It was the constant source of moisture plus rich soil that produced the lush vegetation of Kaua'i and gave it the name Flower Isle. In all directions, miles of vegetation and wildflowers imparted a lovely grace and physical softness to the land.

"How could you ever leave these islands?" he asked.

"That's something outsiders never understand. Life is very hard here. It takes more courage to stay."

They drove to the rim of Waimea Canyon, a natural spectacle, where miles of deep gorges cut in red earth were washed by cascading waterfalls. Eroded by the runoff of rainfall from Mt. Wai'ale'ale, the canyon plunged three thousand feet in sections, its valleys dramatically serrated as if sliced out with giant blades. Covered in green scrub, the series of gorges turned gold and pink as sunlight slowly shifted.

Max shook his head, astonished. "I thought I knew this island. In fact, I was blind to it. Perhaps I didn't feel such beauty should exist after what we did in Bikini, and the Marshalls."

"You saw too much, Max. You cared too much. In a way, you stopped living."

As the days passed, Ana began to relax, braiding her hair like a school-girl. She went barefoot and wore sarongs. One day while they sat on cliffs overlooking the sea, she smelled morphine, the scent of ether on his breath. She laid her head against his shoulder, terrified, and vastly in-experienced.

"I don't know what to say, Max. I don't know how to deal with this."

"Shhh. It's all right, sweetheart. It's when we're quiet that it all makes sense."

Even as he languished, he watched Ana metamorphose into some-thing new. Sometimes at meals he had no appetite and pushed his plate aside, while she recounted ancient legends. Unbraiding her hair, comb-ing her fingers through it in a timeless way, shoulders aglow like running water, she flicked her fingers like fireflies, conjuring and embellishing with such dreamy cogency, Max was drawn into her fables.

He forgot his pain, his body seemed to melt and yield, as she de-scribed a race of little people, the *Menehune*, who had flourished here, perhaps as the first settlers.

"They were small, muscular people, masters of stonework and engi-neering feats. They only worked at night, and built ingenious irrigation systems for wetland farming that still exist today . . . There is a place, called Puʻukapele, high up in Waimea Canyon. It was the home of the Menehune. They gathered there to talk and to debate, rather like the Athenian agora. It's said that on half-moon nights, if you climb three thousand feet to this hill, you can still hear them debating . . ."

She lit a candle. Her voice was soft and soothing.

"The Menehune also built the first lighthouse in Hawaiʻi. They called it Maka-ihu-waʻa. Eyes for the canoe prow. You see, on dark nights they could not find their way back to land when fishing in deep waters. Their chief loved his ocean men, so he devised a plan . . . His land workers dug for weeks and months constructing a platform halfway up a ridge rising behind Waiʻoli River. The ridge could easily be seen at night. Then his workers placed torches all along the ridge, so that its reflection in the river would give the seamen double torchlight . . .

"Some folks say the Menehune were a real people of an ancient time, who had migrated from the Marquesas. Others say they were mythical, children of the Pō, the night, which is also the Realm of the Gods. That is why they only worked at night. You see, in the ancient time, Hawaiian 'day' began at nightfall."

SOMETIMES WHEN SHE LOOKED UP, MAX WAS SOFTLY SNORING. HE often slept for two days straight, then woke refreshed, and sat poring over picture books and maps. In that way he began to understand the layout of the island, a world of breathtaking and treacherous beauty.

When they drove to the Na Pali Coast, the road seemed familiar to him. "This is the way we drove to the Barking Sands Missile Range Facility, which is engaged in intercepting guided missiles from mainland military bases."

"That's right." Ana pointed west toward a place called Mana. "I once told you about this place, sacred grounds where spirits of the newly dead wandered. And where they wander still, in spite of the bombs that land nearby."

It was a region of salt marsh and dunes, of coral beaches that barked like dogs when waves rushed in. Here lay the remains of a great temple that was the gateway to the land of Pō, the dim twilight land beneath the sea where gods watched over the souls of the dead. Now guided missiles exploded in these seas.

She continued on the island's treacherous west coast until they reached the last beach, Polihale. Now they left the paved road behind and jolted through tall, rustling cane fields until gradually a dark ridge of jagged peaks appeared on the right. When she could drive no farther, the beach at Polihale emerged from the base of the cliffs—a stretch of brilliant white powder more immense, it seemed, than the cliffs towering above it. Max fell silent, words seemed so silly here.

"*Polihale*," Ana whispered. "Home of the spirits. Here the coast road ends and our gods begin. Our *ākua*."

There was much more to explain, but she suddenly felt afraid, fearing the gods would look down and see a woman who had abandoned her culture, and her blood.

She turned to Max. "We mustn't stay. The sun is fierce."

Yet in that moment an icy wind enveloped them. It cut right through her, knocking her down. For a moment, she lay stupefied. Max knelt beside her, shouting, and they heard a rumbling from the cliffs. Ana tried to stand but something knocked her down again.

"What is it?" Max cried.

Her lips hardly moved. "We have to leave this place."

She lifted her head, cautiously rose to her hands and knees, and crawled across hot sands away from the cliffs. When she finally stood up, she looked haunted. The gods had leaned down and acknowledged her, a change-face.

SHE WATCHED AS HIS STRENGTH SLOWLY EBBED. EVEN WHEN HE rallied, the bounce back was slight. They began to stay at home where, from their *lānai*, they spent hours looking down on half-moon-shaped Hanalei Bay, its sunshot parquetry of waves, its Titian clouds dazzling as neon. Behind them, rain forests of an astonishing green leading to cliffs called *Hele Mai*. Come Away.

"I can't think what more I could want," he said. "Except more time."

Intense pain came. Nights when he tossed and moaned, when pain threatened to outrun his medications, he swallowed morphine, conservative doses that did not dull his mind. His lung grew more congested. Yet he rallied.

"Tell me more stories of your islands."

Ana was amazed at the wealth of history she remembered from elders who had taught her as a child. "Talking-story" hour after hour, she spoke so slowly and thoughtfully each sentence seemed three generations long.

"Now I will tell you that some folks say much of the ancient life and history of the Polynesians who discovered this island and lived here for two thousand years has been forgotten . . . But, a'ole loa! Absolutely not. Our history is never forgotten. Only hidden . . . Place-names remain, and with them the names of chiefs and chiefesses, gods and demigods. And all their feats and defeats . . . In sacred places, they are still worshipped. Their stories remembered and retold . . ."

Max listened, intrigued, and finally asked, "Why don't your people teach this fabulous history and its legends? Why keep them hidden?"

Ana's lips moved, but her voice was that of someone old and wise.

"*I mea a ho 'oko aku I na makemake o na kūpuna.* So that we might live as our ancestors would expect us to. This is what they wanted. Silence is how we preserve that which is most sacred."

One night she circled the floor in front of him. "Now I will show you the ancient, authentic dance we call *Hula Kahiko*."

". . . *This sacred hula was called ha'a. In the back-and-back days, it was performed only by men, and had deep religious significance for Hawaiians . . . Then certain kapu were lifted and women began to dance outside the temples, using the movements of the hula to express the life force itself . . . This dance and its accompanying chants tied us to the universe, made us one with the powers and currents of nature and the gods. And always, what was so important was the posture in the dance . . ."*

She bent forward slightly, right foot extended and pointed, right hand pointed up with fingers closed, her eyes following her hand.

"There were hundreds of hulas, each performed to celebrate fertility, a marriage, a birth. Hulas to celebrate our gods, our fields, the sea. And Laka, patron of Hula. Watch now . . ."

Ana began a haunting, penetrating chant, her voice eerily low, almost sepulchral, part prayer, part proclamation. Then her voice grew louder as she glided, swayed, and pirouetted in a trance. Moving her hands in all the classic ways of *hula kahiko* she metamorphosed as a bird, a fish, a wave, as Pele—fire and volcano goddess. And as calm trade winds after a storm.

Even as she moved, she felt a deep disturbance. Something calling to her. Something in her responding. She did not know how long she danced. It could have been for days, or only hours. Finally, she sank down to a mat, exhausted.

"You must understand. The hula was our oral history, how we remembered our genealogies. But, for over a hundred years, it was forbidden, along with our traditional art, Mother Tongue, our chants and prayers. In this way the missionaries cut out our tongues, cut off our arms. They wanted laborers, stoop workers for their sugar plantations, not intelligent natives. Our ways were 'pagan' so they outlawed them—on pain of imprisonment, even death—while their children grew land-rich and sugar-rich. Without culture, Hawaiians began to die out. This was how they colonialized our islands."

Max shook his head in silence.

"An old Hawaiian scholar, Samuel Kamakau, said Hawai'i had been 'cut up, salted down, hung out to dry.' White man's diseases did the rest."

"I never knew you gave such thought to your history," he said. "How do you remember all this, the words, the dance . . . ?"

She explained how it was not "remembered," it was just there like breathing, how this knowledge had been passed down for centuries. Each mother "gave" her child this gift of voice, of dance, of *life*.

"I learned the hula in my mother's womb. While she was dancing, I was formed in the rhythm of her fluids. And, in turn, I danced, until a child quickened in my womb. Then my feet stopped moving, my heart turned hard. But, as you taught me . . . genes remember. This knowledge never leaves Hawaiians. No matter where we go, how far we run. And, you know, Max, we did not die out. We survived! In the past ten years there has been a rebirth of our culture. They're chanting the old chants again, reviving the old dances."

He sat back and smiled. "Ana. My 'talking-story' woman. Don't you ever want to come home, to your islands?"

She sat up, looking very young. "I do. When we're here, my body changes. I feel my blood thicken. There's this sense of merging with the land, the sea, I don't feel separate anymore. But, at some point I start to feel strangled. I can't breathe. I'm afraid I'll always be going *makai and makai and makai*, as they say. In the direction of the sea. I don't even blame it on my childhood anymore."

"Ontological security," Max said. "You find it in running, in motion. No one can touch you then."

"You touched me, Max. I no longer need to run with you."

"And what about your daughter? I know you think of her."

She shook her head. "She's a woman now. We're virtual strangers."

Max studied her before he spoke. "Perhaps one day you should try to know her. What good are life's experiences if we don't pass them on to our children?"

That night Ana sat up in the dark, imagining her daughter as a child. *I never "gave" her the gift. I never saw her dance the hula* . . .

MELE KANIKAU

Chant of Mourning

SOME NIGHTS HIS SLEEP WAS SOUND, AND SOME NIGHTS HE WOKE in a kind of delirium. One morning he came awake to find what looked like a huge man-woman standing over him. Eyes like green leaves, a wide 'upepe nose, silver hair billowing to his waist. Under long, yellow robes, he had a massive chest and big copper-colored arms, but the rest of him—his cheeks and lips and chin—were delicate and shaped like a woman's. Max found him beautiful, in a scary way.

Ana spoke softly. "This is 'Iolani. Royal Hawk. I have brought him here for you. He says he cannot heal you because soon it is your time. But he can take your pain, and keep your spirit from wandering."

The priest held a small wooden kiʻi, a sacred image that resembled a howling man. He slipped it inside his robes, then slowly bent and listened to Max's breathing. When he straightened up he took Max's hand in his own leathery hands, examining Max's palm. Agitated by what he saw, he furiously rubbed the palm with his finger as if trying to erase it. All the while he whispered.

"What is he saying?"

Ana hesitated. "He says your lifeline is growing short even as he watches. He's telling it slow down."

The priest pulled him into a sitting position, so that Max was facing the sea. Then he turned to the open windows, raised his heavy arms, and chanted in a high, eerie voice.

"Aloha e ka lā, e ka lā! E ola mai e ka lā, I ka honua nei!" Greetings to the sun, to life, to the earth.

As he continued chanting, she explained. "To greet the sun as it rises, this was the tradition of the ancients. Like people the world over, we believe that the coming of the sun brings *mana*, life force, to the earth each day. With *mana* comes healing, growth, life itself."

Now 'Iolani turned, took Max by the shoulders, and silently studied him. He dug into a large *lauhala* bag and brought forth a gourd full of saltwater he had carried up from the sea, and a leaf cone full of sea salt. He flung the salt around to purify the room.

"He's casting out *'uhane 'ino*. Your demons of delirium."

Then he sat and mixed *olena*, tumeric, in the saltwater. All the while he chanted.

"He's praying to the healing gods. And to his *'aumakua*, the Hawaiian hawk."

The priest seemed to be reading the salt water, staring at images therein. He opened Max's pajama top and rubbed the mixture on his chest. He stopped and prayed, then rubbed again. He did that several times, then finally turned to Ana.

"Child, what I tell you now is so important. He has been a warrior. Now he is frail, an empty vessel. Whatever you put in this vessel must be pure. Of the *'aina* and the *kai*. Nothing else. *Pau la'au haole!* Please, tell him this."

She leaned toward Max. "He says no more food that does not come directly from the land or the sea. And no more 'white man's medicine.' That means your morphine."

Max looked up. "Is this a test? To see how much I can bear?"

'Iolani patted his shoulder. "Be patient, boy. I will come for two more dawns. Healing must be done in threes. And then . . . *pau* pain. Breath will come easy. You'll see."

By the second dawn when he returned, Max was in good spirits. "I feel great. I want to get up and run."

'Iolani pushed him down. "Not so frisky, boy. Be patient. How is your chest?"

Max shook his head in wonder. "No more congestion. I can breathe. I don't have that awful rattle."

He bent and rubbed Max's chest again with the saltwater solution and prayed as he had before. Then he laid his head against Max's chest and listened to his lung. The gesture, the warmth, and weight of the man's massive gray head upon his chest brought tears.

Max wept like a child. "I'm sorry. I don't understand why this is happening."

'Iolani sat up, gathered the tears on his fingertips, and examined them closely. "These come *mai pu'uwai* . . . from the heart. They come when you let your body and your soul relax. When you allow them to believe. You have not believed in much. Did no one teach you? Believing is the final balm."

Ana stood in a corner trembling. When he was finished, the priest took her outside.

"Tomorrow will be third-dawn healing. He will be a boy again, wanting to swim, and run. He will be well, but only for a while. After that I will not come again. I have done what I can do."

She walked to the top of a footpath and took his hand. "How can I thank you, Tūtū man. I would give my life . . ."

He raised his hand. "You offer your life, for what purpose? To atone? I see the past hovering behind you. Things you did, and undid. Not all of it was wrong. Selfish, but not wrong. Only, just now don't think on yourself. Your happiness, regrets. Give all your thoughts to this man who has loved you."

He bent forward and they *honi'ed*, rubbing nose to nose in the old way, then he turned and started down the path. Suddenly he stopped, climbed back, and stood before her.

"Child, you are looking for forgiveness. First, you must learn to forgive yourself. It does not come all at once. Forgiveness comes as opportunities. Things you do or not do. It comes as subtle light in ether. I see tomorrow, third-dawn, as a subtle light. Think how happy you could make this man. One step in self-forgiveness. If you say yes, tomorrow I will join you together in *ho'omale*."

She nodded solemnly. She said yes.

She watched him turn and melt into the rain forest, wild hair floating out like silver moss catching on the barks of trees. His yellow robes astonishing against a hundred greens. She sat down on the ground in shock. *Ho'omale*. To perform the marriage ceremony in the ancient way, with the ancient beliefs. Which meant they were bound forever in life, in death. She would not feel love again for any man.

At the third-dawn, as the sun rose and slid barefoot across the sea, 'Iolani chanted while she and Max stood draped in maile leaves and ginger. And when the sun shone full upon the cliffs, 'Iolani took their hands in his and joined them in the old, old vows.

"*Ho'oheno Pau'ole. Mālama Pau'ole. Ho'omalu Pau'ole.*" To cherish. To honor. To protect. In this life and the next.

"There is only this moment," he said. "There is only ever this moment. All you can fit in the palm of your hand. Go now. *I Hoʻokahi Kahi Ke Aloha.*" Be one in love.

For all of that day they held each other, giving each other pleasure in slow and quiet ways.

"Thank you," Max said. "My love. My wife."

Finally, they lay gazing at the ceiling where, high up on rafters, pale cones of wood powder had been left by termites. A breeze lifted the blond dust and it drifted down. As the sun's rays leaned into the room, the dust became a yellow brilliance showering their faces and their bodies. They blinked, and everything was gold.

Two days later he stood up from the bed. "God! I feel brand-new. I feel like raising hell."

And so they squandered everything. Disregarding ʻIolani's warnings, they made noonday runs into the little town of Kapaʻa to "Sharon's Famous Saimin," a tiny, two-booth luncheonette where they ate delicate *char siu* and tofu soup from giant bowls, while the owner tossed tangles of noodles into boiling pots. They drove to Hanapepe for "Green Garden's" lilikoi chiffon pie, the lightest texture in the world. They sat like youngsters, eating giant cones of blue-and-purple shave-ice, and one day they drove to a famous cattle farm and bought thick beefsteaks from a woman who still roped steer at eighty-two.

They swam for hours in seas so calm it was like being led to prayer. They passed a group of octopi volleying a glass ball back and forth between them. A shark lifted its snout and eyed them, weaving in and out in that old shark way. Lazily, they strolled on long promenades of beaches, their footsteps agitating grains of sand so they left prints of flashing phosphorescence. They lived without discretion, holding nothing back. Only at night did they slow down.

Some nights she placed the oxygen tube in Max's nose and read to him from old tattered books left behind.

"And so it was greed that killed the forests, and the common people. China wanted more and more of the highly prized sandalwood, and Hawaii's chiefs wanted more and more worldly goods, all the things white traders had. Ships, and nails. Rum, silk, and chinaware . . .

"The perfume of sandalwood came from the oil in the heartwood of the tree. The wood nearest the root had the greatest fragrance, making the lower

trunk most desirable. Each tree grew slowly, reaching maturity every forty years. But, these beautiful giants were uprooted from the ground, the heartwood carved out of them, the rest of the tree discarded . . .

"*Commoners wept out of hunger and hardship, and they wept for the death of their great sandalwoods. Each day men and women were driven like cattle to the mountains to cut the trees. Chiefs demanded that they haul them on their backs down to the shore, where they were loaded onto ships . . .*

"*Great calluses grew on naked backs and shoulders, and they became known as the 'Callus Backs.' Many people died of exhaustion. And many died of sickness from the damp, cold mountains. The people had no time to plant their fields, so they ate ferns and roots until the ferns and roots were gone. And there came famine . . .*

"*One day the chiefs looked up. The mountains were exhausted, the hills barren and eroded. The soil began to blow away and this caused floods. And still more people died. These sandalwood years were disastrous for Hawaiians. Generations lost, the lands destroyed. The trust between the people and their chiefs was broken . . .*"

Ana solemnly closed the book. "Unfortunately, that is documented history. Which is why we have no sandalwood today."

Max shook his head. "Jesus. Sometimes I can't wait to get out of this life."

She sat on the floor at his feet. "Please. Don't die regretting everything."

"Oh, I know I've done some good," he said. "I still have a conscience. It's a wonderful thing, it keeps us good animals. And now, as 'Iolani said, I'm gathering the best of life in the palm of my hand."

He reached down and stroked her hair. "The way you look when you come out of the sea, your limbs glowing from sheer joy. That baby octopus wrapped round your wrist—the way its skin went violet to blue to mauve, as if a cloud were passing overhead. The sun leaning into the forest, lighting up the backs of trees. That blue-eyed spider that keeps spinning its web in my hair while I sleep. And all the hours of you breathing beside me. It's all in the palm of my hand."

ONE MORNING HE HAD TROUBLE INHALING, HIS LUNG FILLING UP again. She hooked up the oxygen until his breathing was stabilized.

"I know this sounds crazy, but while there's time I'd like to fly."

She leaned closer. "Max. Tell me what you mean."

"I'd like to see the island from God's point of view. See exactly what he had in mind."

"You want to go up in a plane."

She thought a while, then made some calls. That afternoon she helped him dress, helped him to the car, and held his hand as she drove past the town of Lihue to the heliport. An hour later they stood in the office signing releases, then climbed into the chopper with the pilot. As they settled in, Max bent forward slightly, wincing. The man looked at him, unsure.

"My husband's recovering from a cold," she said. "Today's his birthday. He wants so badly to go up . . ."

"Okay. Well, buckle up, and just sit back. I'll show you terrain you never dreamed of."

She strapped Max in beside the pilot, where they sat floating in a glass bubble, able to see on all sides while she leaned over from the backseat, keeping her hand on his shoulder. Shuddering, the chopper lifted up and turned, heading north, delivering to them coasts of ancient serrated valleys, green velvet cliffs, then tiny, hidden beaches like opals. Some scenes were a tapestry barely imagined—a mountain goat poised for an instant in a ravine, a giant 'iwa bird soaring. Orange-and-purple cliffs etched by centuries of wind and rain standing like giant remnants of a lost world.

Max took it all in silently, too enraptured to respond. They flew up to waterfalls hanging like slender silver ribbons, then swept a dozen curves of pure white sand. They headed west to the Na Pali Coast, and just in front of the Polihale cliffs, the chopper suddenly swerved, shaken like a giant's toy. It seemed to be flying on its side. Ana banged her head against the seat, while the pilot struggled with the controls, righting the craft and flying on.

"What the hell was that!" he shouted.

She sat behind them shaking, feeling the gods had blown their breath right through her, a change-face, telling her to stay away. She squeezed Max's shoulder as they looked down on irrigation canals and tunnels carved into the mountains centuries ago. Clouds flew above them and below them, enhancing the island's beauty with daggers of dark and light.

She kept checking Max's responses, unable to hear his breathing in the craft, but knowing it was labored. Yet, when he looked back at her, he seemed transported. After an hour, the pilot touched down in a field paralleling the sea, so they could stretch their legs.

"Then you and your husband can change seats so you'll really get a view."

She walked Max to a shady grove. He bent forward slightly, trying to breathe in and out, and in that moment Ana was shocked at how distinguished he still looked. His features sharp and bold, his frame still lean, and elegant. But thin, so thin.

"I'll tell him to take us back."

Max refused, wanting to go on.

When they boarded, she told the pilot, "We'll both sit in the back if you don't mind."

He glanced at Max, then nodded. It was late afternoon as they lifted off. Now the light was changing, colors becoming more spectacular. She took Max's hand and they gazed out like children as small clouds gathered, hundreds of them tinged with peach and gold. Then they dispersed over shimmering fields of silver cane as late sunlight deepened, intensifying everything.

"Look! The rain on those cliffs . . . it's falling up." Max squeezed her hand so hard she winced.

Like the unveiling of the island's final mystery, the pilot slowly directed the chopper up over the very center of Mt. Wai'ale'ale, then let the chopper settle into its very crater. Here, in dimly lit mists, a dozen waterfalls were born from ever-falling showers. Max shouted as they flew along volcanic walls of the crater, in and out of waterfalls, each one creating a circular rainbow around them.

She leaned close, shouting in his ear, "Max, we are now in the *core* of Kaua'i. The place of its birth from the volcano's eruptions centuries ago."

Then they looked up. Even the pilot shouted. Hovering inside the crater, showered by what seemed ancient rains, they were suddenly engulfed in a double and then a triple rainbow composed of eerie, ancient blends of light and color. For a while it seemed they were entombed in color's very source. Ana opened her mouth. She felt her heart soar.

Max suddenly sat forward, squeezing her hand, his eyes locked on circles of color and color, of light and light.

"Oh, God," he said. "Oh, God."

They sat suspended, outside of time.

After a while, the pilot seemed to come out of a trance, eased them away from volcanic walls, and lifted them up past the waterfalls toward the entrance to the crater.

Max was still, his hand warm in hers. She gazed at him, and smiled. They circled the island one last time.

"There's Wailua River. See where it flows into the sea? Home to the island's kings and high chiefs. They called it *Wailua Nui Hoano*. Great Sacred Wailua. Just up the river along the Path of Chiefs are the ruins of the Birthstones and Birthing House of *Holoholo 'ku*. The house where women birthed children who would be chiefs and kings."

She spoke more softly now.

"Oh, look. A little farther north is Sleeping Giant Mountain. Do you see his outline? And now we're over Moloa'a Valley. How beautiful it is. Legend says that here they had the most delectable *limu*, or sea-weed, in the islands, so precious, it was put under a *kapu*, reserved only for royalty. Commoners were killed for eating it. Battles were fought for the right to gather it. They say thousands died in the Great Seaweed Wars."

She saw the pilot glance back at them. She pulled Max's collar closed and held his hands in both of hers. They were approaching Hanalei Bay. Ana leaned toward him, pointing out their bungalow cantilevered over the cliffs, nestled just inside the rain forest.

"Look, Max. There we are."

The sun now painted the sky gold and orange above ragged volcanic spires. Boats glittered and dipped in the bay below.

She pulled his head to her shoulder, and kept her hand there. "I'm glad we took that house. It's been perfect."

Then she fell silent, staring at the sea.

When Ana spoke again, her voice was very tired. "Look at the ocean, Max, how it crests and falls, crests and falls. How waves break so indif-ferently. What does it tell us? Shouldn't it tell us something?"

She rubbed his hands. His palms were smooth as if he had polished them with sand. Then very tenderly, she slid her hand down his face, closing his eyes.

"I'll be all right," she whispered. "I was built for this."

After a while she continued. "I'll try to remember everything you taught me. About character, and self-respect. I'll do my best."

She was still holding his hands when they landed. The pilot opened his door, climbed down from his seat, and pulled it back, leaning in toward Ana.

"I'm sorry," she said. "You'll have to call an ambulance."

He leaned in closer, staring at Max. "Is he . . . ?"

"Yes. He's gone."

She rested her cheek against Max's head, and thought of a day when termite dust spilled down from the rafters. How sunlight showered them with gold.

PART TWO

EIA KA PILIKIA LĀ

Here Are Our Troubles

ALOHA ʻĀINA

Love for the Land

AN ASIAN GIRL STRUGGLED TO BALANCE HER MORTARBOARD ATOP a mythological hairdo. When her name was called, she tiptoed to the stage in too-tight shoes. Then Ana's name was called. She would vaguely remember walking to the stage past archipelagoes of families on the sidelines, some wearing rubber slippers so their feet pushed out like ginger roots. Applause as she accepted a scholarship to the John Burns School of Medicine. And she would remember a sudden chill. The sense of someone standing in wavering sunlight and shadow.

Even from a distance, she felt her mother's presence. She smelled her perfume. Her eyes scanned the crowds. She did not see the woman, but knowing she herself was seen, Ana stood tall and threw her shoulders back. Then the family flooded forward—Rosie, Ben, everyone—moving with implicit pride.

Hours later, she stepped from the car at the intersection and started walking up Keola Road. Along the way they waited, neighbors, children, old *tūtū* and uncles who had watched her struggle up and down that road for years. They stepped out and embraced her.

"So proud, Ana! Good fo' you."

A grandpa with one eye stitched shut pridefully pounded the tip of his cane in the dirt. Kids emerged like little dust-ghosts, draping flower *lei* around her neck. Others stood silent, in their eyes deep emotions they could not articulate. Then a big woman stepped from the crowd, sweeping her up in a breathtaking hug. Ana had always thought the woman hated her; for years she had shouted curses from her front door.

"No, honey girl! All dat time was *chanting* fo' you. Now you going tell da world what and what. Dat Hawaiians real *akamai*. Dat we going rise again!"

They flooded into the yard, carrying pans of food and rattling ice chests. The yard seemed to flow into the house, supporting a river of human traffic. And in the midst of it, Lopaka. Big and muscled, thick dark skin. Leaning on his arm brace with the quietude of ironwood, he smiled so brilliantly his handsome face looked young. He didn't speak, but for a moment he stood so close, when he moved away the air still held his scent. And maybe that was her best gift. His deep pride in her.

Inside the house she found kids kneeling at the toilet, whispering down at their reflections. They flushed, watched with fascination as their reflections whirled away, then ran screaming to a mirror to see if their faces had disappeared. And Ana saw how life came back and back, how they still did the things she had done in small-kid time—rubbing mulberry juice on their lips, turning them a ghoulish blue, smearing green mold from the walls onto their eyelids, then pinning *pua* in their hair and slow-dancing in couples like the grown-ups.

She kicked off her shoes, slid into a sarong, and danced hula with half a dozen aunties. Some rinsed their mouths with beer and spat on her hands for luck. Ukulele and guitar, the old songs. One by one, folks got up and harmonized.

A gang of cowboy cousins came, *paniolo* smelling of saddles and horses. They brought a roasted boar, roped kids with their lariats, and sang their *paniolo* songs. Then, a thundering locomotion up the road. Tattooed bikers all in black roared into the yard on Harleys. The Turks of Nanakuli, gleaming with sweat like muscled crows. Several bikes were slung with freshly caught red snappers, which they presented to Ana. In their nose studs and topknots, they unfurled the Hawaiian flag, and raised their fists and shouted *Huli!* Then they broke out ukuleles and sang in sweet falsetto like castrati.

Hours passed. The food they had planted and sowed, and raised and slaughtered, and caught in the sea and called the gods to bless, now came alive. The air was coated with the odor of singed skin as Panama and Florentine Chang grilled mounds of *hulihuli* chicken. Roasted meats burst out of the night by the light of their dripping fats. *Poi* glowed purple in big, deep bowls. Fish scales grew into piles like pink fingernails, which kids stuck all over their bodies and their faces so they glowed.

And in the steam clouds of *kālua* pig, the sounds of people physically responding to their food. The lip-smacking saltiness of *lomi* salmon. The ho! of fiery *kimchee* clearing their sinuses. The zsss! of flip-top soda cans. Men opened Primo bottles with their teeth. The ping! as they spat the metal tops at empty Crisco cans, then heartily drank, dark throats moving like shifting gears.

Ana dished out food, filled bowls and glasses. She drank too much and danced until her feet were scraped and numb. Hours later, she flung herself into a chair and gathered kids around her, faces like dark flowers as they dozed against her legs.

THE NEXT DAY SHE AND ROSIE WALKED THROUGH OLD NANAKULI Homestead Cemetery. They knelt at Emma's grave while Ana spread flowers.

"I did it, Aunty. And I will keep on doing. I will never abuse the *mana* you bestowed on me in the Ritual of *Hā*. I will make you proud."

They strolled the grounds and stood in front of Ava's grave.

"Mama was so beautiful," Rosie whispered.

"Your mama was insane."

"It could happen to me. It's in our blood, you know."

"Rosie, blood can change."

"How? How can it change?"

"Determination. Human will is a powerful medicine. It heals."

"And what about forgiveness?" Rosie said. "Does forgiveness help us heal?"

For a moment, Ana fell silent. "She was there, at my graduation. Wasn't she?"

"Could be. And so?"

"She's like some kind of extinct species that's come back to haunt. It's been nine years. What . . . in . . . the . . . world does she want?"

"She came back from time to time but you refused to see her." Rosie stared at the ground. "Ana. Tell me something. Do you want kids? As far as you know?"

"I take the Pill to avoid having conversations like this."

"Well, your mama didn't want kids either. A lot of women don't. She got pregnant by mistake, tried to raise you alone and couldn't do it."

". . . Maybe she should have thrown me out and raised the placenta instead."

"*Kuli kuli!* Hush now. Stop being so clever. She's proud of you. She's not trying to take credit for it."

Ana tapped her foot impatiently. "Then, what does she want?"

"Maybe in the little time we have on earth, she might just want to know you. After all, she gave you life. She didn't try to *take* it."

She moved closer now. "Rosie, I'm sorry. I forget what it was like for you."

"Sometimes I look at my daughter, Makali'i, so pretty and so smart. I wish Mama were here to see her. I know she was seriously disturbed, the way she beat me and little Taxi. But when you have a child . . . you want to hold it up and shout, 'Look, Mama!' We women, we're the *bridges*. The connections. But you want to tear down that connection, out of meanness."

"I don't even know her," Ana said. "What would I say to her?"

Rosie laughed. "Oh, you. You're worrying about the thickness of the *poi* before you even plant the taro."

SHE BROODED OVER NOTES ON THE ETIOLOGY OF RHEUMATOID arthritis. For a few minutes she felt very clear about things. An hour later, nothing made sense. Each page of her notes reproached her. Ana sat back depressed, sure she would not last through four years of medical school.

Molecular genetics. Immunosurveillance. Chromosomal clustering. She could hardly pronounce the words. They were branches of research for highly trained specialists, not for doctors of general medicine. Yet in almost every course, professors threw these terms at them, expecting students to absorb and understand them.

In class, she raised her hand. "I don't understand how knowledge of these new, esoteric sciences will help me as a doctor. I need to learn how to treat a parasite, not how to clone a titmouse."

The professor smiled indulgently. "You see, I'm trying to show how the line between biology, chemistry, and physics has, in the past few years, been totally eradicated. Understanding human cells helps us understand disease. But to get there we had to combine all three sciences."

He wore an aloha shirt and a reddish toupee, which Ana avoided looking at. Rather she looked to the side of his head, wondering why *haole* seemed to like wearing other people's hair. Students muffled their yawns as he droned on.

"We now have in our hands the keeper of the keys to life. The double helix or twin spiral, of the DNA molecule . . ."

Later, one of her classmates complained, "Another visiting professor on sabbatical from Stanford, or Columbia. To them, we're just a coconut med school. They want to show us how backward we are."

Ana thought he was probably right. The John Burns School of Medicine had been founded only in the past five years. Administrators were still proposing ideas for the curriculum, while frustrated students transferred to mainland schools.

"Meanwhile, we're falling behind in the important stuff, microbiology, immunology. All we do is stab needles into fruits. If I inject one more nectarine, I'll die."

Yet she pressed on, feeling a small transformation with each thing learned, a milestone in her life. For hours, she sat emptied of everything but the text before her. She studied through a hurricane, glancing up dreamily when a cow flew past her window, when the lights blew and she had to read by candlelight.

In spite of her apprehension, Ana approached her first cadaver with cool finesse. Even the word *embalmed* intrigued her, suggesting something hidden inside a tomb, so that when she sliced into cold, gray flesh, cutting deep into the abdomen, she felt she was slipping inside a mausoleum. The smell of formaldehyde swept over her. A young man beside her was violently ill, but Ana stood her ground. She bent for hours probing the flesh carefully as if the nerve ends were still alive, and when she finally stitched up the abdomen, she patted the cadaver's stomach thoughtfully. The anatomy instructor singled her out for her "professionalism."

"Of course," Rosie said. "It's in your blood. Your mama wanted to be a doctor."

She did not respond, hoping that without words to sustain it, the subject of her mother would eventually die out.

LOPAKA STARED AT THE MOUTHPIECE OF THE PHONE, THEN HUNG up and rubbed his leg thoughtfully.

"That was Philomena Lobo's husband. He wants to know if he's got legal rights to sue her doctors."

Ana looked up from her books. "What's wrong?"

"Cancer. It started in her leg. Doctors wanted to take it off, she said no, and now it's in her lungs."

Rosie spoke softly so the children wouldn't hear. "That's the third case I heard of in this valley. Over toward Lualualei, that boy with muscle cancer . . . doctors say it's real rare."

The next day Ana walked down the road to Philomena's house. A huge Hawaiian with a lovely face, she was known to consume a whole baby pig, and a coconut cake in one meal. Her husband sat on the porch, looking lost, a clean, rather handsome man who always seemed to be covered with flies. She set down a fresh-baked pie and hugged him. Inside, the house was dim but clean and stark as if everyone had moved away. Seeing Philomena, Ana stood still. The woman had lost all flesh, the skeleton of her face now hovering just behind the skin. Ana smelled the other thing. It had already taken over.

"Ana. Come. No be shy."

She sat beside the bed and took the woman's hand. "I am so sorry. I just found out. I . . . I brought you a pie."

She laughed softly. "Dey nevah tell you? No mo' appetite. Philomena dying."

She said it with such candor, Ana hung her head

"Dey give me plenty pills fo' pain. When get real bad, dey going shoot me up wit' big-time drugs."

"My God. How did this happen?"

She shrugged and pointed to the ceiling. "When He call, we go."

Walking home, she watched children spinning hula hoops, and wondered how there could be such a thing as death when every evening angels chased their halos into the dusk.

DAYS LATER SHE SAT WITH A GIRL NAMED GENA MELE, WHO WAS working her way through law school.

"If I was already practicing, I'd have a major class-action lawsuit against the military. Those bastards are the ones polluting the soil and air, making everybody sick."

Ana was not sure how much she liked this girl. She did not have the gift of inquiry. She was hot-tempered, made friends and enemies too fast. Men called her "sexy" but her dark eyes glowed with a cool perversity.

She came from the town of Wai'anae farther up the coast between Ma'ili and Makaha. But Gena seemed to come from another country, someplace unnamed and difficult. They had met through Lopaka, and Ana saw they were infatuated; they tended to stare at each other a lot. That was why she had befriended her: to find out what kind of woman appealed to this cousin she loved.

Both girls had found jobs at a steakhouse near Waikiki, and after classes they waited tables, then took a late bus home to the coast. Some nights they stopped at the Humu Humu Lounge, where locals gathered. Over beers, Gena cursed the lack of law-school scholarships for native Hawaiians, the lack of brown faces among her professors. The fact that their educational system, like their lands, had been almost totally appropriated.

"And now they're killing us off with toxins."

Ana thoughtfully sipped her beer, thinking the girl was too much of a firebrand to make a good lawyer.

"Gena. You can't change things overnight."

"They'll change. Sooner than you think."

"How's that supposed to happen?"

"The way it did with the antiwar movement. The Civil Rights movement. Constant vigilance. Resistance."

"Well, I'm planning to be a physician, not a revolutionary. Education is the way to fight back. Even Lopaka says so."

At the mention of his name, Gena calmed down.

He will tire of her, Ana thought. *She will take away his peace of mind.* She didn't see that, in many ways, the girl was a mirror image of herself: her impatience, the way she expressed her passion and her anger. She didn't see how together they cut a swath, two smart lower-class girls on the rise, not yet aware of it.

That weekend folks were gathering on the beaches at Mākua, up the coast, in support of homeless Hawaiians living there. Hurricane 'Iwa had destroyed their makeshift shanties and encampments, and they were attempting to build new ones. It was rumored that the state was sending in police and bulldozers to stop them.

"We're also mobilizing to protest the Army's bombing of Mākua Valley. You've got to come."

"I have to study," Ana said. "Mondays are my heaviest class load."

"Mākua is more important than Monday."

Ana felt her face flush. "Listen, Gena, you've got two more years of law school. You're not careful, you'll flunk out. Or be kicked out. Can't you see they're just waiting for us Wai'anae girls to drop the ball? Remember, we're supposed to be pregnant and on Welfare."

She leaned in closer. "Ana. You didn't hear what happened? Kids sneaked up into Mākua Valley after the Army had been shelling. You know what they brought home? An unexploded ordnance—a bomb the size of a football. They found it lying on the open ground and thought it was a dud. Cops called in a bomb squad, evacuated half the town. You know how many folks could have been killed? Come on! Take a stand."

That night while the family sat discussing the live bomb the children had brought home, Lopaka reminded them how in 1976 folks had begun to wake up.

"That's when they staged land occupations on our island of Kaho'olawe during Naval war maneuvers there. Remember? That same year they filed a lawsuit against the Navy for bombing that island relentlessly for thirty years."

Ana had been sixteen then, and it was somewhere in that time that the phrase ALOHA 'ĀINA began appearing on bumper stickers. Love for the Land.

"I tell you now," Lopaka said. "Kaho'olawe was just the beginning. We will never stop reclaiming what is ours."

ANA PUT HER BOOKS ASIDE AND LEANED FROM HER WINDOW, pondering Nanakuli Valley. With its parched earth, its harsh, near-barren fields, it was ugly and beautiful at once. It would always be her history, her conscience. And some nights she thought of the silent beaches and valleys of Mākua, farther up the coast. For almost two thousand years it had belonged to *kānaka maoli*, the true Hawaiian people, who considered it *wahi pana*, a sacred place.

The valley still contained sacred *heiau*, temple sites, and ancient altars of worship. Deep in caves that had been blown open by military explosives were the bones of ancient chiefs. She imagined their skulls graveled by shrapnel. Above the bones were petroglyphs showing that the protective walls of the valley had once been a sacred training site for traditional martial arts. It had also been home to diverse and unique native birds and plants, most of which had been destroyed forever. Below the valley, the beaches themselves held numerous burial sites. Artifacts found in the waters offshore proved they had once been sacred fishing grounds.

In the 1930s the U.S. military began using Mākua Valley as a gun emplacement. Then, during World War II, they had expanded into the entire valley, using it for "war maneuvers," aerial bombardments, exchange of live ammunition between troops. In order to do this they had evicted several thousand farmers and torn down their homes. Old valley *kūpuna* still recounted the "Murder of the Church."

"Dey painted one big white cross on our Mākua church. Den, swear to God, dey bombed dat church fo' target practice. Bombed it to dust."

Just down from the valley, homeless families had begun using Mākua Beach as a temporary residence, a *puʻuhonua*, or refuge. The elderly and the sick were brought here to lie in the nourishing sea and in the rock pools on the beach. People healed, and stayed, sweeping their beaches clean of garbage. They became once again *kahu o ka ʻāina*. Stewards of the land.

Now these settlements were under assault by the military and state police. It made Mākua a double symbol of resistance, exposing the contradiction of local poverty and homelessness alongside the military occupation of Hawaiian lands. Each time the military scheduled war manuvers at Mākua Valley, or the beach, they found large groups of Hawaiians there, braced for confrontation.

IT WAS A MONDAY, AND THEY WERE GATHERING ON THE HIGHWAY, making their way out to Mākua Valley near the northern tip of the coast. As the crowd moved closer, they saw patrol cars at regular points parked along the highway.

Lopaka slowed his truck. "The main thing is to keep everybody calm. It's a vigil, not a conflict."

"It's a confrontation," Ana said. "We're going to face down police, and the Marines."

Crowds of people shuffled down the road. A woman holding a child stepped up to their truck, tears tracking her dusty face.

"They tore down our shack! No place to go. Rural assistance program full . . . I got two boys in high school trying graduate this summer. How they going finish school if homeless?"

Lopaka gave her the number of a priest taking in families and watched two cops approaching.

He stuck his head out the window and lied. "We're looking for cousins living on the beach, want to take them home."

They motioned for him to pull over off the highway. "Find your folks and get them out of here, quick. Marines are landing in four hours. That beach has got to be secured."

They pulled off the highway just before the beach, a long stretch of undeveloped coastline where bulldozers were flattening wooden shacks and tents. Dozens of eviction-notice servers roamed campsites, shouting at the homeless through bullhorns.

"YOU ARE OCCUPYING LAND UNDER THE JURISDICTION

OF THE STATE DEPARTMENT OF LAND AND NATURAL RE-
SOURCES. YOUR RESIDENCY HERE IS UNAUTHORIZED. YOU
HAVE ONE HOUR LEFT TO LEAVE."

Ana watched families forcefully escorted off the beach. She looked
out to sea where just ten years ago great schools of dolphins had leapt
and played, and whales had come with their calves. Now the seas were
empty of marine life.

"What is an amphibious landing, anyway? The Marines land. Then
what?"

Gena followed her gaze, then looked up at the valley behind them.
"Then I guess they crawl up the beach 'under fire' and make their way to
their 'objective.' One of the hills behind us they're assigned to take."

Ana stared at scorched and cratered sections of the valley, then
turned to Lopaka. "What do you know about O.B.O.D.?"

He watched a cop handcuff a woman trying to kick him in the groin.
"OPEN BURN/OPEN DETONATION. How do you know about
that? It's supposed to be classified."

"I read your files . . ."

"It's a twelve-acre site up in the mountains behind Mākua Valley,
part of those four thousand acres the Army took from us. That's where
they openly burn spent ammunition. Spent rockets. Even Chinook
choppers carrying nuclear-weapons parts that exploded up there on takeoff. Pilots, their clothes, everything. All carefully incinerated, so there's no
proof. They either bury it or burn it."

"And toxic poison is released in the smoke of those fires. We inhale
it, ingest it. It's in our fields, our food . . ."

He put his hand on her shoulder. "That's why the military calls this
coast 'Death Row.' "

In the silence, they watched burly cops with rubber truncheons bat-
tling big, angry men.

"Those cops are Hawaiians. Even they've been turned against us.
We're either dying or trying to kill each other."

Behind them, almost one hundred demonstrators spread out along
the beach, pretending to be looking for homeless relatives. Then, on
cue, they slowly unfurled their banners. NO MORE MILITARY BOMB-
ING. GET OFF OUR SACRED LANDS. They stood waiting for the
Marines to land and come ashore, wondering why the cops ignored
them, why they lingered in the background. Finally, hot and tired in the
sun, they formed small circles and sat down.

In that moment, the gentle, graceful curves of the sloping lower hills reminded Ana of a woman. A nurturing, caring woman of *kahiko* time, the old days. She felt the breath of Mākua, felt the landscape turn to her, imploring.

In the absolute silence, a powerful explosion ripped the air. The ground literally shook beneath her. Then another, so strong her chest vibrated with each concussion. People shouted and staggered to their feet, hills of red soil erupting in the air. They saw Mākua bleed.

Lopaka shook his arm crutch at the sky. "Those bastards tricked us! There's no amphibious landing today. They're bombing up in the valley."

In the background, along the access road to the beach, dozens of cops stood laughing. News reporters with camcorders hanging by their sides looked clearly disappointed. Then groups of deputies approached.

"Okay, you clowns. Go home. You had your day."

Lopaka spun around. "You assholes."

One of them grabbed Lopaka's arm, hustling him along. Lopaka flipped his hand off, swinging wildly with his crutch. It missed, but anger turned the man into a bull. He spun Lopaka around, tried to pick him up by his armpits and throw him facedown in the sand. Gena ran up with a rock aimed at his head, and cops swarmed over them.

Ana remembered glimpsing a fist, a bleeding nose, then she went down. She woke handcuffed, her mouth full of dirt, as they loaded her into a van with half a dozen injured people. A cop slammed the door, then sat facing them with his rubber truncheon.

"You're a brother," she said. "How can you do this?"

His shoulders sagged, his face remained resolved.

"*Auwē. Auwē,*" an old woman cried. "Our own boys, trying to kill us . . ."

Ana bent down to her and held her hands, so full of rage her body shook. As they sped down the road she looked back at the valley, bombs still exploding in the mountains. Again, she felt the suffering of Mākua, felt the land imploring her.

KA HĀ O KONA WAHA

The Ritual of Hā

THE YEARS OF MED SCHOOL SEEMED A BLUR, A LONG BAD DREAM OF scutwork at the teaching hospital—running blood samples back and forth to labs, trotting up and down for X-rays. Most of the doctors were white or Asian males with a continuing disdain for female physicians, but Ana stood up to them, challenging them in lectures. When her diagnoses were questioned, she defended them aggressively, confirming her reputation as a "toughie" from the Waiʻanae Coast.

Observing procedures, she constantly elbowed her way ahead of male students so that during an emergency thoracotomy she leaned in so close the chief resident asked her to step back. Instead she leaned in closer as he inserted a metal spreader between the patient's ribs. When they were far enough apart, he dipped both hands into the chest cavity and squeezed the heart. Blood shot out of the patient's chest, spraying Ana's face. Afterwards, she calmly walked down the hall and threw up in a bedpan.

But during clinical rotations, she found she was not drawn to cardiology, anesthesiology, obstetrics. Internal medicine only partially engaged her. Ward rounds were a bore. Mostly she came alive in the "pit," the hospital's Emergency Room, liking the pressure, the way doctors made split-second decisions, the way they relied on intuition. By her fourth year as a subintern, certain procedures came easily. She seemed to have a knack for finding veins, intubating, and inserting central IV lines. The one procedure she dreaded was giving an intracardiac injection: sticking a needle directly into another human's heart.

The first time she attempted it, the chief resident bullied her. "Come on. You did it with cadavers."

"This man is alive," she whispered. "I can't see his heart."

"Doctor, this is ER. You hesitate, the patient dies. Aim blind, and do it."

After a while she began approaching patients as if they were victims. *I am learning on your body. I will cause you pain. I may even harm you.* A woman went into seizures when she injected the wrong medicine.

"You have to hurt them," the resident said. "That's how you learn to do it right. Then somewhere down the line, you'll save a life."

In time, most procedures became second nature to her and Ana was able to step back, get a broader picture of the ER, a subculture with its own argot and cryptic codes. A place that sometimes seemed staffed by misfits, borderline personalities. The receiving room was a cross section of humans that only accidents, semi-suicides, or crimes of passion could provide. Hawaiians, Samoans, Filipinos, whites—all holding together their body parts, bullied by big, taciturn triage nurses slapping down junkies petitioning for drugs.

She began to understand that no professional who survived ER would be the same as they were before. Its madness was the alkaloid that transubstantiated them. One entered it a rube, an innocent, and came out a husk. Eyes on a stalk. In between fractures and infarcs, ODs and hemorrhages, patients were grossly misdiagnosed, even mislaid. And then, the real nightmares. A child attacked by a pit bull was missing half his face. What would his life be after this?

In that year, six people in her class dropped out. Each day Ana feared she had caught a different disease. Patients spat and bled on her. They vomited and urinated. She scrubbed her hands until they were red and cracked. She wore surgeon's gloves, carrying her papers and books in plastic bags. Some days she wore surgical masks, seeing patients as the enemy. The thing to avoid, not heal.

"I feel no compassion at all. I'm becoming conscience deficient."

"Get out of ER," Rosie advised. "It sounds like a war zone."

Yet, day after day, she watched fascinated as the chief resident performed CPR on a patient while simultaneously orchestrating the expertise of interns, residents, med students, clerks, nurses, even a priest. This was what she wanted. Not to play God, but to mobilize random professionals into a single healing machine.

———

By her second year of internship, Ana had learned to regard death as a nebulous thing. Sometimes they pronounced a patient dead who still had heart activity, electrical activity. She began to wonder, *When precisely does the last cell die, and is the soul intact till then? And when exactly does the soul depart and the body become just a container?*

One night a team stood over the corpse of a man with a crushed chest. When they tried to get at his heart, blood sprayed on monitors, instrument trays, the walls. It poured out of the body so copiously it lay congealed on the floor in black lacquered clumps. After someone called time of death, and everyone cleared out, Ana pulled off her bloody gloves and mask, and gazed down at the body. She turned to a rubber-gloved man with bucket and mop who had entered the room.

"Juan. Do you believe humans have a soul?"

He was slender, quiet, and efficient. He paused in mopping up the carnage. "A soul? Yes, sure I do."

"Well, when do you think it leaves the body?"

He looked down at his mop. "When I come in."

Sometimes she couldn't let the bodies go. Suppose Juan was wrong? She walked beside them as aides pushed them down the hall toward the morgue. On the down elevator, she chatted with the aide, but she was really talking to the corpse.

"Well, the crappy part is over. Now it's just the long, long sleep."

Still, she was not satisfied. *If we really possess a soul, how does it feel when the newly dead body is violated?*

One night the EMS team brought in a suicide, a woman dead from overdose. As soon as the attending declared her dead, they physically ripped her apart. The resident sliced her chest open, using a vise to spread her ribs so students could practice heart massage.

Ana heard the ribs crack. She watched them toss around the heart. They performed half a dozen procedures, injecting her, intubating her, reintubating, over and over. All this on a woman so unhappy she had taken her own life. Wasn't this violation a second death? How did a soul survive this?

Later she stood outside ER, smoking a cigarette. Another intern joined her.

"Brutal, huh? They couldn't even wait till she was cold."

His name was Will Chong, from Kailua on the island's east coast. "I kept wondering how they'd clean her up for viewing. Her family's going to ask what happened to her chest—that huge, ugly scar where they sewed her up."

Ana shrugged. "They'll lie. Say they tried everything to save her."

"Well, don't let them get to you. They always try to break down female interns first."

He was tall, boyish-looking with lovely golden-yellow skin. His father was a neurological surgeon who wanted him to follow in his footsteps. Will said when he chose Emergency as a specialty, his father stopped supporting him.

"He calls it the loser's specialty of medicine. I don't care. When I'm attending physician in ER, I'll do my twelve hours on, twelve hours off, and have a life. No one tracking me on a beeper."

They had been interning at Queens, the largest, and best-equipped hospital in Honolulu. Even into her second year, Ana was still trying to adjust to the grueling schedule. On-call round the clock for thirty-six-hour stretches, then a few hours' rest in between, she lost all track of days and weeks. Her skin broke out, she grew depressed.

Sometimes she came off duty so wired, she could not sit still. Will saw her dancing round the canteen and brought her coffee. She drank three cups and deflated; her eyes flickered and slowly closed. Sometimes she fell asleep at the table, leaning on her elbows while he watched. He began to find it soothing, and rather intimate, watching her sleep.

He did not find Ana conventionally pretty, though she should have been. Black, curly hair pulled back in a twist, a natural tan as if she were tinted from the sun. The full Hawaiian nose and lips. Her slightly slanted eyes were pale above wide cheekbones, she even had a dimpled chin. But she possessed a penetrating no-nonsense gaze that made her face seem hard, as if she were taking someone's measure.

Her body was nice, he thought, long legs, small breasts—full-bodied though, not slender. He imagined rainwater following the line of her hips. But what had first caught his attention was her height. That is, she was average height, but seemed much taller because of her beautiful wide shoulders, the proud way she carried herself. He looked down at her big, lū'au, "townie" feet and smiled. All in all, he found her rather beautiful, but in a scary way.

One day after a postmortem, they stood scrubbing their hands. "Now for a stealth injection of caffeine! Then, sleep."

Will glancd at her. "Maybe we should try that together sometime."

Ana slowly leaned back. "Is that a proposition?"

"Could be. Aren't interns supposed to be sex maniacs?"

"Not this intern."

He laughed, half joking. "Ana, can't you see we're fated? We're locked up in here like savages, confused and half-insane. Forced to sleep in our clothes and filthy shoes. We kill more patients than we save. Who else would want us?"

She looked down at their shoes like walking petri dishes of biohazards. She laughed back, attracted to him against her will.

When it eventually happened, it seemed natural and easy because they had learned to like each other first. The first night they slept together, Will collapsed in her arms before he got his pants off. She found it touching, holding him, listening to his snores. It had been so long, just feeling a man's head against her shoulder was a shock.

Nights when they couldn't sleep at all, they made love frantically, listening for the pager. Then they lay back, discussing patients, procedures, and mistakes. And unrelenting fear. A man with eruptions over his body had yanked the IV from his arm and jammed it into Ana's butt. She was put on antibiotics. Will helped resuscitate an overdose who then nearly strangled a nurse to death.

"I'm beginning to see the downside," he said. "Even nurses say ten years in ER, then burnout."

One night she woke in a sweat, unable to identify familiar terms. *Posturing decerebrate . . . Peritoneal lavage . . . Esophageal reflux.* Her mind completely blank, as if her brain had died. Will found her shaking, nearly incoherent, and asked for Emergency Time-off. For hours, he walked her up and down the streets of Honolulu, both of them amazed. They had forgotten the sound of healthy humans, the noise of traffic. The feel of soft trade winds on their skin. They stroked the rough bark of a tree, they waded in the ocean.

"Think about this seriously," he said. "We've still got two years of residency ahead. I wonder if by then we'll still be human. Maybe you should get out of ER, specialize in cardiac, or OB-GYN. You'd be excellent at that."

She folded her arms and stared at him. "You think Emergency is a man's domain? That a woman can't do the job?"

"I think it's a job for animals. Look at us. We hardly have time to bathe. Half my friends own their own homes. They've already been to Europe. I don't even own a decent watch. I've never owned a car. We'll be old by the time we accomplish these things. We'll be burned out, and angry. All this sacrifice for people we'll never see again."

He took her hand, unable to look her in the eye. "You know, I've come to love you, Ana. More than love you. We've been like soldiers side by side in battle. I would trust you with my life. I don't want to see someone like you turned into a . . . grunt."

His words touched her so deeply, Ana could not speak. She turned away so that they seemed apart, though their feet touched in the sea.

SOME NIGHTS FOR AN HOUR PEOPLE OUT IN THE CITY STOPPED trying to kill each other. The Emergency Room fell silent, interns and nurses slumped in chairs, asleep on cots. On such a night, Ana stood beside a corpse waiting for the gurney to the morgue. A slender young man thrown from a truck, whose heart had been pierced by a sliver of metal. By now she knew the procedure by rote. They had stabbed him full of needles and tubes, slammed him with defibrillator paddles, then tore him wide open, cracked his ribs and broke into his chest. They passed around his punctured heart, then pronounced him dead. While Ana closed and stitched his chest, the resident pulled off his gloves and called time of death.

"He was DOA, but what the hell. Can't say we didn't try."

Then everyone cleared out, leaving the young man naked, spread out like a crucifixion, the airway still clamped between his teeth, his chest a ragged line of stitches.

Ana stepped closer. "Now we are alone. And where is God? How could he do this to you? How could we?"

First do no harm. Hippocrates. Yet she constantly watched doctors slice into bodies with a kind of vicious glee.

"For students," they said. "And interns. This is a teaching hospital."

She didn't always believe it. She saw the expressions on their faces— victory when they revived a patient, or sour defeat.

She wet a cloth and gently wiped the young man's face. "I'm sorry there's no God to comfort you." She covered the body with a sheet. "I'm sorry we didn't honor you in death."

Then she stepped back and looked around. *This is it. The life I'm training for. This is probably all there is going to be.*

She moved to the intern's lounge and stood in a bathroom terrified. She looked down at her legs, trembling so badly her knees knocked. Her arms shook uncontrollably. She slid to the floor hugging herself. From deep in her throat strange sounds issued, like a small, sick dog trying to bark. Her whole body sobbed.

That night she clung to Will. "Am I having a breakdown?"

He rocked her gently. "You're just throwing out emotions you won't need. You're becoming a professional."

When Will transferred to a Chicago hospital to do his residency, Ana spent a year of such visceral loneliness she felt someone had removed her vital organs and given them to her to hold. In that year, the first heart transplant was successfully performed in Honolulu, but seventy people died of AIDS. Surgeons stood with human hearts pulsing in their hands, yet actual contact with human blood became an ana-thema.

Rosie shook her head. "It's what you wanted, life in the pit."

By then, Ana had even learned to preempt her sense of smell: the fruity breath of diabetics, the musty scent of liver failures, the ketone odor of anorexics—a faintly rotten smell. Sometimes her mind went blank, her hands froze in the middle of procedures. Little moments of an-archy. She wondered if she had made the wrong career choice. But then, back aching with fatigue, she remembered her Aunt Emma who had passed on to her the healing gift in the Ritual of Hā.

In her second year of residency she dreamed of Emma with disturb-ing frequency. She woke in the dark remembering how, when she was twelve, the woman had been diagnosed with cancer. Surgery had left her a virtual invalid. Rosie said she was sick in her chest, that doctors had taken off her breast. Ana did not believe her. One day while Emma slept, she had crept into her room and carefully pulled aside her nightgown.

Looking down, Ana's whole body had trembled, she felt a buzzing in her ears and momentarily lost her vision. They had cut out everything. Not just the woman's breast, but the lining of the chest muscles and all the chest muscles themselves. They had cut out all of the lymph nodes under the arm that formed a network of adjacent tissues. They had scraped the woman to the bone.

What had been left was a vertical scar almost two inches wide that plunged from her left shoulder down to her stomach. It was intersected by an equally wide horizontal scar extending from midchest across to her armpit and down under her arm. As the scar had healed, keloids formed—big knots of fibrous scar tissue adding to her terrible disfigurement. Ex-cruciating pain from the badly healed scar had kept Emma from lowering her arm. For months she had lain with the arm outstretched so that the scar resembled a knotty crucifix hung from her left shoulder.

Ana had stood at her bedside, transfixed, feeling her own body go damp and cold. She smelled the salt and rancid odor of the woman's flesh and wondered what awful sin she had committed to deserve this. Sinking to her knees, she had crawled from the room and sat in a closet for hours. She never told what she had seen. Months later, Emma died floating inside an oxygen tent like a withered doll propped up in an aquarium. In her last moments they opened the tent and she drew Ana close, expelling her last breath into the girl in the Ritual of Hā.

Now dreams of Emma persisted, so did a nagging pain. During a checkup, a small mass appeared on Ana's mammogram.

"A macrocalcification," her gynecologist said. "Which indicates a tumor."

A biopsy was performed after which Ana lived with the image of Emma; the large, knotted crucifix hanging from her shoulder. Lab results were positive. She sought a second opinion, which confirmed the need for surgery. She was barely twenty-nine years old.

In the past year, Ana had broken an internal rule and gone out with a patient, a plumber who had come into ER complaining of back pains. During her examination, she had noticed small nicks on his cheeks and neck, and that he was clean-shaven. Somehow that touched her, that he had taken the time to shave before coming to Emergency. She had imagined him lowering a razor into soapy water, twisting it clean, then commencing to shave, calmly scraping his cheeks and neck. She imagined him nicking, then circumnavigating troublesome spots round the thyroid mound while wondering how serious his back pains were.

To put him at ease she said something harmless and funny, and he had laughed. A lovely laugh. A lovely man named Sam. She had called for X-rays, and while they chatted he half flirted with her, self-consciously covering his razor-nicked cheek. She found the gesture so endearing that—with a kind of inward drunkenness, a longing to share, to talk, to listen—she had written her phone number on his wrist. She knew him for only two months when he was diagnosed with kidney cancer.

Ana would always remember the moment he told her, how his eyes looked huge, the wrong size for their sockets.

"How bad is this," he asked. "Don't sugar-coat it."

"Sam, it's one of the worst kinds of cancer. Nothing stops it. Not surgery, not radiation."

He had sat very still, groping for words. "How much time do you think I've got?"

"There are always exceptions . . . but most people die within two years."

He had died within six months. Afterwards, Ana wondered if he would have lived longer had she given him more hope. Had she said she loved him. It might have given him endurance with which to draw the fluid of his life along the course of time a little longer. Time to pray a little harder, time to gather poise.

Now she picked up the phone and called Rosie in Nanakuli. Her cousin was riding her Exercycle, watching *Days of Our Lives*.

"Remember Aunty Emma," Ana asked. "Did doctors ever say what caused her cancer?"

Rosie huffed, one eye on the TV. "A hundred things cause cancer, you know that. All I know is, it's like an epidemic out here."

"I guess what I'm asking is . . . do you think it's contagious? I mean, if you slept with a man who had inoperable cancer, do you think you could catch it?"

Rosie stopped cycling. She swallowed something in a glass, then chewed an ice cube. It sounded as if she were crushing stones between her teeth.

"Ana. You're the doctor. Why are you asking me such silly questions?"

"I'm sorry," she whispered. "I'm confused."

"Honey, we're all confused. In ways we don't even know."

Silence hung, and in those moments Rosie felt a chill. She clicked the genie. The TV died. "So. You had sex with someone who had cancer?"

"I'm not sure . . ."

"Not sure you had sex? Or, not sure he had cancer?"

"Rosie, it's me. How did I get cancer?"

NIKOLAO

Nikolai

He had been traveling for months, through southern Asia then down to Australia—filming its cities and frontier towns. Finally wearying of crowds, he headed out to the desert, driving for days, the sun so white-hot it threatened to blister his eyeballs. He drove with wet rags over his mouth until he reached Alice Springs, a makeshift town in the dead red heart of the Outback.

There he took up with Aborigine trackers who lived in their camp-sites outside Alice. Most days before dawn, they left to hunt game—goanna lizards, even kangaroo. Then, in the heat of the day, they lazed in the shade of acacia trees, eating witchetty grub and honeyants. At night, the incredible heat stepped back, so the sky seemed a great black belly of cold, and the trackers sat at their campfires drinking and laughing at jokes Nikolai never caught on to.

He didn't mind. He played with their dingoes and listened to their deep melodic voices and found their musty odor comforting. Their faces were old and wise, their fingers extremely long and black, making their gestures graceful as they spoke of their history, how carbon-dated paint-ings had proven their claims that Aboriginal ancestors had walked this land for forty thousand years.

Nikolai forgot about moving on. A languidness overtook him, a feel-ing he had not known since early childhood. There was nothing extra here, nothing hindered them. At night, the stars were close enough to freeze their cheeks; the moon so huge they saw its craters clear enough to name them. Here was humor, conversation, food, and warmth. A place where the arc was perfect, where human beings were generous to one another with no motive. He felt absolved, at peace. Weeks passed. He did not even lift his camera.

IT WAS DUSK WHEN, RATHER DREAMILY, ONE OF THE TRACKERS leaned back and flipped on his transistor. The static sounded brilliant in the hush, then the remnants of a broadcast. A word repeated and repeated.

"Chernobyl . . . Chernobyl . . ."

The Aborigines sat up. They stared at the radio, listening, then turned to Nikolai. Hearing the news, he fell silent. When he woke in the morning, they were gone, their saucepans, dingoes, everything. They had not even said good-bye. When he stopped for gas in Alice, the attendant heard his accent and narrowed his eyes.

"Well, mate, looks like your country's bent on blowing itself up. Probably poisoned the atmosphere for good."

He went to a bar looking for his friends; the owner shook his head. "You won't find any Abos now. Gone into hiding. Happens every time they hear that word 'radiation.' "

He explained to Nikolai how Aborigines had been poisoned back in the 1950s and '60s when the British were testing atomic bombs in the deserts of Australia.

"No one warned them. Whole tribes of Abos out there going 'walkabout' in that filthy toxic fallout. Thousands went blind, or slowly died . . . set off a whole new generation of mutations. That stuff is still in their genes."

Everywhere he went, the talk was of Chernobyl. And everywhere, he encountered a new word. *Radiophobia*. Fear of radiation. As a Russian, he was no longer welcome anywhere, and so he went home to a government in shreds.

IT WOULD HAVE BEEN EASY TO SLIP OVER BORDERS, TO SLIP PAST security and film Chernobyl's aftermath—contaminated villages, the unnumbered dead, and dying. But Nikolai was interested in the larger canvas, wanting to record how Russian peasants had, for decades, generations, been sacrificed in the name of progress. He suspected that the real tragedy was in the provinces where they still lived in medieval squalor, vast stretches of land now desolate, abandoned. Since the time of the Tsars, their history was unchanged. Enslavement, starvation. Stalin had only made it worse. How, he wondered, would the fall of Communism affect them? Would it touch their lives at all?

He had learned of two places said to be the most hazardous in all of Russia, both located in the vast region of Kazakhstan, far southeast of Moscow, bordered on the west by the Caspian Sea and on the east by China and Mongolia. A state compromised of one million square miles of steppes, deserts, and mountains rich in natural resources.

Nikolai flew south, crossing the border into Kazakhstan, where he traveled to the town of Muslyumovo on the Techa River. A town that seemed composed of mud, it stood fifty miles downstream from a once-secret complex named Chelyabinsk-65, a producer of weapons-grade plutonium.

For decades, workers at the complex had poured wastes containing millions of curies of radioactivity into the Techa River—so that even now riverbanks and fields were still alive with long-lived cesium and strontium. And for decades, people had swum with their children in the river. From the Techa, they had irrigated their fields and taken their drinking water while scientists studied them and told them nothing.

A second town, Oskemen, most eastern city of Kazakhstan, was just southeast of a nuclear weapons test field called Semipalatinsk. Since the 1950s, almost five hundred nuclear bombs had been tested there, and fallout from these bombs had rained down on the people. So many tests, and so many accidents, land surrounding the town for five hundred miles was a moonscape, uninhabitable perhaps forever. For three decades people were exposed, their children exposed. Scientists had monitored them, watching them suffer and die.

Nikolai would not be able to distinguish in his memory one town from the other. Each town a living bouquet of horrors. One group of children seemed intelligent, coherent, but where their eyes should have been were pouches of flesh hanging from their brows. Their spines had not developed; they could only squat.

"I'm fifteen," a boy told him. "I have been asking to be put to sleep since I was ten. But they would only do that if I was a cretin."

And there were cretins, thousands. In decrepit clinics in each town, doctors dragged him from ward to ward pointing to children whose conditions they had no names for.

"Our next generation. A brand-new species."

He aimed his camera, but each day less of him emerged from behind it. He traveled back and forth between those towns for months, and everywhere he encountered "funny dust," the air and soil still alive with contaminants.

"It's like pollen covering fields and livestock," a doctor explained. "It covers humans and their food. Open your mouth—do you feel it on your tongue? Look, how I sneeze it into my hands!"

When he could not bear to film the children anymore, Nikolai filmed the ravaged faces of the old. They allowed him, wanting the world to know. Finally, exhausted and depressed, he went back to Moscow.

Alone in his shabby room, he lost himself again in mathematics, brooding over the theories of Descartes and that old intuitionist, Poincaré. He spent whole evenings dwelling on Möbius's theory on mathematical ability, debating out loud with himself. Were most abstract ideas developed through mathematical reasoning? Or word reasoning? Did Helmholtz's rest hypothesis still hold up?

Math lifted him out of a world that seemed to be dying. For him, it was human reason in its highest form. He felt only great music could approach it. In the years at university, he had come to love Mozart, Bach, and that shy, unshined-on genius, Satie, whose compostions he felt were like math—each note pure, unhurried. Music in the background calmed him down, helped him focus and root out certain mathematical equations. One seemed to spill into the other.

But always he was haunted by the children he had seen. The "new species" that doctors did not have a name for. *This is what my country has come to.* He did not leave his room for weeks. Finally, an old "roofer" friend tracked him down, saw what shape he was in, and dragged him to the Moscow Circus.

NIKOLAI WOULD ALWAYS RECALL THE CROWDS, AND CIGARETTE smoke that turned the night into a dream. He would recall a lion tamer in high boots that he was sure concealed cloven hooves. And bareback riders bursting into the Big Ring on jangling, feathered Clydesdales. Then everything receded.

He lifted his eyes to a young girl soaring overhead. When she looked down, he imagined that their eyes met and, through the glitter of spangled lights and sawdust, she seemed to shower him with gold. It was his first glimpse of the girl, and he gazed up in silence at a creature that seemed like a delicate moth floating out of the pages of his old composition book. In that moment, he experienced such a sense of wonder, he felt his brain step back to reconnoiter, fearing that maybe the ceiling, those artificial stars, would fall down on his face.

At times she sailed so high he could hardly make her out. Yet he had such a feeling: that this graceful, fragile form might give him reason to live again. For suddenly his whole life meant nothing, just sweets gone soft in his pocket. He stood up slowly as she paused on her platform looking down, her face hanging pale and lovely. He raised his arm, cupping his palm so the girl became a small statue of a bird held in his hand. Security men stiffened and moved forward, then they saw his face. A fool in love!

The band played, the girl floated out again on her trapeze, and Nikolai was struck with spasms like the frog when Galvani discovered electricity. The rest of the night in that crowded tent each time he looked up, her eyes seemed to touch his forehead. Green, then yellow, then scarlet spotlights followed her, turning her into a flying chameleon. The announcer called out her name. Irini.

To the amusement of his friends, thugs who came to the circus to work the crowds, Nikolai returned again and again until he knew her routine by heart. One night when she stepped from her trailer he was waiting. That was how he learned that she was deaf. She had been born deaf. She was beautiful, eighteen, but with the sweet faltering voice of a child. In time, she taught him to read lips, and how to sign-talk. And Nikolai came to believe that hearing had nothing to do with balance, for she was extraordinary in the air. Immune to gravity.

As a youngster she was very smart and athletic, and so had been schooled in gymnastics. She had dreamed of training for the Olympics, and when the Deaf School refused to recommend her, Irini had run away and joined the circus. Now on cold Moscow nights they lay together, while she told him in sign language and simple words punctuated with sighs of the vast steppes of the Gobi Desert in Mongolia, where her father had come from when he traveled the trade routes to Kazakhstan.

"Kazakhstan . . . where he met my mother. So, I was born."

When she told him the name of her village, Nikolai's breathing changed. It was one of the places he had filmed, just outside the city of Oskemen. Now he began to understand the cause of her deafness, and he understood that she would probably not grow old. Nonetheless, they fell in love, they married.

He gave up filming and "roofing," and traveled with her circus, working odd jobs, even working as a clown. And like clowns they lived in pantomime, always animated. Because she could not hear his joyful words, love for them was spectacle. Deep passion, laughter, tricks! Time evanesced into magic and glitter, while from dawn to dusk they touched, some parts of their bodies touched.

By then Nikolai had learned sign language, but in fact they did not talk much. Somehow they understood that things were truer when not said. They dreamed of children, a little house. Their nights were as soft as the velvet paws of the big cats in repose.

IRINI ALWAYS HAD THIS LITTLE COUGH. TWO YEARS AFTER THEY married, she miscarried their child. Doctors told her she was ill, that circus sawdust was suffocating her. Since childhood, her lungs had been weak, and now they could hardly absorb oxygen from the air.

They left the circus, and lived how they could, dragging themselves to the outskirts of Moscow. Nikolai swept streets, sold stolen tires, even engines from stolen cars. All the while, he watched his wife's breathing grow worse. Now it was early summer, the first winter thaw, and there was a window open by her bed through which honeybees flew in, in clouds.

In Russia, honeybees were revered for their intelligence, intuition, even the ability to reverse their sex and age. Many bees now settled in Irini's hair. Nikolai would always remember their wings glittering, her hair full of tiny stars of midnight blue. Then, in one cloud the bees flew out the window. And they took her soul.

Autumn came. He sold everything, cameras, clothes, to buy fresh meat and milk for her. By then it was too late. One winter day Irini could not breathe, she lay gasping hour after hour. Nikolai pulled back her covers, and saw her flesh was gone. She rattled like paper, her skin a leaf covering her spine.

That night she whispered, "Niki. Take my life, and make it yours . . ."

She would not go to a hospital. Such places were medieval nightmares—live patients disappearing from their beds, fresh cadavers found sliced open. Gangsters were harvesting human organs, selling them for research. Vowing this would not happen to his wife, he carried her to a field covered in deep snow, and laid her down and knelt beside her.

Tenderly, he gathered her hair in a ponytail with a ribbon, so her hair would remember life as a young, wild horse. Then he undressed her, wanting to lie down and grow cold with her, but afraid their corpses would be desecrated. Wild dogs would come. Or human-organ ghouls.

He knelt there singing old circus songs, his wife's body naked, her head gathered in his lap, her arms slowly falling, letting go.

He scraped tears from his cheeks and laid them on her chest like crystals, and when he looked up, the world was blue, the time of day in Russia when somewhere the sun was setting.

"Irini," he whispered. "Look! How blue is the air. The midnight blue of honeybees."

He knew she was dead. He built a campfire, wrapped her up, and carried her small body to the flames. Soon he could not distinguish what was branch, what was bone. Hours passed. A day. A night. He fed the fire until there were only embers, watching his wife becoming smoke. When there was nothing left but ash, he threw her ashes to the wind and watched her soar, recalling her young face, her lips moving slightly, telling him to live, live for her.

She took everything with her, his dreams, his silly habits. He was left a man without reason. After that, Nikolai thought only of dying, so full of rage, he wanted to take all of Russia with him. Instead, sleep became the major event in his life. For months he slept twenty hours at a stretch.

Then one day he woke and went into the streets, wanting to tell the world what they had done to her, what they had done to all the damaged children. He bought a new camera. And he began to film again.

'OKI I NA MAKE

To Cut Out Death

WHEN SHE UNDERSTOOD THAT HER TUMOR WAS MALIGNANT, ANA did not cry. Nor did she eat or sleep much. She became like something from the future. Her surgeon, Dr. Lee, was sympathetic; she did not try for irony. But she shocked Ana with her recommendation. Although the tumor was only a Stage Two growth, she did not advise lumpectomy, but rather removal of the entire breast. Simple mastectomy. A phrase so oxymoronic, Ana laughed out loud. Then she leaned forward with her elbows on the woman's desk.

"I'm a doctor, too. I read statistics. Survival rates for the two procedures are almost identical, as long as the cancer is caught in the early stages, and as long as it hasn't spread to the lymph nodes. Which, in my case, it hasn't. I want a lumpectomy. Afterwards you can blast me with radiation and chemo, to your heart's content. If the cancer spreads, it will be my responsibility. But I will die in charge of my own life."

"It's your choice, Ana, but don't you see . . ."

"Believe me, I *have* seen. I will never forget my Aunty Emma's body after surgery. She was mutilated. Left for dead."

"That was almost two decades ago. We've made enormous progress since then."

"Well, like you said, Dr. Lee, it's my life. My choice."

"I don't think it's quite that simple." She fell momentarily silent, then pointed to Ana's lab results.

"Please look at these again. You're right, the cancer has not spread to your lymph nodes. That's the good news. But, your particular cancer cells are highly undifferentiated. These are the most aggressive kinds of cells, which means . . ."

". . . they spread like wildfire."

"Exactly. Which is why I'm recommending a simple mastectomy."

She switched on a light box, holding up a chest X-ray and a CAT scan. "This patient chose to have a lumpectomy. She had highly undifferentiated cancer cells, like yours. Eight months later, a simple mastectomy was necessary. Then, the other breast. Within a year, her lungs . . . her brain . . ."

After a while, Ana spoke. "All right. Only, please stop calling it a 'simple' mastectomy. It isn't fucking *simple*."

Dr. Lee switched off the light box. "No. It's not. And, how well you psychologically survive this is up to you."

She tried to smile. "So. Do you think it will make me a 'believer'?"

The surgeon sat down and clasped her hands together on the desk. "Religion doesn't hurt. Whatever gives you strength, grab it. Use it. Because afterwards, there will be grief. You'll feel mutilated, ugly . . ."

She paused, looked out the window, then continued.

"At first you won't be able to look at yourself naked in a mirror. For a while, maybe years, you won't even think of men. Then, because you're a fighter, something will begin to happen. You'll change your focus from what you lost to what you want to keep. Your *life*."

Ana tried for humor. "I think I know the drill. Meditation. Exercise. I'll develop a warped sense of humor, maybe become a full-blown cynic. I'll give up men. Buy a dog who loves me unconditionally. Maybe take up sky-diving . . ."

Dr. Lee unconsciously pressed her hand against her own right breast. Ana saw for the first time that it was completely flat.

"Oh, God. I'm so sorry. How did you get through it, Dr. Lee?"

"The hard way. First, lumpectomy, which was too late. Then simple mastectomy. In time I learned to forgive myself. You will too. So many women blame themselves, thinking they should have been vegetarians, avoided caffeine, should have had more orgasms."

She patted the flat place rather tenderly. "Losing part of your body alerts you to its beauty, its miraculous intelligence—how it goes on functioning without your conscious thoughts. You begin to really love your body. To honor it."

At the door to the office, Ana turned back. "This may sound unprofessional, even maudlin. But, afterwards I want to see my breast."

"Of course. Many women ask to see the postop photos."

"No, Dr. Lee. I mean I want you to . . . give . . . me . . . back . . . my breast after you remove it."

The woman stared at her.

"It's mine. It's me. I want it back."

ROSIE PUSHED HER SUITCASE THROUGH THE DOOR, KICKED OFF her shoes, and stood barefoot in a *muʻumuʻu*. In spite of periodic diets, her great height and weight seemed to suck all light and space from Ana's small apartment. Her beautiful face broke into a smile, showing gleaming, taro-tough teeth. She spread her massive arms, engulfing her.

She's here. I'm safe, Ana thought. *Even if I die, I'm safe.*

Then Rosie pulled Ana to her side before a mirror. "My God, look at the size of us. A little tumor doesn't have a chance."

Weeks before Ana's surgery, Rosie had begun to call on all the higher forces in the ritual of *kūkulu kumuhana*. She called on friends and family to fast and pray for Ana. Even her drug-running cousins in Halawa High Security Prison prayed. Now Rosie began her most intensive herbal healing.

"You are educated. You follow the modern ways of healing. That is good. You will do what they say. The surgery, the treatments after. But I am your elder, and now you will listen to me."

Ana bowed her head. "I will always honor you."

"From this time forward, we will begin to purify your body. No more whole food which slows elimination and therefore, purification. We will begin to starve the cancer cells. And how? The cancer cells know who they are. They will retreat from healthy cells. The healthy cells know who they are. When it comes time to *ʻoki*—cut!—the parting will be clean. We will *ʻoki i na make*. Cut out death."

On the first night she walked Ana down to a secluded beach where the sea was mirror-calm.

"Now, cousin, kneel and let your knees remember *kou one hānau*. Your birth sands. Kneel so that *ka mahina hou*, the new moon, can see you are a red-soled girl of Waiʻanae. Let her bathe you from the crown of head to soles of feet, and four corners of the body while you pray."

Ana knelt so that her toes rested in the sand. Then she opened her mouth and howled, breaking down doors her mind had tried to seal. Entering bright vacuums of pain.

Thereafter, each morning Rosie pounded the aerial root of the *hala* tree, squeezed out the juice and made Ana drink it five times daily. Three times a day she fed her seeds of whole papaya.

"Chew. Swallow slowly. Dwell on the journey of the cleansing seeds."

At night before Ana slept, Rosie brewed her potent tea from 'awa root, the slightly narcotic tea for curing stress and grief. By the fifth day, Ana felt she was floating just above the ground, her body an empty vessel.

"I feel light-headed. Lighthearted. I feel . . . content."

"Good. We have cleansed you back to innocence."

The morning of Ana's surgery, Rosie was there when they prepped her. And as they sedated her, Rosie bent and pressed her fingers to her eyelids, to her lips, her breast, and her *na'au*, her gut, which was the heart of the healing mind. As orderlies pushed Ana's gurney toward the operating room, Rosie followed behind, slapping the walls with ti leaves for safe journey. Her chanting was the last thing Ana heard.

"*Mauli-'ola*, God of Healing. Hear me now! . . . *Ē ho'i ka'iwi I ha'i I kona wahi iho . . . A pela no ho'i I ka 'i'o o kona wahi iho . . . A pela me ke'a'a olona, e ho'i lakou me ko . . . Lakou wahi iho . . .*"

Return to its own place the bone that is broken . . . and so of course, the flesh to its own place . . . and so, the veins, the arteries, the tendons and the muscles . . . each to their own places. Merciful God. Hear me now.

WHEN SHE WAS WELL ENOUGH ROSIE TOOK HER HOME. *PAU HANA* time, traffic on the freeway crawled, until finally, they reached the coast. Women in crumbling slippers dragged wagons filled with artificial meat. Signs advertising, SPAM SPECIAL. ONE DAY ONLY. And lining the horizon left to right, rusted TV antennas, the unharvested crop of her valley.

They turned up Keola Road, and as tarmac disappeared beneath red dirt, Ana felt a softening—plants reaching out with green spatulate hands as if to take her in. Turning into their driveway, she heard music amplified across the fields, so loud their windshield seemed to vibrate.

Rosie shook her head. "Noah found old records someone left. He's welcoming you home."

They flooded from the house, their arms outstretched. Ben, aunties, everyone. There were times Ana had thought she hated them, their end-less tragedies and scandals. Absent fathers, come-and-go mothers, kids left behind like dog packs. She had hated the way the walls seemed to bulge, as if the house itself kept giving birth. She even hated the way her uncles' fingers, stained with nicotine, left sordid yellow traces on their coffee cups.

But sometimes when she looked at them, there was nothing else. Each elder and child always engaged in some small task that made them unique and important, so that they survived another day with something quietly accomplished. Something that changed them each and all, made them better or worse, proud or ashamed, but left them engraved, and closer. Letting them enfold her now, Ana understood that without this family, her 'ohana, the outside world was nothing.

It had been a drought-filled summer. At night she lay in her girlhood bed feeling the mattress as lumpy as bird bones, but sheets fresh and smelling of wild ginger. The dryness of the land was echoed in the parched, itchy feeling of the stitches across her chest. She squeezed her hands into fists, fighting the urge to scratch them. Instead, she drank Rosie's 'awa tea and let herself relax and drift as one by one, her family appeared and tried to comfort her.

Rosie showed Ana big scars across her buttocks where she had sat on a barbecue grill. "Remember what my mama said. 'Scars makes us inter-esting.' "

One-armed Ben came, bringing the smell of eucalyptus and kukui leaves. These he had twisted till their juices ran, then wrapped them round his stump when it ached, longing for its arm.

"Leaves help da stump fo'get," he said, rubbing it briskly. "One day you going put leaves on yo' chest. I going bless and twist dem fo' you."

He talked to her for hours, softly, as if wanting to be overheard, not heard. He spoke with exquisite politeness about her loss, and how to overcome that loss. He said such wise and noble things she could not an-swer, afraid she would break down.

"Remember, Ana, you get scared, no can sleep. *Waiho kēnā I ke ākua!*" Take it to the gods.

At night she heard the family talking extra-loud, and when they slept they snored to beat the band, reminding her they were there for her. When she lay down they all lay down. She wondered if their lives would ever be vertical again.

Tito came, spinning his wheelchair into her room. Up close, his left hand still had an enduring "ear smell" from wiggling his pinkie in his ear when he played poker. He was wearing a clean white shirt, so that his bronze skin glowed. He struggled to speak "proper" English for her.

"Ana. When I hear you get da Big C, I stood up from dis chair, took four steps, and punched one big hole in da wall. First time I walk in twenty years."

He took her hands and squeezed them. "You going beat dis thing. You hear? You beat dis, I going walk clear to da highway fo' you."

They told her Noah could not come. Always discreet, he didn't want to cry in front of her. But sometimes late at night he stood outside her window, and blew smoke rings into her room. Rosie's girl, Makali'i came. Now thirteen, she had reached the age of defiance and walked around with her shoulders hunched, ignoring everyone. Only Ana gained access to her conversation.

"Mama said you had an operation. You okay?"

The girl had always been devoted to her, and now seemed devotedly awestruck because Ana had her own place in the city. She was going to be a beauty, but just now she seemed timorous and clumsy, slightly over-weight. Ana could see the craving for sexual grace, and attention.

"I'm going to be fine. How's school, Makali'i?"

"A drag. Everything's a drag. I want to die."

"No, you don't. You want to finish school and come and visit me in Honolulu."

She nodded vigorously, she smiled. But somehow her eyes did not participate.

Aunty Pua came with her pedantic cleanliness, her face sad and chalky like old eucalyptus leaves. Having forsaken the Christian Bible again, she sat gripping the KUMULIPO, the book of the Hawaiian Hymn of Creation.

"Ana, this book the only truth. 'He po uhe'e I ka wawa he nuku . . . It is night gliding through the passage of an opening.' That's how we began, so simple. All came from Pō, the night."

She took Ana's hand in hers. "You will never, never be alone. More than a hundred gods stay all around you. Look like they tested you, pushed you into Hikawainui, the strong near-drowning current, to see how brave you are. Then they carried you into Hikawaina, the calm cur-rent, to let you rest and catch your breath. You swam the current well! Now you are mending and at peace, and nothing left to fear."

Some nights Pua dipped into a bowl of fish eyes while she read from the KUMULIPO. "'Hānau ka 'uku oko'ako'a/ Hānau Kana, He ako'ako'a Puka . . . Born the coral polyp/ Born of him a coral colony emerged . . .' "

She savored each fish eye like a delicacy, rolling it round on her
tongue. Then her head began to droop, the book sliding from her lap.
Sometimes in sleep her jaw dropped. Ana watched an eye slip slowly
from her mouth.

AND THERE WAS ONE WHO CAME QUIETLY LIKE A SHADOW. HE
came at the end of a pain-filled day, when she was sleepless and exhausted. He sat beside her bed, and took her hand in his big hand and
held it like a little stone.

"Ei nei. How are you? I thought you might like to know that it is
evening."

"Lopaka. I think I must look awful."

Through her nightgown he saw the golden marimba of her ribs.

"A little thin. But you are always beautiful to me."

Her teeth felt caulked with medications. She struggled to sit up and
smooth her hair. He eased onto the edge of her bed and when he spoke
his voice was soft and low, threatening to break down all resistance. The
trick for her was not to cry.

"I ever tell you how I carried your letters all through 'Nam? I sat in
trenches full of blood, picturing you flying kites the way I taught you. My
Ana, standing in a field."

He moved closer and she smelled his skin, his hair, his maleness. She
studied his brown shoulders and his arms, knowing that any other man
who came into her life would be measured against him.

Now he spoke as he had when she was a child. Their secret language,
a kind of code. He told her how ever since her childhood, she had given
fullness to his life. In dark moments, she had made him want to live.
While he talked, she felt her lungs open, felt herself move back inside a
young girl's skin.

"It seems to me I ought to beg your pardon for the years I messed up
after 'Nam. Drinking, drugging, running with a gang."

He touched the tattoo just below his eye. The shape of a teardrop—
a gang symbol for one who had killed, or maimed, or been to prison.

"After combat, I was just so full of death. Sometimes I sat in the dark
and laughed. I understood that things would never be all right again. I
knew you were waiting for me, Ana. I didn't come to you because I was
ashamed. You had outgrown me."

"I never outgrew you," she whispered. "But I have always wondered . . . how did you finally pull yourself together?"

He hesitated, then slowly rolled up his pant leg, carefully unstrapped his leg brace, and showed her what was left. She had never seen the leg without the brace. Now she stared openmouthed at what looked like a ferociously scarred and pitted, badly dented log. It looked like an artifact.

"One day I came out of a weeklong drunk and this leg was cold and gray. No circulation. I thought of gangrene, how they would have to take it off. For a while after my discharge, I *wanted* amputation. I couldn't stand to look at it. But now I realized it was still my leg. It just looked different. I went back into physical therapy. Stopped drinking and drugging. I got so wrapped up in healing myself, I just kept going. Books. Law school. Who knows why we decide to live again?"

Now he patted the leg. "I'm learning to respect it. Even love it."

He looked down at the leg, and suddenly he sobbed, his big hands covering his face. She had never seen him cry. Had never heard such sounds. Now she reached out to him and held him, and he wept a long hard time. She wept, too, for his lost innocence, for the years after combat when he just stood and stared. And she wept for herself, for things she had lost that she had not had time to value.

Afterwards, they sat back empty and exhausted, heads hanging like they were sharing the same low-grade fever. She dropped her head against his chest. He stroked her thin, damp arms.

"I will be here for you," he said. "I will help you get your bearings."

"I think it will take awhile."

Then he lifted her face and smiled. "Ana, you remember the last time I held you like this? Your face and arms so wet, I wiped them down with cool, wet cloths. Your body so exhausted, I lifted you and held you. I had watched you for hours, thinking it was you, not Rosie, giving birth."

She looked up at him, astonished. "I never knew it was you . . ."

He touched his finger to her lips. "One can know, and not know."

Exhaustion moved aside then. She felt that thing within her. She saw in his eyes he felt it, too. What they could not speak of, did not want to speak of, would never need to speak of. Finally, he got up from the bed and strapped on his leg brace, then stood and smoothed his pants and seemed his old, assured self again.

He leaned over carefully and kissed her forehead. "*Ei nei,* the aku are running. Get well soon, so I can take you fishing."

SOME NIGHTS IN THE SUFFOCATING HEAT, SHE WAS AFRAID TO LIE flat, or to turn on her side, afraid she would pull at the stitches, that they would form keloids, compounding the already awful. In fact, she was afraid to sleep, afraid of the wrench of parting with consciousness. When she dozed off, her dreams had fangs, they hooked into her chest. She slept sitting up facing the fan, wretched and exhausted.

But there were mornings when she was wakened by a skittish breeze and looked up thinking how startling it was to sleep and wake, and be alive all over again. She stood at her window inhaling deeply, watching how dust lay furtive in the fields, turning the light clandestine. How trees and grass hung limp and parched, until the slightest wind brought nature to its feet. Then everything responded. Trees swayed like old showgirls, young green grass exclaimed. Light accumulated in a leaf, and in a bird's wing. All became spectacle.

Ana thought how she had taken it for granted, the light and the rhythms and the motion. The scents and colors, and proportions. The way shadows made plain things interesting, the way space met in empty corners, creating a place for the eyes to rest. She wanted to dwell on these things again. To slow down and understand their "thingness." She understood this would take time; there would be periods of backtracking.

Finally the rains came, thrumming on the roof, on broad banana leaves like huge hands slapping pelts. Ana turned carefully on her side, finding great comfort in the sound. It rained all night, deep as canoes, so the world lay still and listened. In time, her body's internal music and the rain found their right rhythms, and seemed to drum out Ana's individual song, recalling her geneaology, each footprint of her forebears, her name, and the name of each of her organs, her prehistory and her future. A song of rebirth, that went on and on.

She slept for two days and nights and when she woke, her mind felt pure, rinsed clear of everything, allowing only small and simple thoughts, to parse out the large and awful ones.

She had been home several weeks when one evening, carrying a small parcel wrapped in ti leaves, she and Rosie hiked deep into the valley, beyond where chain-link fences barred them from the mountains. They buried her breast beneath a young *kiawe* tree while Ana knelt, relinquishing that blood, those cells. Rosie lifted her arms and chanted softly, *Ē Ala Ē! Ē Ala Ē!* Awake. Rise up. Blessing her flesh so it could rest and recompose, begin to nourish the soil.

SHE SAT WITH NOAH, LETTING HIM CRY, A WAY OF EXPRESSING what he could not say. Finally, cried out, he pressed a knuckle to his nostril, snorting a thick stream of mucus into the dirt, the impact raising a little fleur-de-lis of dust. And then the other nostril. She leaned at his window like in the old days, and they listened while his record player scratched out an old half-warped Puccini, *Madama Butterfly*. Ana liked how it thundered out across the yard and up into the fields, where horses slowed midcanter, turning their heads to listen. Even roosters paused, their bright red combs like ears erect.

Slipping out of her pain and into sound, she talked to him for hours. Noah's silence gave her freedom to confess. She talked of the harrowing years of med school. The terror and loneliness. The lovely men who, one way or the other, always left. She talked of her illness, her surgery. And how death was an all right thing if one were ready, if one had lived a good, long life. She talked of the father she never knew. Of the woman who had been her mother.

When she was silent and talked out, Noah reached into his closet, pulling out a mildewed box he had discovered. Inside, a crumbling snapshot of her mother. A slip the color of old peach skin. Rusty hairpins to which her perfume clung. Somewhere Ana's father had been measured for a hat. Her mother had kept that piece of paper with his name inside the box. That's all she was sure of. Her mother's slip size. Her father's head measurements.

That night while everyone slept, she spread the slip out on the grass, then lay beside it as if they were two females looking at the stars. Carefully, she turned on her side and laid her arm across the slip as if it were a woman's waist. She imagined that woman slipping her arm round Ana's shoulders. She lay like that for hours.

And she began to dream again. One night, moonlight crept across her face. Someone stood outside her window.

Ana sat up, thinking she was dreaming. "Who's there?"

"It's me. I've come."

She called out, half-awake. "Who's that? Who's come?"

". . . It's your mother, silly girl."

HULIKOʻA WAHA ʻAWA

Profile of a Bitter Mouth

FOR DAYS THEY AVOIDED EACH OTHER, THEY EVEN ATE IN SEPARATE rooms. One night she knocked, and opened Ana's door.

Ana looked up frantically. "What do you want?"

"I'm here for you. What do you need?"

"I need you to go back to San Francisco."

Her mother puffed a cigarette and slowly exhaled. "Ana, I didn't come to watch you suffer. I want you to get well. More than anything I've ever wanted in my life."

"And why is that?" Ana asked.

She looked at the cigarette and stabbed it out. "I'm your mother. I love you."

Ana's voice was low and calm. "Perhaps you're here because you want to feel remorse. You're afraid it's an emotion you've missed out on."

Anahola moved into the room, making the air feel lethal. She sat on the windowsill, gazing out. "I know you resent me. Possibly you hate me. I also know the best thing I ever did for you was leave."

In spite of herself she was struck by her mother's enduring beauty. At forty-eight she was still fit in that full-bodied way men called voluptuous. Except for tiny squint lines, her face was unlined. A pampered face, not a mother's.

"Please. Go away. I don't have the strength to deal with you."

"Don't talk to me like that. I'm still your mother."

"Well, yes. You gave birth to me."

That was how it started. The woman showing up, shocking and then intimidating her, so that Ana struck back. Neither realizing that their arguing might be a way of trying to connect.

Unconsciously, her mother lit another cigarette. "You know, when you were a child . . ."

"What do you know about my childhood? Folks say you couldn't even change my diaper."

"That's true. Wet diapers always had the smell of death to me. But I taught you everything I knew. God, you were an active child, but sensitive, alert. One glance from me would calm you down. Like those dogs that herd sheep by eye contact."

Ana studied her. "Did it ever occur to you that the sheep are terrified of those dogs? Look . . . I want to say something that might help you. I didn't get cancer because you abandoned me. It's not something a mother could have taught me to outsmart."

Her voice shook. Normal conversation with this woman was something she could not seem to master.

"So you don't need to feel guilty. My life is in my own hands now. I'm the only one responsible for me. They say this knowledge comes when women hit their forties. But cancer speeds things up, you get smarter fast."

Her mother answered softly. "I see you have a clever tongue. That's good. But don't kid yourself, Ana. You want your childhood back. We all do."

She jumped to her feet, her hands on her hips. "Who in hell . . . do you think you are? Strolling back into my life like this. You are so incredibly ignorant of who I am. Who I have become."

"No, I'm not. I know you better than you think."

"How? By keeping up with me through Ben and Rosie? You should have had the nerve to walk away completely. Instead you cheapened both of us with your random visits, your pathetic checks."

She shook her head. "I never claimed to be sure of every move I made . . ."

"Look, I'm very tired. I wish you'd go. There's nothing left to say."

Anahola moved forward, as close as she dared. "There's a lot to say. Let me do the talking, tell you how proud I am of you. How . . ."

"No. All you had to tell me you said years ago. On your way out the door."

Ana was suddenly aware of the silent house. As if each room, and each thing in that room were holding its breath. She pictured her aunties and uncles listening, poised like strung marionettes. She heard the ticking of a clock, a boar-hound's labored breathing. Through the window she saw a rusty van drive past, letters painted on its side. NOW SELLING FRESH PORK. What had they been selling before? She swayed and sat down in a chair.

"Don't you understand? In the end, you're not that interesting to me. I don't love you. I don't hate you either. I don't really think about you."

Anahola tried to hold herself together. "Of course you do. As a mother, I did not fulfill my obligation. I lacked a moral sense of indebtedness, and I have influenced you incredibly by my absence. Forgive my immodesty, but I'm probably the most important person in your life."

She sat shaking till the woman left, then locked the door behind her. That night she wept so hard, her chest ached deep inside where tissues were still mending. Finally, she sank into a half sleep remembering how, as a child, she learned to swim with her eyes open, looking for her mother's body on the ocean floor. Aunties said she had crossed the ocean on a ship, and since she never sent for Ana, the girl thought maybe she had fallen overboard.

Then letters came, and she waited to be sent for. Each day she swam underwater, listening to the clicking of the reef. Maybe her mother was Morse-coding her from California. Months had passed. She and Rosie eavesdropped as their elders discussed her mother.

"Big city . . . many folks . . . she'll have to beg for work . . ."

She had pictured her mother kneeling, and begging. Her face eye level with the waists of white men.

She heard her aunties whispering again, "Buggah is keeping her . . . *haole* hands all over her . . ."

She had imagined her mother with white man's fingerprints all over her body. The first time she came back to visit, Ana had glanced at her arms and legs looking for telltale prints like dabs of flour. Each month letters came, and in time, postcards from foreign countries. Through the years, the myth of her mother grew, embellished and hung like tapestries. And as they grew older, Rosie's attitude to Ana's mother changed.

"Not easy for her, on the mainland all alone. Who rubs her back with *kukui* oil in that spot between the shoulder blades you cannot reach? Who *lomis* her feet, and scalp? And brushes coconut oil through her hair? This man, he probably don't care if she lives or dies."

"She made her choice," Ana said. "She's free."

"Free? She's a brown woman in a white man's world."

Now Ana stayed locked in her room, waiting for her mother to be gone. Through the walls, she heard her in conversation with the family. Heard how she had erased herself, her origins, speaking island Pidgin like someone who had learned it as a foreign language. Days passed, but the woman did not leave. One night Ana packed her bags and drove back to Honolulu.

SHE FOUND THAT HER ILLNESS ENGENDERED A RATHER WARPED but healthy sense of humor.

"Cancer's very liberating," she told friends. "Except for dying, there's not much more life can do to you."

She began to be aware of each thing she ate, how deeply she slept. She policed her thoughts, blocking out the negatives so that by sheer force of will she did not think about renegade cancer cells. She did not think of her mother. Each morning she met the day serenely. She meditated, watered her flowers. She went back on duty part-time.

Knowing her hair would fall out with radiation and chemo, Ana cut it short, then bought a wig. She began to reexamine her life, how narrow it had become, how each day, each hour had been circumscribed by her work. She looked at rigid pantsuits in her closet, all hung with hysterical precision. She tried on the wig and cried. It looked like a helmet. She threw it out, threw out half her wardrobe.

One night she came home and cautiously opened her front door. Her mother barefoot, in a suit, vacuuming the rug. Ana stood paralyzed then half ran across the room.

"What . . . are you doing here?"

Anahola shook her head. "I don't know what I'm doing here. I just know I've got to be here. I want to help you, show you how to be . . ."

"What? Disfigured?"

She reached down and pulled the plug on the vacuum cleaner, then grabbed and shook her mother's arm. "You cannot do this. Get out. Get . . . out!"

Her mother struggled to pull away. "Whether you like it or not, I'm here to see you through your treatments. And everything else, until you're healed."

Ana's voice turned deadly and calm. "I could kill you for invading me like this."

"Go ahead. Hit me if it makes you feel good."

"You'd like that, wouldn't you. That would validate you. Maybe you'd even slap me back. A little mother-daughter confrontation."

They stood paralyzed, afraid of where the next few words might take them. Anahola leaned against the wall, feeling her lip where she had accidentally bit it in the struggle. She carelessly wiped at the blood, blurring her mouth so it looked as if she had two mouths.

"You want me to grovel. Say I'm sorry. I can't. I don't possess the 'sorry' gene. Neither did my mother. Neither do you. I'm not sorry that I left. But I'm here *now* because I don't want you to die."

Ana sank into a chair. "I'm too exhausted to die."

Her mother sat down on the rug, hugging her knees. "How many letters did I write you through the years, trying to explain it? That not every woman is meant to be a mother."

"Oh, I remember them. Interesting reading for a ten-year-old girl."

". . . how some of us don't have that drive, that urge. I never had . . ."

". . . a role model."

"That's right. I didn't know who *my* real mother was until . . ."

". . . you were sixteen. They had lied to you."

She knew her mother's history by heart.

"Ana, do you think my life has been easy?"

"Yes. And irresponsible. You're smart. You have a college degree. What did you do with it? Besides become some white man's mistress."

Anahola smiled. "Such a quaint, outmoded word. In fact, he was a brilliant man, a researcher in immunology. He put me through university, made me his lab assistant. It was fascinating, a job that gave me dignity and income. To most of his colleagues I was just his 'brown girl.' Sometimes they mistook me for the maid. But he was honorable, he loved me. And in the end, I married him."

Ana stared, taking her full measure. "That's how you could afford to send those monthly checks. So, where is your . . . generous husband now?"

"He died, several years ago."

She had always predicted that her mother would pay. Yet Ana did not feel the bitter rapture she had anticipated. She got to her feet and moved to the kitchen, pausing in the doorway, struck by the figure of her mother on the rug. Barefoot like an island girl, her curly hair undone. The sun lay on her back and cast her face in shadow; in that moment she looked fragile and bewildered. Something caught in Ana's chest. She felt the tug of her fresh scars. She came back carrying cups of tea, and placed one on the rug beside her mother.

Anahola sighed. "You know, it could have been much worse. At least I left you with 'ohana . . . folks who loved you, and doted on you. That's why you've remained intact."

"Of course. And, because of having been abandoned, I'm now somewhat cynical and hard. Which, I suppose, is good. It will help me make it in medicine, which is so competitive."

"And make it out in the world."

"I'm not going out into the world. I *know* where I belong. And who my people are. And who I am."

Anahola sipped her tea. "I see. You're going to play the martyr. I'm the fall guy, the one who warped you. So you will always cling to this safe and limited island life."

Ana put her cup down. "I'm fighting cancer. How fucking *safe* is that?"

In the silence she stood. "Well, we've had our little chat. Our cup of tea. Now, why don't you go back to wherever you call home. However empty it may be."

"On the contrary, Ana, my life is full. I have friends, a career, projects for the future. But right now my only concern is you. I'm not going anywhere."

Ana closed her eyes, her lids fluttered with exhaustion. "Then, it's too bad I didn't get cancer when I was four years old."

Her mother finished her tea and slowly stood. "I see I was wrong. You don't want your childhood back, you want a better version of it back. Your childhood is over, Ana. So is mine."

She carefully dabbed on lipstick, pinned back her hair, and stepped into her high heels. At the front door, she squared her shoulders and stood straighter, looking somewhat formidable.

"You've told me I don't interest you that much, so this might cheer you up. In time I will become even less important to you. It's called 'cell fatigue.' The brain slowly flushes out the pain of hurtful memories so you remember things, without the pain. And after a while, you even stop remembering them. So, why not use me while I'm here? While you still remember me."

SHE WATCHED CHEMICALS DRIP INTO HER BODY, KNOWING THEY were weakening her immune system, killing good cells as well as bad. She felt they should have been taking things *out* of her body, not putting them in. Feeling sudden affection for what now seemed endangered, Ana cupped her right breast thoughtfully. Then she remembered it was all endangered, her brain, her liver, her lungs. Sometimes she lost all sense of herself. No longer remarkable, or unremarkable, she was a simple organ fighting for its life.

Her mother didn't bother her again. Ana hoped she had gone back to San Francisco. Then she began to hallucinate, seeing women everywhere who resembled her. A woman in sunglasses on a bus, a woman under an umbrella. One day she realized the woman approaching her *was* her mother.

"I rented a studio nearby."

Ana watched cars passing in the street. "How can you humiliate yourself like this?"

"Humiliation is healthy. It keeps us realists."

After her third chemo treatment, her hair began to fall out. Now she was wearing a baseball hat, but her mother could see thin wisps protruding round her ears.

"How are the treatments? Is there much nausea?"

"Not bad. I'm back on duty working light shifts."

"Well, do you . . . want to have a drink, and chat?"

Ana stared at her. "What in the world would we 'chat' about?"

"The to-and-fro of life. The in-between."

With no sense of it, she reached out and touched her mother's arm. "I know you're concerned. But, please, go back to San Francisco. Rosie will keep you up to date."

On the phone, Rosie tried to smooth things out. "Ana. Let her help you."

"It's too late. I'm a full-grown woman, not some doll she can play with when she feels maternal. She makes me want to scream."

"Maybe you folks should drive back to the house, sit down with the family. Maybe it's time for *ho'oponopono*, talk things out. How else you going to cleanse yourself of rage?"

She felt the skin on her head retract. "It's *my* rage. I'll do what I want with it. Maybe it's what keeps me going."

Her cousin answered thoughtfully. "Have you considered that maybe your rage is what caused the cancer?"

For the first time in her life, she hung up on Rosie. Then she sat in the dark, her fingers tenderly walking her scars, thinking how angry she had been as a child, then as a woman. She thought of her meager store of lovers who had come and gone and hardly left their prints. Feeling terribly alone, cut off from her own intelligence, she stood on a fire escape

looking down, imagining the pavement against her sudden cheek. She
wanted whatever was coming to be quicker.

EACH TIME THEY SHOT HER WITH LETHAL BOLTS, SHE THOUGHT
how she was ingesting the same particles that had leveled Hiroshima.
The same stuff that made the military call her coast "Death Row." She
began to imagine she smelled scorched, began approaching people timidly.
She thought if she survived, she would have to live downwind of other
humans.

Now there were clumps of hair on her pillow. She felt with her hand
to see if her spine was curving inward. She began to chew delicately,
afraid her teeth were coming loose. *Vision will go. Then speech.* She heard
her future approaching. The dry cough of tablets in bottles, miniature
tides in encapsulated liquids. She began to think of herself as ash.

Waiting for her treatment, Ana sat next to a woman whose vocal
cords and most of her lungs had been surgically removed. She would
never talk again, even if she lived. Ana's hand inadvertently went to her
chest.

One can live without a breast, she thought. *But how to live without ever
hearing your voice again. No words to light the darkness.*

She leaned over, whispering, "These treatments . . . do you think
they're worth it?"

The woman smiled and wrote down on a pad. "Every extra day is
worth it."

"I still have pain," Ana said. "Do you?"

The woman nodded, bending to her pad again. "Pain is good. It
means we're still alive."

Something in her swerved then, if only a little. She felt a rush of
shame, humility. That night for the first time since her surgery, she stood
naked before a mirror. She held her hands across her chest, hearing the
drumroll of her heartbeat. When she was ready, she moved her hands
away and stared. Then she cried out. Not a loud cry, but a long, lingering, and quiet dirge.

Finally, all of her hair fell out, even her eyebrows disappeared. Her
face looked void of all expression. During a rainstorm, she pulled off her
baseball hat and stepped out onto her *lānai*, wanting to be drenched, to
melt away. Then she looked down. Her mother, standing in the street, in
rain and lightning. In strobelike flashes she saw her mother looking up,

her face lacquered with shock and grief. Ana's hands flew to her head, trying to cover her baldness. The next morning her doorbell rang.

Reluctantly, she opened it. "Don't you ever sleep?"

"I'm not here to sleep."

She saw her daughter's utter fatigue, the nearness of her facial bones. The dearth of flesh. Her baldness.

She took Ana in her arms and held her. "I wish to God it had been me. It *should* have been me."

Ana felt momentary confusion, as if she had been given something promised to her mother.

Without the strength to resist her, Ana allowed her mother into her life, but only a few hours every day. And she was meticulous, keeping her at a distance so that they did not hug again. They hardly touched.

Alone, Anahola thought of Max and how in the moment she understood that he was dying, a fuller knowledge of her love for him had surfaced. She felt that now for Ana, but this love was deeper, more visceral and complex.

When she looked at her grown daughter, she saw her younger self, the lifelong bitterness, the feeling of never having felt essential to her mother. She suspected Ana felt it too: that they were more alike than they could acknowledge, they were nearly identical—so blood-deep and rooted, so inextricably entwined, no one would ever understand them as they understood each other.

And finally Anahola grasped how the death of one's child was so against the order of nature, so incomprehensible, that the mere possibility of it left her seized and shaken. Each night she knelt and prayed. She bargained. She broke down and begged. And she accepted with manifest certitude that if her daughter died, she would too.

HAʻAWINA NOʻONOʻO

An Offering of Thoughts

THE DOGS WERE VOMITING AGAIN.

"Could be from rotting goat," Rosie said. "Who knows anymore." She asked how things were going.

"We know the codes. What to avoid." Ana played with the phone cord. "Sometimes I find her interesting . . . but when she's gone I just don't think about her."

Stitching up patients in ER, Ana felt she herself was held together by stitches. Her spirit and her corporeal self. Her skin was coming off in patches, her eyes still had a yellow cast from drugs and radiation. She felt soiled and hazardous, suspected she might be dying, and that no one had the nerve to tell her.

On breaks, she stood out in the ambulance bay, staring at palm trees twenty feet high, leaves slapping each other like mad, green arms. Maybe they were another form of human, screaming. Maybe this was what awaited her in the afterlife. She slid into depression, the aftermath when everything was over—surgery, treatments. Now there was nothing left to fight with. She was even too depressed to fend off her mother, watching listlessly as Anahola cooked her meals, laundering and cleaning, lingering over her soaps and toiletries, trying to discover the woman Ana had become.

She took Ana out driving, forcing her to talk, which Ana resisted. "You didn't say there'd be conversation."

Her mother laughed. "By the way, it's been proven that after humans converse, there's a marked increase in their muscle tone."

"I don't believe that. Most conversations are mindless secretions that actually *keep* us from thinking."

"Well, Ana, maybe that's the point."

One day on Nimitz Highway, they drove near the piers where ocean liners docked.

Ana glanced at her. "Let's stop here and take a walk."

They stood beside Aloha Tower, from which cruise ships still arrived and departed. No scheduled ships that day, the place was empty. As they leaned at the railing, looking out at the harbor, Ana felt a stirring, childlike and perverse. The need to be hurt. To know.

"What was it like? The day you left."

Her mother stiffened. "I . . . don't really remember."

"Of course you do."

"I just remember running. Afraid I would turn back. Afraid the ship would sail without me."

"Were there crowds seeing the ship off?"

"Oh, it was packed. I struggled up the gangway terrified, then stood alone. Everyone on deck looked rich. And when we pulled away . . . you can imagine, clouds of streamers drifting down, families waving, the band playing 'Aloha 'Oe.' "

She fell silent then, remembering the cardboard suitcase in her hand, something to hold on to.

"I shared a cabin with three women. Two I think were prostitutes. At night I listened to them talk and understood that in a way, we were all outcasts. On the run, no tribes, no rules. But they were kind to me."

Ana stared at her mother's profile, taking in her beauty. The high forehead, small flat nose, lush lips like a girl's. Skin just slightly golden that, in sunlight, went brown.

"Did you tell them you'd left a kid behind?"

She slowly shook her head. "I don't think it would have fazed them. They'd probably left their lives behind a dozen times. I've seen hundreds of women like that. They pass through life in full armor."

"I wonder how women like that end up."

Anahola looked at her. "You know how they end up. ER. The morgue. Or in trailer parks in front of black-and-white TVs."

"You didn't."

"My life isn't over yet." She tapped her cigarette, the world still her ashtray.

Ana hesitated. "I always wondered . . . where you got the money for that trip."

"An uncle named Keo. A well-known trumpet player. Those are his records Noah plays. He died a few years later, of sorrow I believe. He had lost his sweetheart and their child in World War II. I was named for the child. *Anahola*. Hourglass."

"God, I don't believe the stories in this family."

"Why? We're just like any family. Ordinary people that extraordinary things happen to."

They fell silent, inhaling the smell of creosote, an acrid toying in the nostrils.

"I know what you're wondering," her mother said. "Did I ever regret it. The running away. No, I didn't regret it. But I missed Pidgin, the language of my childhood. I felt like my tongue had been cut out. And I missed Nanakuli magic. Boar-hounds singing up jade mountains. Peacocks sobbing in trees. Folks who knew me, my history. That's the thing about family, there's nothing to explain. You sit together silent and just *be*."

She faltered, then caught herself. "And I missed you. When you were born, you were so beautiful, at first I thought things would be all right. You would make everything all right. I thought I could be a mother. I just . . . didn't know how."

Ana straightened up from the railing, needing air. A different air. They walked to the car in silence.

"You're wearying of me," her mother said. "You're now more bored than angry. That's good. It means you're getting well."

She started the engine, the needles leapt.

"I want to show you something, see if you remember."

She drove for almost an hour along the east coast of the island, out past Diamond Head, then Kōkō Head. Near Makapuʻu Point, she turned down a narrow dirt road and stopped near a deserted place in rocky cliffs. They climbed and slowly crawled, and half slid down until they reached the sea where water was captured in lava pools as waves washed in and then receded.

Her mother knelt, peering into the pools. "Do you remember?"

Images floated to her then. A little girl in slippers, squatting, as her mother taught her how to draw salt from seawater. How to scoop it from lava-rock pools and sprinkle it in moist little mounds to dry in the sun. She remembered her mother humming, both of them in sun hats whose shadows cooled their faces.

She remembered her mother smoothing her arms and legs with *kukui* oil, teaching her how the word *kukui* meant "light." How ancestors had used *kukui* nut oil for torches. And she remembered long periods of sitting there quiet, watching water evaporate, leaving behind mounds of gleaming sea salt. Clean and full of bite.

"I remember I thought I would die waiting for salt to appear."

"Did you ever figure out what I was really trying to teach you?"

"It wasn't about making salt. You were trying to teach me patience."

For years she had wondered why, in those days, her mother had driven halfway round the island. There were salt pools along almost every rocky coast. Then she realized that Makapuʻu Point was the farthest her mother could get from Nanakuli; she had already begun to leave.

ONE DAY THEY DROVE ROUND THE ISLAND TO THE NORTH SHORE, passing dense settlements near Kāneʻohe Bay, then little towns with cloven streets where no one seemed to live. Tiny hand-hewn churches painted blue. A bloodred Buddhist temple set against black, fluted cliffs. They stopped for *dim sum* and crisp duck, then circled back toward Honolulu on the Pali Highway, and ended up parked near the top of Mt. Tantalus. A break in the forest showed Honolulu and Waikiki glittering below in the distance.

Ana folded her arms, knowing her mother was leading up to something. Her farewell speech.

"I always loved it up here." Anahola breathed in deeply. "Pine. Eucalyptus. The air like autumn."

Late afternoon now, sunlight pierced the trees like broken glass.

"Up here I always found perspective. It's where, one day, I understood I had to leave. I didn't have enough nerve to stay. I had nothing to offer this island, it had nothing to give me in return. But you, Ana, have nerve, and drive. You'll do important things here."

She pointed to the land below, waving her hand slowly from left to right. "Look at the size of it, so small you can hold it in your palm."

Then she pointed farther out, to sea. "But look where we came from. Ancestors crossed that ocean without maps, using only the stars and wave motions. Think of it! That kind of courage is swimming in our genes. If they could survive that ocean, *we* can survive anything. Nothing out there in the world is as scary, as potentially destructive."

Now comes the punch line. Ana waited.

"That's all I have to say. I know you've focused on your studies. I know you've never traveled, never even seen the outer islands. Don't deprive yourself of that. If you're curious, Ana, see what's out there. You will always come home. This is where you're meant to be. But if you ever want, or need, to see something of the world, don't be afraid."

On the drive back down the mountain, Ana smiled. She had expected some form of cheap theatrics from her mother, a plea for forgiveness. But all she had gotten was a pep talk. Out of sheer relief, she reached down, retrieving her mother's sunglasses where they had tumbled to the floor. But later she reflected on how it was true, she had never been off-island.

Rosie had encouraged her to travel. "See what med schools are doing on the mainland. Compare training hospitals to what we got in Honolulu."

Ana knew she never would. She would spend her life with her feet firmly planted on the ground, staying close to home. Her reluctance was based on perversity, a determination to point her life in the exact opposite direction from the one her mother chose. But now and then she wondered, *Is it perversity? Or just plain fear?*

She thought of her first lover, Tommy Two-Gods. He went out into the world and it had swallowed him. No one heard from him again. A neighbor's son went off to dental school in Philadelphia. Two years later his parents received a snapshot of him in some tributary of the Amazon, his native bride beside him wearing only a monkey-fur apron and a dinner plate inside her bottom lip. What about Will Chong, her lovely intern? Not even a postcard all these years. What happened to people in the outside world? What quick-witted beast attracted, then consumed, them? Only her mother had returned. Vain, and unrepentant.

THE WEEK BEFORE HER MOTHER LEFT FOR SAN FRANCISCO, THEY drove back to Nanakuli, where Ana ignored her, resuming a cold and unforgiving air. One day, Lopaka took her arm and walked her up into a field. Affectionately, he brushed his hand across her head where soft down was growing in.

"You look good, Ana. Still a little thin, but . . ." He tapped his heart. "In here I'm proud of you. The way you fought, and beat it."

"Time will tell. If I'm alive five years from now, then we can say I beat it."

He glanced down at his feet, scraping the dirt with the tip of his crutch. "Look, I want to ask you a favor. Please . . . try to cut your mama some slack."

She pulled away from him.

"I see what you're doing. Ana, she never forgot you all these years. She wrote you every week. She called."

"Yes. A real long-distance mother."

His voice was soft but firm. "You have any idea what she has done? For this whole family?"

"What are you talking about?"

"How do you think I got through law school? Just on the GI Bill? On scholarship? You know how few Hawaiians get scholarships. Who paid for my extra therapy and leg brace? How you think Tito paid for his new electric wheelchair?"

He opened his mouth, tapped his perfect teeth. "Who paid for my caps, for Makali'i's dental work? Who paid the lease on my office space when I set up my practice? Who do you think paid for your college education, undergrad and med school? The parts not covered by your scholarship?"

He rolled out expenditures like a great, thick carpet. She said something and he laughed.

"You thought what? Our uncles' pensions paid for all that? Oh, Ana. Their pensions couldn't buy new tires for the truck. Your summer jobs, they hardly bought you shoes."

She tried to move. Her legs felt dead. "You're lying. I threw her checks away."

He leaned in closer. "You know I never lie. Well, now and then a lie overcomes me. But, swear to God, it's true. Rosie picked those checks out of the trash and banked them. And a hundred other checks you never saw."

He reached out and laid his hand against her cheek. She saw the inside of his forearm, his veins jacaranda blue.

"Let go, sweetheart. Before that rage becomes another carcinoma."

She turned and walked away from him, out of the field and up the road, until she was exhausted. Then she lay down in tall grasses. A *poi* dog trotted up; her sobs impressed him. He sat on his haunches, watching her cry.

Hours later when she returned, they were seated at dinner, her mother in the midst of them, like a vastly superior child. Folks looked up. They put their forks down. Ana passed through the room like a phantom. She heard their coughs, heard their talk resume. The scrape of platters being passed.

She sat on her bed, hearing the long procession of their meal. Then she lay back thinking how for over twenty years they had arranged their lives to deceive her. She was a woman created out of their deceit.

When she woke it was after midnight, the house dark and silent. Her arms were cold, her flesh felt blue as if she were an invalid again. She lay still, trying to figure out exactly what she felt. *She has bought the family off, bought their forgiveness.* In fact, no one but Ana had ever condemned her mother. They had only been in awe of her, a woman brave enough to run. All they had done was love her child, and accept her generosity, allowing a measure of dignity to come into their lives.

She thought of her splendid uncles, men who came home from combat and were swept aside. Disabled. Unemployable. Tito, Ben, silent Noah. Men who spent their empty days and years and decades wondering what it was they had so valiantly fought for. Then, Lopaka, disabled but soldiering on.

She thought of Rosie, who had sacrificed her meager dreams to hold the family together. She had physically held the house together when, in pouring rains, a wall collapsed. Ana remembered her pregnant, dragging lumber and tarp, driving rusty nails into wood with a homemade hammer. Then one day carpenters came and built a new wall for the house. Probably it would still be half-collapsed without her mother's checks. She thought of Rosie pushing her to achieve, to go to university. Rosie tending her after her surgery.

They had not always eaten well. There had been small-kid years of surplus cheese and food stamps. Years when the rice bag was only one knuckle full, when Ben bartered his whale-tooth toast rack and old canoe paddles for fresh meat. She remembered Aunty Pua carefully lifting meat from her plate and giving it to Ana. Later she saw the woman in the kitchen, licking juices from the empty plate. She remembered quiet Aunty Ginger going forth to borrow fire, weaving through fields with a neighbor's torch when there was no money for electric bills, when they couldn't even afford matches. And she remembered Noah giving her a quarter for shave-ice while he rolled "cigarettes" of mango leaves.

She remembered that their lives had changed when her mother started writing letters home. Over twenty years of letters, inside of which were folded checks that had bought milk and protein, school clothes, sturdy shoes. Everyone had known but Ana, who never picked her eyes up from her books. Hungry or not, they had loved her unconditionally, had fed and even spoiled her. So how, she wondered, had the family betrayed her? How had they lied to her? What exactly was betrayal? And how did one define a lie?

One thing she had learned in medicine: after a major illness, patients were never the same. The best of them were humble, cherishing
each breath. The word *mortality* entered their syntax. Ana touched her
chest, wondering what her illness had taught her. Maybe cancer was the
cure. The thing that struck her down, shook her like a rag, shocked her
into letting go, letting it all go. Perhaps that's what cancer did: gave people permission to stop keeping track.

After a while she moved through the house and out to the *lānai*. She
stepped down to the yard and stood before the clothesline. She stared at
it a long, hard time, and at the end poles shining in moonlight. Then she
went back into the house and pulled the big sheet from her bed. She
pulled the curtains from the windows. In the dining room she pulled
the tablecloth from the table, and pulled down those curtains, too. She
went to Noah's room where he sat sleepless at his window, a towel
wrapped round his head like a swami.

"Uncle. What's wrong with your head?"

He tapped the towel. "Had one good dream. Like keep it warm,
maybe it come back again."

She pulled the big sheet from his bed, then closed the bathroom
door and filled the tub. She picked up a bar of soap and a scrub board and
knelt beside the tub, and scrubbed each sheet and curtain and the tablecloth. Sometimes she paused, imagining them clean and billowing. She
scrubbed for hours until the flesh of her palms were wrinkled like *cone
sushi*.

She scrubbed till dawn, then laboriously wrung each thing out. She
filled the tub again and slowly rinsed them, wringing and rinsing until
she was exhausted. She leaned against the tub and dozed. Then a final
rinse before she placed them like great, twisted loaves into a basket, and
dragged it to the yard.

Sun coming up, she stood with clothes pins in her mouth, snapping
the sheets to spread them evenly, watching them billow out like spin-
nakers. She snapped and shook and spread each thing, hanging it carefully, meticulously, until they took up all of two clotheslines.

One by one, the family woke and stood stretching at their windows.
Seeing her, they paused. Rosie stepped out onto the *lānai*, watching Ana
move up and down the line, straightening the sheets as they surged and
bellied out. Then she leaned her weight against a pole, shoving it deeper
into the ground so that the sagging line pulled taut. Almost cautiously,
Rosie stepped down to the yard. Ana turned and put her arm round her
cousin's waist.

"I never would have dreamed it," Rosie said.

Big Ben looked out the kitchen window, then called back to Tito. "Ey! Try look! First time dat girl evah hang laundry in her life. First time she *evah* go near dat clothesline."

She and Rosie stood arm in arm, shouting as sheets ballooned into flying tunnels.

THEY WERE A CARAVAN, HEADING TO THE AIRPORT. TWO CARS, three trucks, even Uncle Noah. At the terminal, the men checked her baggage and shuffled back and forth, doing male things so as not to show emotion. Through security, then she stood at the boarding gate, half-buried in fragrant *lei*, looking beautiful and wrecked as they embraced her.

Finally, she put her lips to Rosie's ear. "Take care of her for me."

Then the family moved aside. There was only Ana. She stood very still, not knowing what to do, and stared at this woman who had given herself a second chance. Re-created herself. A woman always in transition. Ana saw the power that independence gave her, the sense of being accountable only to herself.

Still, she wanted to ask why. *I know you loved me. But you loved you more. Tell me why it still seems wrong. Why it seems unnatural.*

Her mother was talking now, her voice soft. ". . . have it in you to change people's lives . . . very, very proud of you."

Ana just stood there.

"Remember, it's only a five-hour flight to San Francisco. Should you ever want to visit . . ."

She stepped forward, drawing Ana close. "I hope you find love . . . I hope you let love in. Live, Ana. Live!"

She watched her mother move into the passageway, legs slim and gleaming like a colt. She watched her turn and wave, a woman stepping from a frame.

'OHANA O KAUMAHA

Family of Sorrow

MONTHS PASSED. DAYS SEEMED BLEACHED A PROTOPLASMIC GRAY, nights mere hours of lidded peace. Only the patients before her were real—the bleeding ulcer, the fibrillating heart. One night at the EMS loading dock, she delivered a premature baby, a tiny, wrinkled thing like a small balloon deflated. It lay silent, still as death, then opened its eyes and screamed. It waved its arms in ecstatic little circles. It was not her first delivery, but in that moment Ana felt an almost unbearable intensification of her senses, a connection to this brand-new life. She leaned down and kissed the newborn, then kissed the paramedic.

Days later, the medical director of the ER called her in. When he asked how she was feeling she said she was having second thoughts about ER.

"That is . . . I've been thinking of switching to OB-GYN. It's not as crucial as breaking open someone's chest and clamping their heart back together, but since my surgery I think I want a branch of medicine that deals in birth, beginnings, that sort of thing."

He nodded thoughtfully. "At the risk of sounding sexist, ER is no place for a female. Even orderlies are burned out in two years."

He paused, and looked down at his desk. "Ana, when you first arrived you were a ball of fire. We had pegged you for a future chief resident. But, with your surgery and follow-up treatments, you've missed important lectures, unit rotations. I want to make a recommendation . . ."

She leaned forward earnestly.

". . . that you repeat this year of residency. You should have top evaluations and skills when you complete this program. Right now evaluations only place you in the upper half of your year. I want you to establish that level of excellence again."

"I think I've been expecting this."

"And you might just want to do general practice for a while. Instead of jumping into three more years of grinding out a specialty."

"You don't think I'd make a good OB-GYN?"

"I think you'd be brilliant at it. It's just you've been through a lot. You should think hard about how much stress you want in the next five years."

"Well . . . what's life without stress."

"It's longer."

SHE SAT AT THE HUMU HUMU LOUNGE WITH GENA MELE. "HE made me feel like a terminal case in brief remission."

"Ana, he's giving you a second chance. You bear down next year, you could call your own shots."

She sipped her beer, fighting mild depression. "My God, will this training never end?"

"Remember, we volunteered for this. Nobody drafted us."

A year earlier, Gena had passed her bar exams and joined Lopaka's small firm out on the coast. Though she was hired as his associate, he kept her in the background, researching briefs and doing paperwork.

"I'm smart. I'm aggressive. He feels threatened and treats me like an intern."

"Then quit. Fight back. Why be his lackey?"

Gena smiled. "If he asked me to clean his john, I would. Something in me wants to give that man everything I've got."

Ana put her glass down. "I can't bear to hear this. Women like us are supposed to be breaking the mold, not kowtowing to the old ways."

"Well, wait till *you* fall in love. Logic goes out the window."

One night Ana had pulled up to his office unannounced. The lights were dim when she entered, calling his name. They didn't hear her, but she saw them through a door in the records room. Near-naked, on a makeshift couch. Lopaka down on his knees like he was waxing Gena's floors, sobbing and thrusting inside her, shouting magnificent things, that he was hers, hers unconditionally. Ana had stood there paralyzed, watching Gena's legs flailing round his shoulders, watching him wait until she came before he allowed himself to come. Then he collapsed as if she had reached inside and wrung his heart. They never heard Ana leave. Now she stared at the girl, clinical and detached.

"That catchall word again. Do you know that hearing the word 'love' can actually slow a patient's bleeding? It constricts blood vessels. In operating theaters in the war, when morphine was short, it proved to be an anesthetic."

Gena studied her. "Is that all you think of when you think of love?"

"I think it's the oldest delusion in the world. Folks use it to free themselves from common sense."

"Ana, sometimes you make me feel real sad. You seem determined to go through life without experiencing certain human emotions."

She toyed with beads of condensation on her glass. "Well, now, maybe that's the point. Maybe what counts at the end of a life is not who loved us, or who we loved. But who did *not* love us . . . and who we did not love."

"You mean how someone without it learns to cope? How not being loved builds character?"

Ana hesitated, feeling the conversation had swerved, that somehow they were discussing her.

In the silence Gena asked, "What about children? That kind of love."

"I'm happy to deliver them, but I don't feel that mythical imperative to 'give birth.' I believe there are women with not much need for men, or kids. The type driven to, oh . . . erase boundaries, strain the limits. Renegades with a certain hungriness of spirit."

Gena laughed. "Well, I'm afraid my 'hungriness of spirit' has been hijacked. I'm just a uterus in *love*."

Something in Ana turned, she spoke with vicious intonation. "It's not just your spirit, Gena. Every time you use that word, you sound brain-damaged. Your horizons have definitely sunk down to your genitals."

She sat very still, then unsteadily rose to her feet. "You know, Ana, you were always too critical, always . . ."

"Polymorphously insensitive?"

". . . something of a bitch. Your sickness didn't change that. You should know that I pray for you, for your complete recovery. But right now I need to get away from you. Good night."

Alone, Ana stared at the choirlike arrangement of liquor bottles behind the bar. They gleamed, as if about to burst into hymns.

SOME DAYS SHE SAT LIKE AN OLD LADY ON THE EDGE OF HER BED, studying a calendar. The weeks, the months that would add up to a year. And then another. Her phone rang. She stared at it until it stopped. She looked in the mirror, amazed to find a face there. Amazed when she felt hunger, thirst. In bed her fingers gently walked her scars. It was the *absence* that always took her by surprise. The surgeon had suggested leaving a "skin flap" in case Ana wanted a breast implant in the future.

She declined. "No leftovers. Please. Just a nice, neat scar."

In fact, there were two scars, each five inches long. Rather like an upside-down T-bar on a slant leaning toward her underarm where they had removed certain lymph nodes to be sure. Stitch marks made the scars appear as luminous white railroad tracks that intersected. The tautness of stretched silk, no surface feeling when she touched them. And there was still discomfort, a vague pain deep within where tissues had been cauterized.

She watched her hair grow into a wavy crew cut which she nervously coasted her hands through before each checkup with her surgeon. Each time she tested negative she experienced exhaustion, a downsurge of adrenaline, and then guilt, because surviving had somehow put her on a lower plane. Lower than that of women who had died. She was learning that the truth of cancer was never told by the living. The truth was what was finally apprehended by those who did not beat it.

WHEN SHE MENTIONED THE INCIDENT WITH GENA, ROSIE SIGHED. "Try to be kinder. That girl lost a baby couple months ago. She keeps it from Lopaka."

"Why didn't someone tell me?"

"Oh, Ana. Look what you've been through. But, maybe you should drive out soon. 'Park boys' beating up soldiers. Another killing over drugs. Lopaka's got his hands full. And Makali'i—that girl's suddenly got eyes for older boys."

She promised to visit, then put it off, exhausted by a double workload. Then she read of more arrests in Nanakuli. More drug busts. She thought of oxidizing Quonset huts deep in the valley where no one dared to venture. Huts where drugs were bought and sold, where gangs kept their arsenal of guns, and where they took their girls. Thinking of Makali'i, Ana called Rosie and drove out for the weekend.

No high-rise buildings, she often forgot how on the coast the sky was everywhere, sunlight so blinding folks could not think. They just lived stunned. She saw children leaping in the sea that paralleled the highway, their skin so coppery and shimmering they seemed to be covered with mirrors. She felt herself unwind, reentering a world that required no effort of her. Yet, it required everything.

She passed big, husky road workers wearing yellow hard hats, sweat pasting their shirts to their massive dark backs. She thought how beautiful Hawaiians were, then almost hit the brakes in shock. It had been a long time since she looked at men sexually, studying the shape of their bodies, reflecting on how they each smelled differently yet the same, with the same underlying odor of maleness. She had almost forgotten the warmth and roughness of male skin, the texture and density of male hair. Yet the idea of making love, of baring her chest to a man, appalled her. She did not want that intimacy in her life again.

As she turned up Keola Road, the house, her touchstone, came out to meet her. In broad daylight all the lamps lit, every room aglow. Noah blasting Louis Armstrong across the fields, so the house seemed a big, pulsing jukebox. Sitting with Rosie, Ana realized how much she had missed in the past few years. How little attention she had paid. An aunt had died. Two cousins had married and moved to the mainland. Another cousin in prison.

"Changes not just in our family," Rosie said. "But up and down the road. Panama Chang married an Italian girl. Now only three nights a week are rice nights, other nights she cooks him pasta. Ho! the fights. He throws her pasta to the chickens."

"Where did he find an Italian girl?"

"Ana. Pick up your eyes. We got all kinds here, always did have. Look at your father, the handsome cop—Hawaiian/Chinese/*haole*."

Rather dreamily, Ana recalled her first love, Tommy Two-Gods. "His father was Jewish, from New Jersey. His mother, Catholic, a local Hawaiian-Japanese girl. He wore a Star of David and a Christian cross."

"He's back, you know, in Nanakuli."

In the silence, the falsetto plaint of a mosquito.

"Been halfway round the world," Rosie said. "Places like Libya. Beirut. I don't know why, but that boy came home a radical."

"What do you mean?"

"Said he hated the military, saw too much what he called 'racism.' Against him as a mix-blood, and a Jew. When he heard you were a doctor he was proud, said you were always two steps ahead of him."

She swallowed twice before she asked, "Did you tell him about . . . my surgery?"

"No, Ana. That's for you to tell. Now he's hooked up with that group Mālama Mākua, trying to force the military to stop bombing up the coast. He's working with Lopaka."

She thought of his eyelashes, long as a mule's, while Rosie chattered on.

"Everybody talking bombs, radiation. Nobody paying attention to our kids. They're not dying from bombs. But from drugs and bullets. Too many gangs rumbling out here, even in the schools."

Ana came alert now. "How is Makali'i?"

"Never home. I feel like I'm losing her."

In those moments, Ana saw how her cousin had aged somewhat. Now midthirties, she was still unmarried, still devoting herself to holding the family together, keeping peace between elders and their kids. She had become the vessel of wisdom and patience in the family, the one who dispensed forgiveness and love. Tall and husky as a man, Rosie's face was still beautiful, and when she entered a room folks felt an immense and sudden calm that seemed to shelter them. But something had faded from her eyes. The gleam of youth, expectation.

Ana, put her arms around her. "Tell me, cousin. How are you?"

"Oh, a little lonely. No time to meet a good, serious man."

"Now, listen to me, Rosie. Bye and bye, you're going to meet someone. You're going to be happy."

"Oh, Ana. Do you think so?"

She paused, then granted her cousin the precious amnesty of lies.

"Of course. I have seen this in my dreams."

In the yard a peacock spread its brilliant tail. Ana yawned and stretched out on a mat, feeling a yogic completeness. When she woke, shadows were long, rectangles of light on linoleum lengthening perceptibly, measuring out the afternoon. Doves warbling in guava trees. The piping voices of children playing in the yard. *Pau hana* folks shooting the breeze as they walked up the road. All sounds that spoke with sweet recall of childhood.

She heard the soft rumble of a rolling pin on dough. The rich, solid sounds of plates being set on a table. The rattle of chopsticks, the clattering splash of spoons. Then the throaty waterfall of milk being poured from a pitcher. She smelled stew bubbling on the stove. A meal that would be full of starch, and good, good grease. She sighed, feeling safe, back in that small-kid time that kitchen sounds recaptured.

IT WAS AFTER 2:00 A.M. WHEN SHE HEARD A DOOR SLAM. THROUGH her window, she saw a truck painted with skull and bones slowly pull away. Then, soft footsteps on the *lānai*.

She moved to her doorway. "Makali'i. It's Aunty Ana . . ."

She drew her into her room, and when she switched the light on, the girl flinched, her eyes not quite focusing.

"Have you been smoking dope?" Ana asked.

"Only one puff. Everybody smokes at school."

"You're absolutely stoned! Maka, you're still a minor. You can't be doing this."

She backed up and sat on Ana's bed, her face so lovely Ana's heart broke. "Doing . . . what?"

"Hanging out with 'gang boys.' At the huts."

With effort, Makali'i focused her eyes. "I . . . never did."

Ana grabbed her arm, fighting to keep her voice down. "I know who owns that truck. He's one of them."

"I . . . only went there once."

"Everything is once with you. Meanwhile, you're breaking your mother's heart."

The girl suddenly stood up. "She doesn't care. I'm just another mouth to feed, another kid to yell at. Who ever notice when my grades were good? When I fought off boys to stay a virgin. Nobody! So I think, what for? May as well be like the rest of this . . . house of illegitimates."

Ana sat back stunned, as if the girl had slapped her. "Maka. Life is something very dear. I'm *begging* you, don't throw yours away. Finish high school, you've only got two years. Then come and live with me in Honolulu."

Makali'i's voice grew small. "You promised that before. You never called."

"This time I swear to God I will. Just promise me you won't go near the Quonsets anymore."

"Okay. I promise . . ."

Ana made a promise to herself, as well. She would call the girl each week, come home more often. The next day Makali'i seemed so easy and affectionate, Ana had an awful feeling that she did not remember her promise. That she did not remember their conversation at all.

SHE FINISHED THAT YEAR NEAR THE TOP OF HER CLASS, PASSED the board exams, and was certified. Feeling she needed a rest before starting an OB-GYN specialty, Ana joined the staff of Queen's Hospital as a general physician. On her thirty-first birthday she looked in a mirror, amazed. She had passed another postsurgery year, her test results negative.

In a celebratory mood, she drove out to the house, and as she pulled into the driveway she saw a man take off across the field, riding a piebald with a quirky trot. A storm was due, the sky becoming lead. Huge drops fell, biting sudden webs into her windshield. She made a run for it and found Rosie on the porch swing, her lovely face aglow, as if she were sitting in brilliant sunlight. Seeing Ana, she dropped her head like a woman waiting for sentencing.

Puzzled, Ana moved into the house. Ben dozed on the couch, where a gecko with a livid blue tongue lolled on his forehead. He woke up startled and brushed the gecko off.

"Uncle Ben. What's up?"

His lips parted and hung there. He looked out toward the *lānai*. Ana turned to Tito in his wheelchair. He nervously shuffled a deck of cards while flipping through an old *National Geographic*. Rain poured in the windows, newspapers blew round the room. Cousins sat dead still, avoiding Ana's eyes.

"What's going on?" she asked. "What's wrong with you folks?"

"Whooo, da rain." Ben closed his eyes, inviting sleep.

She slammed down windows, then checked on Noah, who sat behind his nicotine-yellowed curtains.

"Uncle. What's going on? Rain pouring in the house, folks sitting there like dolls . . ."

He turned and smiled, showing teeth ambered from tobacco, the scorched satin of their sides. He pointed out the window. Wishbones of lightning were suddenly shot with sunlight, turning the day berserk. Rain thundered hard for several minutes, then began to slow until the valley was bathed in liquid sun, fat drops evaporating as they fell.

He put his arm round her shoulder, his smile radiant.

Rosie . . . *hāpai!* We going celebrate. With *hulihuli* chicken."

She started to ask who the father was. Then she saw the human head bouncing in and out of tall grasses. The man on the piebald with a quirky trot coming back across the fields. High in the saddle, he held his arms out to his sides, each hand gripping the legs of an upside-down chicken. Each chicken's wings outstretched and beating, trying frantically to break free.

As Ana watched, the horse leapt a narrow stream, momentarily airborne, so that the rider holding the outstretched wings appeared to be flying. That's how Ana would remember it.

"Tommy . . . Suzuki . . . Goldberg . . ."

"Yeah!" Noah grinned. "Tommy Two-Gods."

Days later she and Rosie sat side by side on the porch swing.

"You don't hate me?" Rosie asked.

Ana slid her arms around her. "Rosie. Tommy and I were kids. It was puppy love back then."

Rosie sighed with relief. "When he first came to visit we talked about you. He said what I told you, that you were always two steps ahead of him. You were meant for better things. He came again with flowers. Conversations so natural, everything as it should be. Oh, I fought my feelings! How I fought them. Two months we talked, and never touched. Then, Tommy said he loved me."

In her eyes, a resurrected glow. Rosie looked like a girl again, caught at that perfect moment of combustion when beauty and youth burn hardest.

"Rosie. *He's* the man you've been waiting for. Remember when I used to bring him home? Tommy always stared at you. You were the one he was in love with."

And, looking back, Ana realized that what she said was true.

THREE WEEKS AFTER THEY MARRIED THEIR BABY WAS BORN, A DATE Ana would remember because, that night while the family celebrated, Makali'i came home very late. She moved in slow motion, as if she were stoned, her eyes not quite focusing. Ignoring her instincts, Ana held her tongue. For the rest of her life she would feel that, had she spoken out, she could have saved Makali'i.

One night the sound of sirens screaming up and down the road. Cops had busted up a drug deal back in the valley and gave chase to one of the dealers whose truck was painted with skull and bones. During the pursuit, he took a curve too wide. The speeding truck crashed into a ravine and flipped over, crushing the girl beside him.

Ana squeezed Rosie's hand as the surgeon spoke softly, measuring each word for tact as he explained Makali'i's condition, her shattered skull, her chances of recovery. In the following weeks Rosie sat silent, tended by the family while Ana watched her child, a strapping boy named Koa Jacob Jesus. He would be a three-god child. As she held him, she watched cars drive slowly past, like in the old days, the ogling of unregenerate voyeurs.

People pointed at the house where the "gang girl" lived, the one now rumored to be brain-dead. Ana imagined how they appeared to strangers: maimed and warped, a family of illegitimates. She suspected that Makali'i would be their icon when they spoke of bad blood, the downward spiral of that family's genes.

The girl remained in a coma for weeks. Her body, hooked up to transparent tubes, appeared smaller yet somehow larger—an immense absence in her presence. Whatever part of her still alive was no longer in the room. In that time, Rosie sat on the porch swing like a statue in repose, eyes slung low, her mouth and lips weightless. Sometimes she sat out there all night. In humid mornings, steam rose from her shoulders, air rippled with her body heat like concentric afterimages of herself. Her odor so strong they smelled her pulse.

No one in the family seemed able to speak. All they knew was pain. At night there was only the sound of cicadas like scorching heat rendered into sound. Even youngsters—little beauties dark and electric—moved on tiptoe, their expressions at the window sad. Lopaka's face was so mythical and harsh, Ana moved close, wanting to press the tattooed teardrop near his eye as if it were a doorbell. Wanting to gain entry and share his pain.

She tried to talk to Rosie, to draw her out. Finally, she just sat with her, rocking back and forth. Afraid she was losing her, that Rosie's mind would go, Ana began to pray. She even stopped using profanities. She waited. What would happen waited with her.

THE DAY WAS OVERCAST AND MOODY WHEN THE PHONE RANG. Lopaka answered it, then left the house. Hours later he returned, switched off the ignition of the car, and sat staring through the windshield. Then he slowly walked up to the screen door and asked Ana to come out to the yard. In the kitchen, she was suddenly aware of the smell of wet drain-boards.

She stepped out to the *lānai*, and moved down the steps. She searched Lopaka's face as he placed his hand on her shoulder. Then she sank slowly to the ground, folding like a paper doll.

Anticipating her question, in a confused reflex, he asked the question instead. "She's dead, isn't she?"

"Is she?" Ana asked.

"She is."

PART THREE

HŌʻIKE NA KA PUʻUWAI

Revelations of the Heart

MAKANI PĀHILI

Hurricane

FOR YEARS SHE WILL DREAM OF FLYING OVER MILES OF TREMBLING, *turquoise skin. Of planes stacked upside down like smashed toys. Boats sprawled belly-up across wrecked piers. A body floating in a harbor. She will remember buckled tarmac, her plane skidding sideways, coming to a bouncing stop. Relief crews stretching bright blue tarp over miles of roofless houses.*

She will remember the crunch of shattered glass as they climbed through the rubble of hotels, searching for survivors. Winds moaning through thousands of caved-in rooms. The wrecked and ringing chandeliers. When flashlight batteries went dead, they searched by candlelight. And when generators failed in makeshift hospitals, they performed surgery by candlelight.

Ever after, when she sees flickering candles, she will think, 'Iniki. 'Iniki brought him to her. He was not in her life. And then he was . . .

THE HURRICANE HIT EVERY ISLAND—TAKING RESORTS, ENTIRE towns. It shaved the island of Kaua'i to the bone—whole forests denuded and flattened, buildings crushed like pickup sticks. For days highways were knee deep in water and debris, undermining the efforts of relief workers. And everywhere surfaces glittered with shattered glass, giving devastation a diamond shimmer.

Twenty-four hours after Hurricane 'Iniki passed, across the blackedout island homeless people huddled in armory shelters, or at campfires, or they walked the beaches, numb. Near the ruins of the Coco Palms

Hotel, Ana sat at a campfire holding a child who had been pulled un-harmed from a nearly flattened house.

She rocked her back and forth, half crooning, "Shh, soon your mama and papa will come for you. Meanwhile, I will tell you a story."

The child stopped struggling as Ana stared at the campfire.

"Now . . . shall I tell you of our island winds? Oh, there are so many they are worshipped as gods. Elders can name two hundred different kinds of winds. There is the *Kona* wind, warning of winter. It blows long and hard, brings gray, humid weather, torrents of rain! And there is *Ha'i Mo'olelo*, the 'telling wind,' that makes a haunting sound like bamboo nose flutes heard at night."

Ana spoke softly, watching the child's eyelids flutter. She prayed her sleep would last until her parents were found, that they would be all right, that she would never know the terror of thinking they were dead. While she gazed at the child, a stranger approached and stood listening, just beyond the light of the campfire.

". . . As with our winds, there are hundreds of rains. Each one is a god, and has a god-name . . ."

The child slept now, Ana felt her soft snores against her chest. She looked round the campfire at people needing comfort, and continued "talking-story."

". . . Just now we have been in the 'punishing rains and hurling winds,' the time of *Makani Pāhili*, the hurricane. But now the hurricane is *pau*. We are in the gentle winds of healing."

She covered the child with a blanket, and long before dawn a priest brought her parents, who took her in their arms. Ana had talked for hours, and now sat back exhausted. And that is when the stranger stepped out of the dark, his sudden face a match-strike, like a painting revealed on the wall of a cave.

He sat down at their fire and began to talk. He talked in mixed accents—the argot of a drifter—his words seeming to bob in the phlegmy workings of his lungs. At some point, almost shyly, he told them his name, then continued spinning tales, distracting them from the wreck-age all around them.

The storm had left polluted rivers, water shortages, and, in the day-time, killing heat. Yet this stranger was dressed head to toe in black leather so stiff it creaked. His teeth were big and crooked, his face pale, slightly sunburned. Under thick, dark hair, his eyebrows shot out in ec-static skyward angles. She found his eyes uncanny—black, intense—the eyes of someone who could carve his life into another human's skin. He handed out cigarettes and chain-smoked, the movement of his hand slow, almost tender, as he brought the cigarette to his lips. He seemed to anticipate each long inhale like someone who had known deprivation.

Ana glanced round the dying campfire at faces sad and dark as angels, as folks listened, intrigued by this man's stories. He saw they were exhausted, newly homeless, some even wounded. Maybe he saw them as childlike, needing comfort, to just sit still and listen. So he continued, his long-winded yarns slipping through the hours. And listening, they learned how war and hunger had invented him. How his past seemed to give him permission.

He coughed, shared a warm beer, then talked again, rolling up his sleeves and pants. In growing light and heat, sweat cataracted down his neck, soaking through the leather shirt. Ana saw he was lean, of average height, snakes of muscles in his arms and legs. Yet, his hands were remarkably huge and scarred. As morning temperatures continued to rise, he slowly pulled off his leather boots, and then his socks. Even his feet were scarred.

A big red ball of sun ascended, yet he continued telling tales as if he needed to talk himself empty. The sun began to hover, then hammered overhead, the fire slowly embered. National Guardsmen in fatigues passed with chain saws, dragging chopped-up utility poles. The stranger paused in his telling, his eyes darting to armed Marines scouting for looters across the road. They stood laughing at a couple with shotguns in their laps, dozing in front of their dry-goods store. A slapdash sign stood between them, NOTHING HERE WORTH DYING FOR!

The storyteller yawned and someone asked him, "Tired, fellah? Where you from?"

He fell silent as if there were a right and a wrong answer. Now folks slowly stood, preparing to meet the new day's manifesto of tragedies. A thousand more people homeless. Another dozen missing. Another body found. Ana gathered her things and glanced his way as dusty leaves fluttered overhead, casting the stranger in dappled sunlight. In that moment a kind of beauty gathered round him, the beauty of bright sky reflected off black stubble on his chin. He would lose them now; she saw his panic. It was like seeing the whole curve of a man's life pass through him.

She kept her face neutral, hoping it looked kind, the particular kindness one extends to loners and the lost. He bent, helping someone fold a blanket. His shirt fell open; his bare chest looked skinny, almost adolescent. He helped stamp out the fire, then leaned forward offering his hand, telling her his name again.

"Nikolai . . . Volenko."

A name that seemed to fit his stories.

She shook his hand. "I'm Ana. Well, I've got to get back to the med team . . ."

"You are doctor?"

"Yes."

"You live here on Kaua'i?"

She shook her head. "I'm one of the volunteer medics from Honolulu."

"So. What I can do to help you?"

The island was already glutted with branches of the military, the National Guard, Red Cross. So many disaster-relief organizations, storm victims were complaining that these people were eating all their rations.

"What did you come here to do?" she asked.

"Normally, I make films . . . documentaries."

Ana looked up at half a dozen helicopters with camera lenses hanging from their bays. The media had swarmed in like locusts. She shook her head, picked up her backpack, and walked away.

He ran alongside her. "Wait. I am not ghoul like them. I flew in before hurricane. Was trying to get footage on . . . something else."

"Like what? Our local drug trade? Our women's prison?"

He skipped in front of her, blocking her way, then stood so close tiny shafts of dust danced between them.

"I am not sensationalist. My films are very relevant, very sympathetic." Then he smiled. "You liked my stories?"

She thought of the amazing things he had told them. "They weren't stories one would like, or dislike. Were they true?"

"Yes. And no. I watched you. You are very good listener."

She started to ask what he was doing on the island, but was afraid it would turn into conversation and she would not be able to get away.

She stepped back, half joking, "You'll die in this heat, in those clothes."

He slapped the leather pants and grinned. "Yes. They are killing me." Then he looked around nervously. "So. You do not need help?"

Ana shook her head. "But, thank you."

Reluctantly, he bent to gather a canvas bag and backpack. For some reason she stood there, watching him prepare to go.

"Then. Is better I get off island quick. How I will find you in Honolulu?"

Before she could answer, he saw two Marines approaching from the distance. He suddenly wheeled and headed off.

Ana hesitated, then lifted her arm, calling, "Wait."

He was already a scribble on the landscape.

NIKOLAO

———

Nikolai

SOMETIMES WHEN SHE FINISHED HER ROUNDS ON THE WARDS, ANA wandered down to the ER, lending a hand when they needed backup. Since Makaliʻi's death she had not moved forward with her plans to do a residency in OB-GYN. She had not moved in any direction, grief and loneliness bonding like crystals, creating an overwhelming sense of stasis.

At night, she walked Honolulu's quiet streets, thinking how loneliness was so much a part of human existence it seemed to have a life of its own, an organism that reproduced. She wondered if that's why she had chosen medicine, to remind herself that others were lonely, too, and that they suffered. To see someone suffering when she was not filled her with relief. All she had to do was heal them.

One day her surgeon shook Ana's hand. She had survived her fifth postsurgery year still cancer-free. She had a quiet drink alone, went home to an empty apartment, and stared at what looked like a giant teardrop hanging from her wall. Since surgery, her left arm had grown slightly stiff, so a cousin who taught boxing at the Nuʻuanu Y had brought her a speed bag, a little hanging punching bag, and gloves.

Screwing a platform to her wall from which the speed bag hung, he had wrapped her hands in bandages, showing her where to land her fist.

"But don't go at it with anger. Remember when I was a kid, the punch bag hanging from the mango tree? Mango season, I'm punching, all the mangoes falling down. So. When you come at the bag, think 'mango time.' "

At first she was clumsy and impatient, striking the bag angrily as if it were a human face. But once she mastered the punching rhythm, Ana began to relax. It began to be almost fun. Then she went at it with conviction, her upper-body muscles growing taut and strong. The muscles under her scars began to feel resilient, no longer tight and tender. The speed bag woke her body up, made her want to swim again.

Out in the waters of Ala Moana Beach she lazily stroked, feeling the sea melt into her. In the distance, Lē'ahi, Diamond Head, that glowing old cadaver. And miles down the coast to her right, the rugged Wai'anae mountain range, reminding her where she belonged. In the parfait colors of a going sun, she floated on her back, eyeing skyscrapers behind her, glass monoliths reflecting kaleidoscopic blue of sea. This time of day the city seemed soft and giving, and Ana realized she had come to love Honolulu. It let her breathe. It left her alone.

On a humid evening as she walked home from the beach, it began to rain a warm, blue evening rain, so soothing she broke into a half trot, then a jog. She jogged past her building and kept running, remembering how as a kid she loved to run in *lokuloku* rains. Moving along the Ala Wai Canal, Ana thought how parts of Honolulu had long ago entered her and were now secretly owned by her.

The invisible city—the sexual one, its geography—was forever fixed in her memory by early acts of love. The Honolulu Zoo, where as a student she had made love nearby in a young man's car while primates chattered in their cages. Makiki Street, where in a borrowed apartment that same young man had ultimately scorned her. Queen's Hospital, where in the intern's lounge, she had made love to Will Chong. Even Atkinson Drive, down which they walked to reach the sea where Will had said he loved her, that he would trust her with his life.

Where were those young men now? Did they remember her? They had each been ambitious and focused, and would be successful, not prone to sentiment. Her memory would not be essential to their lives. Panting and breathless, she jogged back to her building, and stood looking up at her windows as if waiting for a signal, some code to tell her how to live, how to shoulder the burden of time.

SHE WAS ON THE WARDS WHEN SHE HEARD THEM PAGING FROM ER. A man with nonspecific pains was asking for her.

When she pulled back the curtain in the exam room, he smiled and raised his hand. "Hello, Doctor."

At first she did not remember him, then she recognized the big, scarred hands. "Oh. The campfire, after 'Iniki. You're . . . Nikolai."

"*Da.*" He half sat up, then lay back down.

"What seems to be the problem? Are you in pain?"

He touched his heart. "Only here. You broke it that day. What you will do to me this time?"

She put her stethoscope to his chest, then thoughtfully sat him up and pressed it to his back.

"You've got congestion in your lungs. Have you had flu? An allergic reaction?"

He shook his head. "Only frustration in not finding you."

Ana called in a nurse. "Let's get his vitals and a Chem-24."

He tried to pull away. "Not necessary, Doctor. I am here for you."

"Look. We're very busy here. I don't have time for jokes."

As the nurse drew blood, he winced. "I am not here for jokes. Your cousin, Lopaka, told me where to find you."

Ana paused, then pressed the stethoscope to his back again. "How do you know him?"

"We have things in common . . . environmental things . . ."

"Breathe in deeply." She listened, then frowned. "Sounds like you've got low-grade pneumonia. I'm sending you for X-rays."

She leaned close, staring at a yellowish cast to the whites of his eyes that often meant anemia. He waited till the nurse had left, then took Ana's gloved hand and spoke in careful English.

"I will save you time. Blood counts low. Well . . . normal-low. It is probably going to get worse. Not enough red cells to be carrying sufficient oxygen to vital organs. Not enough white cells to be knocking out infections. Eventually, immune system will be going . . ."

She felt her fingers sweating in the glove.

"I should not have looked for you. Should not be remembering you. Probably I am dying."

She withdrew her hand and tried to joke. "You can't die. We just met."

She walked him to the X-ray unit and, when her shift was over, met him in the hospital coffee shop. A low-dose steroid shot had temporarily stopped his wheezing and his face seemed more relaxed. A rather handsome face, wearied by lines. He looked fifty but she suspected he was younger.

He told her how he had looked for her ever since 'Iniki, but all he knew was her first name. Then, out on the Wai'anae Coast, he had met Lopaka and mentioned this doctor, Ana, he was searching for.

"Of course, nothing is coincidence. All is ordained, no?"

Coming on the bus to find her, he had experienced wheezing and shortness of breath. "And look, already you have saved me."

Ana sat back, studying him. "You never told me what you were doing on Kaua'i. You said you were shooting footage . . ."

He carefully lowered his throaty bass voice. "Yes. Was shooting Army Missile Test Range at Barking Sands. Was caught by military police climbing over security fence. Soldiers took video camera. They shove Colt .45 in here." He pointed his finger like a gun into his mouth.

"Were taking me for interrogation when 'Iniki hit. This hurricane saved my life. Was still running from them when I see your campfire."

"So . . . no footage."

"None. But I am working with Lopaka now. Will be other opportunities. I am making documentary, Ana. Very extensive. Including many places."

"That's impressive. But how long have you had this problem with your blood count? Do you know what caused it?"

His voice turned soft, almost elegiac. "How long? Since a child in Russia. Swimming in coal-black rivers. Breathing coal-black dust. Even sheep in fields are black. Other causes? You would like a list? Contaminated soil. Leaking waste. They are calling it 'toxic exposure.' Old-fashioned word is poison."

"We have it here, too. On a smaller scale."

"*Da*. This is why I am going to your Wai'anae Coast. Why I go to Kaua'i. Is all across Pacific. Everywhere, and never-ending."

She asked if this documentary work was dangerous and he shrugged. When she asked if he made a living at it, he shrugged again.

"So-so. Swedish TV is airing my tapes on coal pollution in Russia, because is same thing now in Europe. German TV is airing tapes on acid rain poisoning forests, rivers, streams."

Only, no one seemed eager to air his tapes on nuclear pollution, or radiation.

"And why? Because all major countries are being guilty of such things."

"What about networks in the U.S.?" Ana asked.

He laughed. "Americans. They are wanting fairy tales. They are so dear . . . so innocent. What will it take, I wonder?"

He told her he had shot footage in French Polynesia. Micronesia. Wherever there were nuclear test sites. He had even interviewed Australian Aborigines, who had been exposed when the British tested H-bombs in Australia in the 1950s and '60s.

"Still sick people there, and no one tells. No one cares."

Unconsciously, Ana touched her chest. "We care. It's just, we have so few resources with which to fight back."

Nikolai leaned forward now, rubbing his hands. "This why I plan to make definitive film on death of modern human morals. Am shooting five years now. In my country you cannot imagine the horrors . . ."

She sat back and gazed at him thoughtfully. "You say you're recording the 'death of human morals.' But . . . these people in your films are *victims*. Just aiming a camera at them is immoral. Isn't it?"

He smiled. And then he frowned. ". . . Yes. Maybe I too am guilty of exploitation. But, world has to be knowing, has to be informed. I want to be showing what was done to us. What Russia did to *own* people in race to be world leader. How is happening all over world. I want people looking at these victims, so they are understanding they are seeing their future." Warming to his subject, his face grew flushed.

Ana gave him a moment to compose himself before she asked, "Tell me, how do you get in and out of Russia to make these films?"

He patiently explained how, since the Communist collapse, Russia was now one big black market. Anyone could purchase passports, exit visas.

"Also, I have sympathetic 'official' friends who recommended me for grant, which I received for one year here at East-West Center."

The Center was part of the University of Hawai'i, an international think tank that attracted foreign scholars.

"This grant is to give series of lectures and finish 'book I am writing' on Rise and Fall of Cinema Engagé, political filmmaking in Europe in 1930s."

"Are you really writing such a book?"

"Impossible! Who would read such outmoded thing. This grant is subterfuge. Everything is subterfuge."

"Well, then . . . what happens when your year is up?"

"I go back to Russia, then leave again. Everyone is doing this. Though one day they will be cracking down when we get rid of that drunk, Yeltsin, and get decent president. Who, of course, they will then assassinate."

She noticed he kept switching from "we" to "they," perhaps the love/hate, pride/shame dilemma of being Russian.

"My dream? To one day be showing my films in Russia. Ninety-nine percent of Russians don't know what was done to us. TV is controlling all news. Is absolute power now, like Peter the Great. One television station reaching eleven time zones. One hundred million voters."

Ana began to feel overwhelmed by this man's "foreignness," his intensity.

"Is no more Russia now. Today, my country like big drag queen. All is 'let's pretend.' "

He explained how a colonel in the army, a man in charge of massive weapons, made a salary of only fifty dollars each month.

"He can destroy world, but cannot feed his family! Military officers begging in streets, but bureaucrats eat steaks. Russia now so corrupt, even gangsters begging for law and order. This the reason why we leave."

At the start of their conversation, she had been somewhat fascinated by how luxuriantly he rolled his r's, and how he lengthened his vowels so they seemed to quiver as if suspended from the end of an eye dropper. But when he became excited he seemed to mix his tenses and drop his articles, "a" and "the," so that his English became a caricature of a Russian speaking English.

Ana played with her food and studied his big, scarred hands, drawn in by his eyes, dark and beautiful, and wide, full lips, behind which lurked big crooked teeth that, miraculously, were not capped in gold or silver. She asked if he knew any of the recent Russian émigrés to Honolulu, most of whom lived in Iliwei over near the canneries.

"Da. Good people, but . . . not interested in my projects. They are trying to forget. To live barefoot in Paradise. Gospodi! What a joke."

"Why a joke?"

"Russians cannot assimilate. Unless you are Russian aristocrat, then is not really Russian. You can always spot us. Still blowing our noses in our hands. Forgetting how to button our flies. Ten years in new country, still dressing like refugees."

While they talked he had finished his sandwich, then stabbed each crumb left on the plate and licked them off his fingers. He had squeezed his tea bag almost to a pulp, stirred his tea and gulped it in one swallow. Then, during conversation, he put the tea bag to his lips and elaborately and audibly sucked it dry. She wondered if the tea bag thing were some sort of ritual.

"Look, Ana. While we talk, I have blown my nose in my napkin, then tore my napkin to shreds from sheer emotion. Next, I will ask if you want that half of your sandwich. Then I will finish it, and want to lick your plate."

She laughed and gave him the rest of her sandwich. "Tell me, is your family still in Russia?"

He inclined his head. "Dead father was highly decorated soldier, defending Leningrad during German siege. Mother was famous actress, beautiful. Now lives in Moscow, in the past . . . No wife. No children. You?"

She shook her head. "Only my work."

Nikolai clapped his hands. "So! We can begin."

She laughed again, shook his hand, and went back on duty. She was not attracted to him then, a wanderer, a dreamer, not a man to take seriously. Or perhaps she *was* attracted, because he seemed guileless, flirting like a boy, leaving himself open to hurt, or insult. And perhaps because he was slightly crude, yet somehow elegant, his answers to her questions extremely thoughtful, as if each question were, for him, a gift.

Two days later they went over his X-rays and blood tests, the results of which necessitated further tests. By then she had called Lopaka, asking about this Nikolai Volenko. Her cousin had known him only two months but said he was a filmmaker of integrity. He had rented a room near Chinatown, and one day Ana met him there for lunch.

"Lopaka is very respectful of your work. I'd like to see one of your films."

He hung his head modestly. "Thank you, Ana. For such interest. In two days I leave to shoot more footage in Moruroa, Tahiti, where France continues testing bombs. When I return, two weeks, I show you film."

SHE ASSUMED SHE WOULD NEVER SEE HIM AGAIN. BUT ONE NIGHT when Ana glanced outside, he was standing in the rain with a bouquet of flowers, looking up at her window. She met him at the door with a towel.

"How wonderful to watch," he said. "So happy at your punching bag, content to be alone. I did not want disturb you."

He was soaked from head to toe; his cheap shoes squeaked across her floor. She made him shower while she hung his clothes, and when he came out wrapped in her oversized robe, perhaps for the first time Ana saw him clearly. The body of a laborer, not muscular, but naturally wiry and strong. As he padded round the room she noticed again his scarred legs and feet, even scars on the back of his neck.

His hair was like black paint slicked against his head, only a few strands of gray. His big straight nose seemed to balance his full lips. She saw his skin was large-pored and rough, the skin of someone who had lived out in the weather. He struck her as not handsome, but rather someone who had once been handsome. Now he just looked weary.

She heated stew and poured them wine. He started to tell her about his trip, then fell upon the food, ravenous. He ate so fast, Ana wondered if he understood food; he seemed to regard it merely as fuel. Over lunch in Chinatown, she had noticed that when he finished eating he took his pulse. Now he took his pulse again, feeling his heartbeat in his wrist, its accelerated pounding. She had seen this before, the habit of people who had known extreme hunger.

The rains had stopped and Nikolai hung his head out the window, inhaling deeply. "Such air! So pure it hurts."

He helped her with the dishes, explaining his initial fear of Honolulu. "At first, air here was terrifying. So invisible, so subtle and subversive. From Russia, I only trust air I could see. And water. Here, it tastes like *water*. Very suspicious."

She folded a dish towel. "Tell me, Nikolai . . ."

"Niki. Please."

". . . is anything real to you?"

He refolded the towel and hung it carefully. "Only silence is real. And, no such thing as silence. Listen!"

Gently, he cupped both of her ears with his hands. "Minute worlds exploding. So how you can imagine human language, human mind—so infant to old universe—can begin knowing what is *real?*"

Ana backed up, laughing. "You know, you're like a deck of cards. You come up different every time."

"I promise you," he said. "I am real. I have eked out everything I am."

He left again, trying to raise more funding for his project. Each time he returned he seemed more relaxed, his English slightly improved. Some nights he followed Ana through the apartment like a child, playing with her TV, the appliances in her kitchen.

He opened her freezer and stared dreamily inside. "Makes me very nostalgic. You see, I was born inside ice."

He asked about the cost of her furniture, her clothes, the cost of her groceries. He asked about her work, her income, then turned her answers back on her, making her question her values. One night, Ana sat him down.

"You know . . . at first I thought you were naïve. You're not, you're very clever. You have a way of boiling things down, so that I end up feeling guilty. For being employed, and healthy, for being . . . free. Niki, I don't think I can see you anymore. I feel you resent me. I understand your resentment, but I can't change who I am. And neither can you."

His hands flew to his face, covering his eyes. When he looked up she saw such pain it took her breath.

"I will change. I am learning." He gripped her hands desperately. "Ana. Please. Be patient with me."

"Why? What is the point?"

"Because. One day you are going to love me."

She inhaled so sharply, the hollows near her collarbones grew steep and filled with shadows. She pulled her hands away, and stood.

"Are you mad? I don't even know you. I don't believe half of what you say is true."

He took her hands again, more gently now. "Is true. I swear is true. But, if I told you everything, you would want to shoot me out of kindness."

HOʻOHĀMAU, HOʻOLOHE

To Be Silent, to Listen

SHE WONDERED HOW THEY'D REACHED THIS POINT SO FAST, A stranger strolling into her life, telling her he might be dying. And that he loved her.

"It was the way how you held the child that night at campfire. The way how you listened. You look at me and listened. Is years since someone did that for me."

They had known each other several months, cautiously easing into each other's life. In fits and starts, Ana told him about Makaliʻi, how she blamed herself for the girl's death.

"I didn't take the time for her, like Rosie did for me."

She talked about her dead father, her mother who abandoned her. "Since she left, I hardly think of her. No . . . that's not really accurate. What I mean is, as a kid I used to dream that she would come back for me. I've learned most dreams don't come true, we just outgrow them."

"*Da.* Is accurate, but very sad," Niki said. "And why, I wonder, must we make dreams come true? Is *all* a dream, no? We need to make our *life* come true. Need to know are we really living it. Is there more to it than this? There has to be."

"What do you mean?"

"Well . . . we look closely, we see there is life inside this life. Something wriggling between these spaces. We know is there, but don't know what to call it, how to reach it."

"Are you talking about God?"

"No. I am Russian after all. My background is mathematics. This the only God."

"Hold on," Ana argued. "I've read that there's a whole area of mathematical propositions that can't be proven. They're neither true nor false. Even Einstein was stumped. That means at some point, mathematics fails. It isn't absolute. So how can math be God? Or vice versa?"

Niki smiled. "Ana, you don't see? Answers are there! But even Einstein did not want to see them. And, why? Because if he find all answers, then is no reason for God. He does not want to do this to humanity."

"You're a trickster," she said. "You say life is entirely a dream. Then you say it's mathematically absolute."

He liked that she challenged him, kept up with him. He tried to kiss her. When she pushed him away, he laughed.

"Okay. I am patient. I see you are afraid. So unprepared for love you look right through it."

"Niki, you use that word too easily. You 'love' my apartment, my appliances. You 'love' my speed bag . . ."

"Then I try to be more discreet. But not give up. How I can convince you of my feelings?"

She looked at his stained fingernails, his rather worn-out clothes. But his skin was clean and glowing, and he smelled like old, polished leather. Against a slight sunburn, even his teeth seemed whiter. She wanted to ask why, of all the women in the city, he chose her.

Instead she said, "Slow down. Slow down."

Alone at night, her hands cupped her shoulders, then moved down her waist to her thighs. She wondered if other lonely women did that, imagining how their skin felt to a man. It had been over five years. She tried to remember how a man's hand felt—its weight on her skin, its warmth raising her body temperature.

Her hand came to rest on her scars. They had healed relatively smoothly, no keloids, but in the dark she *felt* their whiteness, the stark absence there seeming to signify the absence of many things in her life. Mostly she dreaded telling this man because she did not want the disease to define her. Each time she looked at Niki, Ana did not want to see it in his eyes. *Here is a woman who had cancer.*

THE NIGHT THEY FINALLY BECAME LOVERS, AT FIRST THEY LAY TO-
gether fully dressed. Ana gazed at the ceiling.

"Niki. I need to tell you something."

He turned somber, folded his arms across his stomach, and waited.

"I've had surgery. For cancer. They removed my breast. It isn't pretty."

He slowly raised his head and looked at her. "How long ago . . . the surgery?"

"Almost six years now."

He turned on his side, facing her.

Now he will be very kind, because I have ceased to interest him.

His eyes were riveted to hers, his face near brute with feeling. He took her in his arms.

"Thank you! Oh, Ana. Thank you . . . for surviving."

When they were finally undressed, she turned her head away. He studied her chest, then very tenderly followed the lines of the scars with his lips.

"Heal, little ones. Heal. Grow strong above your beating heart."

There was no feinting and no barter. He kissed her scars, and remained erect. In time, she would relax, not look away when he touched her there, but on that first night she was stunned. At first she felt like a woman in a fairy tale captured by a beast with massive paws. Yet his big, scarred hands were gentle, his movement endearingly shy and courtly. As if he planned to worship her, to lay down at her feet as an offering his entire history.

But then, in the deepest throes of passion, he became a primate. Screaming. Leaping. Caterwauling like something being slaughtered. He even lifted her by the shoulders, shaking them, as if to make sure she was paying attention. Finally, he was a thoughtful lover, considerate of her pleasure, slowing when he saw where she liked being touched. But then he grew wild again, leaping and shouting, even sobbing when he came.

Exhausted and spent, she watched him blow his nose, still weeping with emotion. "My God. Is that how Russians make love?"

He drew her to him. "Forgive me. I have been with many women, but only once before did I love. We acted out emotions. She was deaf."

". . . What happened to her?"

He turned his head. "Another time. Not now."

DAYS PASSED, THEN WEEKS. AS THEIR FEELINGS SLOWLY DEEPENED, he expanded on his impressions of her that night at the campfire. At first he had found her intimidating—big-boned, proud, her hair dark and wild with a life of its own. When she had looked at him, she squinted like a woman sighting down the barrel of a rifle. And even when she had relaxed, there was an edge, a visible hardness in her gaze. But when she held the child, her features had grown soft and lovely.

Then, as Niki had told his Russian tales—how people drank human blood in the famines under Stalin, how in Arctic cold, his *babushka* chopped off her hand when it froze to a rabbit trap, how wolves still ran in the streets of that old Tartar town, Moscow—he had watched how the fire did strange things to Ana's face. Her eyes going pale to dark as she listened, her native blood drumming to the surface so her cheekbones glowed.

"You looked scary. Maybe even beautiful, but scary. Then slowly I see how good you listened. Your lips apart, expression softening as interest grew. So. I left that night thinking, 'maybe I find her again.' Then I think, 'Why her? Why life is throwing someone like that at me, a drifter, bouncing off life so many years?' But I keep thinking, 'Ana.' "

While he talked, he pressed her hand against his cheek.

"When I get back to Honolulu I decide, 'Okay. I take a stab. I look for her. See if I can be normal again. Laugh discreetly, walk in step. Learn to be like other humans, not scare her away.' I don't know, maybe was time. I'm bloody tired. Tired makes man humble, maybe more sincere."

And finally, Ana admitted how, at first glance, she had disliked him.

"That leather getup. Your slangy accents—Russian, Australian, American. Nothing about you seemed plausible. I've seen men like you from all over the world pass through our islands. They take our hospitality, our energy, and give nothing back. The type of men I would walk through."

She hesitated, feeling shy.

"Then you began to tell those tragic stories. You told them so movingly, so humanely, I didn't care if they were true or not . . ."

"*Da.* Is very Russian thing. We live to story-tell."

EVENTUALLY, WITH HER PRODDING, HE BEGAN TO TALK ABOUT HIS life, giving her a new version, a fable. He told how he was born in a city almost frozen to extinction. This was Leningrad, under siege by the Germans for nine hundred days during World War II. His earliest memories, he said, were of campfires burning inside gutted buildings, so that each building seemed to resonate and breathe.

". . . I remember coffins being trundled down streets on sleds, until even sleds were used for fires. Then coffins used. Corpses formed blue pyramids along these streets."

Without plumbing, clean water disappeared, so there was thirst, de-grading thirst. He recalled how people died stuck to the ice they were trying to chop from the rivers. The living began to drink their own flu-ids. And finally, half-crazed, they carved out thighs and buttocks of the dead, then covered them with snow.

"There was this man, with ordinary face, dragging red woolen shawl from building to building, selling unspeakables. One day he stands with my mother, holding out part of large thigh, cursing softly as she bargains. Then he continues on his way, dragging red shawl. My boyhood is tele-scoped into this moment, the two of them bargaining over human thigh. I have dragged that shawl behind me in my dreams."

Ana tried to imagine such a childhood where all he knew was lice, hunger, time that lay over him like a frozen coat. Then Niki spoke of his beautiful mother, a once-famous actress, who worked with the Under-ground.

"Each night she pull me to my knees and we pray for my father, brave officer leading Russian troops against Germans. And you know, these prayers are answered. Germans finally withdrew, they could not take our Leningrad! When war ends, my hero father comes home, reunited with his wife and son."

In time his parents saw how bright he was, a boy with an affinity for numbers.

"They send me to state school, then university. Very proud. In time I am groomed for Novosibirsk, famous city in Siberia built for scientists, physicists, their families. Very exclusive. But today? A ghost town."

He explained how he began to grow disillusioned.

"I see they are teaching us only to make weapons that destroy. To make Russia number one. You remember what we did in Poland? Hun-gary? Czechoslovakia? This is long before we rape Afghanistan. So I shame my parents. I drop out of university. I give up mathematics. Num-bers now futile, a search for infinity cheap as religion."

Finally, he had dropped out completely and ended up a black marke-teer, then bodyguard to gangsters.

"Nothing touched me. You understand? I would have shot my best friend for money. Years passed. I don't remember them."

Sometimes Nikolai fell silent, as if worn-out by his history. Or, he skipped back and forth in time, omitting years, recalling the mid-1980s when Russia began to splinter.

"Decades of Cold War were a farce. Across Russia, all receptors quiv-ering, H-bombs at the ready, while we stir annihilation into morning coffee. Was in our milk, you see. In this milk is strontium 90, iodine 131. Food-chain contamination running rampant thirty years. This was the joke. Our bombs could not protect us! Our fields already sown with radioisotopes."

It would take weeks before he talked about his past again—traveling through Russia, filming its polluted towns and rivers, its devastation. How he had sat listening to the stories of elders.

"You know what I hear? Nostalgia. Human longing for the past—the clean kill of wolf packs. Even of war."

He showed Ana footage of the faces of Kazakhstan. The young. The old. Eyes that were shell-shocked, completely dead. Bodies so wrecked and poisoned, they seemed devoid of human attributes.

Finally, she shook her head. "I can't watch anymore."

He sat back and sighed. "So, Ana. You want to know my life. This was my life."

"That isn't all of it."

". . . is all I can bear just now."

SHE HAD BEGUN TO KNOW WHEN HE REACHED THE END OF CON-versation. Something in him turned its back, moved to a corner, and sat alone. Some nights she crawled into bed while he sat looking out the window.

"Sleep very hard. Sometimes it look too much like death."

They stayed apart till dawn. Then he lay down and gathered Ana to his chest and spoke to her in Russian. Half-asleep, she asked him to translate and he searched the ceiling for the words.

> ". . . We don't know how to say good-bye/ We wander on,
> shoulder to shoulder . . .
> Let us sit in the graveyard on trampled snow, sighing
> to each other.
> This stick in your hand is tracing mansions in which we
> will always be together . . ."

"That's beautiful," she said. "Is it Pushkin?"

"That is Akhmatova. Now sleep, my Ana. Sleep."

PALAI

To Turn Away in Confusion

HE COUGHED SLIGHTLY, THEN TURNED TO SHAKE HANDS WITH people entering the room. Some folks looked apprehensive. They had heard a Russian would address them and half expected a great, shaggy bear risen up on its hind legs. As he bent over his notes Ana studied him. A man who slept sitting at a window, one who loved poetry but ate with his mouth open. Sometimes he forgot to change his socks.

Tonight he was wearing a shirt so bright it seemed as though objects could bounce off of it. She saw he was nervous by the veins in his neck, the way his heart made his shirt vibrate. She watched him shake Lopaka's hand, his overeagerness. Next to the Russian's big, scarred paws, her cousin's hands looked new, unused.

Folks had come from up and down the coast, even neighbors from Keola Road. Ana's family came, the smell of grief still clinging to Rosie, heady and unnatural. She still played dead for days. Some nights she sat with the moon cupped in her palms, her arms enmeshed in darkness. Grief gave her license to withdraw. And silence gave her eloquence; she sat amongst them like a priestess.

Now Gena Mele moved to Ana's side. "Sly mongoose! Imagine you with a Russian."

Lopaka stood, scanned the room, then tapped the mike. "Okay, folks. You know who I am. You all know we're here tonight to support Mālama Mākua, and other groups whose aim is to end military bombing of the valley and its beaches, and to demand return of the valley to the people. This is not just for cultural reasons. We're fighting for our lives.

And, we've also gathered here to show support for people across the Pacific."

He pointed to half a dozen men and women in the front row.

"Our brothers and sisters from French Polynesia, from Kwajelein and Rongelap in the Marshalls. And our Aborigine brothers from Australia. They want to tell you what has happened to their islands and their people."

Finally, he acknowledged Niki. "Before I present our guest speakers and get embroiled in debates, I want to introduce Nikolai Volenko, from Russia."

Niki stood, then confused, sat down.

"Mr. Volenko is a documentary filmmaker. For several years he's been shooting footage all over the Pacific, of average people like you and me. People sick, their children sick. Today he will show you footage of his *own* country, whole villages of people suffering and dying. Think of what you are going to see as a warning, of what could happen here."

Polite applause as Niki approached the mike. "My English . . . not so good . . . forgive me . . ."

Folks leaned forward, encouraging him, and in that moment, Ana forgot his loud shirt, his worn-out pants. She forgot how he ate with his head over his plate like a hungry dog. In that moment—his voice slightly rattly, his face tense with the effort not to cough—she wanted to stand beside him and take his hand.

His mouth worked furiously as he struggled to articulate.

"We were always poor people. Real Russia is mostly peasants, farmers . . . not demonstrating Muscovites you see on TV. In hundreds of villages across Russia, they never hear of such a thing as dial tone. Do not know what is a zipper. But! Long ago our forests were *magnificent*, going on for miles . . . our soil dark and fertile. Great herds of wildlife roamed our lands, we hear their thundering for days. We called our rivers 'the sea' because they were so endless, crystal clear and full of fish."

He paused, looking out at individual faces. His English had improved dramatically. Ana suspected it was because, for Niki, English was a language without memory. It did not hold his past.

"So. I want to show you . . . what is Russia now. What was done to us. Please, pay attention."

Lights dimmed. The tape began as he narrated slowly, allowing images to inscribe themselves. Towns where everything was black—people, even sheep. Coal towns, steel towns. Towns where humans resembled something else.

His deep, bass voice resounded. "From Vilnius to Vladivostok, over eight million square miles . . . now mostly environmental horror. Even seas are poisoned. Even Arctic Ocean. Death is now exceeding births in Russia by over one million each year."

The camera froze on a sweet-faced boy squatting on his haunches. He was ten or twelve, his gaze off center of the camera.

"Victim of food-chain contamination. Chemicals from river leached into the soil. His sin? Eating produce from his father's field. Now, re-tarded. Friends call him 'firefly' because at night he glows."

Niki cleared his throat. "Forgive me if you have been offended. All you have seen is true."

Lights came on. Men placed their elbows on their knees and held their heads between their hands. A mother rocked her child and wept.

Later, a woman named Reiata Huahine rose and talked about her is-lands of Tahiti and the Tuamotus in French Polynesia, and how the French government's bomb testing had damaged many of her people. Since the 1960s children as young as ten and twelve had been conscripted to work at test sites and never given protective clothes. When they began to die, their bodies were so contaminated they were buried in lead coffins. Then the coffins disappeared. They were flown to France for research.

Her voice was deep and strong, like a beautiful wailer. Yet she kept it controlled, her emotions in check.

"Our lagoons are irradiated, our coral dying, we are afraid to eat our fish, to nurse our children. And France will not even give us back our dead."

She was stout, big-hipped and beautiful, with the bronze skin and broad features of Tahitians and Hawaiians. Even the two languages were similar. The earliest settlers to Hawai'i had migrated north from Tahiti, the Tuamotus, and the Marquesas. These were Ana's closest Pacific cousins, yet she had never been curious about their customs and their Mother Tongue, so similar to hers. She had never longed to see Tahiti.

Later, several Aborigines spoke of how their people were still being "monitored" by the British and Australians from the effects of atomic bombs set off at Monte Bello, Western Australia, in 1952, and in the Great Victoria Desert of Australia in 1953.

"Nobody warned us. They just exploded the bloody bombs. Thou-sands of our clans were out there living in the desert."

Only in 1985 did the British government publicly admit that such tests resulted in radioactive fallout that rained down on them for miles.

"And how did they apologize? With subsidies, and *deep indifference.*

And still we are forced to live within the hazard zone of nuclear-support facilities. Uranium dug up from our sacred lands is still used in nuclear warheads."

By the time the Marshall Islanders got up to speak of the atomic and hydrogen bomb tests at Bikini and Eniwetok in the 1940s and '50s, and how—shifted from island to island—they came to be known as "nuclear nomads," Ana was overwhelmed with anger and grief.

Later, she talked to Reiata Huahine, a doctor herself, an internist. She asked about Ana's practice, why it had taken her so long to start her fellowship in OB-GYN.

"I was sick for a while. Then . . . a death in the family. Practicing as general physician allowed me to function by rote."

"Sometimes we need such pauses, to catch up with ourselves," the woman said. "But you will find great fulfillment in your chosen field. Nothing is more mysterious or exhilarating than the machinations of the female anatomy. And nothing is more tragic than when that system fails, or is invaded."

Ana spoke of a plan slowly forming in her mind: to one day open a women's clinic on the coast. "A healing place for birthing and nurturing. I want midwives, licensed doctors, and *kahuna la'au lapa'au*. Ancient and modern medicine. So women will have a choice."

AFTER THE CONFERENCE, NIKI MADE PLANS TO RETURN TO TAHITI, wanting footage of demonstrations taking place in Papeete, capital city, as Tahitians challenged France's plans to resume bomb testing.

"Please come, Ana! I invite you. You will see how I make film."

She wanted to go, she thought she did. "I'm sorry, Niki. I can't."

His voice changed, sounding almost challenging. "Ana. Can it be you are afraid?"

"Of course not. I flew to Kaua'i for the hurricane."

"And that is the only place you ever been. Only time you stepped off this island. Perhaps you are afraid of newness? Afraid to . . . expand?"

Her voice turned ugly and dismissive. "Well, cancer was pretty new. I think I *expanded* somewhat there."

He stood in shock, then turned and left, quietly closing her door.

WHILE HE WAS GONE, SHE THOUGHT OF HOW, AFTER THE FIRST time they made love, she had felt unscarred, desired, even cherished.

She had felt passion. But he was not an average man, not average anything. She saw him as a kind of scavenger, so warped by his past he had no context for normality. What was cancer to this man, a woman's mutilated chest, after what he had lived through?

She thought of his dark, haunted eyes. Of all she did not know about him. The scars he never talked about. She thought of his laughter in unguarded moments. Deep belly laughs like a child, and how in sleep he enfolded her, like a fragile teacup in his big hands.

She tossed back and forth, remembering a day they had toured downtown Honolulu, and how they found themselves in front of the police station. Standing there, she had told him again of her young father dying in the line of duty. Then, abruptly, on a busy street, Ana broke down.

"My father. I don't even know where he's buried."

She had cried so hard, protracted sobs shook her body. Niki surrounded her with his arms, holding her head against his chest, whispering in Russian.

"... *fortushka* . . . *fortushka* . . ." a word sounding soulful and extravagant.

Then, almost desperately, he had guided her to a small park, sat her on the grass, and rocked her back and forth.

"Cry, Ana. Cry. It is a way of honoring your father. We will find his grave. We will take flowers."

He had whispered that word again in Russian and as she calmed down, he slipped back into English, trying to distract her, talking with his head, his hands. Unfolding a tissue, he carefully wiped her nose, then dug deep into her shoulder bag.

"Let us see. Let us see."

Finally he had pulled out her hairbrush with a wide, blue, plastic handle. He held the handle to his eyes.

"Look, Ana. Such magic! All becomes Monet. Yellow street sign is melting green. Clouds now are violet. How beautiful it is."

He put the plastic handle to her eyes and it was like seeing the world through a rainbow lens, everything washed in pastels. She looked at trees, a passing car, a little wild-haired man in slippers. Through the plastic handle, refracted light was broken so that palm trees looked like exploding blue cigars, the car a purple tuna floating by. The little man approached, a bouncing gingerroot of pinks and greens.

Niki had twisted the handle, further distorting things. The gingerroot man waved as he passed by; through the blue handle his hair became green flames. Ana laughed out loud. They had sat like that for hours, holding the handle to each other's eyes, exclaiming like children at a world eclipsed into a fabulous lunacy.

Walking home at dusk, Niki had kept his arm round her shoulder protectively. "Remember, Ana. Even when grief tears us apart so we want to die, there is always something left that soldiers on. Some human rag of hope, of heart, imagination. Look. Today a hairbrush made us happy!"

Her hand inside her bag held tight to the blue handle. "Tell me, what does that word . . . *fortushka* mean?"

"It is pastry filled with chocolate. Very sweet."

Then he stood still. "Forgive me. That is a lie. In Russia, farmers huddle in houses through long Arctic winters, very little air. No one dare open window or door. Outside, humans freeze to death in fifteen seconds. So, tiny, trap windows are built, only one inch square, through which people can breathe fresh air. The little window, that is *fortushka*."

"But why did you say it to me?"

He glanced away, embarrassed. "You were suffering. I want to take away the pain. Make you breathe, feel life again. I want to be your . . . *fortushka*."

Now she lay sleepless, thinking of this man wandering the Pacific. Perhaps he had always been a wanderer because he had no notion of what it was to come to rest. Later, she got up in the dark and rummaged in her bag, and fell asleep holding the brush with the blue handle.

ONE NIGHT SHE WATCHED NIKI'S TAPES ON THE FALL OF THE So-viet Union. An old survivor of the *gulags* talked about Russia's history, how for centuries they were serfs, then with Bolshevism they were freed, to be murdered in the tens of millions. Those not executed in the *lags* had rarely survived Siberian winters.

"How can outsiders know what we have suffered? How can they know what is mass famine in country this size? And so you call us backwards. Cynical and fatalistic. You laugh because we still eat with our hands . . ."

She watched soldiers on Soviet tanks moving into Moscow, prepared to shoot down Russians fighting for democracy. Then, as if in slow motion, the soldiers lowered their rifles, handing them over to the crowds. She watched as they helped old *babushki* climb up on the tanks and ride them down boulevards into Red Square. Standing beside the young soldiers, while huge crowds cheered, the *babushki* did not cry or wave triumphantly. In their leathery faces there was only exhaustion, resolve, a final calm that surpassed all understanding.

Ana replayed that footage again and again, wondering how she could even begin to understand such a country, its history, what its people had endured. How could she compare her tiny islands to such vastness? If she could not comprehend the country, how could she ever understand the man?

AIA NO I KE KO A KE AU

Time Will Tell

HE DID NOT CALL WHEN HE RETURNED FROM PAPEETE.

"He feels you need breathing space," Lopaka said, then laughed. "Also, he needs to do his laundry. I said we have a washer, but Niki said, 'A*'ole pilikia*. Not problem! Not problem!' "

He had no phone and so she went to Chinatown to his hotel. The deskman showed her the stairway to the laundry room. Down a long basement corridor of cement blocks she saw him, a slouched-over man wearing a sleeveless undershirt and rumpled pants, framed by a lavender-painted doorway. A naked bulb shone down on his shoulders, making his ears look translucent and vulnerable.

The iron was chained through its handle to the wall, the chain just long enough to allow its movements back and forth across the ironing board. As Ana watched, Niki took a mouthful of water from a glass, bent and spat the water out in a spray across a shirt, then pointed the iron carefully and slid it back and forth.

She didn't move. She couldn't. It was like a scene from a penal colony. Naked cement walls, a bare bulb hanging, a man's movements restricted by a chain connected to a wall. And there was something heartbreaking in the caring way he ironed, inspecting each crease. Something touchingly maternal in the way he held the shirt up to the light, then carefully arranged it on a hanger.

She backed up slowly, afraid he would look up and see her watching him. She left a note at the desk, asking him to call her. Ana did not know what she felt. She knew you could miss someone without loving them. You could miss their conversation and humor, or just the animal comfort of being with another human. You could feel affection for someone because they needed to be rescued, or needed to be healed. She did not think that constituted deep abiding love between a woman and a man.

They sat in a Japanese restaurant and he struggled with his chopsticks, poked at a slice of squid, then bent and wolfed it down. They drank sake, and as it slid down her throat and warmed her ribs, she felt herself relax. Niki's trip had left him looking thinner. But he smelled fresh and clean and his shirt was meticulous, so starched it looked as if it could stand up by itself. He sat back and smiled, in that moment he was almost handsome.

"Ana. It is so good to see you. I have much to tell you. But, slowly. I will build it up in increments."

She played with her napkin. "Look, before anything, I want to apologize. I was rude the day you left. I'm sorry."

He waved his hand. "No, no. I was the rude one. Who am I to tell you how to live?"

"But you were right. I *am* afraid to travel, to expand. I hide behind my work and get so tense I almost choked a patient."

He looked concerned. "But now? You are all right?"

"In a support group. For anger management."

"Good. Good. A doctor's life is stressful. You need to decompose."

She thought he meant decompress.

"I watched some of your tapes, Niki. I was stunned. You have such an important film here. A real indictment. I think it should be shown in every country in the world."

He looked down, touched. "Yes . . . I hope. Only, there is one more segment, very important. Then I start final editing. My God, it's long. It will have to be shown in several segments."

He coughed slightly and shook his head. "You have no idea what I have gathered . . . almost two thousand still photographs, one thousand pieces of archival footage, several hundred interviews . . . doctors, scientists, environmentalists. Even military personnel. Plus, there is narration, voice-overs to be read by professionals. God knows, we cannot use my voice. It will be exhausting work. Could take one year. Three years . . . depends on funding."

"How can I help you? What can I do?"

"Just to talk with you is good. Soon I need to bear down, really focus. As long as health holds out . . ."

"Tell me, how are you feeling?"

He shrugged. "No appetite this trip. Now look, is huge! Soon I will lick my plate, then reach for yours."

"Listen, I want you to come back in for tests. Have you had any colds?"

"First two weeks, I wheezed. Very damp in Tahiti. But those medications you gave me, very good. And now to see you again . . . I feel much better. I missed you, Ana. We have much in common."

She played with her chopsticks, not knowing what to say.

"It's okay. I don't expect . . . I know you are meant for more than some crazy Russky with camera."

"It's not that. It's just, we're very different. I watched that tape on the week Communism fell. Those *babushki* riding on the tanks. I watched interviews with survivors of the *lags*. It was devastating. I wonder why you feel we have so much in common. My people have suffered yes, but our islands are so small. Our biggest struggle is to remain visible. Your Motherland is huge. Your suffering was massive. Tens of millions starved, and murdered. There's no comparison."

He clasped his hands on the table, straining for near-perfect English.

"Ana, Russia is made up of many languages and states, many different cultures. As your Pacific Ocean is made up of different island tongues and cultures. Each is important to the human race. So. Each culture that dies affects each of us."

She started to respond but he put up his hand, explaining how such cultural deaths began with the breakdown of families when they were forced apart, leaving their fields, their homelands, to find work. Then, the taking away of their language. And then their land.

"Fourth, maybe most important," Niki said, "is the taking of religion from the people. Missionaries took your ancient gods, and loaned—*not gave*—you their gods."

He talked about how Stalin closed all churches, turned them into factories, garages. How thousands of Russia's monks and priests were murdered, or starved to death in hiding.

"In late 1980s, priests and monks begin returning to their villages. Churches slowly opened. Icons brought out of hiding. Now people openly worshipping again. Yes, we still starve, but at last we know what *hope* is. Bell-ringing is now revived in churches and cathedrals. This signifies human freedom. They can never again stop bells across Russia. Never!

Even if they stop the bells, our people have heard them ringing. They will move forward, remembering the echo of those bells."

He leaned across the table.

"Ana. Your people are struggling so they will not be wiped out of history. People have also struggled in Latvia, Estonia, Lithuania, many Russian states. What does it matter whether is one small island, one region, or huge continent? Extermination of each unique culture is another death of human conscience."

He took her hand with such force she felt pain.

"*This* is what you and I have in common. This struggle. Look. Who would have thought Communism could be shattered? As long as your people fight back, each step forward is small victory. Hawaiians, too, have heard the bells."

In that moment, so much inside her responded to him she could not speak. She watched him sit back, his face flushed with emotion, and wondered what it would be like to utterly let go, let this big, tender, damaged beast take over and consume her. She thought she might be happy for a while. But what would come after?

ONE DAY HE LEAPT FROM THE SEA LIKE A BOY, THEN DIVED BACK IN and came up shouting, "Hit me! Hit me!"

Waves pounded his chest then dragged him under, and threw him back onto the beach where he lay laughing and exhausted.

"The undertow . . . so strong it pulled me out, but then I thought, 'I cannot drown. Today we have a mission.' We go to visit your father's grave."

On his own, he had researched in library archives, old newspapers, even police records. "You see, Ana, he was buried with great honor. There are even photographs."

He showed her blurred copies of a parade of uniformed police, someone standing at a podium, women with their faces in their hands. One of them could have been her mother.

Later that day, they stood over her father's headstone at Diamond Head Memorial Park. *John Ing Keahi*. She followed the letters with her fingers.

"Ben says he was handsome. After his death his folks moved far away."

"Come." Niki pulled her down beside the grave.

She didn't cry. Instead, she thought of her mother. "I think she loved him. Or, maybe he was her way of paying back her parents. As I told you, they waited sixteen years to tell her who she was. Whose child she was. All that time, she thought her mother was her sister."

Niki shrugged. "Sixteen is not so late. Look how interesting her life became, made deeper by truths it did not have before."

"I don't think she saw it that way. She saw cruelty and lies. She turned her back on them, had me, then ran away."

"Imagine. A simple girl, taking off across the sea. How scared she must have been."

"She was never simple. And probably nothing could ever shock her again. Nothing could be added to her, or taken away."

"Except you. She came back, saw you fighting for your life, and realized how much she love you."

Ana neutralized her voice with a calmness bordering on meditation. "Niki, she doesn't even know me. Probably, she has never loved."

He gazed at her. "You say she never sacrifice, never pay for what she has. How do you know what her life has been in California?"

Ana looked into the distance. "Maybe you're right. When she was here, a great sea of what I didn't know opened up before me. She had been married, then he died. We didn't really talk about it. One thing I learned: Parts of me *are* like my mother. Our childhoods were similar, both abandoned in a way, so we both learned to be survivors. We're both vain. She said women like us don't possess the 'sorry' gene. And, it is hard for us to trust."

"You have trusted me a little."

"Only a little. So much about you puzzles me."

"*Da.* I understand your fear. Depending on another human creates much expectations, very troubling atmosphere."

Ana leaned back on her elbows. "We try so hard *not* to be like our parents. Yet, like my mother, I have gone my own way. Folks have learned to leave me alone. I have my apartment, all the privacy I need. When I want family, I go home to Nanakuli. Maybe I'll just spend my life observing, taking stock of other humans."

"This would be a tragic thing."

"Why? I'm achieving what I set out to achieve. I've regained my health. I've never felt so balanced in my life."

"Yes, Ana. You are truly admirable. I think everyone would like to have their lives so under control as you."

She looked to see if he was joking, but he seemed earnest.

"I had to earn that control, Niki. When they first told me I had can-

cer, the only relief I found was lying awake at night planning my suicide."

"Stop, please!" he cried. "Don't you understand what life is? Just
being is a miracle, a gift."

He pulled her down so they lay side by side, looking at the sky. After
a while he began to sing an old Russian song about a broken soldier coming home from war. As he sang, he translated it for her.

". . . *His family dead. His home blown up. His fields and livestock gone.
Everything he love is gone. He is so weary. He puts rifle in his mouth, wanting to end it. Then it begins to rain . . . He sees something on ground in front
of him, one single leaf on dead plant. Then he sees leaf move. Sees it slowly
turn its underside up to receive this rain. He puts his rifle down . . ."*

He fell silent, then he sang another song, his voice sounding so sentimental she thought of a picturesque drunk poised, hand to his heart,
under a balcony. Still, Ana would recall that day in detail, Niki beside
her at her father's grave, their heads pressed together, the sky going on
and on above them until, where the earth curved, the sky touched the
tips of Niki's shoes tied with broken laces. She would recall his voice
floating out among the dead, telling them they were remembered.

That night they were so full of emotion, at first they lay still. Then
he leaned up in the dark and kissed her shoulder, her breast, and then
her scars. He moved down and kissed her belly, and laid his face there as
if listening for a code. His face tipped down. His tongue gently probed
then slid inside her, moving back and forth, so little satellites exploded
in her brain. A radiance ran down her spine.

She moaned, and grasped his head with both hands and he kept
probing with his tongue, as if there were something inside her he must
find, something that would give him answers. Her moans became protracted until she shouted out. Finally, Niki reared up on his knees, and
laid his chest warm on hers, letting their skin experience the static poem
of texture, rough and smooth, dark and light, the minor symphony of
sound, skin rubbing skin. The miracle of that skin expanding and con-
tracting, fever-flushed, then chilled.

Then Ana reached down and gently wrapped her hand around him,
guiding him. The outline of his shoulders hunched in concentration as
he lowered himself down farther and, moving gently, found his way. Her
legs went up around his chest, she arched her back, then pulled him
closer.

"Niki."

His hands under her buttocks, he moved inside her until he was deep as he could be. They slowed down then, rocking back and forth in rhythm while he crooned softly, memorializing this moment, him and her, and this, and this, and nothing more. His pace changed, quickening, and Ana clung to him, feeling the sudden cataracts, the spasms. Then he was shouting, his words seeming to run ahead of him.

"I am yours. I am so very yours."

Now she felt self-conscious and vulnerable, and so she was relieved when he left for the coast to spend time with Gena and Lopaka. They drove him to strategic points from which he shot footage of armed military guards, electrified fences surrounding arsenals in the hills of Lualualei. He went deep into Mākua Valley, dodging military patrols, shooting sites of ancient *heiau*, sacred land transmogrified into cratered holes in shocked, parched earth. He shot footage of live bombs—unexploded ordnance lying in the woods—waiting to blow up in the hands of scavenging children.

He returned to Honolulu exhausted, and Ana took him home, laundering his clothes while he slept. She bought new laces for his shoes, then changed her mind and bought him new shoes. She reversed a fraying collar on a shirt. When they made love again, she identified what she felt as passion and affection, nothing more.

ANAHOLA

Time in a Glass

NIGHT AUGURING TOWARD DAWN, THE SKY PART FLESH. THE BAY A great kettle seething with fog. It is a view she cherishes, in a city she has come to love. At night, hills round the bay glitter like coals of fiery lava flung into the wind. Then dawn extinguishes the coals, the gray fog lifts. The bay, a prismed diamond.

She always wakes at this hour, an hour that takes solitude to its purest extreme. A dreamlike time where she feels, but does not quite acknowledge, the cold, ethereal strangeness of being palpably alone. She has been alone for years now, has tasted solitude to the dregs. And maybe that will be her fate. Still, she finds joy in her work, and in travel. The going and doing, the convulsive motion, the courage to want to penetrate life—break out of one's living shell—that is still the challenge.

Sometimes she enters Max's rooms, each thing untouched, the same. Silk scarves with hand-stitched labels, "A. *Sulka, 2 Rue de Castiglione, Paris,*" embroidered on them in cursive. Cashmere sweaters retaining the scent of his cologne. She holds a sweater to her face. And it's all right, it is enough to have been loved so well, and to remember.

Now she wraps her body in an amber-palmed kimono, then brushes her dark hair, the middle part covertly gray. She sits down, inclines her head, and tries to begin a letter. There are nights when she has called her daughter on the phone, but such conversations leave her stranded. She does all the talking, Ana merely listens. She prefers writing letters, letting the blank page before her silently instruct her. She has discovered that certain things remain unknown to her until she writes them down.

In that way, she sees what she has chosen to omit. Which is equally revealing.

Sometimes Anahola writes through an entire night. What matter if she misses a night's sleep? She is alone now, she can do anything she wants. In that sense, she is still who she always was—a rather self-indulgent woman, but one with ambition, a curiosity about the larger world, the knowledge that each moment is her life.

Yet, some shift in attitude has taken place within her. Max's words keep haunting her. *What good are life's experiences if we don't pass them on to our children?* Now when she writes to Ana, she is someone she has never imagined—a mother, trying to give motherly advice. Sometimes she wonders, is she saying too much? Offering too much? She tries not to sound too candid or too blunt, not wanting to remind the girl, ". . . you are part of me, like it or not."

Midsentence she leans back, closes her eyes, and prays. That God will look down on her daughter, see that she has paid enough, been tested enough, and will leave her alone. Then she broods over the letter. It is always an exhausting task. Profound exertion in the writing, and rewriting, and then the anguish of wondering how it is received. For they are never answered, not one in over thirty years.

> "My dear Ana,
>
> I recently heard from Rosie that you have passed the six-year mark and remain cancer-free. I cannot describe how happy this news makes me . . .
>
> I am doubly grateful for your recovery because you have so much to do in life. Important tasks to accomplish that will give dignity to our people. Rosie writes me of your plans to one day open a women's clinic on the coast. I am so very proud of you. I will help you in any way I can . . .
>
> I'm sorry we could not see each other on my recent trip to Honolulu. I understand how busy you are. You may have heard that I returned for my mother, Malia's, funeral. I had not seen her or my father since before you were born. It seems my mother died out of vanity. Her teeth were old and stained. She wanted a perfect smile, perfect dentures, and so she had all of her teeth pulled, a drastic step for a woman her age. Something went wrong. She bled to death in her sleep . . .
>
> At the funeral, my father did not know me. Then he did. What's

left is just a sad old man. He's almost eighty now, still big but stooped. He said he tried to visit you at Uncle Ben's when you were growing up, but you would not see him. Probably you were afraid. Of course, my mother never tried to see you. While we talked my father cried . . .

I believe he always loved me. But he was weak, deferred to her, and let me go. And now he asks my forgiveness—this old man who seems a child. As if I have become the parent. This is how life tricks us. This is how we become kind. Perhaps you're wondering why I'm telling you these things. Because he is your kupuna kane, your grandfather. And he would like to know you, know all that you have become. And, though this knowledge comes so late, I would like you to know whose grandchild you are . . .

Ana, you are now outpacing me, experiencing things in life that I may never know. I have little left to offer you, except the knowledge that there are stories we must tell and years when we must tell them. And there are years when we must listen. I know you blame yourself for Makali'i's death. Perhaps you are part guilty, as we all are. As I was guilty of leaving you. In trying to survive, we make mistakes. Yet, I believe each human is worth more than their worst act. Each life is part tragedy, part riddle . . .

For now I will tell you three things I have learned. One, is that we must never get too nostalgic for childhood, because usually it's the childhood we never had. Secondly, I believe the most important thing you can ever accomplish is to know who you are. What you want. The world will always step aside for a woman who knows where she's going . . .

Lastly, I repeat what I said at the airport the last time I saw you. Live, Ana. Let love in. Let it all in before it's gone, because each thing in our lives is stolen gradually and silently. It is the natural course of things. Please remember I am here for you. I will always be here, offering my love.

Your mother, Anahola

Ana glanced at the handwriting on the envelope. In the past few years, the letters began to arrive more frequently. The woman had no husband now, maybe she wrote these letters in order to exist more convincingly.

Through the years she had tried but could never *not* read her mother's letters, could never entirely turn her back on her, perhaps out of curiosity mingled with awe. She still wrote on thick, expensive stationery on which her perfume lingered and haunted. Five thousand miles away, and she still *announced* her presence.

Ana skimmed over the letter, then got up and made a drink, remembering the adolescent years when she had hated the woman. When she had hate to burn. *What happened to that hate?* Perhaps she had come to see her mother as a free pass: no one could judge Ana too harshly because she had been abandoned as a child. In return, her hate had matured into a wariness and deep resentment.

She read the letter again, more carefully, picturing Anahola approaching her father, whom she had not seen in over thirty years. Ana felt she was looking in on such a private moment, she closed her eyes imagining her mother as a young girl, unloved, and banished to an arid coast. *What would it be like to be so reduced? To have so little left?*

For years she had wondered, by what genetic predisposition, what skid marks on her DNA, her mother had been able to abandon *her* in return, to exempt herself from moral responsibility. But then Ana thought how, through the years, each letter served to remind her that she had never actually felt the absence of the woman's love, only of her presence. She would never quite understand her, would always be somewhat intimidated by her. Still, this woman had a claim on her. *She's in my blood. She* is *my blood.*

Ana folded the letter, and sighed. In the dark, a soft breeze buffeted her shoulders and her cheeks. Tides in her body shifted. Something accumulated in her veins and in her nerves. She thought of her mother's recent visit and how Ana had scrupulously avoided her. Avoided introducing her to Niki. She imagined how her mother would have silently appraised him—his shabby clothes, imperfect English—with inscrutable reserve. How, with a glance, she would have diminished him.

Which, somehow, would diminish me.

NĀ MEAHUNA O KA PUʻUWAI PŌLOLI

Secrets of the Hungry Heart

Now THERE WERE NIGHTS WHEN HE SAT UP FIGHTING FOR BREATH, a distinct rattle in his inhalations. On such nights she gathered him to her like a child, wanting to drag him into her lungs and breathe for him. Wanting to rescue him, and heal him. One night they sat like that till dawn. And, feeling the profound beneficence of her arms, Niki began to talk.

"I have said that if I told you everything, you would want to shoot me out of kindness. But now, whatever happens, I want you to know who is this man who loves you . . . I did not tell you about Irini, my first love. A circus girl from the region of Kazakhstan. She came from one of the villages I filmed and, like many of these children, she was born deaf. Even now I wonder how can aerialist be deaf? Hearing controls our balance."

He described how he had first seen Irini at the Moscow Circus, a small, exquisite creature glittering above the crowds.

"It may be she relied on something else for balance. Maybe molecules in the air. Maybe ancient gods, for she soared like an angel."

"How long were you together?" Ana asked.

"One moment. Forever. Who can measure such things? Irini was my wife. Now, I will tell you how she died. Come close. Put your head here on my chest and close your eyes."

His voice low, Niki recounted in great detail how they had fallen in love and married. And how he gave up his life of "roofing" and filming so Irini could continue traveling with the circus, soaring above the crowds who loved her. How he had worked odd jobs, even as a clown, to be with her. He spoke of their passion together—life lived in pantomine. And how they had dreamed and hoped—a child, one day a little house.

"Now I understand that those dear moments of wishing, planning, hoping . . . that is the happiness."

He described her cough, how she had miscarried their child, and how in time they were forced to leave the circus. Sawdust had infected her weak lungs. He recounted the night of the honeybees, the "little winged prophets," how they flew in through a window and settled in Irini's hair.

"I remember their glittering wings, her hair full of tiny stars of midnight blue. I knew then, she would die. In one cloud, they flew away and took her soul."

In the stillness Ana heard herself swallow.

"One winter day she could no more eat, no more breathe. So thin, she seems transparent. Such pain, she beg me take her life, and make it mine."

He explained about hospitals in Russia then, live patients disappearing, the human-organ ghouls. He would not let this happen to Irini. And so he had carried her to a field blanketed in snow. He had undressed her and laid her naked there.

"I kneel and sing old circus songs to her. For this she smiles, then very slowly she turns blue. My tears drop down, turn to crystals on her chest. Then I build a fire. I carry Irini there and gently feed her childlike limbs to flames. And I watch over her, a day, a night, until she is just smoke and wind that soars. She will always soar . . ."

He turned to Ana, his face devoid of emotion.

"Maybe then I died. I do not know. But after many months, I decide to live again. To look at life again, try to record it. So I have continued. For her. For you. For some kind of human future."

For days Ana moved in a kind of stupor, images of the girl, Irini, haunting her. She wondered how Niki had survived such loss, how he had carried on.

SHE BEGAN TO BE AWARE OF TIME. HIS YEAR AT THE EAST-WEST Center would soon end. He would have to return to Russia. He grew less active, more reflective. One night he sat her down again.

"Forgive me if my story made you sad. Time blunts pain. We live again, learn to feel again. I have given this much thought. And what I think is this: Each of us has one love in our life that haunts us. One love that died, or one that walked away, because love was not possible. I used to wonder, what is the good of this? Why have emotions at all if we are crushed so terribly? Now I think there is good reason for this love that breaks us. It teaches us humility, makes us better humans, preparing us for who comes next."

She sat quiet, thinking of Lopaka.

"Why I am saying this? Because Irini's death prepared me for you. It taught me deep humility, I see that now. So, Ana, whatever happens, there is something more I need to tell you."

She took him by the shoulders. "Niki. Nothing is going to happen. You're going to get well and live. What are you making this film for, if not for your future. For all our futures."

"But just in case . . . I need to tell you something more."

"What more?"

"I need to confess that . . . I am serious liar. Very Russian thing. We lie in order to survive. For us, this is an art. After Irini, I became pathological liar. Was thrilling! Bending reality to implausible extremes. Each day new life, new name. Was better than old days of gangsterhood."

He took her hands and squeezed them. "Do you understand? Telling lies brought back sensation to my nerve ends. Feelings of euphoria, like drugs. I was this new man, born of lies, then topping them with better lies! Look. Even, I am here at East-West Center as a hoax, a lie."

She leaned back slightly. "You mean the things you told me, things you said while we made love . . ."

"No, Ana! All of that is true. I did not lie in my deep feelings for you. Or what I told you of Irini's death. But much of the rest . . . my mother was not celebrated actress. My poor father, not decorated hero of the war. Please listen. Let me say the truth, so you will know.

"When World War II begins my mother was a nurse. But with this strange, asymmetrical face. One eye lower, one nostril lower. Like two mismatched halves from strangers. When wounded soldiers see her face, they faint, thinking death has come. Doctors banish her from hospital. During Siege of Leningrad, nine hundred days of bombing by Germans, she was sent to Street Services Corps, dodging bombs, running errands back and forth across city. Running bandages and blood, even food to basement of Hermitage Museum . . .

"This the way how she met my father, who was carpenter. Poor peasant, his feet so flat he walked on insides of his ankles. Could not march, could not fit in military boots. So. Army train him to build artificial artillery to fool German spy planes. With planks, plywood, papier-mâché, he and hundreds of carpenters build warships, tanks, painting them gray. They build wooden heads and painted faces and stand them up in 'tanks.' They build entire artificial battle scenes. From the air such battles, tanks, and ships look *real*. Our armies and artilleries look massive. That's the way how we saved our city from Germans. With magic! And so my father *was* hero in a way . . ."

He told Ana how one day on the street, his mother was wounded by flying shrapnel, and how his father dragged her into the basement of the Hermitage Museum. He had been sent there to help build wooden crates, for here were hundreds of curators and restorers hiding priceless works of art. And so Niki's mother stayed there with her bandaged leg. They lived by candlelight.

"And it may be that in such flickering light, bombs exploding around them, my mother becomes beautiful. Maybe in her face, my father sees his feet. This allows them their humanity. And so they fall in love midst Rembrandts, Tintorettos, starving curators eating glue from bottles, eating their own shoes. In basement of Hermitage they begin to stack the dead. When my father goes back to build more artificial tanks along Neva River, my mother follows him . . .

"This is their true story, swear to God! A nurse whose face could kill wounded soldiers. A carpenter who built toy tanks to fight a war. But even then—where tens of thousands perished from starvation, food supplies cut off, coldest winter in two hundred years—even then, there was sorrowful majesty and beauty . . ."

Niki took Ana's hands.

"Imagine fabled onion-domed cathedrals. The Hermitage, and Winter Palace, bombed but still intact. This fairy-tale city covered in ice, then snow, then upon that, ice again. A city so cold and deep in ice, it glows. Like Japanese vase that glows from depths of eighteen layers of resin . . .

"Leningrad. People so weak they dump refuse and excrement from shattered windows. Buildings became streaked with mounds of waste frozen down their sides. In time, new snow covers this awful slop so it becomes like ruffles of frosting on gigantic cake. Buildings now blurred and lost their edges. Great city floated like a dream. Then light hit ice covering the snow, and all of Leningrad turned blue! . . ."

He described how humans grew pale, transparent, so they too turned greenish blue. How they dragged sleds with pots and pans, searching for water, and even these turned blue. Immobilized streetcars, buses stood like blue whales, cast ashore in snowdrifts. At night when the full moon shone on the Neva River, the Winter Palace, former home of the Tsars, and the Hermitage, their beautiful museum, all stood intact on the river's embankment, snowed under, frozen blue. Like a mythical sleeping dragon.

"Most ghostly were huge battleships immobilized in ice on frozen Neva. Real Russian battleships, not my father's cardboard toys. Summer so short, nothing thawed. They sat for three years, moaning like prehistoric monsters. People beside them, stabbing at ice for water, their dying cries echoing like choruses. Even light round those ships was choral . . ."

As if stepping from a dream, Ana gently interrupted him. "But, Niki, you weren't born yet. How do you remember all of this?"

He shrugged. "Ah, but life does not just stop and start, it is a thing in continuity, always in progression, no? I *was* there, in my parents' genes.

"I watched through my mother's eyes as she ran through burning streets, dodging bombs and shrapnel. I felt broken glass and rubble underfoot. I remember coldness of the nails my father hammered into wood, making artificial tanks. I see mouths emerging as he painted faces on dummy soldiers, using his own blood to rouge their cheeks, glittering light from frozen Neva almost blinding him . . .

"And I remember city was grisly, cut off from the world. Germans had surrounded us. For three years no one did bathe—scurvy, typhus everywhere. And horrible hunger. All pets, even rodents, disappeared. The starving eyed the newly dead, tender-fleshed corpses of children . . ."

Niki glanced at her, then lowered his eyes.

"Yes, Ana, there was this man with red shawl who bargained with my mother. Yes, I dream of him. There were many men with shawls, full of the unspeakable. People dragged themselves to barter at place called Hungry Market. Here were 'sausages,' 'meat patties' sold by pink-cheeked, bright-eyed vendors. Yes, one does such things to live . . ."

Then one day they heard sirens. Russian soldiers came on tanks. After three years, the Germans had withdrawn, defeated. Niki explained how it was almost too late. Leningrad was an open grave. People had no flesh, neither the dead nor the living.

"This what I remember, blinking skulls, walking sticks. Nonetheless, they thought they had survived, my father and mother. That they would have future together. Now carpenters were ordered to tear down all artificial wooden ships and tanks, and burn them. My father was carpenter, yes, but great lover of trees. One day he carelessly passed judgment. All trees they had felled for lumber for toy tanks, toy soldiers, were a waste, he said. 'Tragic waste.' These two words sentence him to death. He was denounced as traitor. Dangerous subversive. Stalin's paranoia killed more millions than Germans ever did. . . ."

Niki bent forward, shaking his head.

"They sent my father to nightmare place up near Barents Sea, below Arctic circle. A *gulag* called Archangel'sk. Stalin already sent two million *kulaks* here to die. Though west of Ural Mountains, was bleak, forbidding as Siberia . . .

"At Archangel'sk, armed guards dragged prisoners to woods where stood great stands of fir and pine. Each day, chained men were forced to chop them down. In time, whole forests disappeared. Men died from starvation, beatings, horrible disease . . ."

He spoke more slowly now.

"After his sentencing . . . my poor mother, Vera, she follows my father, Sergeivitch, from war-torn Leningrad to this place, Archangel'sk. Ana . . . how I can explain such incredible journey? Thousands of war wives—wounded, crippled, tubercular—dragging selves across the land, following condemned husbands. Across *taiga* and *tundra*, through great virgin forests. Through Vytegra, Savinskiy, Novodvinsk. They trudge through ravaged towns, mined fields, till half of them were dead. This journey taking over one, two years."

Niki recounted how, in time, his mother had found his father in chains, in the forest, chopping trees. How they had made love beneath giant firs, and that was how he was conceived. He never knew his father. What he remembered most indelibly from those years were the women who rubbed bear grease on his cheeks and taught him how to hunt and trap.

"They were like Goths, so fearless! But when they learn their husbands have perished in the camp, they give up . . . lie down and turn to logs. Or they step out into arctic winds. Some nights I smell these women in my sleep. I hear their hunter heartbeats. I see them frozen into standing blocks of ice."

While Niki talked, Ana had covered her face with her hands, and shook her head, disbelieving.

"So, Ana, this was my birthplace, and it was my father's grave. Starving humans dragging their chains. Guard dogs sporting with a corpse. Yet it is where I believe I have never felt so safe, so cherished."

He fell silent for a while. Then finally, he described the two-year struggle back to Leningrad and how, so young, he watched his mother taken as Stalin purged cities of the wounded and deformed.

"But I was clever. I survived. You see, long before Irini I learned how lies were my salvation."

THAT NIGHT ANA LAY SLEEPLESS. SHE FELT PHYSICAL PAIN, FELT slightly beaten-up by Niki's stories. Her heart hurt for him. She wanted to reach out and somehow heal him, but she was not equipped for such a task. She wondered what a man like this would ultimately ask of life, of a woman who shared his life. He would probably ask too much. He would take her hostage. Knowing he would soon return to Russia, she felt a deep sense of remorse, and yet relief, already imagining her days filled with the quietude his absence would create.

MIHI

Remorse

THE RADIOLOGIST WAS BALDING, A CENTRAL STRAND OF PEWTER hair. He held X-rays to the light, trying to be tactful, but seemed handicapped by a congenital brusqueness.

"See these small cavities in his lungs? From toxic invasions. Without proper treatment, he could become susceptible to viruses, bacilli, even pulmonary edema . . ."

She studied the X-rays. "What else?"

"Well, his liver . . . typical Russian. Years of oversmoking, overdrinking. And I would say he's borderline anemic. You want the rest?"

Her heart turned.

"His immune system is weak. White cells aren't reproducing fast enough. Soon they'll be too low to fight off infections."

"Is there any good news?"

"Amazingly, he's got the constitution of a bull. I'm not saying he's dying, but he could begin to fail if he's not looked after."

He saw the expression on her face. "I've seen much worse. Toxic-exposure victims, radiation, people so polluted, or fried, they have no immune system left. Your friend is not that bad. He could recover."

"What exactly does he need?"

"Rest. Clean air. Diuretics to draw the fluids from his lungs. AZT or Interleukin to build up his white cells. Iron supplements, calcium. Fresh fruits, vegetables. Beef, liver, leeks. And he needs to check in for a complete workup, and to review his medications."

"He has no medical insurance."

"It could be done on an outpatient basis. Still, it would be expensive."

Ana gazed out the window. "He was on a grant here at the university. But his year is up. He has to go back to Russia."

"*That* would be a death sentence. Tourists are coming back with serious respiratory problems."

She looked down and sighed.

"He needs real supervision, Ana. Someone to pay his bills. A big responsibility."

Later, she stood in her apartment, everything tasteful, but bought secondhand. Even her car was secondhand. Most of her paychecks went back to Nanakuli, young cousins—their education, clothes. She helped the family buy a van when all the trucks broke down. She had no more room for responsibility.

WHEN SHE TOOK HIM IN FOR HIS LAB RESULTS, SHE FELT PART OF herself step back.

The radiologist spoke softly, asking Niki to sit down. They hunched forward eye to eye like two men at a chessboard, discussing his X-rays, his blood count.

"You need rest, Niki. And stronger medication."

"*Da.* Perhaps in Russia . . ."

The man half laughed. "My friend, Russia will kill you."

Something surfaced then, long-buried and resentful.

"Kill me? My own country kill me?" He rose to his feet and spoke softly. "This is what you think of Russia only? That all is death? That we don't dream of little houses, rose gardens? Is true, when you look at Russian, you do not see a rose. But we are not cliché. Russia is not cliché. We are not all dying. We have hope. And dreams."

In the silence, he felt Ana's acute embarrassment and clasped his hands.

"Sorry! I am dramatic. I sometimes abash myself. But look. It is not so bleak. Soon I return to Moscow to finish important footage for my film. We have national health, hospitals are free. I will get proper medication . . . life will be good."

The radiologist shook his head. "Just breathing that polluted air again . . ."

"Not problem. Not problem." He shook the man's hand. "*Spasibo!* Thank you. Thank you."

As they walked down the street, she allowed him to talk to cover her embarrassment, the fact that she was letting him go.

"Don't be sad, Ana. Russians are like *wolves*, takes more than dirty air to kill us. I will go back, finish film, get well. You will see."

Taking his arm, she spoke halfheartedly. "Niki. You won't get well. Stay here. We'll fix your visa. We'll raise money for your medical expenses."

He turned away, insulted. "Please. Like you, I have learned to survive alone. But most importantly, I must go back. There is final footage I must shoot. It will define entire documentary."

"More victims?"

"The scientists themselves. Many are dying. Leukemia. Bone cancer. They want to finally speak the truth, of what ungodliness they created. Such a coup if I can pull it off."

"How can you? Such interviews will be admitting to the world that your leaders self-destructed."

Niki laughed. "All over Russia, bigwigs selling their confessions. And, these scientists not so important now. They have been erased as serious cases of mediocrity."

"But how would you get such tapes out of the country?"

"Same as before. Make copies, friends acting as 'mules' smuggle them out. Besides, today anyone at Customs, Immigrations can be bought."

She saw that he was really leaving. And she began to draw back, so that their nights were nights of tempered passion. They became more like friends lying side by side trying to talk, but with a confused sense of not being able to understand each other.

Finally, he took her in his arms. "Ana. Don't despair. You are strong and true. You have taught me to be true. To embrace *pamyat*, memory, instead of lies. With you, I finally honored my mother and father by telling their true story. And I have honored my dead wife, Irini."

"I wish I could give you more," she said.

"You have given me riches. You have shared your childhood, and your dreams."

"I mean . . . I wish I could end your suffering. I wish I could offer you some kind of future."

His voice turned soft, trying to hide his sadness. "One day when you are ready, you will find a man deserving. I know it would not be me. But you have saved me for a while. And maybe now and then you will think of me. Maybe that is the reason we exist at all . . . to be remembered."

Now he moved through her apartment carefully, his hands lightly touching objects, memorizing them. Ana watched, suspecting that in some far-off time these moments would be recalled as exquisite, barely capturable. How he clasped his elbows when he stood silent, like a boy with a chill. How he smiled down at a glass of pure, clear water just before he sipped it. How tenderly he held a bar of soap, marveling at its scent.

One night he took her to dinner at a nice hotel. A band played, and after their meal they watched couples on the floor. During a fox-trot he asked her to dance.

Ana looked astonished. "I didn't know you knew how . . ."

Niki laughed. "Does a Russian dance? Is the pope *Cathol . . .* ic?"

He danced beautifully, daringly, holding her like something rare. Then he asked the band to play a tango and swept her down the floor, turning her hip to his hip, the two of them gliding in profile. When she stumbled, he lifted her, carrying her over the misstep, so that their movements were unbroken, even seamless, bodies melting and molding, their rhythm sheer. Couples stopped dancing and watched. How they fit. How they moved as one.

Ana felt immense calm descend on her, wanting to stay like that forever, in that rhythm, in that time. She glanced up at his face, almost stern in pitiful decorum. He seemed to have stripped himself of everything, as if he were naked, offering her all he had, all he was. At the end, she felt so weak and vulnerable she abruptly let go of him and walked off the dance floor. She saw how the gesture shocked him, how it hurt him. This would be the hardest thing to remember. This moment.

That night as they fell asleep, he whispered, "You have been my guide, my companion. But finally, we are each alone. We are all paupers in the end."

At the East-West Center, he gave his final lecture on his "book in progress," attended farewell dinners, got thoroughly drunk with colleagues. The morning he left Honolulu he was wearing a shirt that smelled so clean, Ana wanted to bury her face there. She could not take him to the airport, could not bear to, and so she had scheduled early appointments. Gena and Lopaka waited downstairs in their car.

She suddenly felt desperate. "Niki. You'll write, won't you? And you'll come back. We will always want you to come back."

"Of course. When I am well. When I have means. One day I will come back and show my film."

Gently, he took her by her shoulders and spoke to her in Russian. "That was a poem to your shoulders. You wear them with such pride. Oh,

Ana. You must give all you have to life. Work to exhaustion. Think to exhaustion. And one day you will love to exhaustion."

She stood dumb, afraid to speak, then walked him to Lopaka's car and finally embraced him.

His hand was still waving as the car pulled into traffic.

NOW, THE SLOW RAIN OF DAYS. THE LONGING FOR SO MUCH THAT was incomprehensible. Some nights she woke alarmed. *I must have been crying. My cheekbones ache. Was I crying? Well, it will pass.*

Some days she worked double shifts, but it was just her body. She was somewhere else. She started driving the freeway very late when there was little traffic, wanting the sensation of moving past things with velocity. Some nights she swung onto off-ramps and swerved down roads, looking for streets without lights where she entered a void, leaving the world, her conscience, behind.

She looked for stoplights, a sudden red eye, through which she sped, uncaring. She drove for hours, fingers nimble on the wheel, the radio dial, the gearshift, as if they were separate from her, small intelligent aliens working as a team. One night she pressed the accelerator to the floor, blood drumming in her head, which seemed to match the tires drumming on the road.

Eighty miles an hour, eighty-five. She pressed down harder; the car had nothing more to give. It started shimmying, the steering wheel seemed ready to come loose. She stared at her bare foot on the gas, feeling her particles rearrange. Life would soon be over. Her chest ached, the sole of her foot began to burn. She did not have the nerve.

She drove the freeway till dawn then, with a kind of homing instinct, headed to her coast. As the freeway became a two-lane highway, the tin-roofed houses began, the run-down stores. She pulled into a parking lot and dozed. When she woke, she saw what looked like a corpse under a car, an exhaust pipe in its mouth. Then sunlight shifted and the body crawled into the shade.

School kids passed, sword-fighting with broken car antennas. "Park boys" swaggered by, spectacularly tattooed, scored with pins and studs, their girls cosmetically pierced, some bruised with using. They glanced at Ana, eyes glinting with hate, then seeing she was local, they relaxed. Finally, she started the engine and headed up Keola Road.

Lopaka stood out on the *lānai*, stretching his arms and yawning, a towel draped over his deltoids in a girlish way. Seeing Ana, he turned and went inside. When she walked into the house, Rosie looked away. Ben glanced at her without expression. She sat down to breakfast making small talk, the others so still, she heard herself swallow.

While they sat there, Gena pulled into the driveway, saw Ana's car, and slowly drove away. Lopaka finished eating, then stood in the kitchen yelling into his cell phone, clicking it and cursing.

"I hate those things," Ana said.

No one responded. Pua gazed at her, then slowly stood, turned her chair around and ate with her back to the table. When she finished, she got up and walked her gerontological delicacy to her room.

Ana stared after her, her shining silver braid reaching the backs of her knees. "Aunty, you like I brush your hair today?"

The old woman paused, then turned and shouted. *"Hila hila male!"* For shame.

Ana followed her to her room. "But why, for shame?"

"Because . . . your bitter mouth has leaked into your heart."

"Niki *had* to leave. Besides, you said he wasn't right for me. He was not Hawaiian."

Pua shook her head. "Not Hawaiian, true. But one good man. Your moment of good taste."

Ana sat in her girlhood room where she always came to when she hurt. Eventually she had brought Niki here. She remembered how his booming voice had filled the house and startled them. How his laughter had infected them. And how his stories of Russia, told with feeling and pain, had stilled them.

And she remembered her elders speaking out, telling him bits of their histories, stories Ana had never heard. His keen interest in them, his attendance when they talked, had made them feel visible, important. Eyes glittering, they had clasped his hands and talked for hours. He and Noah had listened to old warped records, leaning at Noah's window while Louis Armstrong and even Puccini blasted across the valley into dawn.

Ana remembered how the walls had trembled when Niki danced his Russian dances. How children had sat wide-eyed, then got up and joined him. They had tried to teach him the hula. Somehow his presence had made each human and each object step forward, showing their dimensions. When he sang his sentimental songs, old koa furniture had glowed as if newly polished. Faded walls seemed splashed with color. The house itself seemed celebrated. Now everything looked gray.

She listened to the family talking softly, knowing as soon as she opened her door, they would fall silent. Finally, hearing the house calm down, kids off to school, she ventured into the kitchen.

Rosie appeared behind her in the doorway. "Not on duty today?"

Ana touched her temple as if making sure it still housed her brain. "I called in sick. I was driving the freeway all night."

"How very extravagant. Considering the price of gas."

"Don't you care why?"

"I know why. I'm sorry, Ana, I don't have the strength to comfort you. I'm too busy holding this family together, keeping the young ones out of crime and drugs while Lopaka keeps telling me radioactive parasites are living in our brain stems. I don't even know if these kids are going to grow up to be normal."

She placed her hands on her hips. "And why should I comfort you? You threw that man away. You sent him back to Russia, where he'll die."

"I didn't *send* him away. Look, I'm a physician. I'm not the Salvation Army."

Rosie studied her. "A physician, but what kind? First you were an Emergency Room doctor. Then a doctor of general practice. Now you're preparing for OB-GYN. What will you be next? What are you really committed to? All you do is paddle round and round in your sea of self-indulgence. Why don't you just open a practice in Waikiki, catering to tourists?"

Ana sat down in shock. "Maybe I have been self-indulgent, but I think I paid my dues . . ."

"Yes. You had your mastectomy. A lot of women out here have had them. And quite a few have died. It's time you faced facts, girlie. You *survived*. Why not stop whining and move on to the next phase of your life. My God, I'm ashamed of you. Niki was good and decent. A wonderful man."

"His year was up. He had to leave."

"You could have got an extended visa. You could have married him."

She looked down at the floor. "Rosie, he wasn't like you and me."

"That's right. He came from a country where nine-tenths of the people are starving. Stealing rags off their corpses. He talked funny. His clothes didn't always match. But, he was a tender, moral human being, trying to do an important thing. He loved you. He said you brought him back to life."

"We had good sex. That always brings a man to life."

Rosie reached out and viciously shook her arm. "What is *wrong* with you? Why are you afraid of men? It's women who are deadly. Sometimes I think men were put here to distract us, so we don't destroy everything."

Ana rubbed her arm "Is that supposed to be food for thought? If so, I'll leave the thoughts to feed themselves."

"Close that bitter mouth of yours! Listen to me. When I lost my daughter, a large part of me died. But what is left, what survived, is learning how to cherish things again, how to be equal to the earth's provisions. Now, I want you to tell me. What did you survive cancer for? You turn your back on everything that's beautiful and meaningful."

"I don't."

"You do. Your whole life has been a full-hearted rejection of anything too 'messy,' too human. You come home when you're lonely. Otherwise, we don't see you, you send checks. You punch your speed bag when you're angry, and I suppose when you need sexual release, you have affairs. Niki was a novelty for you. Now he's gone, and what have you got? What do you hold on to?"

She had never heard such cold, derisive comments from this woman. "Rosie, why are you talking to me like this?"

"Because it's time. You keep saying you have us, your 'ohana. You don't have us. We were your origins. We're not your destiny. One day you'll be forty, and you'll be alone, because you think the worst thing in life is to be used by another human. Let me tell you something. To be used is what we're here for. That's what humans do. We use each other. Depend on each other. You got things all mixed up in your head."

She stood towering over Ana, Amazonian and Junoesque. The second child had doubled the size of Rosie's breasts and hips, turning her body into a massive fact. Then Makali'i's death had taken her down to the bone so she looked nearly skeletal. In time she had gained back the weight; it made her face fleshy and somehow more beautiful.

"You know, Ana, I hardly get out of this house and down the road. But my life is twice as rich as yours."

Ana threw her arms around Rosie and, like a child, she clung. "Don't hate me! You're all I've got. All I ever had."

Rosie gently pulled away. "I don't hate you. You're my love. But I can't wet-nurse you anymore. My God, Ana, you're a doctor. You save lives. Wake up and save your *own* life."

"How? I don't know how."

Rosie sat down across from her. "First off, you've got to recognize one thing. You take after your mama."

"That's a lie."

"No one ever had the nerve to tell you. You're both searchers, always looking for answers. And . . . you're selfish like her. You do not like, and will not accept, responsibility."

Ana shook her head. "You're wrong. There's no job with more responsibility than mine."

"You get paid for that. If Niki had walked into the ER homeless, and needed medication to save his life, you would have given him the meds for free. Right?"

"Of course. I've done that many times."

"But this man needed more. Your time, your love. My God, he must have been terrified when he couldn't breathe at night. You, of all people, would know how much he needed care, and comforting."

"I did care. I cooked, I sewed his clothes. I gave all I had to give. There wasn't any more."

"Which is probably why he left. He knew you didn't love him."

"How could I love a man who's had a dozen lives. A drifter and a dreamer."

"That's what men do when they have no place to stop. They drift."

"Maybe I did love him. But not enough. Besides, people throw that word around too much. They use it like a crutch."

"It *is* a crutch. That's what you never understood. Without it, we're just fornicating apes."

Ana sat back, so exhausted she felt nauseous. In that moment she could not think of a good reason to get up from that chair, to go back to the city, to go on living.

"How do you know when you love someone? I mean, truly, unerringly. How did you know you were in love with Tommy?"

Rosie turned thoughtful. "At first I was in a daze. It's like I was temporarily blind, and deaf. I felt stolen from myself. When I came out of it, I felt different, changed. Even my footprints had changed. I didn't care what people thought. Tommy was a mess when he came home. The military had trained him to kill. He got up each morning and thought 'Who can I kill today?' I decided to rescue him. Nothing mattered but Tommy."

"Weren't you afraid?"

"Ana, I was terrified. I'm no beauty queen. Uneducated, never been off this hill. Tommy's been halfway round the world, slept with women in countries whose names I can't even pronounce. Folks said he would use me, then leave me. I took a chance. That's what you do—take a chance, fill in the blanks with faith. You know the man is not perfect, still you promise yourself to love him. Maybe even improve him."

She reached over and took Ana's hand. "Listen. It is not a fairy tale. Smart women do not *fall* in love. We choose the man, and leap. It works because we make it work. Your mama once said something very wise. She said most men are eighty percent good and twenty percent dreadful. That women should not look for the hundred-percent man, he doesn't exist. We should look instead for a man whose twenty percent we can live with."

She sat back and smiled. "So I chose Tommy Two-Gods. I'm working on his twenty percent."

"But, Rosie, how did you know he was the one?"

"There is no *one*. I told you, I chose to rescue him. And in the end, I think we most love the one we rescue. They make us rise to our full height. Make us see how human, how heroic, we are."

Ana stared at the floor. "That all sounds very noble, but I don't think I have the guts. Maybe I don't have the heart."

Rosie leaned closer. "You were happy with that man. You didn't even know it. And you were wonderful to him. Like Pua said, he was your moment of good taste. Ana . . . it isn't heart you lack. It's imagination."

WAIHO KĒNĀ I KE ĀKUA

Take It to the Gods

THEY WERE MARCHING TO MĀKUA. FOLKS LINED THE HIGHWAY AS far as she could see. By now almost four hundred people were living there in tents and shacks. Homeless in their own lands, they were facing "a final eviction" by armed state, federal, and county police. The National Guard stood ready as Coast Guard ships patrolled the coast.

Ana studied the faces of her people, light browns and dark, high-yellow browns, and browns as pale as cream. Outsiders called Hawaiians "golden-skinned,": infused with sunlight, or wet from the sea, their skin appeared copper-colored, brass, or bronze. But in reality they were brown, rich, luscious brown. Watching them as they moved along—tiny bird-like aunties, and big, husky athletes—she saw how their movements had a natural grace. How their steps fit into invisible grooves, attuned to the inhalations of the sea.

We are water people. And we are tribal. We protect our bones, worship our ākua and our 'āina. The world sees this as backward. For this, they make us pay.

She shifted her backpack and water bottle, as Rosie huffed alongside her. Their older uncles had stayed home. Old stalwart vets, they stood neutral on continuance of Mākua's live-fire war maneuvers.

"Those soldiers need practice," Ben argued. "We need be in state of readiness."

Ana had stared at the stump of his arm. "Readiness for what? For whom?"

"Fanatics. Terrorists. Anybody who don't like America. Ana, you got to understand, men get bored wit' peace. Even governments get bored."

Uncle Tito had agreed. In that house of wounded men, only Lopaka was steadfast in his hatred of war, his concern for the land. Now she watched as he passed in a truck, shouting through a bullhorn.

"Okay, you folks. Stay in line! Stay calm . . . Remember Gandhi, and his march to the sea."

They advanced slowly up the highway, passing through the towns of Ma'ili, then Wai'anae, on toward Makaha, ever north to Mākua. Occasionally they stopped in small groups and rested in the shade while Lopaka spoke from the back of his truck. A news reporter asked why there wasn't more support. Why thousands of Hawaiians on the coast were not marching with them.

He answered through his bullhorn.

"We don't have more support because folks want to continue believing in 'Paradise.' Hawaiians as well as *malihini*. We tell them our rivers and ponds are polluted, our soil poisoned, people sick, then where's their Paradise? We've stolen their innocence and they hate us."

As he talked more people gathered, for his voice was strong and deep, resonating like a striking bell. Ana saw how he touched them at their hearts, binding them all together.

"I've just been told that sheriffs and the National Guard have blocked the road starting at Kaneana Cave, cutting us off from our brothers on the beaches. They're going to use a pincer movement. I saw it a thousand times in Vietnam. They'll descend on the homeless from both ends of the beach and also the middle. They'll come by land and sea and air. They're going to squeeze them out. Anyone who resists, they will arrest."

He raised his voice, looking over the crowds.

"We're not going out there to start a riot. Don't let them corrupt you into violence. If a cop strikes you . . . do not hit back. Remember, we're not just marching for Mākua. We're marching for our lives."

A man shouted up at him. "Ey! Lopaka. Why listen to you? Your house is full of war vets, men who killed. *You* killed in Vietnam. So, who are you to talk about nonviolence? Who are you to stop the Army from protecting us?"

Ana saw his bodyguards move in. A chill went through her. She saw that same chill passing through the crowd. Lopaka was becoming a force strong enough to need protection. When he spoke even cops listened, though their faces registered contempt. For here was a man who moved crowds. Ana saw how, without meaning to, he had been lifted to another level. He had become someone they looked up to, and would follow.

"Yes, I come from a family of soldiers, men who fought in every war. We tried to be honorable, to serve our country when it called. But in return, our country has not honored us. It is not serving us. If you are not with us, step out of the way. We will not be divided!"

A wave of excitement shifted the crowd. Sheriffs unsnapped their holsters. They had heard him speak before. Perhaps he didn't know the power of his voice, how it seemed to touch a moral center. Today a crowd of only several hundred had gathered, but what if one day he raised his voice, inciting half the island to rebel? The sick, the unemployed, the disenfranchised. He had that kind of power now.

"Justice is all we are asking for," he shouted. "We will march until we reverse this domination. And if they knock me down, someone else will take my place. Victory is just a two-day paddle home!"

The crowds pressed on until they saw the barricades ahead. Lines of police blocking them from further progress. Folks massed and stood there shouting as Ana worked her way forward, then stood paralyzed. Tactical-unit SWAT teams, state police, highway patrol. And almost every face, Hawaiian. Now half a dozen bulldozers made their way up the highway. The drivers, too, Hawaiian. The military and state were clever, pitting brother against brother so that, to the outside world, there was the impression of total disunity amongst the people.

Using her elbows to break through, she continued pushing forward, finally confronting a wall of men in full battle dress. Bulletproof vests worn over thickly padded shirts and pants. Holstered guns and gas canisters at their hips, and in their hands big rubber truncheons. Metal helmets covered their ears and necks, and attached to the helmets were dark, convex visors protecting their faces. They looked like man-size beetles. A killer species facing unarmed people.

Ana stared at the man before her. "How can you do this to your people? How?"

Through his visor, she saw perversely absent eyes. "Back!" he shouted. "All you folks get back!"

Ahead, bulldozers turned in at the beach gates where homeless women herded into police vans shouted as their men battled federal marshals and deputies. She felt crowds pushing up behind her, threatening to crush her. She didn't think the cops could hold them back. A big brown arm flashed before her, something projectiled from the hand.

Then all around her objects flew, the sky suddenly full of rotting fruit. A cop staggered back, his visor hit by a large exploding papaya. Another swiped at something yellow dripping down his chest. The wall of uniforms retreated, blinded by cataracts of garbage. The shouts of the crowd a wind-driven song. She saw a truncheon raised, a man go down. The crowd condensed in panic. The thud of hard rubber on soft flesh, the moans. Then sirens, choppers overhead.

She heard Lopaka shout, "Stay calm! Stay calm . . ."

She saw him grapple with a cop, his arm crutch kicked away from him. Then someone threw her to the ground. In an instant, the highway had become slick, the sky overcast by waves of papayas, exploding grapefruits. In slippery leather boots, the uniformed men could not find traction on the ground. They skidded back and forth like skaters, swinging their truncheons, their visors dripping with runny produce. Folks were knocked down, knocked out. The next wave of folks moved in, armed and aiming. It seemed to go on for hours. Then Ana heard the horns.

They came from a long way off and as they neared, folks pulled back, confused. The horns grew louder, and down the highway crowds began to cheer. She shaded her eyes, looking in the distance. Ten trucks speeding up the highway, blasting their horns. On the back of each truck stood old tūtū—grandmothers and great-grandmothers. Tiny, wrinkled women and some who were stately and huge.

In billowing, faded muʻumuʻus, brown faces glowing with sweat, they stood with their gray hair flying in the wind. On each truck, half a dozen old women braced themselves, holding a flagpole steady as the Hawaiian flag flew over them, each flag flying upside down, the international signal for distress. In truck after truck, they stood firm, facing forward like the prows of ships, looking like harridans and angels of wrath.

Ana stepped back in shock, recognizing Aunty Pua, her profile immaculate and stern, hair flying out like a silver shawl as she sped by. Their horns blew and continued blowing, and in that moment Ana felt a tug, some memory she could not clearly summon. Folks began shouting again, running beside the speeding trucks headed to the barricades. As the drivers lay on their horns, demanding to be let through, a second and third line of SWAT teams moved in with German shepherds, blocking the trucks.

Federal marshals pushed forward, warning the drivers, "Back up or be arrested."

The old women never spoke, they just stood there, wind lifting their hair and fluttering the flags as they stared at Mākua Valley, the desecrated bosom of their ʻāina. SWAT teams stood patting their palms with truncheons. Attack dogs strained at their leashes. Then one of the old women began to chant. A dirgelike chant that grew louder and louder, her voice vibrating until it seemed not a chant but a terrible portent echoing across the land.

The crowd fell back. Another *tūtū* took up the song until dozens of them were chanting in unison. Eyes resting on the valley, their voices slowly rose, deep and terrible, like voices from the dead. Then slowly their heads shifted, their eyes came to rest on uniforms surrounding every truck.

One of the old women raised her hand and pointed her finger at a cop. His eyelids fluttered, he seemed to sway, and dropped his arm, his truncheon useless at his side. Still chanting, she pointed at a snarling German shepherd; the dog whimpered and lay down, its head between its paws. All around, the armed forces stood there dazed. And still the old women chanted, their voices a roar that bounced off the walls and ridges of the valley.

"*Ē mau! Ē mau!* . . . *I Mau Ka Ea I Ka 'Āina I Ka Pono . . . !*"

We must strive! We must strive! So that righteousness will fill the land again.

And they continued chanting in Hawaiian. "Rise up! Rise up! Do not submit to insult and ignominy. Rise up until there are no more people left to rise. And when we all have risen, then the stones will rise! Then Earth will rise up with us, too!"

Along the highway, folks stood dumb. Three women went down on their knees. Federal marshals looked around, unsure. Out on the beaches, women still shouted from police vans, their men grappling with cops as bulldozers leveled their shacks and tents. Then, it suddenly grew quiet. Only the voices of the *tūtū* were heard, calling to their gods.

They called on *Kāne*, creator of man, keeper of the earth. They called on *Kū*, god of war, of chiefs and chiefesses. They called on *Lono*, god of agriculture, of clouds and weather. And *Kanaloa*, god of the ocean, of the life therein. They called on *Hina*, first female god of the ancients, and on *Hi'iaka*, goddess of healing, restorer of life. In those moments, no one moved, no one seemed to breathe.

It was then that the wind came, answering the old women. It blew soft as breath, stilling everything. It was *Makani Hau*, the cool wind from the uplands of Mākua issuing from deep inside the mountains. It blew the people calm, blew children sleepy in their parents' arms. It blew the armed, uniformed men a sudden ease, so that they raised their hands, stifling yawns.

All along that troubled coast, everything was still. Brothers looked each other in the eye. Moments ago they were prepared to maim or kill. Now they just felt sleepy. And when *Makani Hau* was ended, people felt it lift away. And they felt the coming of her sister wind, *Makani Malu*, the wind of peace, and of protection.

And in that peace and quiet, came a voice. One so deep, so ancient and resounding even *tūtū* turned their heads, raising their arms as if surrendering. They listened and they heard.

"*'Olaaa . . . Nā . . . 'Iwi. 'Olaaa . . . Nā . . . 'Iwi.*"

The words repeated and repeated. An urgent litany echoing across the land.

"*'Ola . . . Nā . . . 'Iwi . . .*" The bones survive.

People moaned. The hair stood up on Ana's arms. Sheriffs covered their genitals protectively. *Mākua*, their Mother Earth, their parent, was telling them she knew. She saw. How the people were offering their *aloha*, their *mālama*. They were offering to take care of her. She saw they were prepared to die protecting her. For them, she would live on. Deep in the soil, and in caves where bones of their ancestors rested, she lived on. A woman knelt, stretched out, and laid her cheek against the ground. Many others followed.

Finally, as the voice died down, the old women in the trucks resumed their chanting, and people in the crowds composed themselves, prideful and determined. Ana set her shoulders wide, and as she watched, deputies and National Guardsmen holstered their truncheons and took a brother's arm, asking them to go home peacefully. The marshals stepped back, gazing into the valley with wondering eyes.

On the beach, bulldozers resumed their destruction. Tents and shacks were razed, and some of the homeless were arrested for resisting. There were minor scuffles, injuries. But on this day, folks felt victorious. They had risen up, the land had risen with them. And so, too, had their gods.

And so it was that on a day when lives could have been destroyed, when brother might have maimed or murdered brother, people stood intact. For years, parents would tell their children, and their children's children what they had witnessed here. How their gods had rallied. *Mākua* had rallied. They had been granted progress, not slaughter.

The trucks slowly turned around and headed down the highway, the old women silent, fierce-looking and triumphant. Cops ran beside each truck, trying to clear the way. But to Ana—watching how they gazed up at the old women with a kind of awe—it seemed as if they were running in support of them, ready to throw off their gear and join them. As crowds slowed the progress of the trucks, people tried to clamber aboard. Several young soldiers hoisted themselves up, and stood protectively beside the old women and the flags.

In that moment, Ana remembered footage from Niki's film, the fall of the Soviet Union. She remembered uncanny scenes of Russian soldiers capitulating, handing their rifles to the crowds, turning their backs on the Russian army forever. And she remembered old grandmothers, *babushki*, climbing aboard armored Russian tanks, young soldiers pulling them up, embracing them, as the tanks rolled into Red Square.

Ancient women who had known only slavery for generations had, in those moments, become the *symbol* of liberated Russia. As they passed through the crowds flooding into Moscow, they did not wave. They stood proudly atop the tanks, their faces sober and determined. Now, as old Hawaiian *tūtū* passed in trucks, gray hair streaming out behind them, they seemed to see right through the world.

ALMOST MIDNIGHT AS THEY CLIMBED KEOLA ROAD. ANA'S CHEEK-bone hurt, she felt the beginning of a shiner. In the house, youngsters had gathered at Pua's feet, seeing her with a new eye. She had a different air, one of quiet authority, as if she had been keeping her power a secret all these years, and suddenly unveiled it. No more the mixed-up aunty, one day quoting from the Bible, next day from the KUMULIPO. Now she had precision, like a blade-sharp stone. She marked each thing, each person with a glance. Ana saw what she had missed for years, that Pua was wisdom-full, that she possessed *hanohano nui*. Great dignity. In all her years of searching for truth, she had earned much *mana*.

She sat down and rubbed Pua's dusty feet. "Aunty, so proud of you today. Watching you, I understood we've been getting it all wrong. Our future doesn't lie with my generation, or the kids coming up behind us. It lies with you, our *kūpuna*."

With a trembling and exhausted hand, Pua reached out and stroked her head. "So it has always been, child. We are old fools, but wise fools. One day it will be your turn."

"Do you think we'll win? Will we ever get Mākua back?"

"Oh, yes. Remember what Lopaka said. Victory is just a two-day paddle home. Meanwhile . . . Ē *mau! Ē mau! I Mau Ke Ea I Ka 'Āina I Ka Pono.*"

Gena came out of the kitchen with a beer, exhilarated from the march. They sat out on the steps in the jungle of tattered slippers and running shoes.

"A good day," Ana said. "The gods marched with us. Lopaka must be proud . . . Where is he?"

"Passed out. That boy's been up four days and nights. We'll celebrate tomorrow."

They gazed into the night, a coiled indigo shimmering through fog. They heard a peacock scream. In spite of her euphoria, Ana felt great fatigue and a recurring sense of nausea.

Gingerly, she touched her eye. "Passive resistance really works. I always thought some of us would have to die to make our point. Well . . . what good is life without a point?"

Her voice was soft, devoid of edge. Gena silently reflected on how Ana had changed in the past few months. She came home to the coast more often, sitting in at community discussions on women's health issues, on ways to combat crime and drugs amongst the young. She addressed folks more caringly.

Looking back, Gena saw that the change had begun with Makaliʻi's death. After that she saw an idling in Ana's gestures, a hesitation in her walk as if not sure which way to turn. Since Niki's departure, she watched her sit for hours staring out of windows, as if the calligraphy of windswept leaves would tell her what to do, how to behave.

"Ana, remember those long-lost nights at the Humu Humu Lounge? The two of us counting our waitress tips?"

"I remember. What happened, Gena? How did we drift apart?"

"I've got a theory about that. We're role models, you and me. First-generation college grads. First-generation not-hula-girls-or-chambermaids. We're talented, ambitious, but not too confident. We don't have enough peers to bounce ideas off of . . . so we disagree, and take it personally."

She played with her beer, scraping the label from the bottle.

"And then, there is Lopaka. I have always known how much he loves you. It's deep, real deep. Maybe I've been jealous."

"He lalau! Nonsense," Ana said. "You're what he wants. And what he needs. He loves you! I'm sorry for that thing I said way back, that where he's concerned your brains were between your legs."

"Well, where he's concerned, sometimes they are."

"I see now I was lashing out, at everyone. Trying to hide how terrified I was. Even six, seven years after surgery, sometimes I'm afraid to fall asleep. Afraid I won't wake up."

In the silence, Gena moved closer. "Ana. I've got to tell you something. I mean . . . I've got to give you something. If Lopaka finds out, he'll kill me. I don't care."

Ana leaned back slightly.

"I stole something. It's for you. He doesn't think you deserve to have it. That's not for him to say."

Gena held out a long, white envelope. "I took this from his files."

"What is it?"

"A letter. From Niki. The day he left, he asked Lopaka to give it to you."

"But that was five weeks ago."

Gena looked down, embarrassed. "When you let him go, I thought, 'the hell with her.' Now I realize, it's not for me to judge. Not for Lopaka, either."

Ana stood holding the letter as Gena slid into her car, her head thrust out the window. "Whatever happens, whatever you need . . . I'm here for you."

HŌʻIKE NA KA PUʻUWAI

Revelations of the Heart

Beloved Ana . . .
 It is late at night, and I depart tomorrow. I write this by candle-light so I do not wake you.
 I look at you across the room, lying on your side. Outline of your shoulder and your hip. You will always be beautiful to me. A woman of extravagance and moral force. Though I think you do not know this. When I have seen you coming down the street, I think, "She is my lover, and my friend. A miracle!" I do not know why you chose me. I maybe will never understand.
 Yes, I have been a liar all my life. Is how I survived. Until I met you I never knew this luxury of speaking truth. I was impaired. My past, my poor homeland, these made sense of my impairment. I think my behavior does not make sense anywhere else. This is why Russians do not adapt. But every word I write now is from my heart. Puʻuwai . . . as you say in your beautiful language. And I hope you will hold a long time these words in your heart.
 I leave you my collection of Pushkin's poems. And those of Anna Akhmatova. They speak from the very soul of my country. Rare birds who froze to death midflight. In Moscow, I will read them again. Maybe you will be reading them, too, and we will be connected through their thoughts.
 ". . . I loved you with such purity, such passion/ As may God grant you to be loved once more."—Pushkin.

Oh, Ana. I have wanted life too much. I have wanted you. Maybe with completion of my film, you will see a better me. Maybe in such work, I will become the man I wanted you to love.

In Moscow I will return to Old Arbat district. Friends are there, many ill like me. They cough, smoke cigarettes, drink vodka, like good Russians. Probably some of them are dying. Some have already fled, but those who stay continue painting, writing poetry, pretending there is a future.

My friends will call me mudak, fool! for coming back. Will tell me how that neo-Tsarist, Yeltsin, is starving everyone to death. But they will welcome me, ask about my travels. There is an old, smoky shashlik restaurant. I will sit with friends, remembering you but will not talk much about you. It would make me joyful, and joy is so exhausting.

Now you turn in sleep, flinging your arm across the bed. I remember first time I saw you after Hurricane 'Iniki. Your hair so wild, your face so stern and angry, at first I found you scary. But then I listened, how you comforted that child. And I watched how you listened when I told my stories, some of which were lies. Maybe I began to love you then. O! How to conjugate that great, slow word. Yes, even then I wanted to stand beside you, help you do something, maybe something you could not do alone. These were new sensations.

After Irini died, I was like an animal. Even filming sick and damaged people, I sometimes spoke brutishly to them. She was dead and they still lived. I walked out of people's lives in middle of their sentences. I was again that scavenging orphan with head of lice, knowing only how to scratch. But that campfire night in my cheap leather clothes, I was already adoring you.

Now I wonder, will you remember me? Will you remember my sad stories, life seen through a dirty glass? You said I have lived very hard. Yes, I lived enough for two. I see that now. If there is afterlife, I have already lived mine. When I'm dead, I'll just be dead.

I always thought I would die young. But those who loved me died young instead. You came in the part of my life when death seemed to be sleeping. Maybe I felt safe too soon. But you brought out my innocence, that unbreathed part of me strangled as a boy. I was my best self with you. Was someone I had never been. Not even with Irini, because first I had to know deep suffering.

I understand now, much of my life I hated myself. I longed for everything which stood outside me. You taught me how in some ways

I am lovable. I could be witty, people could be drawn to me. I know you could not love me, but you cared. Enough to make me think that on my own I will be all right. That maybe I can stand myself. You helped me see parts of my past I had forgot. Little miniatures that made me happy. Moments when I made others happy. You taught me many things. Only you did not teach me how I should forget you.

This was meant to be thoughtful letter of farewell. It seems instead letter of extreme longing. Maybe this is good for me. You said without longing, bones lose calcium. If so, I will grow well! Maybe, if granted time, I will go back to mathematics, study of which expresses human will to live. Once this old professor told me a place is nothing but a place. Is just long chains of molecules occupying space. Beach resort, prison cell. Both same. Just occupied space.

He said we think of things, places, as composed of solids. But are not solids, are just energy trails. By the time we see them, energy is moving on. So. A place is just where our corporeal bodies exist at given moment while our minds explore past, present, future. "Remember that," he said, "and you will never be unhappy." I try to remember such a thing as I prepare to leave you.

Ana, you have just sat up in your sleep, talking to a patient, then lay down again. This makes me smile. There is such quality, such depth to you. You do not know yet how to reach it. It is in the darkness waiting. One day it will come to you through work, or love, or sacrifice. Something will challenge you, make you rise to your extreme.

Einstein said all knowledge floating in the universe will only amount to half of what we are. Half of what I am is that boy born in ice hut in Archangel'sk. Half of me is my parents. And maybe part of me is gangster, stealing, maiming for a living. Part is a young man undressing his wife, watching her turn blue in snow. Flinging her ashes in the air so she will soar forever.

And part of me is coward. Who then lay down in grief and snow, trying to join Irini in her soaring. Should I tell you my scars were from Afghanistan, when I as mercenary soldier was taken prisoner of war? But I was never soldier. My scars are wild-dog scars. Who knows why I came conscious when he gnawed my frozen flesh? Or how I found strength to fight him while he lunged and danced away with bits of me. All I remember is warm cadaver breath, his mouth of clashing knives. My fingers closing on his throat.

Farmers found me mummified in frozen blood and insects. They carved this hard pelt of filth from me and with it came sections of my skin. They bathed my raw flesh in vinegar. Is true, a half-dead man can faint, many times. An old babushka poured oil in my furrows like how in the Bible. And, slowly, in such a way I healed. Sometimes even death does not want us. This is my true history. So maybe part of me is also dog, part insect. These were truths I kept from you. Now you even know my scars. My real name is Nikolai Volenko. I, who have loved you.

I used to lie beside you full of plans. I would fix my crooked teeth. Learn how to dress. Stop carrying spoon in my pocket. I would eat like human, not a wolf. Would cook for you, keep house for you. Would teach high-school mathematics. I would marry you. We would make love on little beaches in moonlight and would aways cry out so nature thinks we are virgins! Our children would be made in acts of love. Now my exalted dreams abash me. I am only a stranger looking in window. A man passing who leaves his face hanging there with longing.

I think of St. Petersburg, called Leningrad when my parents were alive. If I begin to feel less well, I will go there. I will want to die there. I will make my way from Moscow, relive their lives for them. Surely as children they were hungry. Did they steal offerings from cemetery graves? Did they suck icicles to quench winter thirst? And did they play the icicles like bells? As lovers, did they crawl half-starved from catacombs of Hermitage, scavenging for food while Germans bombed their city?

Leningrad no longer exists. Renamed Petersburg, is now a city of gangsters. But Leningrad must still exist, because I remember it! I will go and blow dust from its magnificent palaces and cathedrals. I will breathe in moldy air of rivers, parks. My cheeks will shine from light reflected off golden wings of bronze lions on Griboyedov Canal.

Ana, if you think of me, think of me there. Probably I will live to be an old man who sits down to urinate. But if my body begins to fail, if lungs to weaken, I will go where instinct takes me, to my mother and my father's past.

I want to sit under a special tree in tiny garden, behind old Sheremetievsky Palace on Fontanka Canal in heart of the city. In this garden is a huge old maple tree. Here Anna Akhmatova sat, cold and hungry, writing her poems. If I can see this tree, I will be happy. I will drag my feet through the drowned city of Leningrad, shouting Russian *curses at the past. Your face beside me to correct my grief. I will go out singing Russian songs of joy.*

Maybe one day in some great obscurity we will meet again. We will stroll aimlessly by an endless sea, freed from all things so important to humans which we soon forget. We will talk openly like monks at confession. You will tell me your secrets and I will tell you mine. Then maybe you will finally understand me. I have been living in a world not mine. I have not earned your world. Even so, you thought you could rescue me, and heal me. I did not want just healing. I wanted you to love me. Again, my dreams abash me.

Already I feel Russia reclaiming me, two squeezing claws of an eagle on my shoulders. I will take very little back. Back there nothing I possess will help me. There are not yet words to describe our new condition. Yet all Russians ever wanted was to be normal, to work, have food for our children. To have a bed, and sleep with our windows open. To talk in our sleep and not be afraid. Was it so much to ask, I wonder? It seems so little.

I feel chills, hours pass. The candle growing smaller. The dark becomes inquisitor, examining my thoughts. Forgive me, everything is pouring out. I don't know why I write this. Why I fight to stay alive. Maybe living is just bad habit I cannot break. Maybe only Lopaka understood me, having seen real devastation in his war. Many nights we sat for hours, saying nothing, understanding everything. He will always be my bratlich, my dear brother. Gospodi! What a beautiful man he is. His children will be beautiful. He and Gena will make many children.

This, too, is my regret. Other than this film I make in bits and pieces—this film which will one day fade, because other, better films will be made about these crimes against ordinary people—other than this, I leave nothing behind. No family, no roots in time. I have nothing. You, Ana, have who you are. Family. Tribe. Hold these things precious. Fight for them.

For a while your Wai'anae Coast, your Nanakuli, saved me. I stood in your life and even sometimes lived it. In your big house, I saw real closeness of humanity, all of life condensed. Joy, grief, rapture, love, and hate. All found expression here. How much you are! How much your people are!

Mine is a huge land. Your islands are small. We have lost almost everything. Your people will not lose. You must not lose. Remember what I told you. Death of each culture is a death of human conscience. In Russia they killed everything, but not our need to worship. Our churches are open again, the world now hears our bells. Each time your people march, the world will know Hawaiians, too, have heard the bells.

I bend close to candle now. Its flame shivers with my breathing, as if my life is balanced on its tip. I have spent this night writing so much my words walk around with a life of their own. I feel desperation. I feel like something skinned. I will lie down beside you now. And maybe for that while I can ignore my terror. It will ignore me. Yes, I am terrified. Not for where I go. But for what and who I leave.

We have Russian word, Pamyat, memory, much like your word, Ho'omana'o, to remember. Another beautiful Hawaiian word I will take with me. Ana. I will always remember you. You have been a riot in my heart. I have pictured us growing very old together, me still desiring you. I carefully pin up your silver hair, then take it down again, so slowly. Pin by pin.

My wrinkled hands cupping your hips. My lips kissing your dear scars, healed long ago. Your splendid laughter and your warmth making me a boy again. Innocent, unknowing boy. I have pictured us holding hands, staring down time together, carefully turning it inside out. For what is time, except this name we give our heartbeats?

One day when you are reading this, I hope it will stitch together pieces of this spreading night when you breathed soft, and I watched over you. I hope these written words will in some way tell you what my poor Russian tongue could not convey.

Oh, Ana, so much of life is foolish, except what is known by the human heart. Honor. Loyalty. And love. Thank you so deeply for honoring me. For allowing me to love again. In the little time we had, you gave me splendor.

I am truly yours, Nikolai Volenko

HOʻOHOLO

Decision

A starless night, the moon a half grape, eerily green and watery. Lights on in Lopaka's office, she found him and Gena discussing a case involving civil liberties.

"Please. I need to talk to him alone."

Gena quietly gathered her things and left.

He tilted his head, half smiling, a flicker of impatience. "Ana. What's up?"

She moved closer as he took off his glasses and folded his arms, alert. His crutch leaned against the desk. She picked it up and flung it hard across the room. It hit a window that spawned a jagged crack. She picked up a paperweight, a hunk of shrapnel from his war. She stared at him, then put it down.

"Looks like we're going to have a scene," he said. "Can we handle it?"

She leaned over his desk. "Who told you you had the right to dictate other people's lives?"

His eyes caught and held hers in an admonition not to pursue this, whatever it was.

She chose her words carefully. "I . . . I used to feel safe with you. Certain things you said could change my thoughts completely. Maybe I grew up. Now I find you vindictive, even cruel."

"Do you want to break this down for me?" His eyes shifted back and forth, then came to rest on a filing cabinet.

"That's right. Your files. Where you kept his letter."

"What letter?"

She closed her eyes, then opened them. "Niki's. The one he left for
me. How could you do that?"

Lopaka slowly shook his head. "Such passion. I didn't know you had
it in you."

"Don't patronize me. You have no idea how much I hate you right
now."

Even saying it, she realized how hatred seemed to operate the same
glands as love. It even produced the same reactions. She was perspiring
and weak.

"For chrissake, Ana. Calm down."

"Calm down? You kept something that was mine."

"Yours?" he said softly. "When did you claim ownership? Of anything? You who are so attached to your detachment. So free of demands."

"That's not true. I cared for him."

"Your feelings come and go like weather. Even *you* can't tell if they're
real."

She backed into a chair and slowly sat down. She would not be
quick-tongued. There was too much between them, barriers, deep feelings, that prevented surrender and forgiveness.

"That letter was written to me, meant for me."

"You don't deserve that letter. You allowed Niki to go back to Russia, where he'll probably die."

" 'Don't deserve'?" she whispered. "Who are you to say?"

"You played with him. You didn't love him."

"I did. I was learning . . ."

"Ana. You can't 'learn' love. Maybe you picked up a certain residue . . .
that wasn't love. That's why he left. The man was proud."

"He had to go back. To finish that documentary."

"Maybe. Or maybe that was his excuse to let you off the hook."

"Oh," she said. "I see where this is going. You're the one who's guilty,
but you want me to apologize. You forget, Lopaka, you don't intimidate
me like you do everyone else."

". . . Don't I?"

In that moment she saw how much alike they were, or had become—
ambitious, coldhearted, each a spiky complex of defenses.

Now he tried to dismiss her. "Look. It's over. I did what I did because . . ."

"What you did was immoral. And illegal."

He leaned forward. "Do you know I even asked him to let me find a
local girl to marry him. So he could stay here legally, get medical atten-

tion. He laughed. Like I said, the man was proud. So what does it matter to you now? How has reading his letter changed your life?"

She lifted her head and met his gaze. "It matters because you broke my trust. You made a decision about my life without my knowledge."

His jaw tensed, a vein pulsed at his temple.

"I'll tell you why you did it, Lopaka. You wanted to punish me. You like playing God. You say you're committed to our people, but you're only committed if they do your bidding. You don't really care about your fellow man. You don't care about *anyone*. There's something missing in you."

She saw him flinch.

"I care about a lot. I came to love that crazy Russian. We grew close, we had things in common . . ."

"Devastation. War. You think I betrayed your 'brother from the trenches.' Your war is *pau*, Lopaka. It's been over for twenty years."

"You know, that's something women just don't get. Men come home, but our war is never over. It's in the smell when my feet sweat. It's in my dreams. Why do you think Ben drinks? Why has Noah sat at his window all these years? Because they know. Because war taught us."

"What did it teach you?"

"That nothing's out there. You see young soldiers dying in the thousands, and you know that humans are totally and completely alone. That we will never be *not* alone. That's what you live with."

"Then what's the point of other humans?" Ana asked. "What is all this talk of love?"

"That's what keeps us from sitting in dark rooms, wringing our hands. Another human allows a little tenderness in, a softness we don't know we have. Someone telling us it's okay to be idle, to lie back, a little quietness, a sweetness . . ."

She knew he was thinking of Gena.

"Maybe having someone say they love you means you found a reason not to kill yourself."

She thought how only a woman with a huge tolerance for conflict would choose this man. "You don't deserve her, you know."

"I know that. But some women don't back off. And they are *rare*."

Her head hung. Anger could not sustain her now.

"You know, Ana. Niki was the first man I ever met who I thought might deserve you, though he's not Hawaiian. He was trying to help us, but when he needed help, you let him down. You could have saved him. I guess I lost respect for you."

"And I, for you."

Finally, he cleared his throat. "Okay. Maybe I was wrong. But I hated the way you kept him at a distance so he wouldn't burden you. You do the same thing with the family."

"You're crazy. I'd die for any of them."

"But you don't live for them. Sure, you visit. Then you leave. They're too *real* for you up on that hill."

She suddenly felt exhausted. "I don't care what you think. I loved him. I didn't know how much till he was gone."

"Well, Ana, sometimes life doesn't wait. Funny, I always thought of you as fearless. I was wrong."

"Then, tell me . . . how do I stop being afraid?"

"You have to start living like you mean it."

DAYS PASSED IN PARENTHETICAL FLASHES OF REMEMBRANCE AND regret. She recalled Niki's flesh against her flesh, his grumbling sighs, words he whispered against her temple while she slept. Her body seemed to mourn with her. An aching in her breast, a tightening in her belly. Each morning she threw up. Recognizing the signs, but too incredulous to believe them, she arranged for a physical exam. Afterwards, Ana stared at her face in a mirror as the realization took hold that she was carrying a child.

That night she dreamed she was moving fast, without the pull of gravity . . . *A skater on sharp blades, a sea of ice, moonlight sowing a path ahead. A voice compelling her to go. Go on. A forward motion. Neverending . . .*

She woke in a state of shock to find it was a dream. And maybe that is when she set out on her journey. It was simply a matter of focusing, taking each thing in order of importance. A travel agent. A lawyer. Emergency passport, visa. In a heightened, breathless state, feeling slightly mad, she arranged a leave of absence from Obstetrics.

One day she delivered a premature baby, and holding it up to the light—skin so transparent she saw its tiny, fluttering heart—she turned and smiled, handing it to its mother. And while she stood there, Ana felt the sun lean on her back, a warm explosion in her spine. *This is what hope feels like . . .*

She called Lopaka. "I need to know. Have you heard from Niki since he left?"

"No. I wrote, but he warned me letters don't get through. Postal workers open them looking for currency, they steal stamps off the envelopes. His phone is out of order."

"Then . . . as far as you know, he's still in Moscow at that address he left?"

"As far as I know . . ."

She tried the Moscow number several times. Nothing but static, then a disconnect, international operators telling her all circuits had been broken.

SHE DROVE OUT TO NANAKULI AND SHOWED ROSIE THE LETTER. When Rosie looked up, her eyes were wet.

"Lopaka had that letter all this time. He said I didn't deserve it."

"And, what do you think?"

"I think I have been very selfish," Ana said. "I thought surviving cancer entitled me to that."

"Maybe it did, for a while. When Makali'i died, I wished all children dead so parents could suffer like me. But then time passed. What will you do now?"

"I'm going there. I'm going to bring him home."

Rosie seemed to take it calmly. Distances were all the same to her— Los Angeles, Moscow, all a million miles away.

"I knew you loved him. I knew before you knew."

"You aren't shocked I'm going?"

"Oh, Ana. What is left in life to shock me. And you have always taken the hard way. Only tell me you'll be safe."

"It's safe. Tour guides day and night. They'll bus us everywhere like children." She suddenly moved close. "Rosie, I'm scared! Suppose I can't find him?"

She took Ana in her arms. "You will find him. Life will help you."

She thought of telling her cousin about the child, but its existence was so new to her—so seemingly miraculous—that Ana felt furtive and protective.

"Would you go, Rosie?"

"For a man like that? I would go in a minute. Ana, this isn't just about your heart. It's about saving a life. However selfish you have been, there's something magnificent in you lurking just below the waterline. Something that finally needs to come up for air. I'm very proud of you."

SHE WOKE AT FIVE, PLACED HER LUGGAGE AT THE DOOR, AND WHEN the cab arrived, she went downstairs. Outside, she saw Lopaka paying off the cabbie, sending him away.

"Wait! What are you doing?"

Seeing Gena get out of their car, Ana stepped back. "Don't try to stop me, Gena. Don't."

She called out to the cab disappearing round the corner as Lopaka carefully picked up her bags.

"Don't touch them," Ana cried.

Gena moved forward with her arms out. "Ana. It's okay. We want to drive you to the airport."

She watched Gena take Lopaka's crutch, watched him struggle into the seat behind the steering wheel. Then reluctantly, Ana slid into the backseat. Once they were moving in traffic, Gena turned round and took Ana's hand.

"We sat outside your place all night. Afraid we'd miss you. Ana. We're here to kōkua. We love Niki, too. I only wish we could go with you."

"Who told you I was going? Rosie?"

"She called us hysterical when it finally sank in. You are doing the right thing. It's just . . . we're concerned for you."

Ana glanced up at Lopaka. In early-morning light, his black, curly hair hung oily and disheveled, his big, 'upepe nose and forehead appeared gray like granite. He looked exhausted and mean.

At Honolulu Airport they checked her luggage and followed her through security to her gate. People wearing name tags, EASTERN TOURS, seemed to be gathered in a group. Two Chinese American couples, a Hawaiian couple, three women young enough to be students, assorted other locals.

She glanced at her itinerary. "I guess I'm with them."

Gena moved close. "What happens when you get to Los Angeles?"

"Two-hour layover, then straight to New York City." She checked her itinerary again. "Then it says we switch to Finnair."

"Finland? Are you sure?"

Ana nodded. "In Helsinki we switch again to . . . Aeroflot. A one-hour flight, then we land in St. Petersburg. Eight days there, then an overnight train to Moscow."

Gena seemed to panic. "Ana. Do you have any idea what you're getting into? You don't need to do this."

"Yes. I do."

"But, what will you do when you get to Moscow?"

"Go to his address. Go to where his friends are."

Gena left them for a while, and Lopaka sat down beside Ana. Since they picked her up, he had not said a word. There was nothing she wanted him to say. Everything between them had been said.

Now she recalled the scene in front of her building as they piled her luggage into the trunk of the car. The practiced harmony with which Gena had taken Lopaka's arm crutch as he slid behind the steering wheel, her silent, concentrated overseeing as he settled in, dragging his damaged leg in after him. She recalled how, on cue, they had nodded to each other, tacit acknowledgment that he was comfortable, before Gena handed him the keys and closed the door. And the way she quickly opened the back door, placed the crutch strategically on the seat so as not to obstruct his vision in the rearview. Then she had guided Ana into the car.

It had taken only three or four minutes, but in those minutes, she had witnessed a timeless ritual: two people so attuned in rhythms, thoughts, habits, that they moved together automatically with no need for words, or touch. They had seemed then like dancers, each step fluid and assured, each recognizing that they could not perform this human dance alone. It was the first time she had seen evidence of their deep, maturing love.

Gena returned with a thick carnation *lei*, placing it carefully round Ana's shoulders.

She whispered in her ear. "I'm so damned proud of you. Please, be careful!"

Ana placed her hands on Gena's cheeks, her face still dark and beautiful, but softer now. Life was slowly erasing all the harshness.

"Take care of him," she said.

Hearing the boarding call, she moved to stand in line. They stood beside her as the line slowly advanced, and she suddenly thought her heart would burst. Her face began to tremble. She felt her legs begin to go. It was then that Lopaka reached out and took her arm, holding it steady and firmly until she felt his strength flow into her. Then, very gently, he pulled her from the line so they stood in a private space.

He lifted her chin and spoke softly as their eyes held. "I ever tell you I carried your letters all through 'Nam? I knew them by heart, they saved my life. I have them still. Ana, remember Aunty Emma. She had real *mana*, the gift of healing, and when she died she passed it to you in the Ritual of Hā . . ."

Even as he said it, he blew softly in her face.

"Do you understand? You were *meant* to rescue, and to heal. Take that *mana* with you. It is very powerful. It will keep you safe."

He took her in his big, bronzed arms, and held her tight against his chest. He pressed his lips against her head.

"I am so proud of you. You who I have loved in ways we never spoke of. And I will always love you. Always."

His words gave her the strength to go. She turned back once and waved, then moved down the pleated passageway.

HA'I A'O

To Give Advice

SHE WOULD REMEMBER EVERY DETAIL OF THE TAKEOFF, WATCHING her island and her coast diminish. In those hours she saw for the first time the immensity of what encompassed her small world. At Los Angeles Airport, she hung close to her group as they pushed through darting, feinting crowds.

Then someone touched her arm. "Ana."

Dreamlike, she turned to her mother's voice. "Rosie called me. I flew down from San Francisco."

Ana opened her mouth to speak, then closed it. Silently, her mother moved along with Ana's group until they found their gate.

"You've got almost two hours. Come and sit down."

Ana held back, confused. "You're not going to talk me out of this."

"No. I'm going to try and help you. You won't find your friend alone, in Moscow."

In a trance, she followed her mother to a café along the concourse. For a moment they sat watching a man out on the tarmac semaphoring with batons. A huge plane looming, responding to his movements. Then gradually, the crowds, the din, fell back. She turned to her mother whose lips were moving, languorous and full.

She was wearing a smart khaki suit, sheer stockings, and high heels. Her hair was now tinted, a show of vanity and vulnerability that made her seem less formidable. She leaned forward so Ana smelled that same haunting perfume. And she realized that somewhere in the long-lost years she had forgiven the perfume with which her mother's letters came.

Anahola was discussing Russia, the conditions there.

"Yes. You're safe on a tour, it's not Communist Russia anymore. But, understand, you're not going to a resort. Conditions are appalling for the average Russian. They'll try to hide this from you, show you only tourist sights. There is a man named Eric Dancer. I've already given him the names of your hotels. Hopefully, he will set wheels in motion. His father, Hubert, was a physicist, my husband's best friend."

Ana had no idea what she was talking about. It occurred to her that her mother was fighting hysteria.

"Eric is in and out of Russia. Imports, exports. And . . . sometimes he helps people get out."

"You mean he works for our government."

Anahola shook her head "Let's say he's an . . . entrepreneur. He does favors, people pay him back. He will contact you, Ana. Trust him. Yeltsin's government is collapsing, they're tightening emigration. Unless your friend has contacts, Eric is his only hope of getting out."

She dabbed her lips with a napkin, trying to sound calm. "This Niki sounds like an honorable man. You'll probably be saving his life. But to go off to Russia . . . all alone! My God, you've never been out of the islands."

Ana stared at her. "Neither had you."

They fell silent, wishing they could rewrite all the angry words they had exchanged, the looks that had rejected an intimacy so longed for.

"I thought of going with you, but I know you don't want my interference. *Mine*, least of all. Actually, I've wanted to go back since Max died . . ."

Ana let her chatter on, it seemed to calm her somewhat.

". . . Rosie told me about Niki's film. Ana, he doesn't need the testimony of Russian physicists. People know they're dying from contamination. They're dying in every country, that's how my husband died. His film needs to end with a message that's the opposite of despair."

She hesitated, as if about to ask a favor. "I was thinking . . . maybe Niki could shoot footage at this research clinic in Honolulu that I help fund. It's called the Hope Institute, where children damaged from radiation are fighting to survive. They bring them there from all over the world. I would help him in any way I can."

Ana listened, trying to grasp the deeper implications of what was said.

"I'm not offering to do this just for you. I'd be doing it for these children, and for my husband, Max. For once, please try to rise above your
resentment toward me and see the larger picture."

While she talked, Ana studied her mother's face. Lips a bit thinner.
Tiny time-lines fanned the corners of her eyes, but she was still lovely.
Ana wondered if her child would favor her.

She checked her watch and stood. "It's time to go."

Then she sat down again. "I have to tell you something. I found my
father's grave. It made me feel more . . . real."

Anahola looked down at her lap. "I should have married him when
you were born. But then, my own parents never married. Obviously, I
was *their* mistake."

Ana slowly shook her head. "It seems we've both gotten a lot of
mileage out of that word *childhood*."

They walked the concourse in silence, not noticing how people
stared because they were so striking, so similar, except for Ana's lighter
skin. At her gate, she saw the tour group had swollen now to almost
twenty people.

Her mother suddenly took her aside. "Let me meet you there. *Please*."

Ana gently pulled away. "I'll be okay. You and I . . . we'll always have
our history. But seeing you reminded me how strong I am."

She stepped across the chasm of unsaid things and took her daughter in her arms.

"Ana. You have no idea how strong you are. Yet, in some way . . . I
don't feel you're saving this man's life. He's saving yours."

PART FOUR

E PULE I KĒIA MANAWA

———

Now Is the Time for Prayer

PIKELOPOLO

The City of Peter

MOONLIGHT LAY ACROSS HER FOREHEAD LIKE A HAND. IT MADE the passing landscape bone. The train took a slow, languid curve and she saw her reflection in the window like a remnant of her soul. She leaned her head there, as the Red Arrow to Moscow ratcheted softly through the night, its long, low oboe chords sounding deeply wounded.

The compartment was stifling, suffused with a rich, crotchlike odor. The walls glimmered yellow, like soft human skin. Slumbering in their bunks were three virtual strangers from the tour. Ana took her pulse, thinking how close to the outer world her blood was circulating. But she no longer knew what world she was in, having left all borders behind.

She had entered timelessness over New York City, night making it a living jewel. At Kennedy Airport, she had dozed upright until dawn when they boarded Finnair for Helsinki. People began to look distinctly different, long-boned Scandinavians, and others whose bodies had a hefty, rural magnetism. They spoke in Balkan and Slavic tongues, rather guttural and harsh, and wore strange amalgamated clothes that looked as if they'd been assembled by committees. They moved with the lethargy of centuries.

In Helsinki, a tension had settled on the crowd as they lined up at Aeroflot for the hour flight to St. Petersburg. Even the small group from Honolulu grew alert. As their plane approached the "Venice of the North," Ana saw how St. Petersburg spilled across the banks and islets of the Neva River Delta and into the Gulf of Finland, an arm of the Baltic Sea.

"A city of islands," her neighbor said. "Eight hundred bridges lace it together."

Niki had said that, too. It was just a collection of islands. She held on to that; it made the city less frightening.

Now she sighed and stretched her arms, then half sat up and leaned her head against the window, peering out again. Great robber forests of fir and pine, deserted little huts bent sideways. Moonlight gave it all a talcumed beauty, a seeming endlessness. They passed little villages where people stood beside the tracks waving lanterns and small torches that, through grimy windows, flickered blue.

Ana waved back, then dozed again, her mind drifting over the week since her arrival in St. Petersburg. Immigration and Customs a blur, her group had huddled close like goslings following their Russian tour guide to a bus, where the driver sat cursing in the dirt, replacing a tire slashed by the "taxi mafia" looking for customers.

The guide had introduced herself as Zora, a small, energetic brunette with blue eyes reminiscent of Byzantine mosaics. Yet there was a tightness in her smile, fatigue in her sloping posture, suggesting that youth had already flown, that her energy came from her will to endure. With childlike candor she tried to divert the group's attention, describing the city's excellent restaurants, its grand cathedrals, and Peter itself as "most beautiful city in world." For hours passengers sulked, their breath stirring up the stagnant time inside the bus, until finally they departed.

The outskirts of Peter had rushed at them—medieval ruins of peasant huts dotting miles of concrete high-rises resembling penal institutions. Crows roamed the skies like bandits, swooping down on fresh roadkills. And in gray fields, *babushki* in fearsome tapestries of rags swung picks at the earth, then paused and blew their noses in their hands. When they looked up Ana saw eyes red and raw, wrinkles deep as saber cuts. Children with dirty faces ran beside the bus, offering bouquets of broken buttercups. Others just ran, holding out their empty hands.

They moved into a city layered in grime—bridges, boulevards, even cars stuck in traffic. It was summer, yet everything looked entombed in a dream of granite and mold. An overriding quality of despair, decay. Then their bus turned a corner and through the shimmer of linden trees, Ana was confronted with the haunting echo of Russia's past. Gold-domed cathedrals of a size that made people seem antlike. Forty-foot monuments of bronze and marble. A landscape of grandeur frozen in time. With a soft lurching of brakes, they came to a standstill in front of a huge, pistachio-colored wedding cake.

"Mariinsky Theatre," Zora announced. "Famous for Kirov Ballet . . .
Pavlova, Nijinski. You are fortunate to be seeing a performance there
this week, where you will see *nine hundred pounds* of gold in gilded interior walls and façades!"

Ana's lips parted in wonder as they passed cupola'ed and onion-
domed jewels, great baroque and neoclassical palaces still magnificently
intact, hints of crimson, blues, and yellows rinsing through the grime. In
pearly, northern light, each palace had an eerie, otherworldly beauty.

"Beloselsky-Belozersky Palace . . . Stroganov Palace . . . Menshikov
Palace . . . Each set in splendid, private park."

A sense of melancholy majesty and attending death formed a strange
alloy in her head. Fairy-tale palaces and their vast pollarded acreage set
midst crumbling decay and poverty gave this dreamlike city a disturbing
hybrid quality. Like a deadly poisonous yet alluringly beautiful, fading
orchid.

At the end of the main thoroughfare, Nevsky Prospekt, they crossed
the Neva River to their hotel. Halfway there, the driver stopped and
they looked back across the river at the jewel of St. Petersburg. The
Hermitage Museum, which melted into the magnificent Winter Palace. Fronting the river, the Hermitage and Winter Palace were perfectly
reflected in its waters—a graceful baroque edifice of soft chartreuse
greens. Punctuated by white Doric columns topped with allegorical
bronzed statues and window surrounds of gold, it seemed to extend for
miles.

From the front of the bus Zora spoke. "You are feeling awe, no? In
monumental scale, in architectural beauty, in quality and encyclopedic
display of culture and art, Hermitage is rivaled in world only by Louvre
and British Museum. But we have something more . . ."

She threw up her hands in a gesture of wonder so that her breasts
stood out.

"Hermitage was also Imperial Residence! Winter Palace for Peter
the Great. Later Catherine the Great. Alexander II was dying here of as-
sassin's wounds. Russian history is walking these corridors. You will be
feeling emotional charge of Imperial past when you are entering it tomorrow. Only several rooms to take all day."

Ana stared. As in a dream, she saw them.

*. . . There is the nurse with the strange, uneven features, outrunning
the bombs, bringing them bread and candles . . . And there is the carpenter
with bad feet, building crates in the catacombs to hide priceless paintings . . .*

· · ·

She imagined the nurse and carpenter meeting.

. . . The two of them making forays to the haunted galleries upstairs, hammering plywood over shell holes, sweeping out piles of shattered glass . . . They stand before an empty wall, imagining the portrait that had hung there. The Return of the Prodigal Son. The nurse traces with her finger the Rembrandt's shadow on the wall . . .

Ana shook herself, suspecting that this was how she would experience the city—borne to her through the memories of Niki. She would find him by listening to the cellos of the past.

THE HOTEL OKHTINSKAYA WAS NONDESCRIPT AND HUGE. ARMED guards were posted at the entrance and scattered round the lobby—big, scarred men with the restless gaze of wildlife that had not tamed their focus down to meet the human eye. They took her passport, gave her an entry pass and key. At the desk, she asked if there were any messages for her. The receptionist stared at her, then shook her head. On her floor, in a kiosk that sold magazines and vodka, two husky women sat knitting.

"*Dobraye utra,*" they said. Hello.

Big-breasted sentries, they watched her progress down the hall, then listened as she struggled with her key. Her room was small and musty, the bedspread retaining the sorrowful smell of sleepless humans in transit. The closet door hung by one hinge. Her window looked out on a treeless park eight floors below where people carefully side-stepped manure and ran their scruffy dogs.

Ana sat down and tried to call Niki. Static, then voices shouting back and forth. A phone rang, then it stopped; the operator said the phone was out of order.

"Then . . . is there any other listing for a Nikolai Volenko?"

The woman laughed and spoke in fearless English. "Is very common Russian name! Maybe two hundred of this name in Moscow."

She lay back feeling helpless, then showered and went down to dinner, where she found the cavernous dining room closed. They had run out of "tourist" food. A guard pointed her to a market half a block away and, cautiously crossing the dog park seeded with broken glass, the staggering swoon of couples, Ana entered a crowd of wild-looking men and women.

She was in a *gastronom*, a people's market, not meant for tourists, gamey with the odor of stale meat, humans reeking of sausage and unwashed flesh. Valkyries in steely white hairnets and bloodstained white coats stood behind low counters, hacking at chicken parts. They flourished their knives, shouting abuse at unruly crowds as people waved chits, grabbing up greenish bottles of kefir and small knots of potatoes.

Ana turned back to the entrance door, but in the frenzy of the crowds—expressions mean, determined—she was thrown against a counter. Her cheek slid down the belly of a hanging hare, its peltless corpse flayed blue and red. She screamed but in the general shouting no one heard. Then, in the swelter of bodies, a white-coated woman leaned over a counter and hacked at a huge, singed pig, a sunflower protruding from the moldy star of its anus. In his desperate grab for a slice of pig, a man knocked Ana down, then someone knocked him down. She lay stunned in a chaos of muddy boots.

But in the obtuse violence of the crowd someone took pity on her. One of the Valkyries mounted a box and shouted, waving her knife over her head as if preparing to aim and throw it. The crowd fell back, someone helped Ana to her feet. The white-coated woman laid down her knife and leaned over the counter, offering Ana a yogurt cup.

"Eat! Be strong like Russians!" Then she stepped back, still yelling at the crowd, and slapped a big cream cheese into shape.

Working her way back through the mob, Ana made it to the door, where someone grabbed her yogurt and thrust several *kopecks* in her hand. She staggered out into the sodium halo of a streetlight. She had been frightened but not mortally so, for there was something palpably alive in that crowd. Something that wanted life, not death. An enormous strength that stemmed perhaps from the memory of want.

Dizzy with hunger and fatigue, she wandered down the street and entered Last Kiss Before the Revolution Café. A dark vestibule, a cavernous dance floor, and a bar. It was empty except for a couple with shaven heads. The waitress wore exaggerated platform heels that sounded a clunky staccato as she crossed the floor. She was dark and pretty like a young, Greek boy, but when she bent close, Ana smelled the fruity breath of a diabetic.

Seeing three words on the menu she understood, she pointed and ordered.

"*Borscht, shashlik, I chashka chaya.*" Cabbage soup, shish kebab, and tea.

"*Da.*" The waitress nodded vigorously and disappeared through beaded drapes into a small, dark coffin of a kitchen.

The shaven-headed couple seemed to be licking each other's faces. The barman studied his profile in a mirror, left, then right.

It seemed only a matter of minutes before the waitress gently nudged her. "*Uzhin!*" Dinner.

Ana looked down at a dingy glass of beer, a tomato from which it appeared a bite had been taken. And what looked vaguely like a plate of dog ears, long mustard-colored petals covered with singed fur.

She shook her head. "*Nyet.* Not what I ordered."

"*Da*," the waitress insisted. "*Da!*"

In that moment, she remembered Niki's words. "In Russia, logic does not apply. Only the improbable is real."

She sighed, picked up her fork and speared one of the furred things, hoping it was some kind of vegetable. It was like chewing rubber covered with singed fur. She gagged into her napkin, ate the tomato, slowly drank the beer, and left *rubles* on the table.

Walking back to her hotel, she saw a solitary window lit up in the dark and, midst a white meringue of curtains, an old pressed flower of a face. It smiled, then waved its hand, a tiny envelope of bones. Ana waved, then crossed the dog park, trying vainly to grasp this mysterious, timeless heartache of a city.

Exhausted, she undressed and sank into a sleep that seemed a series of interrupted naps. Russia was in its "White Nights" of summer when, for a week or so, the sun barely set. Night was a pinkish dusk that lasted several hours before the sun rose again. She woke and dozed fitfully, Niki's face appearing and dissolving.

BY THE NEXT DAY PETER BEGAN TO OVERWHELM HER. A CITY OF too much exhausted beauty, too much history. She could absorb it only in sidelong glances, little sips, finding similarities to her islands.

Zora explained how rough-hewn Peter the Great had envisioned his city as a "window on Europe," and how his successors had followed him. Aristocrats of early St. Petersburg had learned French and English, and married their children off to European nobles, hoping to absorb their dress and manners. Studying the portraits of Russian "noblemen," Ana recalled the history of Hawaiian kings and queens, how they had copied the British to the point of adulation.

In 1882 when Kalakaua had completed construction of 'Iolani Palace in Honolulu, he had even crowned himself king with a full coronation ceremony. His successor and cousin, Queen Liliu'okalani, a friend of England's Queen Victoria, had dressed exactly like the queen. And like England's queen, Liliu'okalani had been a noble and imperious ruler, so threatening to Americans they had dethroned and imprisoned her.

As they progressed through the Hermitage, Zora expanded on Russia's history.

"Please understand opposing forces of our geography. Always we are being pulled two different ways. Pull of Europe on western borders. Pull of Asia on eastern borders. This is making us always a little what you are calling . . . schizophrenic."

Ana thought how Hawaiians, too, had been pulled in different directions. Set in the heart of the Pacific, they had always felt the ancient pull of Asia, and after being colonialized, the massive influence of the United States.

That evening at their hotel, Ana quietly took Zora aside.

"I'm trying to reach a friend in Moscow. The hotel operator says the phone is out of order. But I heard it ring! Could you please make the call for me again? Perhaps, since you speak Russian . . ."

The woman stared at her until her silence seemed extreme. "Sorry. I am guide only. I do not tamper in such things."

THE NEXT DAY SHE STOOD IN A FADED PINK CATHEDRAL MIDST flickering tapers and the rich brocade vestments of an Orthodox priest lifting high in the air the *ikonostasis*. Beside him acolytes swung urns of smoky incense. Engulfed in a sea of *babushki*, Ana listened to the soaring of old Slavonic chants as hundreds of voices sang out in quavering trebles archaic words of adoration.

After seven decades of silence they were allowed to worship openly again, to fill a human need for beauty and pageantry, a sense of the miraculous. A need that had proven indestructible in most Russian hearts. She closed her eyes, dizzy and nauseous from the suffocating odor of incense, acrid candle wax, the oils of tired human flesh. And with no sense of it, she prayed. *Please. Help me find him. I will not ask for anything again.*

Each evening she asked at the reception desk for messages. It seemed to amuse the security guards. Now, when they saw her, they grinned broadly, and shouted, "No messages!"

When she finally got through to Rosie, her cousin's relief was palpable. "Thank God you're all right. What is it like?"

"It's not like anything. I've seen real palaces . . . and people begging

in the streets. Have you heard from my mother? There's a man who's supposed to contact me . . ."

The connection was broken. She tried several times, but could not
reconnect.

AT PUSHKIN MUSEUM ON THE MOIKA CANAL ANA STARED AT A
life-size portrait of Alexander Pushkin. Dark-skinned, almost swarthy, a
broad forceful nose, he looked more Mediterranean than Russian, even
somewhat Polynesian. The docent explained in perfect English.

"His great-grandfather was Ethiopian, a black slave brought from
Constantinople as a gift to Peter the Great. Peter educated him and he
became a general, for which Pushkin was very proud."

At first the young poet had led a gilded life, then his poetry began to
speak of the abject poverty of Russian peasants. For a time he had been
exiled to Odessa as a revolutionary, fighting to abolish serfdom.

"Eventually the Tsar conspired against him, arranged a duel where
he was shot, and died. We have a saying. 'Tsars come and go. Regimes
come and go. Pushkin is forever.' "

Later, Ana stood on a bridge overlooking the Moika, watching sunlight turn the water rose. And she thought of the poet whose ancestor
had been brought to Russia in chains as a "gift" for the emperor. *When,
she wondered, had the young Pushkin, the dandy, turned his back on his life
of excess? What moment of stillness had served as a kind of pivot? Perhaps it
was a woman's glance, making his dark skin unignorable. Or perhaps it was
simply the whispering in his blood.*

Ana lingered there so long, she missed her tour bus and began walking back to her hotel along Nevsky Prospekt, passing shops for rich
tourists and a smart café where they sat draped at windows, sipping
drinks. She stopped on a hunch, retracing her steps. The café was located in Hotel Europa which she had heard was frequented by expats
and internationals.

Conscious that she was dressed in khakis and running shoes, she
drew her wide shoulders back, hoping she looked robust and confident as
she entered the café. She sat at the bar, where she ordered a beer and
stared at her reflection in a mirror; against a white shirt, her tan skin
seemed pronounced. Scanning the crowd, Ana noticed a loud group in a
corner. Journalists, sounding world-weary and blasé.

Finally, she approached them, introduced herself, and asked if they
had heard of Nikolai Volenko, a documentary filmmaker. They shook

their heads, inviting her to sit down, and Ana told them how she was trying to reach him, how frustrating it was.

A Brit leaned over, patting her hand. "My dear, it's Russia. Remember, they were serfs. You must *tell* them what to do."

One of the Americans took Niki's number, went to a phone and spoke in Russian, then came back, shaking his head.

"Disconnected. You need to go to his place in Moscow. Don't trust the phones."

Desperate, she looked round the group. "Would the American Embassy help me?"

A few of the journalists laughed.

"What about . . . Intourist?"

They laughed again.

The American walked her to the lobby. "Maybe you should give up. After all, he chose to come back. This thing with Russians . . . they always come back."

Along Nevsky Prospekt, crowds grew denser. Legless men whipped by on skateboards, signs pinned to their fatigues: AFGHANI VET. The nasal litany of vendors selling rotgut. Curbside, Alsatian dogs warning off gas thieves were chained to car bumpers, orange flakes of fender rust glittering in their fur.

Ana pressed on, passing old folks with their hands out, hoping for a *kopeck*. Niki had said the country was in chaos, but she had not fully understood. Now she saw people so starved they were beginning to show advanced signs of dystrophy, the disappearance of muscle when the body begins to devour itself. Their hands were clawlike, their faces skeletal. Avoiding a congested intersection, she followed crowds down steps to an underpass.

A man yelled after her, "Hey, tourist! You are entering Tunnel of Starvation."

Here masses of old folks stood propped against filthy concrete walls, their eyes completely blank with want. Dozens of them, some so weak they had collapsed, still holding out their wares, selling anything they had. A jar of teeth. A rusty birdcage. A rotting, blue brassiere. A woman with bleeding ears seemed to be pushing her granddaughter out to strangers, a child marked with the premature wrinkles of malnutrition. Ana shoved *rubles* in their hands and fled.

Exhausted and depressed, she made her way home through a vast park dotted with toppled statues until she was slowed by a young Circassian with Rasta braids playing a kind of bouzouki-mandolin. The sound was so plaintive and haunting it seemed to produce a wavering light, a place to rest the eyes. People paused and listened.

Amber Hindus in white muslim, dark handsome Moldavians with their black, sooty brows. Even a family of Uzbekis, men in sandals and threadbare, quilted coats, their wives holding children in vests and embroidered skullcaps. While the young man sang, bystanders swayed rather dreamily. Perhaps it was a song about a traveler far from home, and perhaps they were remembering a road, a hut, someone left behind.

A breeze lifted Ana's hair and there was suddenly a spiraling down, a cherry tree showering white blossoms on the face of a child, leaving petals on his skullcap. The boy closed his eyes, then opened them and laughed. The mother smiled, shifted the child in her arms, and slowly followed her husband from the park.

Ana dropped *rubles* in the young man's hat as he gazed after the family. "Refugees. But very tough. They come from the famine steppes of Uzbekistan."

He dipped into his hat and bowed, grateful for the *rubles*, then made a place for her to sit beside him. Softly fingering his mandolin, he told her how he had been traveling for years, how he had walked to St. Petersburg from his home in far Circassia, a country in southwest Russia on the northeast coast of the Black Sea.

"An old man when I began, wanting to see all Russia then I die." He grinned, pointing to his youthful face. "Instead my life lived backward. I grow young!"

She smiled, not quite believing as he told what he had seen. Towns where horsemen wore necklaces of human knuckles, where they used human skulls for pillows. Towns where the smell of wet newborns brought wolves in from the night. How their placentas were flung out to the wolves to draw them in.

"So in winter, warm coats of bristling wolfskin."

He had never held a fork, never been inside a running-water house. For a year he had lived in silence and that was when life came clean, and he grew young again.

Now he turned to Ana. "You are journeying, too. Yes?"

She nodded. "I came to Russia to find someone. He's ill. He needs my help."

He leaned close, his dark eyes searched her face. "But no. This journey is for *you*." His finger touched her cheek. "You have been old. At journey's end you will be youth again. Believe."

She wandered in a daze until she found a bridge that crossed the Neva. Dusk now, outside a subway entrance near her hotel, vendors threaded raw mutton onto *shashlik* skewers. Old women sold bunches of hyacinths and tulips. Ana watched crowds carry off red tulips like bright torches in the dusk, remembering folks in a far valley going forth to borrow fire.

That night people strolled along the Neva singing old Russian songs, accompanied by bayans and guitars. Ana threw open her window, smelling jasmine and forsythia. The sun hung just below the horizon where it would stay till it rose three hours later. As far as the eye could see, the river was a flowing pink, and it seemed as if, for these few hours, people slowed down and contemplated life. Perhaps the shimmering twilight gave them hope. That there would be a tomorrow, that it would be better.

A NIGHT AT MARIINSKY THEATRE, A PERFORMANCE OF *LA BAYA-dère*, the dancers so graceful they seemed to float a finger's breadth above the floor. Overhead, tiers of balconies and chandeliers were gilded with inordinate amounts of gold—another Tsarist building that had barely survived the Germans. Sitting in old plush seats, Ana imagined the place half-bombed and boarded up with plywood. Niki had told her of a concert here, the first of only three held during the long siege. She glanced at the audience in the dark, at phantoms that seemed to sit amongst them.

. . . *Musicians limp across the stage. In slippers and ragged boots, their feet are swollen from scurvy . . . They wear holey mittens while tuning their instruments. The cellist has blue lips. No heating, the Mariinsky is ice-cold. But who would miss tonight, no one! . . .*

. . . *The conductor enters. Thin and tired, he is greeted with applause . . . People struggle to their feet, they feebly shout. Tchaikovsky. Stravinsky. During the performances, they weep . . . Sergei, Niki's father, takes Niki's mother's hand . . .*

. . . *It has been a winter of starvation. They know the war is going to continue . . . millions might die. Yet, right now they are alive! Partaking of something beautiful, immortal . . .*

. . .

When Ana returned to her hotel she glanced round the lobby, looking for an American, a man who might be looking for her. She called
San Francisco, a connection that took only five minutes, much easier
than calling Moscow.

"I haven't heard from Eric," her mother said. "I promise you. He's
doing all he can . . ."

THEIR LAST DAY IN PETERSBURG ANA BROKE OFF FROM THE GROUP.
Breathing in the moldy air of Peter's rivers and parks, she made her way
to the intersection of Nevsky Prospekt and Griboyedov Canal. Remembering its description from Niki's letter, she followed the canal until she
stood in sunlight reflected off the golden, outspread wings of great bronze
lions guarding one end of a black filigree suspension bridge spanning the
canal. At the opposite end, another pair of winged lions sat, the four of
them holding in their mouths two gracefully swooping chains supporting
the bridge. Along the canal, misty rococo willows hung over the embankment, carrying the eye to the horizon. A beautiful and haunting
scene.

     . . . I know this place. I know that Niki's parents stood here after the
siege had ended. They talked about their future. I know that down this street
and to the left is a place where they kept instruments of torture . . . Medieval
wrist screws, nail-studded bludgeons. I know they used these instruments in
Stalin's time. They used them on Niki's father . . .

Suddenly chilled, Ana walked back to Nevsky Prospekt, feeling the
urge to run, to get out of this city, yet also wanting to stay, until she finally understood it. She seemed to walk in circles until she found a di-
lapidated palace, then pulled out Niki's letter to make sure.

". . . I want to sit in a tiny garden, behind old Sheremetyev Palace overlooking the Fontanka Canal . . ."

Just past the palace she turned in at a walkway leading to a small
jewel-like garden full of carefully tended flowers. Under the old maple
was a stone bench and plaque, commemorating this as Anna Akhmatova's favorite place, where she came to think and write. Ana sat down
and closed her eyes, breathing in jasmine and flowering limes.

After a while she opened the book of poems he had left her, the pages stained and dog-eared. She traced his fingerprints haunting the margins.

> ". . . I drink to our ruined house,
>   to the dolor of my life,
> . . . to lying lips that have betrayed us,
> . . . and to the hard realities:
>   that the world is brutal and coarse,
>   that God in fact has not saved us."

MOKEKAO

Moscow

Still sleepless in her bunk, Ana watched a stand of trees jump out like a forest of white fires. For a moment the train jolted as if sidestepping a giant pothole. Around her, people groaned. She looked at her watch, 2:00 A.M., then struggled out to the passageway, where gamblers squatted in the aisle, drinking vodka and throwing dice.

A massive man in yellow silk pajamas sat on a jumpseat like a Buddha, reading. She worked her way past him, found the lavatory and knocked. When no one answered, she pushed her weight against the door and it flew open. A man sat on the toilet with his pants down. He was holding a large handgun, and a clip of ammunition.

He looked up, grinning. "*Privyet!* . . . *Kak Dila?*" Hello. How are you.

Ana turned and fled, scattering the gamblers and their dice, then stood trembling over the man in yellow silk pajamas. "Do you speak English? There . . . there's a man with a gun."

The fat man laughed and closed his book. "He is your protection. What you pay extra for when boarding train. So no one rob you, slice you open in your sleep."

Her hand went to her heart.

He laughed again and smoothed his silk pajamas. "Hey, you are Americans. Cash cows of Western world. Besides, all part of Russian adventure, no?"

The gunman appeared, zipping up his pants, calling out to her in broken English. It sounded as if he were asking if she wanted her back

shaved. She found another lavatory, and then stepped out onto a con-
necting platform, inhaling grit and coal dust, the taste and smell of Russia. From the next carriage, she heard singing that lured her on.

At first she was struck by the dimness, then the sorrowful smell of
humans and clothes inadequately washed. It was a "hard-class" carriage,
without compartments, an open barracks on wheels. Two long tiers of
bunks on either side of a narrow aisle down the center. There were perhaps eighty people in the car, each bunk crammed with luggage and
a human surrounded by voluminous, plastic sacks. She saw mothers
changing diapers, men lined up for a stinking toilet. Seeing her, the
singing died. They rolled over in their bunks and stared.

"*Dobraye utra,*" she cried. Good morning.

A couple laughed, for it was night, not morning. The man leaned
forward from his bunk. "You are from . . . what country, please?"

"Hawai'i," she said. "The USA."

They grinned, waving her forward. "USA . . . okay! We practice English."

And so she met Viktor and Darya Patrovich, pensioners in their sev-
enties. Sitting on their bunk, Ana stared fascinated at Darya's row of
flashing metal teeth.

"*Da!* Smile of knives so beautiful I marry her," Viktor said. He had
wide Mongol cheekbones, the cheeks themselves were frostbite-scarred.

His wife slapped him playfully and smiled as people gathered near
the bunk, chattering in Russian and broken English, asking did Ana
drive a Chevrolet? Did gangsters still run Chicago? They asked about her
family, how many children did she have?

Darya filled tiny cups with tepid tea and as they drank, she pointed
to a window. "You see outside . . . beautiful Russian *taiga?* Rich soil from
centuries of human bones. Now history coming back again. For us."

"You understand?" Viktor tapped Ana's knee. "New capitalist Russia
bringing terrible inflation. No jobs, no care for old ones. Government ignore us. Our children ignore us. Old, backward Soviets, we remind them
of bad past!"

In spite of their shabbiness, they seemed tough, resilient.

"Forgive," Darya said. "We wanting nothing. Only you . . . listen.
No one listening no more."

They explained how, with sixteen dollars a month pension, they
were one step from begging. They lived in an abandoned building soon
to be demolished. The cost of water, lanterns, and batteries took all of

their pension. For ten years they had each owned one pair of shoes, which they continually mended. Viktor turned their shoes over, proudly showing the soles.

"Linoleum, from rubble pile!"

At night they stood behind restaurants waiting for thrown-out food. Or they scrounged around abandoned farms on the city's outskirts, raiding root cellars.

"We eat very slowly," Viktor said, "so saliva fill us up. Cannot remember feeling full. Russians cannot even cry. Tears very precious, they have salt."

They had sold everything they owned for this trip to Moscow, where a cousin worked at the Salvation Army.

"We will scrub floors, guarantee one good meal a day."

Darya pointed to the window again. "In villages is mass starvation. Millions dead. No produce anymore, no grain, no food. You see torches? People stand by tracks? They hoping you throw anything from train. One bread slice. Even garbage. Even . . . human shit. Dried, can use as fuel in winter."

Ana recalled the flickering blue lights, how she had waved to them.

Now Darya sighed and laid her head against her husband's shoulder. "Leaders say Communism dead. We now free humans. But no one feeding us. No one teaching us what human is. Freedom very cruel."

She thought of the poverty on her Wai'anae Coast, the sickness, the struggles. In spite of that, elders were cherished, loved, revered. They would never be thrust out on the streets to beg, to live in abandoned buildings. For the first time in her life, she was suddenly deeply conscious of what being Hawaiian truly meant.

And she was beginning to understand why Russians seemed a little crazy, with a violent largeness that knocked things down. They were people who did not know, had never known, what their future was. They could not even see a future. It left them deeply sundered, deeply vulnerable, and helped explain why they committed such noble, honorable, and unfathomably bestial acts. Perhaps she had never understood Niki until now.

She looked at her watch and struggled to her feet. "I'm sorry, I have to go."

She dug down in her handbag, pulling out a wad of *rubles*, folding them within her hand.

"Thank you for listen," Viktor said. "Remember Viktor and his Darya . . . tell your people of."

"I won't forget you." Fearing she was going to cry, Ana pressed the wad into Viktor's pocket. "Won't you take this please . . ."

He jumped back, shocked. "*Nyet!* Not wanting anything from you. Just to be talking."

She clasped her hands before her, begging. "You have shared your food, your lives with me. Please. Take this little gift. For *friendship*. It will make me very happy."

They hesitated, then reached out and hugged her, rubbing their wet faces against hers. "*Spasibo!* Thank you, Ana American!"

At the door, she looked back at where they stood holding hands, waving like children.

She had seen old photos of Moscow with its ugly, Soviet drabness, so this "New Moscow" stunned her. The heart of the city had been transformed into a glittering showcase for entrepreneurs. Towering skyscrapers, hygienic streets with lime-green parks. Monuments so bright they looked shellacked. Ana looked up astonished as they passed under neon banners advertising CHANEL. PORSCHE. ROLEX. Yet, here and there down dingy side streets, old posters of Stalin were viciously slashed with red paint. Statues of Lenin lay toppled in vacant lots.

At the Alpha Hotel, she glanced round the lobby expectantly, but no one was waiting for her. In her room she picked up the phone and asked to be connected to Niki's number. The operator said there was no such number, and no listing for him on Gogolny Street. There was no such street. She put in another call to San Francisco and shouted into an answering machine.

"I'm in Moscow. Your friend has not contacted me. I don't know what to do . . ." Her voice began to break. "I don't know what to do."

Out on the streets, she trembled with impatience, waiting for an opportunity to break from her group. They drifted up a hill of vast cobblestones, Red Square, and past St. Basil's Cathedral, with its schizophrenic onion domes, cupolas covered with gilded and enameled copper, its multicolored bricks and recessed tiles all thrown together by a seemingly mad architect. They stopped at Lenin's Tomb, wherein his body lay embalmed. It was something of a letdown—a lone red granite slab fronted with wreaths. The crypt was closed to the public now, rumors flying that Lenin's body had been "retired" to the countryside.

Ana studied their Moscow guide, a young woman named Raiza who wore jeans and Nike running shoes and looked rather hip. She thought of asking her for help, but she began to notice that wherever the group went, they seemed to be "escorted" by men in white shirts, black pants, and vests, and tinted shades.

A woman in her group said they were "uncles," old, retired KGB, keeping tabs on tourists.

"I thought that the KGB was dead."

The woman laughed. "They just call it something else now. You don't wipe out five hundred years of paranoia in three–four years."

Ana's attention was caught by the crowds themselves, the "New Moscow" where poverty seemed nonexistent. Flashy cars. Swaggering kids of the newly rich posturing with cell phones. They sat at bistros in designer-scruff, throwing peanuts at waiters. No beggars in the streets. But Ana knew from Viktor and Darya that only a few blocks away from downtown Moscow, thousands of hungry, disenfranchised people were scavenging at dump sites, sleeping in drainage pipes.

On the second day she casually broke off from the group and made her way across several boulevards and then through twisting streets to what—according to her map—should have been Gogolny Street. Instead she faced a veritable river of girders and cranes, earthmovers, swinging iron balls. A lone building tottered, its façade veiled in soft green nets like an old coquette. Crumbled bricks hurtled down metal chutes, exploding in tornadoes of dust. She breathed in acrid soot of sulfur, diesel oil, and then the rusty smell of blood. A black-market dealer had slid open the door of his van.

"Gogolny Street?" Ana shouted. "Is this Gogolny Street?"

Waving *rubles*, hard-hatted workers shoved her aside, hoisting upon their shoulders whole carcasses of marbled beef.

That afternoon, she crossed Marx Prospekt and entered the Arbat district, home for decades to artists, writers, dissidents. New Arbat was modern, an outdoor mall with galleries and cafés catering to tourists. Old Arbat Street stood behind the modern shops—more like a wide alley where vendors set up carts, selling souvenirs and lace. Menus hung yellow and faded outside ancient-looking restaurants, and up and down the street, artists hung their canvases on walls and in small, vacant parking lots.

Breathless, feeling faint with apprehension, Ana walked the length of the street, then doubled back. She bought a lace doily from a vendor while watching a group of artists who had hung their canvases in an empty courtyard—sentimental scenes of Imperialist Russia that tourists seemed to love. But one canvas drew her attention, a naked body wrapped in barbed wire that even encircled the face and mouth. "Dissident art," off-putting to most tourists, but the artist's use of light, the shimmering skin of the body had the subtle glow of a Vermeer.

A woman approached her. "You like it?" She turned the painting around. "Done on plywood. Some on tin, even plaster. We have no money for canvas."

"I wish I could afford it," Ana said.

"No need to buy. Please look, just look, and see our talent. We have talent."

Ana moved round the courtyard, then turned to one of the artists, a man with a goatee. "Excuse me. Do you speak English?"

He smiled. "A little."

"I am looking for a friend, Nikolai Volenko, a filmmaker. Have you heard of him?"

He frowned. "Very common name. I will ask."

He moved to a group of artists who looked at her and shook their heads. Ana thanked him and moved on. She stopped several times, asking for Niki, explaining that she was his friend, that it was urgent, that she had only five more days in Moscow. Each time she stopped, she volunteered a little more, casting her net a little wider. Niki was her fiancé, he had returned to Russia to finish a film. He was ill, she wanted to take him back to the U.S., where he could get medical attention.

She began to feel foolish, embarrassed at how they looked at her. She imagined them thinking that here was a woman who could afford to travel halfway round the world looking for her lover. Most of them wore threadbare jeans, cheap vinyl shoes. But even poorly dressed, the women were vivacious; the men had a seedy magnetism.

Hours passed while she moved up and down the street, then she sat at a coffee shop, exhausted. After a while a man passed and glanced at her, then looked back at an artist who nodded. He bought a pack of cigarettes, watching as she continued down the street, querying artists who shook their heads. Finally, she paused before a large red painting. Someone beside her cleared his throat.

"You like painting? It is of Georgian monastery. You know state of Georgia?"

Ana looked up startled. He was big and broad with a rather serene virility. Thick black hair and eyebrows, thick mustache.

"I'm sorry," she said. "It's my first time in Russia."

"So. I am Volodya Tavashvili."

She shook his hand. "Ana Kapakahi."

"You are buying art?"

"Oh, no. I'm looking for a friend."

"He is here? Old Arbat?"

"I don't know. Have you ever heard of Nikolai Volenko?"

Very casually, he lit a cigarette. "I know several Nikolai . . . but different surnames."

Ana moved closer. "Do you know any independent filmmakers? One of them might know him."

"Ho!" He laughed. "Today any Russian with video camera calls self filmmaker. Look . . . come have a beer. Just over there."

She shook her head. "Thank you. But . . . I don't have much time."

He reached out and took her by the elbow, gently, but firmly. "Come, sit down. We all know each other here. I will try to help you."

She sat at a small, sidewalk café while he went inside. She watched him make a phone call, then carry out two beers.

"Someone might know. Be patient. Cheers."

She raised her glass and drank down half the beer. "I . . . I've never felt so desperate. Niki returned to Moscow two months ago. We can't reach him by phone or mail. I came here to find him."

She showed him a slip of paper with the address. "I went there. It doesn't exist. Just blocks of demolition sites."

"Neighborhoods are vanishing," he said. "When your friend left Moscow, perhaps were buildings there. Now they replace it with high-rise for rich, foreign investors. Even rename streets. Tell me, you are American. But, from which part?"

She was suddenly aware of her broad features, her tan skin.

"From the islands of Hawai'i. I met Niki in Honolulu. Have you heard of it?"

"*Da!* Pearl Harbor, your strategic port. But you were saying . . . ?"

Something about him had subtly changed. He seemed more attentive, leaning forward as she spoke.

"Niki was traveling round the Pacific, making this documentary film about . . . I guess you could say it's about environmental pollution."

"Subject Russians know too well."

"He was in Honolulu on a grant while he worked on this project. We became . . . very close. He came back to Russia to finish the film. An important final segment."

Volodya spoke very carefully. "Do you know what was this final segment?"

She hesitated, not knowing who this man was, where he was from. "I'm not really sure. But he shouldn't have come back. He needs medical attention. I'm not sure he'll get it here."

"*Da*. Hospitals real nightmares."

Ana was mildly dizzy from the beer. "He should have stayed with me. But he felt in the way. Felt I didn't . . . care enough."

"And, did you?"

She suddenly felt a need to confess, to purge all her frustrations.

"I didn't know how much until he left. You see, I'm a doctor, still finishing my residency in obstetrics and gynecology. I work long hours. I thought I didn't have the time, the energy for him. And now, I'm here."

She looked up imploringly, as if this man could give her absolution. He lit a cigarette, flicking the match with a yellow thumbnail.

"Ana Kapakahi. Who let her lover go. Now you are here to take him back. Tell me, is life so easy in the West? Make decision, snap your fingers, and it's done? How wonderful."

Inside the phone rang. Someone shouted for Volodya.

He came back smiling. "A friend will join us. She might help you in your search."

Ana wondered if she should offer him money, if that was expected.

As if reading her thoughts, he smiled. "Think nothing. We have idle time, and are very curious to talk to Americans."

Within minutes a striking blonde arrived. Tall, well dressed, with topaz eyes.

"This is Katya."

"Hello, Ana!" She shook hands like a man, then asked Volodya for a whiskey.

While he was gone, she pulled high-tech baubles from her handbag. "Boyfriend calls me gadget-girl. Look what he brings me today! Mini cell phone. Mini-Walkman. Look, this lighter, voice-activated recorder, good for spies! Also wristwatch TV."

She whipped out a sleek, little palm-sized camera. "Latest model Polaroid, tiny, excellent. Wait, I take your picture. Smile!"

She pressed a button, heard a click, then pointed it at Volodya, bringing out her drink. She had Ana take a picture of her and Volodya, then one of him with Ana. Within minutes they had a row of perfect prints.

Volodya laughed. "All hijacked. Sell everything. Before gangster-boyfriend is arrested."

"Never arrested," Katya said. "Will be shot to death. Pride thing with them." She abruptly turned to Ana. "So. You are looking for Niko-lai Volenko."

She felt her heart beat. "You know him?"

"Maybe I have heard of him. Maybe he is out of Moscow. Making film."

Ana leaned forward. "But where outside of Moscow? Do you have a phone number? Address?"

The woman shook her head. "Maybe he call my boyfriend when needing new video camera, black-market price. Maybe he went east. Novgorod. Yekaterinburg. Big cities. Weapons plants, going now to rust."

Ana looked from one to the other. "Please. How can I get word to him?"

Katya shook her head. "I think . . . impossible. Why is so important for you to contact this man?"

"He's sick. He will get sicker. I want to take him home, take care of him."

Almost nonchalantly, Katya examined her long nails. "You know how hard for Russians to leave Russia now? Especially returning Rus-sians. Why coming back? Very suspicious. Old Soviet passport no longer valid. New passport taking months, maybe years. Maybe never. How you would get him out?"

"I don't know. I don't know. He told me anything could be bought. Passports, visas . . ."

"*Da.* Maybe. But you have first to find him, no?"

Ana sat up straight, refusing to break down in front of these tough Russians. "I'll find him. However long it takes."

Then she slumped a little. "The truth is, I wasn't prepared for your country."

Volodya leaned back and smiled. "Ahh, Russia. To understand us, you must listen closely to everything we say. Then, reverse it."

"How far are these cities you mentioned? Could I get there by train?"

"Impossible. Novgorod, eight hours. Yekaterinburg, almost twenty-four hours. You don't speak Russian. You would be robbed. Or, you would disappear."

A dish of *zakuski*, little tasties, appeared—radishes, cucumbers, meats, and cheese, tiny pancakes filled with roe. Toying with the food, Volodya stabbed a radish with a sharp knife, and offered it to Katya. She swal-lowed her whiskey, then wet her lips and took the radish between her teeth, slowly sliding it off the blade.

Almost dusk now, a warm, summer dusk that would draw couples to linger over bridges, to sit together under linden trees. Vendors turned on electric lights. Something passed between Volodya and Katya.

He stood, offering his hand. "Ana. I must leave. I will make more calls. You will come again tomorrow? Katya now will drive you home."

She jumped up and shook his hand. "Thank you. Thank you. I don't know how . . ."

"Not problem! Maybe one day you do *us* favor."

She followed Katya to a sleek new car, and while she struggled with the air conditioner, Ana studied her slim legs, her pale hair that fell seductively over her face. Except for a certain toughness, she was rather beautiful.

"Your boyfriend is lucky."

Katya laughed. "Today gangsters like rock stars. Live hard, then die. He has many girls. I must be clever, get all I can. Liquidate. Then, get out of Russia."

"What about your family?"

"Parents die-hard Soviets. No longer do we speak. Is sad. But life is sad, no?"

As they wheeled into traffic, she beat on the dashboard, cursing the faulty air-conditioning.

"I, too, was artist, Ana. Very *avant*, very good. No one buying. Now I am something else. I help other artists. Buy beef, fresh vegetables, so they are never starving."

Ana watched entranced as she steered the wheel with her knees while working a lighter and holding a cigarette. Then she stabbed a cassette into the player. Asking Ana about her life, her work, she pulled out makeup and looked in the rearview, combing her hair, touching up her lipstick, then waved her fist out the window as they highballed across an intersection.

Searching for a business card, Katya dug deep into her handbag, throwing out all her gadgets. She emptied the glove compartment, tossing things to the floor. Then she reached over the backseat into a leather briefcase. Still steering with her knees, she carefully selected a card, wrote down a number, and ceremoniously handed it to Ana. As they skidded up to Ana's hotel, she took Ana's hand in both of hers.

"So. Ana! I see you tomorrow, yes?"

Then she drove off, hands busy lighting another cigarette, adjusting the rearview mirror. In the twenty-minute drive across the city, Ana had not seen the woman's hands touch the steering wheel.

MOSCOW SEEMED TO HAVE ENTERED A HEAT WAVE; IN AN ALMOST trancelike state Ana threw open her windows. They were still in the ebb of Russia's "White Nights." At eight o'clock the sky was a pale, reverberating green like the dying light of a fluorescent bulb, making everything look ill. In spite of the city's glittering façade, the air was filthy and polluted. Her shoes were covered with grime. Her mouth had the aftertaste of metal. Worrying about the effect on her child, she ran to the bathroom and heaved.

After a while she washed her face, then lay down, exhausted. She thought of the two Russians, how they had humored her, a silly American looking for her lover. And she began to pray for him, for what they had created. She prayed herself into a half sleep. When the phone rang she jumped up as if the thing had bit her.

"Ana? Is Raiza, your guide. We have been missing you. You are coming tonight? Our famous Moscow Circus! Bus is downstairs, forty minutes. We are waiting you with ticket."

A CROWD OF HUNDREDS UNDER THE GLITTERING BIG TOP, THEIR faces upturned to the whirling iridescence of aerialists. Dwarfs rode in on elephants. Clowns threw white mice at the audience. Ten Siberian tigers entered, roaring at the crowd. Magnificent creatures, they snarled and tossed their heads like angry princes. The audience clapped wildly.

Then a girl appeared on a trapeze, soaring alone like a wandering star. The band struck up a waltz as she swung out in a lazy swoop and hung from the bar by her arms, legs stretched in a perfect arabesque. In a return swoop, she hung by the back of her bent knees, then only by one knee. The crowd applauded, calling out her name. She pulled off a bracelet and flung it to them. She threw them kisses and soared.

Ana closed her eyes.

   . . . A small, graceful girl, a glittering moth lifting a young man's eyes. He reaches up, surrendering . . . And they are happy for a while. And then he holds her, naked, until her face becomes the snow . . .

'IMI, 'IKE, MAOPOPO

—

To Seek, to Sense, to Understand

AT 6:00 A.M. HER PHONE RANG. "GOOD MORNING, ANA! I HAVE waked you?"

She sat up instantly alert. "Katya. Do you have any news?"

"Not yet. But we are asking. Meanwhile, I invite you to breakfast. I come at eight o'clock."

Ana glanced at the day's itinerary to see what she would miss. Tretaykov Galleries. The Armory Museum—Imperial thrones, Fabergé eggs. The city was offering her everything but what she needed.

In the lobby Katya stood flirting with a ponytailed security guard wearing a flowered shirt.

"You are looking very *glasnostic*," she told him. "*Molodets.*" Good for you.

Guiding Ana to the car, she laughed. "Such peasant. Ponytail. Aloha shirt. This look went out with Andropov."

On New Arbat Street she took Ana to a smart café. "Boyfriend is partner here."

Bending over an American-style breakfast, Katya wolfed down the food with an endearing greediness, then sat back and sighed.

"Sorry. As girl I grew up on potato peels."

Feeling exhausted, Ana sipped orange juice so fresh it bit her tongue. "How do you sleep in these White Nights?"

"I never sleep. You are tired, Ana?"

Katya's behavior was different today, her voice softer, more intimate.

Yet she seemed slightly nervous, apprehensive. Later, they turned onto Old Arbat Street, as artists yawned and hung their canvases.

"No government support for them," she said. "No official recognition. Same as beggars in the streets. What will future civilizations find when digging up Russia. Poetry? Art? *Nyet.* Only bones. Eight thousand square miles of human bones."

". . . And Lenin's mummy." Volodya came up behind them with two men he introduced as Sandro and Ulan.

They were dark and swarthy, wearing black leather. As Ana shook their hands, their bodies gave off such heat she felt she was standing beside a panting locomotive.

"Don't mind them," Volodya said. "Hot weather makes their thick Siberian blood boil!"

"So," he continued, taking her arm. "We inquire up, down the street like yesterday. Then have a coffee."

As they moved along, she had the sense of Sandro and Ulan hovering, moving to either side of her so that she felt protected, or closely observed. Several artists recognized Ana from the day before, but no one had news for her.

"It's too late," she whispered. "I've wasted too much time."

Volodya placed his hand on her shoulder. "Ana. I ask you to be patient. Today we invite you to lunch. An interesting place . . ."

She shook her head. "I've got three days left to find him. I'm sorry, I don't have time to linger over lunch."

He leaned down close. "Yes. You have time . . . to linger over lunch. Believe me."

His voice was different now, it frightened her. He steered her to a side street, an ancient-looking restaurant whose dining room was underground. *This is where I disappear*, she thought.

It was called the Palace of Small Amusements, its interior perfectly preserved from the 1940s, what Volodya called Stalin Gothic.

"His favorite restaurant."

Through a damp vestibule, they entered a cavernous dining room. Ana looked around amazed. Everything outsized, intimidating, the place looked designed in a delirium of fever. Wide, thick stone steps without balustrades climbed the walls, going nowhere, ending abruptly. Yet farther up, a second flight of steps, again ending abruptly as if on the brink of an abyss. Ana silently stared at the dark upper gloom.

"Yes . . . like a dungeon," Volodya said. "Here, while Stalin dined, he watched his henchmen torture dissidents, 'enemies of the state.' Men. Women. He watched them tortured to death. The place was patterned after Ivan the Terrible's 'Palace of Amusements' inside the Kremlin when it was a medieval fortress."

As the waiter showed them to a table, Ana noticed a man in a corner dressed in a tuxedo, holding a stack of menus.

"The maître," Katya said. "A little dusty."

Ana moved closer, thinking the figure was plaster, but very realistic-looking, except for an eerie paste-gray face and glass eyes with the look of lobotomized bliss. A musty smell hit her with such force, she cringed. A mummified human.

"One of Stalin's henchmen. His sin? One day during torture session, his electric prod accidentally set Stalin's tablecloth on fire. Comrade thought this was deliberate attempt on his life."

She stood there, disbelieving.

"If we had more time, would show you what happened to Stalin's projectionist, who accidentally ruined his favorite Charlie Chaplin film."

They told her that for decades these grotesqueries of Stalin's were hidden from the public in underground vaults. Now they were collector's items, selling for thousands of dollars. Ana sat in mild shock while they ordered from a menu written in Cyrillic. Hare stuffed with bloodberries from Tashkent. Roe from the Caspian. Deer-penis wine from Lapland. Red and very tart. Waiters passed silently. Trolleys with jellied pâtés went quivering by. From somewhere the soft strings of a guitar. Ana kept glancing at the mummy holding menus, wondering what would happen next.

"Forgive our black humor," Volodya said. "Sometimes we Russians even scare ourselves."

"I'm not really shocked," she said. "That is . . . I've been in total shock since I arrived."

"Very different from your United States, no?"

She looked round the table. "I don't know the United States. I'd never been out of my islands till I got on that plane to come and look for Niki."

"Not possible!" Katya said. "You don't know Las Vegas? Miami?"

She shook her head.

"You did this just for Niki?"

"Yes."

"My God. Volodya, tell her."

"Shut up." He leaned forward, refilling glasses.

"Tell me what? Why did you bring me here?"

"We know the owner. A safe place to talk."

Ana pulled her wallet from her handbag. "Here. It's all I have, maybe $400 American, $300 left in traveler's checks and *rubles*. Take it. *Please*, tell me what you know."

"Put it away. And listen. Your Niki . . . is okay. We are his friends. He is okay."

She let out a moan.

"Calm down. We need you to be calm."

Katya reached across the table, taking Ana's wrist. "Ana. It is very serious. Yesterday we were not being sure of you. We show Polaroid pictures to Niki. He hear your voice on minirecorder. He is shocked. He wept. That you have come for him. 'Yes,' he says. 'That is my Ana.'"

She tried to breathe evenly. "I need to see him . . . to talk to him."

"There is trouble," Volodya said. "May be dangerous for him. Officials promise him interviews with high-positioned scientists now sick from radiation. But no one will *ever* interview these men. World will never see them."

While he talked Sandro and Ulan carefully watched the to-and-fro of waiters.

"Was a ploy. To get him back here with his tapes. No one, Yeltsin, future leaders, *no one*, wants world to see what Russian government did to own people. If such tapes are shown, world will see Russia as a joke. We already nuked *ourselves!*"

Ana looked from one to the other. "What happened to Niki?"

"There were meetings. They picked his brain about sickness and pollution in Pacific, in United States, wherever he shot films. They want to see all footage of such films. Good propaganda against U.S. Niki hid them, would not tell where. They said 'Okay, you keep your word, we keep our word. We make exchange. You do interviews with scientists, then after, you show us tapes you have made, maybe give us copies for archives. They set up interviews. Niki never arrive. Afraid is trap to arrest him. Disappear him."

Ana shook her head. "He doesn't need what he brought back. He left copies of those tapes in Honolulu. Why didn't he turn them over and get out?"

Volodya smiled. "Ana. Remember, this is Russia. Here, logic does not apply."

"You understand?" Katya said. "Many journalists, cameramen now recording Russia's devastation. Leaders telling them shut up. Want to keep our filthy history secret. So. They are rounding up such people."

"You mean, they're being shot."

"Not so dramatic. Gulags are finished, yes. But we still have 'penal colonies.' Real nightmare prisons. Someone like Niki, little bit known, they would make of him example. Give him four–five years in prison. So he stop making films."

Ana shook her head. "He would not survive four years in prison. He would die."

"*Exactly*. So he is in hiding. Not knowing what to do."

"Please. Let me see him," she whispered.

"Wait. And listen. They come to Old Arbat looking for him. Posing as sympathetics, network officials offering to help him air such documentaries on TV. They are all assholes. 'Uncles.' "

Katya interrupted. "Then, last week, different type comes. American. Clean-cut. He, too, is looking for Nikolai Volenko. Man named Eric Dancer."

Ana sat back, letting the name resonate.

"This Dancer says he carries letter from American Consulate inviting Niki to America, to make his films. He says there is sponsor for him, someone guaranteeing Niki's income. How do we know this man is not working with the 'uncles'?"

One of the Siberians stood and stretched, then walked over to the draped vestibule, looking left and right.

"I know who he is."

They didn't seem to hear her.

Volodya continued. "I ask this American why such a favor for Volenko, who I pretend 'I never heard of.' He tells me is personal matter. Of the heart. 'Suppose,' I say, 'this man you seek is not allowed to leave Russia, is accused of embarrassing government with "shocking" documentary films?' "

He shook his head and smiled. "This Dancer then names twelve officials, bureaucrats, whose signatures he can buy with *blat*. Illegal payoff. Real opportunistic shits. He tells me he can buy good passport and visa with such signatures. Can do it very fast."

What he said next jolted Ana halfway to her feet.

"He said if he could find Volenko, could have him on plane for U.S. in twelve hours."

Katya gently pushed Ana back into her chair. "He gave us card, but we are still not knowing who he is. Even Niki not knowing who he is. So we play dumb, avoiding him. Then this week, you come."

"Eric Dancer is my mother's friend. She's trying to help me. She said he would contact me in Moscow."

They stared at her, and then Volodya responded.

"If this is so . . . we need you to confirm this. To meet with him. Here is his card. If he is legitimate, we take him to Niki."

"Can't you take me to Niki first?"

Silence fell while a waiter cleared the plates.

Katya spoke again, but softly. "Ana. Every step you now take . . . very crucial. One stupid move. You put him in prison."

"What do you mean?"

"You think you are not watched? Your guides, bus driver are not watched? You think you are not seen leaving tour group, asking for Niki, up, down Old Arbat? You think Russia suddenly wide-open? Free? A joke!"

"Just tell me . . . is he nearby? Does he know I'm here right now?"

"Not important."

Unable to control herself, Ana suddenly broke down and wept. They looked away, allowing her time to pull herself together.

"I have to see that he's all right. I need to tell him I'm . . . carrying his child."

The men sat motionless. Katya closed her eyes. After a while she opened them, and slapped her hand on the table like a warden.

"Okay. Now we begin to mobilize. Ana, no more horseplay. You are not seeing your child's father until he is outside of Russia. Or. We finish with you *now*. We walk away. Agreed?"

She would not remember clearly what happened next. She remembered only calling Eric Dancer's number for hours until they finally reached him.

In the car, Volodya instructed her. "Wipe your eyes. Comb your hair. A little lipstick. We will be in hotel bar across from you. Any problem, you call out my name."

Katya pulled a small, elegant handgun from her bag and slipped it into Ana's.

"My God!" she cried. "I don't want a gun."

"Darling. It's Russia. A *status* thing, like cell phones."

As they pulled up to the National Hotel, Ana gave Katya a letter she had written Niki. "If anything goes wrong, tell him . . ."

"Shh. Nothing going wrong."

The hotel had been refurbished from a shabby Soviet-era pile of rocks to a monolith of glass and steel. Security at the door was tight. They checked her handbag and smiled, relieving her of her handgun as if it were a toy. A man in an expensive suit took Ana's name, then guided her to an area of deep, plush chairs. Snapping his fingers at a bell-boy, he spoke in rapid Russian, then stayed at Ana's side until the American appeared.

"Ana? Eric Dancer."

He guided her to a table in the bar. "What would you like?"

"Nothing. Tea."

He ordered two teas, letting her observe him. Average height. Forty, forty-five. Hair close-cropped, blond going gray. An all-American face, nice-looking, almost bland. A face that would not stand out in a crowd. His clothes well made, his fingernails immaculate.

"Ask me anything," he said. "But remember, time is of the essence." He nodded to the group entering the bar. "Your friends must know the jokers at the door."

"Why are you doing this?" she asked.

"For your mother. In a roundabout way I owe her."

"What did she do for you?"

"Her husband, Max, once saved my father's life. They worked together at Los Alamos, the midforties."

He explained how, after Hiroshima, when Robert Oppenheimer refused to make more bombs, Washington had pegged him a Communist and drummed him out of the business. Dancer's father was one of the physicists who had dropped out with him after seeing what bombs could do to humans.

"During the Red Scare no one would hire Dad. He drank, tried suicide a couple times. Then Max McCormick took him on. His family had money, laboratories. He gave my father his own labs, worked with him in the field of immunology."

In time, Hubert Dancer's research papers were published. He won recognition and finally regained his dignity.

"Thanks to Max, he died a proud man."

This was not rehearsed. Ana could tell by the sudden flush on Dancer's cheeks, the dead calm of his voice, that he was speaking with emotion.

"Then, when Max got sick I went to see him regularly. He asked me to look after your mother. She was what kept him going. He said she was pretty much alone in the world. I guess . . . you two were never close."

Ana looked away.

"I call her every week or so . . . visit when I'm in San Francisco."

"Are you her lover?"

Dancer smiled. "Your mother's got about ten years on me, though she's still beautiful. But no, I'm not her lover. I wouldn't choose a woman like her. Too damned independent. By the way, we're getting sidetracked."

"We've only been talking seven minutes."

His eyes narrowed, half-amused. "I see you take after her. Look, Ana, we can drag this out. We can do lunch and shop while you decide if I'm legitimate, or if I'm scouting for the Russians. Meanwhile, they're closing in on your boyfriend. I understand he's got a health problem. You leave, what? Tomorrow? Next day? I lose track of him, you might never see him again."

She gripped the handle of her cup. "Exactly what is it you do here?"

"I import food. Silly luxuries. Nouveau riche Russians crave New Zealand lamb. Pineapples from Costa Rica. They love California wines. California anything. I bring them that."

"And what do you *export*?"

"Bodies, Ana. Innocent people who need to get out."

"Why did you go to the Arbat? You scared his friends. Why didn't you contact me first?"

"You didn't pick up your messages yesterday. Besides, I needed to move things along. You see . . . we don't really need you to get your friend out. I've been busy waltzing certain Russians, trying to set things up. Frankly, you would have been in the way."

She sat back and studied him. "How can you move around so easily? Are you some kind of agent?"

He played with a book of matches. "Look, this isn't about espionage. It's about love. A wonderful thing. Your story has a slightly different spin. Now all we have to do is locate your friend and buy off a few bureaucrats with holes in their socks. Which will get us a passport, and exit visa. And your Nikolai is free. Your mother's already signed papers to sponsor him. The U.S. Consulate has offered a work visa."

"What about the men who are trying to find him?"

"I would say that qualifies him for political-exile status. It also means we've got to find him quick."

He drummed his fingers on the table, waiting.

"My mother never described you," Ana said. "How do I know you're . . . really *you?*"

He grinned. "You *do* take after her. Sometimes, sweetheart, you just have to go on faith."

OUTSIDE, HIS VOICE TOOK ON AN URGENT, ALMOST MILITARY TONE as he shook hands with the group.

"Volodya, you need to take me to Nikolai right now. There are things he has to do. Katya, take Ana shopping, anything. Don't let her out of your sight."

He turned to Ana and took her hand. "You will not see him in Moscow. Understood? You will not see him till he's safely out of Russia."

She sat in Katya's car in shock, watching the four men drive off in a cab.

Katya glanced at her. "Is going to be all right. I promise. You are going to have your Niki."

As they drove down boulevards, Ana asked, "Do you know Niki well?"

"We all know Niki. Very smart. Very kind to others. At one time, very good gangster."

"Did you know his wife, Irini?"

"Yes. Tragic. All Russians have such stories. Even now."

"So much for your 'new democracy.' "

"Democracy! Russia's final penance. Is only for gangsters, privateers. What you see in Moscow is not real Russia. Ana, you know what is pornography? You ever watch pornography? Longer you watch, less you feel. History of Russia is pornography. No feeling. No reacting. So we make up own history, own reality. Is how we survive without going mad. For Russians, lying very important, is highly crafted skill."

"You haven't lied to me, have you?"

"Only a little. Volodya and me . . . we are not just being friends. Look at him! Who could not love this man so handsome. One day I marry him." She patted Ana's stomach. "Have little babies."

"What about your gangster?"

"I finish with him soon. When, like Russia, I find my soul again."

She had begun to like this Katya, her toughness that hid a sensitive, reflective nature, her wild extravagance in the way she shoved large wads of *rubles* at old *babushki* in the street, the reckless way she drove the BMW, showing a certain disdain for the car and for the life she led.

They drove to a park where, from a terraced café, they watched
swans attack a swimming dog. After an hour Katya tapped buttons on her
cell phone, talked in Russian, then hung up and ordered them a meal.

Ana felt desperate again. "Are they with Niki?"

"All is well, Ana. Is only about right people to be paid."

Later, as they slid back into the car, it occurred to Ana that Niki's
freedom depended on someone paying someone off, that everything
hinged on money.

"How are they paying them?" she asked. "Where is the money coming from?"

Katya looked at her as if she were inordinately dense. "From who
Dancer is doing this favor for. Your mother. No?"

In the silence, they passed a hard hat with a bullhorn shouting at
four women pouring tar.

"Look those women," Katya said. "Bright red lipstick! Peroxide hair!
Even if Russa dying, they are dressing up. Maybe female vanity will save
us."

She suddenly veered left, then right, down several alleys. "Wait. I
show you something special."

They drove to a narrow street where Katya parked and entered a
building, guiding Ana up three flights. The halls smelled of steamed cabbage and fried *kasha*. She unlocked a door, and Ana was swept with the
clean scent of bergamot and lavender. It was a small, cozy room exuding
privacy and secrecy, a sanctuary deep inside the great stone crypt of
Moscow.

Floorboards groaned underfoot, dishes in a tiny cupboard rattled.
Small mirrors gave the room imagined depth. A room that could be
crossed in eleven steps, life lived on an intimate scale. A hot plate on
a desk, bottles of wine, ripe fruit. A fireplace for burning wood. Ana
saw dark windows veiled with spectral drapes. But she imagined how, in
winter, the panes would be flower-scrolled in hoarfrost. Firelight would
gleam on a large bed covered in red satin, causing the satin to shimmer
and dance.

She saw snapshots coming unstuck from a wall—a teenaged Katya in
uniform holding a rifle. An older Katya in an ore-smelting factory, in
headscarf and overalls, her perfect face near black with soot. And everywhere, books—under the bed, spilling from chairs, piled high to the ceiling. A room filled with thought, and with a strange vitality.

Katya gestured toward two sets of *tapochki*, carpet slippers, beside a
pair of men's shoes.

"This room, my real life. Boyfriend finds out, he kill me. So what? Without Volodya, I am dead."

Ana stared at the slippers, imagining the two of them lying together, engaged in long conversations while they gazed at the ceiling. Hopes and dreams that never crossed the threshold.

"Imagine, Ana. To climb a stair. Know he is listening for my foot-step. To be taken in, and held. Close the door, world melts away. What better thing for humans? We are so alone."

In that moment she saw how, in her search for Niki, she had stum-bled on this other life. And this life now revealed itself as precious and terribly fragile, a thing to be fought for, to give up one's life for.

At her hotel, Katya embraced her. "Now I take your letter to Niki. You go upstairs. Lock door, no calls, no conversations. Yes?"

"God bless you, Katya."

"Is nice feeling. God blessing me."

SHE SAT IN THE DIMNESS OF HER ROOM, THINKING OF KATYA AND Volodya, Viktor and Darya, and all of them. Their lives, their country in such chaos each day brought new convulsions. Yet here were people so wrenched by life, they had decided to strike back, to prove there was something more to human existence than suffering.

MANA'OLANA

Hope

THE NEXT MORNING KATYA CALLED, INSTRUCTING HER TO JOIN HER tour group, make herself highly visible. By now Ana's clothes looked dingy; even her fellow tourists had begun to look worn down by grime, bad food. They no longer trusted what they saw. Two Cuban women who had joined the group in New York had disappeared. A man wearing gold chains was robbed by prostitutes. While he slept they cleaned out his room, even his American condoms.

The day was a blur, more cathedrals, and galleries. A performance at the Bolshoi Ballet.

That night Eric Dancer called. "Tomorrow is your last day, right? Go out with your group again. It's important you be seen. Do not wander from the group."

"But what about . . ."

"Ana. All is well. Katya will contact you in the evening."

The next day they drifted across squares, desultorily snapped photos of each other. They stood in a kind of field where statues of Stalin and Lenin had been deposited by refuse trucks. They lay in great pieces, a head, a leg. Inside a large wire cage, hundreds of human heads sculpted from stone were piled one atop the other, the expression on each face one of abject horror. A plaque below the cage read SIXTY MILLION. Ana's group stood silent.

Leaving the dining room that evening, she saw Katya in the lobby surrounded by thuggy security men. They laughed, hunching their shoulders and flirting with her.

Katya waved her over. "Ana! We go for a nightcap?"

Her face looked tired, almost devoid of makeup. As they slid into the car, she lit a cigarette, then tapped her nails on the steering wheel.

"Tell me what's happening," Ana said.

"So far is okay. But these *mudaks*, shmucks! Stupid, greedy bureaucrats. Takes one minute to sign documents. But they are changing minds. Wanting more money, then more. Until Niki is out, I trust no one."

"Katya. Can't you at least tell me where he is?"

"He is fine. A little cough. No more questions."

They stopped somewhere for a drink, then drifted aimlessly across Red Square, a place Ana was now familiar with. They gazed up at flamboyant cupolas and spires of St. Basil's Cathedral, like giant swirling Dairy Queens.

Katya shook her head. "A metaphor for our mad country."

"I could never have imagined Russia," Ana said. "My islands are so small. My town is just some red-dust roads along a coastal highway that goes nowhere."

Through the days she had talked about her homelands to Katya, about her people's struggle to find themselves.

"But you have blue and warm Pacific sea. And family," Katya said. "You say you have many family. All together, laughing, crying. Living life. What is it like, I wonder?"

She had momentarily lost her bravado and her humor. Now she seemed merely sad. "I have no family no more. And friends are leaving. Now Niki goes. Only Volodya means anything."

"But, could you live the old life?" Ana asked. "Could you be happy?"

"Ah, Ana. What is happiness? Maybe just to eat ripe pear with man you love. Maybe just to know he is well. Volodya gives me grief. Make me feel like ashes from his cigarette. But I cut off my hand for him."

"You remind me of someone," Ana said. "Gena Mele, a good friend. She would lay down her life for my cousin, Lopaka. I'm here because of her."

"Like in Russia, always women helping women. Men only move their lips. Poor things, what can we do but love them?"

"Katya, would you ever leave? I mean emigrate?"

She looked out at her city. "*Nyet*. Every human have one country only. Good or bad, I love my Russia. For Niki, is important for his health he goes. And because he have such love for you. And now, the child."

"Were you there when he read my letter?"

She nodded slowly. "He sat in room alone, and wept. My God. I heard."

Ana trembled, trying to imagine it. Then she pulled a small velvet bag from her pocket and handed it to Katya.

"I want you to have this, from me."

She opened the bag and took out a coral-bead rosary Ana had carried with her. "Oh, Ana! Is very beautiful."

"The coral comes from my ocean. You might just want to hold it now and then."

Katya slid an expensive-looking watch from her wrist. "And this for you, Ana."

"No! I couldn't . . ."

She took her arm, sliding the watch over her wristbone. "Of course! Is very Russian, exchanging sentimentals. When you look at watch, you think of Katya. You remember this Russian time."

At the hotel, her demeanor changed. "Now you go upstairs to sleep. In the morning, I await you. Airport bus is leaving eight o'clock."

She panicked. "Suppose something goes wrong? Suppose . . ."

"Nothing you can do, Ana. Now is time to *trust*."

IN THE MORNING, WHEN SHE CAME DOWN WITH HER LUGGAGE KATYA was waiting in the lounge. The tour group slowly moved outside to their bus.

"You will be calm. You will be getting on the bus, no?"

She felt panic rise again, felt tremors run across her cheeks. "I still don't know what's happening. Dancer didn't call last night."

"Everything is moving, in good progress. That is all what I can tell you. See woman in beige suit? She is on your flight. Trust her."

Katya drew her off to the edge of the crowd and put her hands on Ana's shoulder

"Ana Kapakahi. I like you very much. You are good ambassador for your people. Maybe Russians, Hawaiians, not so different. Both struggling to live. Find dignity. You go home, tell them Russians not all gangsters. Not all caricatures. Okay?"

She fought back tears. "How can I thank you and Volodya?"

"Bring our Niki back to health. Make him happy. He has suffered enough."

She motioned the woman over. "This is Sonia. She flies to Helsinki with you."

Up close the woman seemed smaller, and dainty, somewhere in her forties. "Hello, Ana. We will sit together on the flight. Don't be afraid. I have done this many times."

She looked from one to the other. "Can you just tell me, is Niki at the airport? Is he safe?"

"Ana. You promised. No questions."

"Then, where is Eric Dancer?"

"They are together."

For a moment, she almost lost control. "But I've had no contact, no proof! I haven't even heard Niki's voice."

Katya handed her an envelope and a slender ribboned box. "Read note later. Now you open box."

She slowly undid the ribbon. Inside, wrapped in tissue was a new hairbrush with a blue, transparent handle. She pressed it to her chest.

"He said when you see this, you are understanding. You know what he's remembering."

Ana embraced her one last time. "Me ke aloha, Katya. You are my sister now."

"Good. Now I have family. And now is time for old Russian custom. Silence before journey."

For a moment they held hands and stood silent like good children. Then Katya pushed her gently toward the bus.

"Da svidanya, Ana. Udachi vam!" Good-bye. Good luck.

As she turned to board, Sonia fell in line behind her, utterly composed, her English perfect.

"It's okay. I am acquainted with your guide and driver."

As they pulled out onto Marx Prospekt, she turned to Sonia, wanting to ask a dozen things. The woman patted her hand.

"Be calm. That's all you have to do. I am beside you at all times."

"Can you just tell me, will they be on our flight?"

"Is better you know nothing."

The woman saw her struggle, saw how hard it was for her.

"I understand you are physician, used to giving orders. But sometimes it's good to be helpless, to not be in control. Then we are forced to trust other humans. Why don't you read Niki's note?"

She reached into her bag, and opened the envelope.

Sonia leaned closer. "A few words only to assure you. He had no more time."

Ana,
   You have my whole heart. Do everything they say.

                                                            N.

———

THE TWO-HOUR FLIGHT TO HELSINKI SEEMED LIKE DAYS. SHE WOULD remember nothing but a flight attendant whose face was slightly green from years of wearing lead-based makeup.

"Remember," Sonia said. "We will not officially enter Finland. We are only in transit at the airport. Until you are over the Atlantic, anything could happen."

Ana grew calm. She had never been so calm. They landed, gathered their things, and moved down the aisle.

Sonia checked something in her flight bag. "There is a restaurant. We can relax."

They entered a stylish café overlooking the concourse below where tour groups milled in duty-free boutiques. Ana sat down jittery with fatigue. They ordered sandwiches and Scandinavian beers while Sonia pressed buttons on her cell phone, shook it, and tried again. Then she excused herself and went to a phone in the corner. She talked for several minutes and came back looking tense. Ana stared at her, expectantly.

"Everything . . . will be fine," Sonia said.

She unfolded her napkin and delicately bit into her sandwich. She sipped her beer. "Drink a little. Beer is nourishing. Taste your sandwich, very tender ham."

Ana picked at the sandwich.

"Now, listen closely. I'm sorry to tell you, Ana, you will have to miss your flight. You understand?"

". . . No."

"You will not be getting on your plane."

"But Niki . . ."

"He was not on the plane. It was already full. To bump passengers would have drawn too much attention."

"He was *not* on our flight?"

"No."

"So, he is still in Moscow."

"Yes."

After a while she looked up. "Did you know this when we left?"

"I knew they were trying. We have not lied to you. We have tried to do what is safe for him. Had you known he could not get on that flight, you might have tried to stay behind. You might have caused a scene."

"Yes. I'm afraid I would have."

"Everything is in place. Only they have to find two available seats without drawing attention. Planes are crowded. Tourist season."

"Will he get out today?"

"All we can do is wait. I will remain with you however long it takes."

She tried to distract Ana. "They'll hold your luggage in New York City. People miss flights all the time. He will arrive here, and you will both take a later flight. It is desirable that you enter the United States together. He is your fiancé, father of your child. Eric will be with you both through all U.S. formalities."

"Is it possible he won't get out at all?"

". . . In his condition, he should never have come back. Many people have worked to get him out again. Even people here in Helsinki. The tapes are important, people everywhere must see what human damage has been done. He will have to leave those tapes behind. Friends will destroy them. You have copies, so nothing has been lost . . ."

"Sonia! Please. Is it possible he won't get out at all?"

She tapped her cell phone. "Yes. It is possible he won't get out."

Ana stood up. "I think . . . I don't feel very well."

They found a restroom where she bent over in a stall. Afterwards, she rinsed her mouth and splashed her face.

"Come," Sonia said. "There is a place to rest. A private place."

She steered Ana down the concourse to an EMERGENCY ONLY door. It was locked and she pulled out a key. They went down two flights of stairs and unlocked another door. MAINTENANCE SUPPLIES. Inside, leather-jacketed men sat in front of monitors behind a thick glass wall. They waved, and pushed a button. The glass wall slid apart.

"Sonia! You are well?"

"Yes. Busy."

She shook their hands, introducing them to Ana, then guided her through another door into an elegantly furnished lounge. Deep chairs and couches in soft browns and grays, colors meant to soothe. Racks of magazines, a fireplace. In the corner a stocked bar and buffet, apparently just set out.

"There are beds in the next room, showers. Whatever you need."

Ana sat down trying to get her bearings. "Is this sort of a . . . safe house, for people on the run?"

"Something like that, though not so dramatic."

"How long will we be here?"

"Until they get him out. It could be hours. Days."

Without warning, Ana began to cry. "I'm sorry. I must be very tired."

After a while, when she was calm, Sonia moved to a window and opened the blinds.

"Look. Across the way . . . something special. A sort of giant 'greenhouse.' Palm trees. Streams."

Ana was startled to see an atrium, like a small rain forest surrounded by glass.

Sonia took her hand. "Come and see."

They passed through two doors, then a kind of tunnel and came out at the entrance to the atrium, the glass surrounding it so virtually invisible one had the impression of being outdoors.

"Usually it's open to the public. But some days, like today, it's closed 'for renovation.' "

Another leather-jacketed man stood casually at the entrance, greeting Sonia as they passed inside. Ana breathed in deeply. She could have been in the rain forests of Hawai'i. Even the sounds were those of home. Whispering bamboo, dripping ferns. Birds chortling amongst the leaves. It seemed to extend forty feet or so in either direction, dense enough for several people to sit or stroll in private without encountering each other.

"Climatically controlled," Sonia said. "Just like the tropics. Now, I leave you to your thoughts."

Ana strolled a gravel path, feeling nature sigh and breathe. Hanging vines brushed her cheeks. A drop of water slid down a leaf, then clung, reflecting light. She bent and scooped up soil and brought it to her nose, recalling the smell of fields back home, the balm of clean, warm seas. Another hour passed. Sonia came and joined her for a while, then checked her watch and stretched.

"Over there is a fishpond. A hammock somewhere in the trees. Now I will go and make more calls."

Behind lush, giant ferns, Ana found the hammock slung between two palms. She slid off her shoes, sank down and closed her eyes, wondering what she would do if Sonia came and told her Niki had been detained, that he could not get out of Russia. She would keep coming back until she found him. Even after their child was born, she would continue coming back. She did not think about his health. How it would deteriorate. She did not allow herself such thoughts.

Time passed. A man drifted in the background through the trees, then moved close to check on her. Sonia came again, and went away.

ĪNANA HOU

To Come to Life Again

ANA SAT UP WITH A JOLT. HER WATCH SAID ALMOST MIDNIGHT. IT seemed barely dusk, the sky a swirl of purple/pink, as dark as it would get. She leaned forward, listening. Nothing moved. Even the birds were still. She got to her feet, then sat down again, feeling apprehensive. From somewhere, the soft click of a door opening and closing.

Her voice sounded childlike as she called out, "Sonia. Is that you?"

She heard footsteps moving on the path. Then she looked up, and gasped. A man was standing there, misshapen and grotesque. Huge shoulders. Arms extra-long like an ape. His head was large and bald, a heavy beard. He wore thick glasses.

"Ana . . ."

She blinked, then stood up slowly in bare feet.

"Forgive me . . . for disguise. The baggy clothes. They even shaved my head. But it is me . . . it's Niki."

She leaned forward slightly, then moved one foot in front of the other, approaching him.

"How you have waited, and waited. How you came for me . . . Brave Ana! And our child has traveled with you . . . our miracle. Already she is making journeys."

She stood before him with her hands out. She stroked the baldness of his head. Then lowering her hands, she pressed them to his cheeks.

"Yes, Ana . . . it is me."

She kept touching him and stroking him, holding his cheeks between her hands. She whispered his name over and over, as he gathered her to him.

"Oh, Ana. It has hurt very much to be alone. It was most hard in the mornings when my mind was clear. I thought of you and wondered how I could forget you. Now I loved you more for not knowing how to keep you. Then you came. You came."

She turned him slightly so she could see his face more clearly in the light. His beautiful, dark eyes. She studied his oversized hands as if to make sure they were his. One of them held a ring he had pulled from his pocket, an old, shiny band of wood.

"Marry me, Ana. Marry me. Wear this, my mother's ring. Carved for her by my father when they were lovers in Archangel'sk. Worn by my mother when I was born. Worn until she pulled it from her finger, when they threw her on the truck. All I possess of my mother and my father. Now, for you."

He slid it on her finger. The ring was large and heavy, as if weighted down with years of human oils. Tears sat in the wrinkles of his cheeks. His large hands smoothed her curly hair.

"Oh, Ana! Everything that went before was just a dream. Illness, and loneliness. Now we will laugh at the past, carry it like a white rose in our teeth. We will bite into life like a radish! We have not even begun to be young yet. Our lives are starting *now*."

Very tenderly he put his big hand on her stomach, then bent down and whispered. "Hello, little one. My *goloobka*! I am your father. You are going to teach me many things."

Ana looked up at him and smiled. She opened his coat and lay her head against his chest, smelling his dear, familiar smell.

"Take me home, Niki. Stay beside me always."

He held her for a while, as if he would never let her out of the circle of his arms. Then he stepped back and ceremoniously took her arm. Ahead, she saw Eric Dancer and Sonia smiling through the glass.

"Come," Niki said. "Now we must try to live very well, to carry on in the most splendid way. One day our child will be remembering us, retelling our stories. We must leave her fantastic tales, rich and full of detail, for her children and their children."

Ana held tight to his arm, matching his steps as they moved forward.

"Look! Already we are making legends. Who will believe how we met in the wreckage of a hurricane? How we loved, and lost, each other? How you journeyed. And how this crazy Russian, this headstrong Hawaiian, found each other again, in a rain forest . . . in Helsinki."

ʻĪLOLI

Deep Emotions of Gestation

It is true that a highway runs along the Waiʻanae Coast, but it is not the lifeblood of that coast. That is to be found in the quirky, dusty roads branching off the highway, heading deep into the valleys and up into the hills. Here are found the people who give life to the land, who watch the centuries shamble in and out, and never start on time. Yet in that summer, of the last half of the last decade of the century, folks began to feel that good things might be possible, even on their finite coast.

Some people talked of revolution, of taking Mākua Valley back with weapons and guerrilla war. But men like Lopaka knew that the way to win back their valley was not to try to defeat the military, but to win them over to the people's side. To choose the war of nerves instead.

"We must not only liberate our lands, but liberate the military from *fear* of us."

With stealth and slow persistence, the people began to impose their will, appealing to the United Nations, asking them to review the circumstances of Mākua Valley, still under bombardment in military war maneuvers. The U.N. responded, sending representatives to view the ravaged land and the hazardous wastes thereof. Petitions were drafted demanding environmental-impact studies of the valley. Eventually, experts were brought in, and their in-depth evaluations of the land began.

The media followed, and the eyes of the outside world slowly turned its gaze upon Mākua. Under mounting pressure, a federal judge decreed that, for the duration of the studies—a process that would take years—

the Army cease its bombing of Mākua Valley and its beaches. On that day folks stood along the highway, cheering.

"But even so," Lopaka said, "our beach waters are lifeless. No fish do you see here, and very little *limu*. Dolphins and whales long ago left these waters. It will take decades to bring them back. And for the valley, we must never turn our backs. We must be *kahu o ka 'āina*. Guardians of the land."

That island-autumn was a slowed-down time when silence walked the coast. The burned and ravaged land stopped crying out. Some nights in brindled moonlight, sounds issued from the valleys and mountains of Mākua. The sound of humming, the *'āina* humming to Herself. A healing sound. Folks looked up and *they* began to hum, but then they shook themselves clear-sighted, knowing victory was illusory, that truths merged into untruths. And so they left a kind of innocence behind. Henceforth, they would always be vigilant and wary.

LIFE PLODDED ON DEEP IN THE VALLEYS; GRAFFITIED QUONSET huts still warned of gangster turf. There were still shootings, dead bodies found. But there were more police sweeps now, and parents paid more at- tention. On weekends people rallied at the false *kamani* tree at Mākua Beach. It was open once again for spiritual gatherings and cleansings, for swimming and gathering *pōhaku*, and the cleaning out of weeds and refuse to help reopen streambeds.

Each day Gena and Lopaka sat in the sea up to their waists. And she felt her womb respond, felt the sea's healing minerals strengthen her ves- sels and her organs. One day they would hold her husband's seed. Now she watched waves wash his bad leg side to side, like a shell lulled on the ocean floor.

"You been depending on that brace too long. Time you start walking without that thing. Become the man you are in bed."

His eyes momentarily turned to slits, ready for a fight. Gena threw back her head and laughed, her lovely breasts bobbing in the water.

"Don't give me the *stink*-eye!"

Lopaka smiled. He felt his leg bones humming, the warm sea soften- ing his scars. He reached out and grabbed her hand, their locked fingers dancing in the broth of waves.

Up on Keola Road, in front of the Makiki house two Hawaiian flags flew. Inez had finally given birth to twins. Panama Chang still fought with his Italian wife, arguing for more rice nights. And old Uncle Noah still leaned at his window, the windowsill grown shiny through the decades of his forearms.

At night their shipwreck of a house seemed to palpitate, made tremulous by the flickering blue tube of a TV in front of which old Ben slept, and by candles lit in various rooms. Niki liked reading by candlelight, it took him back to student days in Russia. Adoring young cousins mimicked him, doing their homework by candlelight. Sometimes Aunty Pua tottered over, slipped a linty, dried plum from her pocket and pressed it to his lips. He slid his arm around her waist.

"How is my little *babushka?*"

"Oh you!" she cried. "Put your eyes back in that book. By and by, you going be one excellent teacher, when you *pau* making your important film."

She still read the Bible every night, though she would never reach the end. Old Uncle Tito had begun using the thin pages of her Bible for rolling his tobacco. She was reading Chronicles, he was smoking Deuteronomy.

Autumn turned to island-winter, making the ocean rage. White waves stood erect like giant hares. Some days there was only fog, so thick the world outside their windows disappeared. At night they lay staring at the ceiling from which termite dust filtered down, feathering small hairs on the ridges of their ears, and on their cheeks. They watched it sift through candlelight.

"After our child comes," Niki said, "I will resuscitate the house, one room at a time. I am good carpenter, you know. It is your house, and you must honor it."

"Now it's your house, too," she said.

"I will have to first consult the house. See if it accepts me."

Ana saw how carefully he moved. How softly he talked. Even when he brought her a glass of water he walked bent over like a child, careful not to spill a drop. As if he were on probation. As if, if he did not measure up, they would send him back. The years would unbend him. She knew one day he would shout again, stomp around like a Cossack, perform his crazy Russian dances. But this was his quiet time, of coming back to life.

Some nights he jumped up and looked around.

"It's all right, Niki. You dozed off."

"Oh, Ana. How good it is to lie still, listening to weather, and know it cannot kill me. That I am growing strong again. And how very good to lay my head against your belly, hearing our child's beating heart."

The baby kicked, which made her right hip throb. Her body was bloated now, her slender wrists looked wrong. The child felt huge, long overdue. For months Rosie had taken her to the ocean for ʻauʻau kai, her sea bath, letting waves sway her belly back and forth to loosen the child so it would not stick during birth. Now storms prevented sea baths, and she missed the sensation of weightlessness, of all her organs floating.

"My clinic is going to have home births and water births, like in your country. I don't understand why I can't do that now."

Niki implored her, "Ana. This one time I ask you, please. Be prudent. Have our firstborn in hospital with real doctor. We do not know what to expect. With my warped genes, we could be starting brand-new species."

She almost laughed, but flames reached out, her insides seemed to crackle. Then sudden stillness. A capricious child. It had been in the "White Nights" of Russia that her body visibly began to change. A line began to grow upward from the bottom of her abdomen; another started down from the top. Her alawela, scorched path. Now Ana looked in a mirror, at where the dark lines had almost met.

"It's time for kuakoko, bloody back."

Niki looked alarmed.

". . . Childbirth."

"Cannot be! Two more months yet."

"No one is listening to me," she said. "This child wants to be born."

"Too soon," he said. "Too soon."

And yet the family was already in preparation. A pig had been fattened for the birth feast. Old aunties sat around calling on the ʻaumākua, family gods, imploring them to come to her in dreams and give her child a name. Without this, they could not compose her name chants. One night in her sleep, the gods did come, decreeing the inoa pō, the name given in darkness. Ana would not tell them what it was.

And as her body swelled, old tūtū women lomilomied her body, massaging especially the stretched skin of her belly. They gently manipulated the baby, making sure she was in the right position.

"Lift up your arm."

Automatically, her left arm rose.

"A girl! For real."

They studied her right breast where the nipple stood out brown and firm.

"Ah! *Maka puaʻa*. Pig nipple. Means baby will nurse good."

And, they made her observe all the *kapus*. No scaling of fish, or the baby would have rotten breath. No eating mountain apples, or she would be stained with red birthmarks. No eating of bitter or too-salty foods, or she would be born with everlasting thirst.

Ana rebelled and bowed to her craving for *kimchee*, for Hawaiian salt and seaweed. Week after week, she gorged herself.

"*Auwē!*" old aunties cried. "The child will have the face of a crab."

"Rosie, you don't believe this nonsense, do you?"

Her cousin shrugged. "I told you before. *Pēlā paha. ʻAʻole paha.* Maybe. Maybe not. But it is better to believe."

TIME MOVED FUNEREALLY SLOW. NOW SHE COULD HARDLY WALK. Some nights she woke fighting for breath, as if the child were trying to smother her from the inside. Small things began disturbing her. A cousin's haircut. Tommy's whistling was off-key. Rosie's hand on her shoulder did not feel sincere.

One day when she woke her body was numb. It lay there like a log, not getting the message from her brain. The message was fear. The child would be born missing an arm, a leg. Or, she would be too perfect, Ana would love her too much. She would shoot out of the womb like a bullet and keep going, out into the world. And she would take Niki with her. He would forsake Ana for their child. She would be alone again.

She grabbed his hand as he laid a damp cloth across her chest.

"I don't want this child! I just want us. To shout when we're angry, make love when we feel like it, eat when we want. There's a whole life I haven't lived. I want to live it now, with you."

He saw she was panicking. "Ana. Nothing will change. Only what you want. But now you must talk baby still. She is too early."

"I don't want to talk to her. I don't want to have her. I want to change my mind."

Rosie laid a calm hand on her forehead. "You are panicking. And why? It's not the pain. It's not the weight. For the first time in your life, you're not in control. You're feeling helpless."

Ana lay back against her pillow, panting.

"It was the same with me," Rosie said. "At first I hated pregnancy. Makaliʻi's father planted his seed, doubled my size, then deserted me without giving her a name. I felt trapped, imprisoned. I thought of suicide."

"How did you overcome it?"

"Pua. She has always been the wise one, though we made fun of her. One night she came when I was trying to throw out the child. She put my left hand on her Bible, my right hand on the KUMULIPO. And she said 'Pray.' I said 'Who should I pray to?' And Pua said, 'That is your decision. You see, *you still have control.*' It was like a thunderclap. My body was bloated and useless, but I could make decisions. I still had that power. So do *you.*"

"This is a rich time for a woman," Rosie said. "So rich our emotions get confused. Much fear, much guilt. Giving birth is such a sacrament sometimes we think we don't deserve it. It's the only time we transcend the merely human."

Ana shook her head. "I don't want to transcend. I want my life back! My ankles."

"Stop being childish. Embrace these days. And be prepared for what comes next . . . *'Īloli.* That blizzard of emotions that comes in late pregnancy. The blues. Then downright grief. This is a time for flushing all things out."

As Rosie said it would, it came. In waves like multiple assaults. Every source of pain she had denied, perversely turned away from. The grandmother who never deigned to know her. The grandfather she only came to know so late. Her mother, who had not wanted her, had turned her back on her. She mourned that proud and lonely child.

She thought of the plumber, Sam, a man of grace and laughter, whom cancer took while it spared her. She remembered him squaring his shoulders, accepting that he was dying. She should have held him, said she loved him, that he would beat the cancer. What would it have cost to lie? She had deprived him of the dignity of hope.

She thought of Niki, all he had suffered. Parents sacrificed. His young wife, melting into snow. Things he would try to put behind him that would haunt him all his life. She thought how she had let him go, had almost lost him, and how she did not deserve him now, did not deserve his child. She held her stomach and grievously wept.

"*Bedney Ana!*" Niki cried. "You are experiencing immense physical changes. Your brain, and glands, the metabolic system . . . all . . . *yamburg* and *skolzko!*"

And each night, silent as a ray, Makali'i came, easing into a place between Ana's shoulder blades. The niece she had ignored until it was too late. For weeks, she was Ana's nightly execution.

Then came the memory of her surgery, of waking in the Recovery Room, a doctor peering down. Then twilight, Rosie dozing in a chair. It struck her now how beautiful it was to come back from the dead and see someone sitting in attendance. To know another human cared.

What Ana grieved for now was not her breast. What she mourned was her abject aloneness all those months and years that followed. Nights when she sat like an old woman on her bed, turning the pages of a calendar. Nights she had wrapped her arms around herself for comfort.

How could a human survive like that? Like a plant without rain, trying to water itself. Then she remembered that there *had* been someone there with her through months of chemotherapy and radiation. The mother who had come back into her life so late. But, she had come.

'IKE 'IA NĀ MAKA I KE AO

The Eyes Are Seen in the World,
the Child Is Born

ROSIE PULLED BACK THE SHEET AND STARED AT ANA'S BELLY. SHE was huge, her skin stretched tight. She examined between her cousin's legs where she had begun to dilate.

"Soon time. Doctor said bring you in tomorrow."

Near noon Ana heard gravel crunch like things deep-frying, and looked out the window as a car drove up. Earlier in the week, her mother had arrived in Honolulu.

"She's helping Niki finish footage of his film," Rosie said. "At the Hope Institute for damaged kids. And of course, she's here for you . . . to witness this event of childbirth."

In the silence they watched Anahola stepping from her car, high heels sinking in the dirt, her hair exuberantly curling in humid air. Yet her uptilted head accented a certain pride of carriage.

"It seems so little to ask," Rosie said. "She saved your husband's life. She has saved all our lives, one way or the other."

"I know that. I'm very grateful."

Rosie turned to her. "What a meager little word. *Hila hila male!* For shame! We're a clan of proud and headstrong women. Our emotions are *big!* Oh, cousin . . . open your heart. Break this pattern now. *'Oki* all the bitterness that eats each generation of the women in your family."

She took Ana's hand. "Let your daughter grow up knowing her grandmother. If you don't, I promise she will make you pay."

NIKI SAT AT THE TABLE WITH THE FAMILY, AND NOW AND THEN HE gazed at Anahola. Each time he met her, profound gratitude rendered him almost inarticulate. Yet, knowing her history with Ana, he felt concern. During the meal, she seemed almost shy, as if unsure of her welcome.

He cleared his throat and leaned forward. "Your name is very beautiful. *Anahola*. Hourglass."

Pua reached out and took Anahola's hand, recalling her fiery temper when she first came to live with them, pregnant and cast out by her parents. Her beauty that had mesmerized the youngsters. Old aunties remembered how she had swum with little Ana clinging to her neck, teaching her to be alert for stingrays. And how, during *tsunami* alerts, she had tied Ana to her back and run up into the mountains.

While they talked Niki lowered his eyes, touched by how they were telling Anahola they remembered. Hours later, they were still reminiscing, when Ana appeared in the doorway, water cataracting down her legs.

"Her sack has broken!" Rosie stood. "No time for doctors. Someone fetch midwife, and chanters."

"My God, it hurts," Ana cried. "Make it stop hurting."

"Stop? Girlie, it has just begun."

Rosie steered her to her room while folks pushed the table to a corner. The floor was soaped and rinsed and sheets were spread, upon which *lauhala* mats were piled until they were knee high. When the time was right, Ana would squat on them to birth her child.

Youngsters ran for the old midwife while aunties gathered on the *lānai*, noting the shape of clouds, the flight of birds, the way trees bent and swayed. For these all might be *hōʻailona*, omens that foretold the infant's future. Soon the kitchen was fogged by boiling water through which children peered, having an eager, frightened time. Minutes passed slowly and very fast. Then Ana wobbled back into the living room.

"Labor pains begin for real. Now she must walk to and fro."

She dragged her body in and out of rooms, leaning on the walls, her stomach appearing in a doorway, and then the rest of her. After a while she was given tea from the bark of the *hau* tree.

"Makes baby slippery, eases her passage through the narrow place."

Every half hour Rosie laid her down to palpate her abdomen.

"It's good to *hāhā* your belly, make sure baby's in right position."

Aunty Ginger, ever the quiet one, suddenly spoke out. "This going be a long birth. We need gather *pōhuehue*."

Lopaka was dispatched to the sea to gather sixteen leaves of beach morning glory. He picked them swiftly, plucking the first half with the right hand as he prayed to *Kū*, god of medicine. Then he plucked the rest with his left hand, praying to *Hina*, goddess of medicine. The leaves must not be mixed up. Those he had plucked with the right were given to Ana to eat. Those plucked with the left were crushed and rubbed on her stomach.

She lay back chewing, praying the leaves would hasten birth. She chewed until leaves turned to saliva. The pain seemed never-ending. Then abruptly it subsided, and it was like walking through a cool, clear moment of a dawn.

Niki knelt beside her. Even children gathered, big-eyed and attentive. Only her mother kept her distance, lingering outside the room.

Suddenly Ana cried out. "My father! He will never know this child. Oh, I want to see him . . ."

Anahola turned away, her hands went to her face. Then old Ben walked out to the yard; they heard him grunting in the weeds. He came back carrying a hefty stone and put it down near Ana's bed.

"Child. Here in this *pōhaku* is your papa."

She bent forward, staring. Because stones had such *mana* for Hawaiians, she felt her father's presence.

"Please. Bring him to me."

And when they brought the stone, she held it tight against her belly, feeling its warmth from the sun.

"Now he can feel his grandchild's beating heart. He will feel that heartbeat through eternity. She will remember *him*, and always be fond of him."

The *pōhaku* was carefully passed from hand to hand so it would bear the imprint of each of this *'ohana*. It would be buried beside the child's placenta.

Her labor progressed. The chanters and midwife were attentive, but it was Rosie she reached out to. When spasms became intense, the midwife pressed down on her belly, and when they subsided she stepped back, and Rosie took her hand.

Out on the *lānai*, elders argued over who, as oldest living member of this family, should assist in the birth of Ana's child. Pua pointed at one-armed Ben.

"You are ranking senior. It is your duty and your right."

Ben spoke with the modesty of a man who knew he would always be most beloved by the younger generations. For it was he who had delivered them, and loved them, and raised them to adulthood.

He lowered his head, his cheeks were wet. "Such richness in old age! I, who don't deserve it. I am a simple man. But, if allowed, I will teach the child prayers, legends, genealogy, family etiquette, and customs. I will teach her even traditions of land ownership, and how to talk to people in trouble. I have learned much in life."

Pua stood, hair floating round her like a shawl.

"It is decided. This *kupuna*, and his *mo'opuna*, will be one. You will never go too far from one another. You will always be a two-hour paddle home. Henceforth, this child will look to you as *kumu*. Source of all family knowledge."

As LABOR PANGS INCREASED, ANA WAS MOVED FROM HER BED TO the living room. There she took a squatting position on the mats, and placed her arms round the midwife's neck. The woman was so frail and old, she could not take the weight, and motioned Niki forward.

"Think yourself into a sturdy tree! Let her cling to you for strength."

He faced his wife and locked her arms around his neck. Rosie moved behind her as her *ko'o kua*, and sat, legs sprawled apart. With her arms encircling her, she pressed down on Ana's stomach giving her support.

The midwife saw the pain about to convulse her. "*'Ume i ka hanu!*" Draw the breath!

Colors and edges of things blurred beyond the natural. Ana gasped and bent forward. The chanters moved close, wailing softly in Hawaiian.

". . . *Be patient, be patient. We are all here in watchful expectancy. Your husband who loves you is here, and so is your beloved Rosie who is holding you. And so your aunties and uncles who raised you, and your tender young cousins . . . And so your rightful mother is here, and your rightful father in the rock. They have gathered as the gods decreed . . . And so the gods are here, Kū and Hina, gods of medicine, and Hi'iaka, Pele, and all the major and lesser gods. And everyone. And everything. Even the weather is here . . . The sun lying on her side, peeking through the window. The trade winds rippling the shades. All are in attendance just for you. You are not alone . . .*"

SCREAMING IN CHILDBIRTH WAS THOUGHT DISGRACEFUL, BUT NOW she screamed, she howled. Men looked away in order to be able to stand the moment. Some stepped outside, urgently scolding their boar-hounds. Trying to transfer Ana's pain, the midwife called for a recipient.

Gena pressed forward. "Give it to me. I will take her pain."

The old woman closed her eyes and prayed, but nothing happened. Another hour passed.

As her labor began to reach its climax, the midwife instructed, "Push now. Push hard!"

She cursed to restore her courage, pushing to exhaustion. Finally, they knelt her forward on her knees so she could rest. They put her head down on the mat and sponged her neck and shoulders. In the doorway, her mother prayed. Ana turned and glimpsed her mother's face. Decades had passed without her knowing her, and maybe this was a mourning for those stillborn years. *That's what the child will be: a stillborn.*

She moaned and rocked back on her heels.

Then someone moved to the midwife. "Give me the pain," Anahola whispered. "Give it to me. Please."

Now she stood close, larger than life. Ana hung with her arms round Niki's neck, watching as the midwife prayed. Her mother stood expectant, waiting for pain to strike her down, but nothing happened.

The old woman opened her eyes, pointing at Ana. "This pain wants *you*."

Then something wrenched her with such force she momentarily blacked out. They bathed her neck and face again, bringing her to consciousness, then put her head down and let her rest upon her knees. Agony was all-consuming, but still no head appeared. She was pulled back into a squatting position while the midwife implored.

"Draw the breath! The breath!"

"No more," Ana whispered. "No . . ."

Even Rosie was exhausted, her arms and legs visibly trembling. Then Ana felt the thing expand, engulfing her. Her scream was piercing.

"Mamaaa!"

Anahola lifted her head, then moved instinctively. As Rosie pushed aside, she quickly sat and took up the *ko'o kua* position behind Ana, her legs surrounding her, arms wrapped round her stomach, pressing down. Ana's head hung with exhaustion. She panted like a dog.

The next seizure swept her with such force, her feet and buttocks left the floor. "Mamaaa!"

"I'm here."

Her face distorted with effort, Anahola pressed down on Ana's stomach, willing that child to drop, to begin to come out to the world. Her daughter shouted, she shouted back. Each time a convulsion came, Ana's elbows bore down on her mother's knees. Their sweating faces side by side, their cheeks seemingly attached, so Niki saw a two-headed woman giving birth.

And yet the infant would not crown.

Then Anahola whispered in her daughter's ear, "The baby is close to crowning, I can feel how low she is. When I say three! we are going to *make* the head crown. First we rock side to side, together like one body . . . and when you are ready I will count to three. Then, we will press down with all our might. Remember, you are in control, only when you're ready . . ."

Speaking in a low, soft voice, Lopaka took up position behind Niki, arms tight round his waist, providing traction. Ana tightened her arms round Niki's neck. Then she and her mother rocked side to side, so attuned they seemed one body. As they rocked, her mother hummed. And Ana's eyes began to overflow, remembering the sensation of being rocked when she was a child, remembering this same song being hummed, the scent of this same woman rocking her.

Finally, her mother whispered, "Ready?"

She felt pain coming fast, it seemed to gallop. She stood up to it. "Ready. Now."

Her mother counted. "One . . . two . . ."

She would not remember the wrenching push as much as the enormous pressure her mother exerted with her arms upon her stomach. "Now! Press now!"

They threw back their heads and gasped. Then they pressed down, her mouth a gaping rictus. Ana's eyes bulged. Veins stood out on her neck like ropes, her long, protracted groan so primal and subhuman, folks felt hair stand up on their arms.

The midwife bent and saw the head emerging.

The chanters sang out, "'*Ike 'ia nā maka I ke ao!*'" The eyes are seen in the world! The child is born.

She gently guided the body on through its narrow passage as folks leaned close, exclaiming. A strapping infant that would weigh eight pounds. Ana shuddered, then lay back against her mother's chest. Laps and thighs tattooed with blood, they watched as the child was lifted in the air still attached to Ana by the *piko*, the umbilical cord. The chanters sang out one last time.

"Ola ke kumu, I ka lālā hou!" The branches of the tree are green again.

Now Ben stepped forward, and with the guidance of the midwife, he cut and knotted the *piko*, a sacred duty. Then, winding a clean piece of cloth round his finger, he gently stuck it into the baby's mouth, gagging her just enough to disgorge the *nalu*, birth fluid. He rinsed his own mouth and sucked the fluid from the baby's nose. He wiped her tiny eyes clean. She wailed, her wails were loud and healthy. The midwife gently sponged her, counting her fingers and her toes. And she was perfect, and everything was as it should be.

Niki knelt on the floor and held his child. "At last. My *goloobka*. Little dove!"

While they sponged off her hands and thighs, Ana listened to the beating of her mother's heart against her head. And when she was ready, they handed her her child. She knew that henceforth life would be distracted and disordered, that she had lost forever a certain symmetry and focus. But here was this being, this helpless perfection of radiance, her small head covered with a tender down. Ana pressed her to her breast. Here was truth, her deepest truth. And there was no retreat from wonder.

"Now, will you tell us?" Rosie asked. "What is the name the gods have chosen?"

She looked down at her child, and spoke out clearly. "She is . . . Anahola. Anahola Kapakahi Volenko."

Ē NĀ HANAUNA, Ē!

O, Generations, O!

The bombs are silent at Mākua. For several years there has been peace. *Nature slowly begins to heal itself. In the soil, roots take hold, seeds swell and lengthen. Folks say they are the seeds of freedom, and that in time winds will blow those seeds and germinate the land.*

Up and down this red, parched coast, crops still grow, sap still flows. Sounds fill the valleys. The sounds of children growing like plants, rooting and seeding, learning to take care of each other, learning how caring is a holy deed . . .

Some days a girl runs down Keola Road. At her mother's clinic she will witness a water birth. On such days she watches midwives gather, and chanters, the solemn errands of women in an eternal dance of birthing and rebirthing. She watches a newborn slide down that ancient seaway to greet life. She hears its cries. Each birth brings new requests for the placenta. It will be blessed and buried, so the child will not be a wanderer who loses sight of home.

And, some days the girl, Anahola, sits with her elders, even her grandmother, and great-grandfather, spinning tales. For, like those before her, she will be a "talking-story" woman. And even when her elders doze, she continues talking, for the sheer love of it. Small-kid stories of her valley and her coast whose people, from ancient times, have given themselves to dreaming, and to fabulating. She never quite finishes her stories, for she is a knowing child who vaguely understands that stories have no endings, that they go on and on.

Sometimes she stands impatiently in the road, with the tremor of fire in a sunstruck leaf. She is waiting for her father. When he arrives she watches the important way he walks with his briefcase. He is a teacher now, a man who finds quietude in numbers. Often, he tells her of a city called Peter where nights are pink, and where winged lions fly over rivers that are pink. And he tells her how he was born in ice, how his first words were visible. On nights when her father's dreams turn bad, her mother curls herself around him, her warmth correcting the soft ellipses of his nightmares.

And, often she sees her mother take her father's hand. His hands are so massive they seem to hold all of their lives within them. She sees what happens between her mother and her father when their eyes meet. The look they share suffuses her body with such warmth she runs out to the fields, letting her shadow dance across the land. Leaving her footprints there among the ancients.

One night she sits with her parents in a crowd. They have gathered to watch her father's film. A film about sickness and chaos. And even as they gather, chaos is exciting itself again in the world. Near the end of the film, folks grow silent, watching children in a place called Hope. Many of them are bald like monks, some so pale and transparent it seems God has already touched them. And because they are children, each face is beautiful.

Later, as they walk up Keola Road, Anahola's parents discuss the rumors that, "of necessity," they will soon resume bombing in Mākua Valley. Her parents grow tense, hearing the Wup! Wup! of military choppers overhead, the crackle of satellite receivers in the distance.

The child hears nothing. She skips through dappled light from shimmering leaves, loving how moonlight seeks her out, as if choosing her, selecting her. She scoops her hand into the dark and combs the moonlight through her hair.

"Will those kids get well?" she asks.

"Some will," her mother says.

"And . . . why do they call that clinic, 'Hope'?"

Her father struggles with his answer.

"It is a good word, Ana. A big word. It means that, after all, we still love life. That living is a sacred act."

She walks on, pondering his answer, holding tight to her parents' hands.

HAWAIIAN-ENGLISH GLOSSARY

‘A‘AMA (ah-ah-ma) . . . Black, edible crab

AHI (ah-hee) . . . Fire, matches

ĀINA (eye-nah) . . . Land, earth

AKAMAI (ah-kah-my) . . . Smart, clever

AKU (ah-koo) . . . Bonito. Skipjack fish

ĀKUA (ah-koo-ah) . . . Gods

ALAWELA (ah-la-vel-ah) . . . Dark lines meeting at navel in pregnancy

ALI‘I (ah-lee-ee) . . . Chief, ruler

ANAHOLA (ahn-ah-ho-lah) . . . Hourglass

‘A‘OLE LOA (ah-oh-lay-lo-ah) . . . Absolutely not!

‘A‘OLE PILIKIA (ah-oh-lay-pee-lee-kee-ah) . . . No problem!

‘AU‘AU KAI (ow-ow-ki) . . . Sea bath

‘AUMĀKUA (ow-mah-koo-ah) . . . Family gods. Deified ancestors

AUWĒ (ow-way) . . . Alas!

‘AWA (ah-va) . . . Slightly narcotic tea

CHOP SUEY (chop-soo-ee) . . . Pidgin for mixed ancestry

DA KINE (dah-kine) . . . Pidgin shorthand for anything; you know what I mean

Ē HAMAU (ey-ha-mau) . . . Be silent.

Ē KŪ (ey-koo) . . . Stand tall!

Ē MAU (ey-mow) . . . We must strive!

EI NEI (ay-nay) . . . Dear one, beloved

E‘OLU‘OLU (ey-oh-loo-oh-loo) . . . Please

‘EWE‘EWE-IKI (ey-vey-ey-vey-ee-kee) . . . Ghost mother

GEEV 'UM . . . Pidgin. Show your stuff!

HĀ (hah) . . . Breath

HA'A (ha-ah) . . . Ancient dance with bent knees. After mid–nineteenth century called "the Hula"

HĀNAU (ha-now) . . . Birth

HANOHANO NUI (ha-no-ha-no-noo-ee) . . . Great dignity

HAPA (ha-pa) . . . Person of mixed blood

HAOLE (how-lee) . . . Caucasian, white

HĀPAI (ha-pie) . . . Pregnant, to conceive

HAUMEA (how-mey-ah) . . . Fertility goddess

HE HIAPO (hey-he-ah-po) . . . Firstborn

HEIAU (hey-yow) . . . Temple site, shrine

HILA HILA (hee-la-hee-la) . . . For shame!

HO'OKALAKU (ho-oh-kala-koo) . . . Undo evil by prayer

HO'OLOHE (ho-oh-lo-hey) . . . Listen

HO'OMANAWANUI (ho-oh-ma-na-va-noo-ee) . . . Patience

HO'OPAHUHU (ho-oh-pah-hoo-hoo) . . . Ooze forth

HO'OPONOPONO (ho-oh-po-no-po-no) . . . To bring balance, put right

HULA KAHIKO (hoo-la ka-hee-ko) . . . Old, ancient form of hula

HULI (hoo-lee) . . . To turn, to reverse. Also to overthrow

HULIHULI (hoo-lee-hoo-lee) . . . Chicken or meat on spit

HULU KUPUNA (hoo-loo-koo-poo-na) . . . Precious elder

HUMUHUMU (hoo-moo-hoo-moo) . . . Trigger fish

IKAIKA (ee-ky-kah) . . . Strong, powerful

'ĪEWE (ey-ee-vee) . . . Afterbirth, placenta

'INA'INA (een-ah-een-ah) . . . Bloodstains preceding childbirth

'INIKI (ee-nee-kee) . . . Sharp, piercing, as wind

INOA PŌ (ee-no-ah-po) . . . Name, title given in darkness

'IWA (ee-vah) . . . Frigate, man-o'-war bird

IWI (ee-vee) . . . Bone

KAHILI (kah-hee-lee) . . . Feather standard, symbol of royalty

KAHUNA (ka-hoo-nah) . . . Priest

KAHUNA PALE KEIKI (kah-hoo-nah-pa-lay-kay-kee) . . . Midwife

KAHUNA PULE (ka-hoo-nah-poo-lay) . . . Prayer expert, priest

KAI (ky) . . . The sea, seawater

KALAMAI (ka-la-my) . . . Forgive

KĀLUA (kah-loo-ah) . . . To bake in underground oven (*imu*)

KĀNE (kah-nee) . . . Male, husband

KĀNE, KŪ, LONO, KANALOA (kah-ney-koo-lo-no-kah-nah-lo-ah) . . . Four
    major Hawaiian gods
KANAKA MAOLI (ka-nah-ka-mah-oh-lee) . . . true, indigenous Hawaiian
    Plural, KĀNAKA
KAPAKAHI (kah-pah-ky) . . . Crooked, lopsided, askew
KAPU (ka-poo) . . . Taboo
KA PU'UWAI (ka-poo-oo-vy) . . . The heart
KEOLA (kay-ola) . . . Life
KIMCHEE (kim-chee) . . . Spicy Korean cabbage
KOKE, KOKE (ko-kee-ko-kee) . . . Soon, soon
KŌKUA (ko-koo-ah) . . . Help, aid, assist
KO'O KUA (ko-oh-koo-ah) . . . One who gives back support in childbirth
KUKUI (koo-koo-ee) . . . Candlenut. Oil used for lights
KULIKULI! (koo-lee-koo-lee) . . . Be still, be still.
KUMU (koo-moo) . . . Foundation, source
KUMU HULA (koo-moo-hoo-lah) . . . Hula master
KUPUNA (koo-po-nah) . . . Elder, wise one (Plural, KŪPUNA)
LA'AU HAOLE (lah-ow-how-lee) . . . White man's medicine
LA'AU LAPA'AU (lah-ow-la-pa-ow) . . . Herbal medicine
LAKA (lah-kah) . . . Patron god of the hula
LĀNAI (lah-nigh) . . . Porch, balcony
LAULAU (lau-lau) . . . Steamed ti-leaf-covered fish or pork
LIMU (lee-moo) . . . Algae, seaweed
LO'I (lo-ee) . . . Irrigated taro terrace
LOKO'INO (lo-ko-ee-no) . . . Evil, malevolent
LOKULOKU (lo-koo-lo-koo) . . . Downpouring rain
LŌLŌ (lo-lo) . . . Feebleminded, stupid
LOMI (lo-mee) . . . To massage
LONO MĀKUA (lo-no-mah-koo-ah) . . . Fire god
LOPAKA (lo-pah-kah) . . . Robert
LŪ'AU (loo-ow) . . . Hawaiian feast, also wide taro leaves used therein
MAHEALANI HOKU (mah-hey-ah-la-nee-ho-koo) . . . Full moon
MAKE (mah-kay) . . . Death
MAKAI (mah-kigh) . . . Seaward, in direction of the sea
MAKANI (mah-kah-nee) . . . Wind, breeze
MAKALI'I (mah-kah-lee-ee) . . . Seven major stars of the Pleiades
MĀKUA (mah-koo-ah) . . . Mother, parent
MALIHINI (mah-lee-hee-nee) . . . Newcomer

MĀLAMA (mah-lah-mah) . . . To preserve, take care of

MALOʻO (ma-lo-oh) . . . Dry season

MANONG (mah-nong) . . . Pidgin slang for Filipino

MAUKA (mow-kah) . . . Toward the mountains

MAULILOA (mow-lee-lo-ah) . . . Sacred essence of life

MOKES (mokes) . . . Pidgin. Brothers of the 'hood

MOʻOPUNA (mo-oh-poo-nah) . . . Grandchild

MUʻUMUʻU (moo-moo) . . . Mother Hubbard dress, loose gown

NAʻAU (Nah-ow) . . . Gut, gut feelings

NANAKULI (na-na-koo-li) . . . To appear deaf. In hunger years when there was no food to offer strangers, folks pretended not to see or hear them.

ʻOHANA (oh-hana-ah) . . . Family, kin group

ʻOKI (oh-kee) . . . Cut, sever

ʻOKOLE (oh-ko-lay) . . . Buttocks, anus

ʻOLELO MAKUAHINE (oh-lay-lo-mah-koo-ah-hee-nee) . . . Mother tongue

ʻONO (oh-no) . . . Good, delicious

ʻŌPAE (oh-pay) . . . Shrimp

OPIHI (oh-pee-hee) . . . Limpet, a delicacy

PAʻA KE WAHA (pa-ah-kay-wah-ha) . . . Close the mouth

PAHŪ (pah-hoo) . . . Push

PAKALŌLŌ (pah-kah-lo-lo) . . . Local marijuana

PAKE (pah-kay) . . . Chinese

PANIOLO (pah-nee-oh-lo) . . . Hawaiian cowboy

PAU (pow) . . . Finished, ended

PAU HANA (pow-ha-nah) . . . Finished work

PEHEA ʻOE (pe-hey-ah-oy) . . . How are you?

PIKO (pee-ko) . . . Umbilical cord

PŌ . . . The night

POHĀ KA NALU (po-ha-ka-na-loo) . . . Amniotic sac

PŌHAKU (po-hah-koo) . . . Stone, rock

POI (poy) . . . Paste made of cooked, pounded taro corms

POI DOG (poy dog) . . . Pidgin for mutt, mixed-blood dog

POLIHALE (po-lee-ha-lay) . . . Home of the spirits

PRIMO . . . Local beer

PULUPULU AHI (poo-loo-poo-loo-ah-hee) . . . Fire-starters; hot-tempered

PUNAHELE (poo-nah-hey-ley) . . . Favorite one

PUʻUHONUA (poo-oo-ho-noo-ah) . . . Sanctuary, place of refuge

PUʻUWAI (poo-oo-vy) . . . The heart

SHAKA SIGN . . . Fist presented with thumb and little finger extended meaning righteous! Right on!

TŪTŪ (too-too) . . . Grandma, grandpa

ULUA (oo-loo-ah) . . . Gamefish. Pompano, or jack

'ULI'ULI (oo-lee-oo-lee) . . . Gourd rattle used in hula dance

'UPEPE (oo-pay-pay) . . . Wide, flat nose

WAHI PANA (wah-hee-pah-nah) . . . Sacred, or legendary place

WAI (vy) . . . Water other than seawater

WAI'ANAE (why-a-ny) . . . Waters of the 'ama 'ama mullet fish

WAIWAI (vy-vy) . . . Wealth, double water

RUSSIAN-ENGLISH GLOSSARY

BABUSHKA (ba-bush-ka) . . . Grandmother. Scarf worn by such
    Plural, BABUSHKI

BAYAN (by-yon) . . . Zitherlike musical instrument

BEDNEY (bed-nee) . . . Unfortunate, poor you!

BRATLICH (brot-lik) . . . Brother

CHASHKA CHAYA (chash-ka-chy-ah) . . . Cup of tea

DA (da) . . . Yes

DA SVIDANYA (dah-svee-don-yah) . . . Good-bye

DOBRAYE UTRA (do-bray-oo-tra) . . . Hello, good day

FORTUSHKA (for-toosh-ka) . . . Tiny breathing space in windowpane

GLASNOSTIC (glas-nos-tik) . . . Openly, freely

GOLOOBKA (go-loob-ka) . . . Little dove

GOSPODI (gos-pod-ee) . . . My lord!

GULAG (goo-lahg) . . . Slave labor camp system under Stalin

KAK DILA (kak-dee-lah) . . . How are you?

KOPECK (ko-pek) . . . Russian currency, coin

KULAKS (koo-loks) . . . Farmers, forced into collectivization by Stalin

LAG (lahg) . . . Slang for gulag

MOLODETS (mo-lo-detz) . . . Good for you!

MUDAK (moo-dok) . . . Fool!

NYET (nee-yet) . . . No

OPASNO (oh-pos-no) . . . Help! Aid me

PAMYAT (pam-ee-yot) . . . Memory

PAZHALSTA (pah-shol-sta) . . . Please, you're welcome

PRIVYET (pree-vee-et) . . . Hi!

RUBLE (roo-bul) . . . Russian currency, usually paper

SHASHLIK (shash-lik) . . . Shish kebab

SKOLZKO (skol-zko) . . . Slippery, difficult

SPASIBO (spa-see-boh) . . . Thank you

TAIGA (ty-gah) . . . Subarctic forest terrain, south of the tundra

TUNDRA (ton-drah) . . . Frozen terrain between arctic and forest region

UDACHI VAM (oo-dah-chee-vom) . . . Good luck!

UZHIN (oot-zin) . . . Dinner

VOLENKO (vo-len-ko) . . . Boot

YAMBURG (yom-burg) . . . Messy

ACKNOWLEDGMENTS

Special thanks to my agent, Lane Zachary, and to my editors, Elizabeth Dyssegaard and Mark Tavani. Thanks also to Deirdre Lanning.

Mahalo 'a nui to friends and 'ohana for their generous support:
Rosemond Kehau Aho, Braxton Davenport, Lorraine Dusky, Cheryl Gaebel, Polly Gose, Bette Howland, George Kam, Jr., Napoleon Keawe, Polly Kreitz, Dorson Liss, Maria and Marcello Margini, Kathrin Perutz, Marilene Phipps, Koko Poliahu, Lois and Richard Rosenthal, Cary Chandor Savant, Gretchen Dow Simpson, Nani and Don Svendsen, and Ku'uleialoha Tamura.

In Hawaii: For help in researching Mākua Valley, thanks to Kyle Kajihiro of the American Friends Service Committee, the members of Mālama Mākua, Hui Mālama O Mākua, and Aunty Frenchy de Soto. And thanks to the medical staff of The Queen's Medical Center, Honolulu.

In Russia: For their expert knowledge and guidance, thanks to Rosalind Tepper and Eric Tepper. For help in translating archival materials at the Hermitage Museum, thanks to Ivan Spano. And heartfelt thanks to Boris Ozhogin in Moscow, and Rudolph Otradnov in St. Petersburg, for their personal memories of the Archangel'sk gulag in the 1950s.

These books were helpful to me in my research: *Nānā i ke kumu*, I & II, by Mary Kawena Pukui, EW Hartig, Catherine Lee; *Kaua'i, Ancient Place-*

Names, by Frederick Wichman; *Kaua'i: The Separate Kingdom*, by Edward Joesting; *900 Days: The Siege of Leningrad*, by Harrison Salisbury.

For their continuing support, my especial gratitude and affection to Jan and Frank Morgan of the Kohala Book Shop, Kapa'au, Hawai'i.

Cherished in Memory: E. Haring Chandor, Peter Dee, Lee Goerner, Heather Ho, Kawika Ho'opau, James Pili, Norma Wickler.

ABOUT THE AUTHOR

Of Native Hawaiian and Anglo-American descent, KIANA DAVENPORT is the author of the bestselling novels *Shark Dialogues* and *Song of the Exile*. She has been a Fiction Fellow at Harvard, a Visiting Writer at Wesleyan University, and a recipient of a National Endowment for the Arts grant. Her short stories have won numerous O. Henry awards, Pushcart prizes, and the Best American Short Stories, 2000, Award. She lives in New York City and Hawai'i.

ABOUT THE TYPE

This book was set in Goudy, a typeface designed by
Frederic William Goudy (1865–1947). Goudy began
his career as a bookkeeper, but devoted the rest of his
life to the pursuit of "recognized quality" in a printing
type.

Goudy was produced in 1914 and was an instant
bestseller for the foundry. It has generous curves and
smooth, even color. It is regarded as one of Goudy's
finest achievements.